BEFORE

HER

EYES

BEFORE

SHE CAN'T SEE THE KILLER

HER

BUT THE KILLER CAN SEE HER...

EYES

JACK JORDAN

CORVUS

Published in Great Britain in 2018 by Corvus, an imprint of Atlantic Books Ltd.

Copyright © Jack Jordan, 2018

10 9 8 7 6 5 4 3 2 1

A CIP catalogue record for this book is available from the British Library.

Trade Paperback ISBN: 978 1 78649 446 7
Paperback ISBN: 978 1 78649 445 0
E-book ISBN: 978 1 78649 447 4

Printed and bound by CPI Group (UK) Ltd, Croydon, CR0 4YY

Corvus
An imprint of Atlantic Books Ltd
Ormond House
26–27 Boswell Street
London
WC1N 3JZ

www.corvus-books.co.uk

Dedicated to J,
for everything you have conquered

PROLOGUE

*T*he blood on his hands peeled off in flakes like ash from charred meat. He tasted her every time he licked his lips, and remembered the hot splatter of blood against his face as he dragged the knife across her throat.

The spade crunched into the earth. Drops of sweat mixed with the blood and ran down his face in rosy streaks.

The body lay at his feet, skin washed porcelain white under the moon. The fear she felt as the blade severed her neck was locked inside her eyes.

He stopped to catch his breath and looked down at her.

Even in death she was beautiful.

The adrenalin began to wane. Lactic acid burned in his arms and shoulders; his bones ground together at the joints and seized with every thrust of the spade. He wiped sweat from his forehead and waited for the guilt to come. Nothing.

The spade fell to the ground with a clatter. He took her by the ankles and noticed how cold they were, how the skin and muscles had begun to harden against her bones. He heaved her towards the grave, squinting against the sweat. The body landed with a thump. A bone cracked against a rock, the snap *of her neck maybe, or her skull splitting in two. He threw the knife in after her and eyed the moon reflected in the bloodied metal.*

Light flooded the lawn with a flash. He shielded his eyes and felt sweat trickle to his elbow.

Mother stood at the window, her shadow stretched across the grass. He felt her take him in: skin and clothes spoiled with dirt and blood, strands of hair stuck to his face.

Mother knew what he had done, what he was capable of. Perhaps she had always known, known even before he did, and had been waiting for this very moment, sleeping lightly and ready to wake to watch her child bury another.

He had to finish before dawn. Dew was collecting on the grass and the eastern corner of the sky was diluting with the waking sun. The car would need to be scrubbed and bleached, his clothes burned.

He picked up the spade and shovelled the dirt on top of the body, listened to the stones clatter against her bones, ricochet off her eyes, her jaw, her ribs. He watched her face disappear beneath the dirt as it filled the dip of her eye sockets and her open mouth. When the earth was packed tight, he looked up again. The sky was emblazoned with oranges and reds where the sun had risen behind his back.

Mother closed the curtains. He went inside to wash the blood away.

PART I

ONE

Naomi Hannah stood at the edge of the cliff with the sea breeze pushing against her as though it was trying to keep her from jumping. All she had to do was lean into the wind and wait for it to drop.

Not knowing how far she had to fall should have made it easier. Being blind didn't usually come with advantages, but as she stood before death, she was indebted to the darkness.

She stood and listened to the waves crash against the cliff. The sound of them thundered in her ears like taunts. *Jump, you coward. Jump.*

Maybe the waves would be merciful, yank her downwards with the current and rake her over the rock bed until her neck snapped; quick and forgiving. But Naomi knew better than to expect mercy.

She curled her toes over the edge until earth crumbled between them. All it would take was a second of courage to tip forwards. Gravity would do the rest.

Someone would find her clothes and walking boots at the top of the cliff and know she had jumped. There would be no need to scour the beach for tatters of fabric tangled with the seaweed. Someone would find the suicide note tucked in her pocket, the paper stained with dark splotches from stray tears, the words scrawled on the page like the writing of a child. No one would need to find the body she had left behind, dressed in nothing but underwear and bloated skin. The sea would take care of that.

Max ran around the green behind her chasing rabbits, his tail wagging and wet with dew.

He will go on helping people, she thought. *He will forget me.*

Just the night before, she had stood in the very same spot, wondering if it would be better to wait for the tide to go out so she could fall onto the beach and break her spine in one quick hit, or leap then and there for the waves to slam her against the cliff face and thrash the life from her bones. But she hadn't found the courage; she had stood there for hours picking at the skin around her nails until her fingers bled.

The smell of the sea brought with it memories of better times. A day at the beach with her adoptive mother and sister eating soggy sandwiches speckled with sand; playing on the beach with her niece and nephew with her then husband by her side, his voice filled with hope at the thought of children of their own, children she would never give him. She shook her head.

Don't think of them.

Her mother, the woman who had found her and raised her as her own, would never forgive her. The wail of the wind began to sound like distant screams. Maybe that was what her mother would sound like when she learned her daughter was dead. She clenched her eyes shut and covered her ears.

'Please stop,' she whispered.

Her ex-husband's voice seeped in, stalking the salty breeze, whispering the words she would never forget: *I'll never stop loving you.*

Two tears shot simultaneously down her cheeks.

'*LIAR!*'

She shouted the word to the wind until her throat burned.

Dane had been the start of it all. He had been the one to claw up that voice again, the voice that whispered of death and how easy it would be. She had existed for two long years, isolated, single and friendless, but loneliness had finally got the better of her. To successfully quieten the voice inside her head, she had to die.

Max's bark echoed over the barren clifftop. If she turned, he would run towards her and make her give up. She couldn't give in to the fear. Not again.

'Max, go away!'

She covered her face with her hands and felt the wind curl around her body like a cold embrace. Even the wind pitied her.

Max barked again, closer this time; she felt the heat of his breath on the backs of her legs.

'Stay away! Go!'

His high-pitched whine sliced through her chest. She landed on the ground with a dull thump, sending crumbs of dirt from the edge towards the sea.

Max nuzzled her hair with his wet nose and licked her tears.

She hadn't brought him with her last night for fear of not being able to go through with it with him so close, but then the guilt had eaten away at her when she thought of him locked up inside the house waiting to be found. What if no one realised she was gone? What if he wasted away waiting for her to come home? She imagined her mother entering her house and being hit by the smell of him, decomposing in his bed.

The sun hid behind a cloud and left her to the mercy of the breeze drifting in from the sea. She stood up and began to dress.

'Tomorrow,' she whispered. 'I'll do it tomorrow.'

She forced her feet into her socks and walking boots. The laces fumbled between her deadened fingertips, numb to the bone.

The suicide note teetered on the edge of her jeans pocket and whipped up with the breeze, carried briefly about the green before it launched over the edge of the cliff and danced in the air, right before her eyes. All she saw was darkness.

'Come on,' she said, searching for Max's service harness on the wet grass. 'Let's go home.'

She fitted Max's harness and walked away from the cliff edge. Another failed attempt. She took a deep breath and held it in her lungs until her chest burned.

Tomorrow, she thought. *I'll do it tomorrow.*

TWO

Naomi walked from the cliff to town, shivering against the wind as it drifted in from the sea and through the streets, the blood in the town's veins. She missed the serenity of the clifftop, with nothing but the sound of the waves crashing to shore and the squawk of gulls as they glided in the morning sun. In town, life crashed around her and invaded her every thought.

Balkerne Heights was an incestuous wasteland at the edge of the county, but to Naomi it was the edge of the world. The town had been picturesque once, with stone cottages lacing the lanes and colourful terraced houses framing the seafront, their bay windows reflecting the chopping waves and the sun as it set. Photographs of the cliffs had been slapped on postcards, and the yellow ribbon of beach had once been crowded with tourists. All it had taken was one crime to suck the life from every brick and cobble. The cliffs crumbled and the sea greyed. The townspeople locked their doors and scared the tourists away. The town didn't just lose its beauty; Hayley Miller, the teenager who had gone missing, was never seen again.

Naomi trudged on with clenched teeth to stop them chattering. She listened to the rush of cars splashing through puddles, the mutter of voices blending into one incomprehensible hum. She never seemed to be a part of the life that vibrated around her. She was always on the outside listening in.

'Naomi!'

She heard Wilson's voice through the noise, mumbling around the cigarette between his lips. He would be waiting by his garden gate for the milkman like he did every Monday. They always talked on Mondays.

'Good morning, Wilson,' she said, forcing a smile.

'You got a cold?'

Her voice was raspy from screaming into the wind. 'A little,' she lied.

'Hot water and lemon, that'll do the trick.'

'Thanks, Wilson.'

She passed his garden gate and breathed in his ashy exhales. She could smell sleep on him: dried sweat, stale in the folds of his skin.

'How've you been?' he asked.

I want to die, Wilson.

'I'm fine. How're you doing?'

'Grand, sunshine, grand. How's the pup?'

'Just fine. He's going on seven.'

'I don't believe it,' he said.

'Time flies, doesn't it?' she called behind her, a false cheer in her voice. 'See you soon.'

They had the same conversation each week. No one else seemed to notice that their lives rewound every Sunday night and replayed the next morning, recycling each smile, word and breath. Naomi wanted to scream at them, wake them from the hold the town had over them. They were a town of nobodies.

She had battled against her suicidal thoughts for two years, but last night she had finally given in to the persistent whispers and trekked through the night with only her cane to guide her until she reached the cliffs. Just the act of accepting her fate had lifted a weight from her shoulders, and even though she hadn't gone through with it, knowing that she would succeed tomorrow made each breath a little easier.

She listened to footsteps pass by, the scratch of coats as they brushed against hers. Perhaps it wasn't as suffocating for the rest of them because they had opportunities that she would never have.

Naomi's life wasn't out of control; quite the opposite. Her mother and sister chose her clothes and submitted her online supermarket shop, ordering the same food each week. Her dog and cane took her everywhere she went, led her to her dead-end job in the café because no other employer would take her. She couldn't just jump behind the wheel of a car; if she wanted to go somewhere, she had to be driven. And how could she move on from Dane and meet someone new? For everyone else, it was as easy as catching someone's eye. All Naomi could do was wait for someone to breach the darkness, someone she couldn't even see coming. The only aspect of her life in her control was the decision to live or die.

Max's tail swished against her knees and Naomi knew that they were approaching the bus stop where Joanne waited for them each morning. She wouldn't be surprised if Joanne let several buses pass just so she could catch a glimpse of Max.

'Here's my beautiful chap,' she said, her voice creeping through the noise.

Max's tail beat faster against Naomi's legs. He sat and fanned the ground, and waited for the treat Joanne always gave him.

The bus stop smelt of cigarette smoke and stale urine, but Naomi could still smell the peppermint on Joanne's breath and the sweet lavender perfume dabbed behind her ears.

'Hi, Joanne.'

'How are you, darling?'

I tried to kill myself today.

'I'm fine.'

'How's Max been?'

'He's great.'

'I'm so pleased.'

Naomi could hear from Joanne's voice that the old woman was stooping, her spine slowly curling in on itself like an insect shrivelling in the heat of the sun.

'Can I give him a treat?'

'Just one, he's getting fat.'

Max sniffed around Joanne's bag as she rummaged inside. Naomi's shoulder brushed against the side of the bus shelter, and the memories flooded her mind like stagnant water.

She could still feel the softness of her biological mother's fur coat caressing her cheek as she was carried through the night. Her mother's heartbeat and the vibrations from her cries had sent Naomi to sleep in her arms, lost in the warmth of her. When she woke up, she was alone, huddled in the corner of the bus stop, wrapped in the coat, which smelt of stale cigarettes and cheap perfume. She called out for her mother and cried until she wet herself. On bad nights, she could still feel the warmth of the urine soaking her thighs and hear her calls for the mother who never came back for her, even in her dreams.

'Naomi?'

'Sorry, what did you say?'

'I asked if you were going to work today.'

Max finished crunching on the treat and licked the tarmac for stray crumbs.

'No, no work today.'

'How about tomorrow? I could drop by the café and say hello to Max.'

'Yes, I'm working tomorrow.' *But I'll be dead by then.* 'I'd best be off.'

'Oh.'

'We'll see you again tomorrow.'

'Yes, tomorrow.'

'Come on, Max.'

Naomi had to stop herself from smiling at the thought of never having to walk down that street and talk to those people again.

Max stopped suddenly and sniffed the air.

'Keep going, Max.'

He pulled at his harness, dragging Naomi behind him as he darted to the left. As she tightened her grip on the harness, she mentally retraced the steps she had taken thousands of times before. She could smell fresh pastry from the baker's shop drifting across the street, and fresh coffee from the new café next door, but Max wasn't led by greed. He wanted to go into St Peter's Alley.

'No, Max.'

A whine rumbled in his throat, strained from the harness.

'Max, come on. We don't go that way.'

The dog pulled until Naomi struggled to stand in place without moving with him. She heard his claws scratching against the pavement and imagined them filed down to nubs, dusty scratches left in the tarmac.

Passers-by moved around them freely. A man grunted as she blocked his path. The hard corner of a briefcase knocked into the back of her thigh.

'Max, please,' she whispered.

Max forced himself against the harness until his breaths escaped in desperate hisses. Her boots slid on the pavement. The harness began to slip from her grasp.

'*Max!*'

He gave up with one final whine and shook his fur to rid the sound from his ears.

Don't be angry with him, she told herself. It won't matter tomorrow.

She thought of everyone watching her, a blind woman who couldn't even control her own dog.

'What's up with you today, huh?' she asked him as he carried on up the road with his tail between his legs.

Max was trained to ignore his instincts and lead her around safely. The change in him was worrying. Perhaps she couldn't put all her trust in him. What if he did it again and ran off? What would happen to her then? But it wouldn't matter for much longer. Tomorrow she would be dead.

THREE

Detective Sergeant Marcus Campbell had never been to a murder scene before, though he had seen his share of the dead. His first was a drunk driver slumped behind the wheel of a car, his neck snapped from the impact of the airbag. His last had been an elderly woman stiff on the floor days after falling, her hand frozen like a claw reaching for the phone to pull it from the side table and call for help, help that would never come. But although Marcus had seen plenty of bodies, he had never seen so much blood.

The woman was lying on the ground, tucked up against the brick wall of the alley with a deep gash in her neck, curved like a toothless smile. The strands of blonde hair stuck to her face were red with blood. Eyeing the white of the bone within the wound gave him the sudden urge to stroke the skin on his own neck to check it was still intact.

A school kid found her, he thought to himself. *He won't sleep for months.*

'What a waste,' Detective Inspector Lisa Elliott said, her eyes on the body by their feet. Her auburn hair glimmered in the setting sun. The lank black suit hung from her frame as though it was still on the hanger. The only bit of colour on her was the gold ring wrapped around her wedding finger. If she behaved at home like she did at work, Marcus didn't envy Lisa's wife.

'We got a name?'

Forensic pathologist Dr Ali Ling looked up at them from the ground where she was crouched beside the body.

Marcus had only met Dr Ling once, when he had first joined the force in Balkerne Heights two months earlier. It was a quick exchange, sharing names as they shook hands, but there was something genuine about her that put him at ease; he could see it in her eyes, hear it in her voice.

Being in a small town with even smaller resources, Dr Ling and her team were also trained and employed as the crime scene evidence recovery unit. Men and women dressed in white suits filled the alley, snapping photos, bagging possible evidence with gloved hands and metallic tools. Someone was taking photographs of blood splattered up the bricks. They all looked the same, dressed in white from head to toe. The flash of the camera blotched Marcus's vision and followed his eyes.

'Driving licence says her name's Cassie Jennings, twenty-five years old.'

'Anything stolen?'

'Not that I can see. We found two phones and a purse filled with notes.'

'Two phones?' Lisa asked. 'Why would she need two?'

'One's a high-tech smartphone. The other is a cheap pay-as-you-go.'

'You'll need to check the call records from each phone,' Lisa said to Marcus without looking at him. 'I want to know why she has two.'

'Could it be a work phone?' Marcus asked.

'Perhaps, but I want to know for sure.' She looked down at Dr Ling. 'Did she die from the neck wound?'

'It appears so,' Ling said, tucking an imaginary lock of hair behind her ear. Even though the white plastic suit hid her hair, it didn't seem to break the habit. The mask over her nose and mouth muffled her words. 'No signs of sexual activity at this stage, but I'll confirm that after the post-mortem. I have yet to find any other wounds from the weapon that cut her throat, though again, we won't know for sure until I flip her over.'

'You'll get your time with her,' Lisa said. 'Let us have a few minutes at the scene.'

Dr Ling stood up and removed the mask from her mouth, leaving it dangling around her neck. 'I wasn't suggesting we hurry.'

Marcus shook his head. *Let it go. She's on one today.*

The setting sun reflected in the dead woman's eyes as if they were burning inside her skull. St Peter's Alley was getting colder by the minute.

Dr Ling cleared her throat. 'There are no signs of skin deposits under her fingernails, but there's bruising on her neck to suggest she was—'

'Strangled?' Lisa cut in.

'No, but held with force. The splashes of blood on the wall –' she moved up the alley and pointed to dark, crusting splatters against the bricks – 'suggest she was first attacked here.'

'So someone grabbed her and cut her throat, and she wound up over there.'

'Probably trying to escape,' Marcus said from behind them.

'So the killer just let her get on with it?' Lisa asked.

'Watching her die might have been part of his motive,' Dr Ling said. 'All he had to do was step back and enjoy the show.'

'He?' Marcus asked. 'How do we know it was a male killer?'

'This scene doesn't suggest a female,' Lisa said.

Marcus looked at the puddles, the lifeless eyes in the young woman's skull, the wasted life splattered up the walls.

Dr Ling watched him eyeing the crime scene for answers.

'Female killers tend to choose people they know, and for a particular reason: rivalry, jealousy, obsession. Crimes between women tend to be … messier. This is more of an execution.'

'What Ali is trying to say,' Lisa said, 'is that if a woman did this, our victim would look like a dead pig used for target practice.'

Marcus looked down at the body apologetically.

'Yes, it would most likely display multiple wounds, more rage.' Ling made her way back up the alley. 'What I did notice –' she knelt beside the body – 'was that the wound seems to have been made quickly but nervously. I wouldn't be surprised if this was our murderer's first kill, or his first kill in a while.'

'But we don't know if it'll be his last,' Lisa said. 'Any initial signs of hairs or semen?'

'We won't know for sure until—'

'The post-mortem, I know,' Lisa cut in. 'I asked for *initial* signs, Dr Ling.'

'Semen?' Marcus said. 'I thought you said you hadn't found anything to suggest sexual activity?'

'Masturbation, Campbell,' Lisa said coldly. 'Just because he didn't violate the victim doesn't mean he didn't stroke the pony while she died.'

Marcus blushed.

'Nothing yet,' Dr Ling said. 'Either sex wasn't the motive, or he is good at tidying up after himself. The downpour last night didn't help. We'll examine the body for any traces.'

'Okay, call me when you've cut the cake,' Lisa said and made to leave.

'Do you ...' Dr Ling paused, chose her words carefully. 'Do you think this could be the same attacker as ...'

'Not a chance. That was twenty years ago.'

Marcus looked between the two women, watched them speak without words.

'All right,' Ling said finally.

Lisa walked off with a confident stride. Marcus followed behind her, building up the courage to ask what she meant by cutting the cake, until it came to him: the post-mortem.

He looked back at the body and felt a pang of guilt for leaving her there. He wondered if it was possible to be lonely in death.

'Well, that was useful,' Lisa said wryly as Marcus shut the car door behind him.

Sitting next to her in the confines of the car made his skin itch. He wiped his palms on his trousers.

'No evidence at all. That place could be a gold mine in the right hands.'

'You don't think Dr Ling is qualified?'

'I don't think she's smart,' Lisa replied as she turned the key in the ignition. 'There's a difference. She looks for the obvious, not the hidden clues.'

'But what if there aren't any? What if the murderer is good at cleaning up after himself, like she said?'

Lisa looked at him as though a child was buckling itself in beside her. 'There are always clues, Campbell. You just have to find them.'

She pulled away from the scene, thrusting Marcus into the back of his seat.

'What was Dr Ling talking about just now?' he asked.

'The past. It's all they do in this bloody town.'

FOUR

The sounds of the sea called to her in soothing whispers. Her nightgown flittered in the wind and brushed against her thighs. The wind tickled the palms of her hands and laced between her fingers, like warm hands leading her towards the cliff edge. When it appeared beneath her toes, peace washed over her until she was completely submerged in it, in the totality of what it meant to step into the unknown. For the first time, she wasn't afraid to die.

She rested into the wind and breathed in the salt of the sea. The waves were lapping beneath her, beckoning her down. Her right foot crept out. The breeze sent a shiver up her calf. She let the wind tip her forward and smiled the whole way down.

Naomi woke screaming. It had all changed when she plunged into the sea. She had screamed for help beneath the waves and clasped her throat as the water forced itself inside her and choked the air from her lungs. As she sank, her ears popped with the pressure and the sea salt clawed at her eyes. She inhaled until her lungs burst, just as her feet reached the sea floor and kicked up a flurry of wet sand.

She sat up in bed and felt cold sweat snake between her breasts. A part of her was still in the sea, screaming beneath the surface, and for a moment she mistook the sweat for seawater dripping down her body.

The house was quiet except for the sound of her neighbour, George, shuffling around on the other side of the wall. The chill in the room snuck into bed with her and cooled the damp sheets. She took her phone from the nightstand and asked for the time. It was late; she had crawled into bed the moment she got home from the cliff that morning, too exhausted to face the day, only to return there in her dreams.

She patted the other side of the bed and felt nothing but sheets. Two years had passed and she still struggled to call the bed her own. In the slumberous limbo between sleep and waking, she sometimes forgot that Dane was gone. She thought of him in his own bed, a bed he shared with someone else. Now it was Josie who felt the warmth of his skin at night, and listened to the softness of his breaths as she drifted off to sleep with his arms wrapped around her. That was enough to make Naomi hate her, the woman she had never met, whose only crime was loving the man Naomi herself had discarded, at the price of breaking her own heart.

She picked up his pillow and breathed in the scent. The aftershave he had worn since he received his first ever pay cheque evoked every memory they had shared, and the safety she felt when he was near. On bad nights, she spritzed the scent on the pillow; it was the only way she could sleep. She used to spray it every night, but now she only had half a bottle left. The line had been discontinued; when the shop assistant had told her, she'd had to bite back tears.

She longed to move on, but couldn't seem to let him go. Leaving him behind would mean losing a part of herself. She hated who she had become without him, and dreaded to think what would happen to her if she severed herself from him completely.

Naomi crept out from under the sheets, wrapped herself in her dressing gown and made her way downstairs. Max rushed from his bed to greet her with his tail thrashing into the banister.

'Hello, Max.' She rubbed his head.

She grabbed an armful of logs from the stack, arranged them in the fireplace, and waited for the flames to take hold before heading for the kitchen. Max followed her every step of the way.

Once the fire began to eat away at the wood, she crept through the dark house and let Max out into the garden before feeding him quickly so she could return to the fire.

The doorbell chimed. Max gave a bark from his dinner bowl.

She was so used to being alone that she froze on the spot. The only visitors she had were her mother, her sister and Dane, none of whom she was expecting. The bell rang again. Naomi smoothed her hair and checked her breath in a cupped hand. She opened the door and closed her eyes as the night air hit them.

'Hi, are you all right? I heard a scream.'

George.

'I'm fine, I ...' She considered lying, but swallowed it down. 'I had a nightmare. Sorry.'

'That's a relief. I was worried you were hurt or something.' He shuffled on the spot. 'How have you been? I haven't seen you in a while.'

George was new to Balkerne Heights. He was in his mid-thirties, but had something about him that made him seem like an older, wiser man.

'I'm fine,' she lied. The tie on her dressing gown fell slack around her waist and the wind fluttered the hem of her nightgown. She crossed her legs and squeezed the silk of it between her thighs. 'How are you settling in?'

'Fine.'

'That bad, huh?'

He gave a nervous laugh. 'People here don't half fight friendliness from strangers.'

'It'll get better. Give them time. We're not used to new faces.'

'I'm sure any other neighbour would've slammed the door in my face.'

'Well, I'm blind. I didn't have the opportunity to peek through the curtains.'

He laughed. 'I'll let you get back to your evening. Good to see you.'

'You too.'

Naomi shut the door and turned on the answering machine as she headed for her armchair by the fire. She angled herself so her feet dangled before the flames.

'You have two new messages.'

One of them would be from her mother. Rachel was her

mother whether they were blood relatives or not. She had been the one to find Naomi hidden in the corner of the bus stop, her small body hiding behind her jittering knees. With the fur coat and her eyes filled with terror, the little girl had reminded Rachel of a cornered feral animal. Despite that first impression, she'd taken her home and domesticated her until she learned to love again. Social services had called the adoption *a match*, because like Naomi, Rachel and her biological daughter Grace came from African descent. Years later, she still remembered the phrase with disdain; they had been seen as a match because of the colour of their skin, above their ability to love and nurture. She often thought how much better off society would be if everyone were blind and incapable of making judgements on a person's appearance.

'Hi, darling, it's Mum. We missed you at the party today.'

Naomi closed her eyes and sighed. The twins' fifth birthday party. She had forgot all about it. Their presents were waiting on the sideboard by the front door.

'Give me a call when you can so I know you're okay.' Her mother paused and took a small breath. 'I don't know if you've heard, but there was a murder in Balkerne Heights last night.'

Naomi sat up in the chair and tucked her feet beneath her. She thought of her immediately.

Hayley Miller.

'People are saying it was Cassie Jennings. Poor girl. She was on her way back from her niece's funeral, as if the family didn't have enough going on. Make sure you keep yourself safe. You're vulnerable, darling, so don't go out after dark. At least until the person responsible has been found. Give me a call when you can, and don't worry about the party. Grace will get over it soon enough. Love you.'

Grace.

Naomi wondered how her sister had taken the news of the murder. It had been twenty years since her sister's best friend had gone missing. It was inevitable that those memories would be clawed up with Cassie's death. Grace and Hayley had been as close as siblings until the night before her disappearance. Something had happened between them. Naomi had found Grace at midnight, sobbing into her hands in the dark.

I can't tell, Grace had whispered when Naomi asked her what had happened. *She made me promise not to tell.*

Naomi had never told her mother about that night. Whatever her sister had done, she had to protect her – Rachel and Grace had taken her in when she needed them most. But whenever Naomi thought of her sister, she wondered about the secret she had harboured for twenty years.

She turned on the TV, pressed the numbers on the remote for the local news segment, and held her breath so she could hear every word. The news broadcaster introduced a tape of a police press conference, headed by the lead detective on the case.

'At three thirty this afternoon, the body of twenty-five-year-old Cassie Jennings was discovered in St Peter's Alley. At this stage we do not believe the murder was motivated by robbery. We ask that anyone who knew Cassie, or anyone who was in the area between eight and ten p.m. yesterday evening, come forward with any information they may have, however seemingly insignificant. Balkerne Heights is a small town that doesn't hear news like this very often, so I ask you all to be vigilant while my team and I work day and night to bring justice for this horrendous crime. I understand this is unsettling, but I want to assure every resident in the community that we will find the person responsible for Cassie's death. In such a small town, there are few places to hide.'

'Oh my God.'

St Peter's Alley.

Max's claws tapped on the wooden floor as he entered the room.

'I'm sorry, Max.'

He crossed the room and rested his chin on the armrest. She stroked the soft fur on his head, thinking of what had happened just last night in her town, so close to where she slept.

That poor woman.

The broadcaster spoke again in her neutral tone. 'The murder isn't the first major crime the town has experienced, with the controversial case of eighteen-year-old Hayley Miller still unsolved twenty years on.'

Naomi turned off the television.

To think that just that morning she had passed Cassie's body, lying in the alley. Max had smelt death in the air. She thought back to the desperate hisses straining from his mouth, his claws raking against the path.

Thank goodness I wasn't the one to find her.

She noticed the shaking of her hand as she pressed the button on the machine to play the next voicemail message.

'Where were you today?' Grace asked. 'I know you're there. Pick up.' Heavy breaths crackled down the phone. 'You're their auntie, Naomi. You need to be there. Everyone was asking where you were.' She sighed again. Naomi could almost feel the heat coming off the phone. 'I'm sick of covering for you every time you hide away in bed. You can screw Mum and me around all you want, but don't hurt my kids. It's not fair. I needed you today. Hayley would have been there for me. I should have known you wouldn't turn up. I don't know why I bother, Naomi. I really don't.'

Naomi flinched as the message ended with a bang as her sister slammed down the phone.

'I'm sorry,' she whispered.

Grace hadn't said the words, but Naomi had felt them rippling beneath her message. She would rather Hayley was alive than Naomi.

Twenty years had passed, and still the town spoke of Hayley's unsolved disappearance. Naomi struggled to pair the Hayley she had known with the Hayley who stoked the local whispers. They seemed like two different entities: one a sweet, vivacious teenage girl, the other a manipulative and promiscuous young woman who had slept with half the town.

She jolted in her seat as booming thuds thundered on the other side of the door. She hadn't heard anyone at the door in days, and now she was about to receive her second visitor of the evening.

Max rushed to the door, barking as he went. Naomi headed after him and took him by the collar as she opened the door.

Cold wind whistled through the crack between the door and the frame.

'Hello?'

Max pushed his head through the gap and barked hot breaths into the night.

Dead leaves rustled down the path. The air was moist with rain.

Max continued to bark. Someone was out there.

'Hello? Is anyone there?'

She could hear someone breathing. Excited breaths consciously slowed, rattling through the stranger's nostrils, vibrating with the beat of a heart.

'Who's there?'

Max's bark echoed down the empty street, bouncing against every closed door, every curtained window. No one would see the stranger push their way inside. No one would know.

The wind rustled the trees lining the road and battered the leaves with rain until the quiet street turned into a rush of noise. The iron gate at the end of the garden path slammed and creaked, slammed and creaked.

'Tell me who you are.'

Naomi stood in the doorway on shaking legs, listening to the rush of the rain and her own frantic breaths. Adrenalin leeched the moisture from her mouth until the insides of her cheeks stuck to her teeth.

Footsteps headed down the path. The gate squeaked on its hinges and slammed shut. The last thing she heard was the footsteps walking steadily back up the road until they were nothing more than a whisper, leaving her staring blindly into the night as rain collected on her cheeks like tears.

FIVE

Marcus filed into the stuffy incident room behind his colleagues and took the seat closest to the door.

Balkerne Heights had been his home for only two months, and yet he already found himself looking for any opportunity to escape. His car always faced the road on the driveway, and his clothes were folded and arranged so they could be packed up at a moment's notice. There was something about the place that kept him on edge.

The incident room was cramped and hot, with a table that took up the majority of the room, forcing officers to squeeze into seats or stand against the wall until their toes went numb in their boots. The walls were scuffed from the backs of chairs and the table was scarred with scratches of ink, like small blue veins in the wood.

Lisa stood at the top of the room and waited for the last of the officers to line up against the wall. Marcus had learned early on not to take that spot; Lisa made direct eye contact with those standing at her level.

Once everyone had assumed their positions and the door was shut, silence rang through the room as they waited for her to speak.

It was an impressive number of people to work on one investigation in such a small town. But without the uniformed officers in the room, the truth would be revealed. There were only four people dedicated to the case.

'Settled? Good.' Lisa scanned the faces. When her eyes fell on Marcus, a muscle twitched in his neck. 'Campbell, give us the run-down on the case.'

All eyes turned to him, a sea of faces with straight set lips.

'Twenty-five-year-old Cassie Jennings was killed between eight and ten p.m. on the thirtieth of October 2017.' He noticed the shake of his voice and cleared his throat. 'Cause of death was asphyxiation by drowning.'

'Drowning?' an officer asked. Marcus had yet to memorise all their names. He eyed the officer, her brown hair tied in a bun, her hazel eyes with flecks of gold. The name was on the tip of his tongue.

'Drowned in her own blood,' Lisa cut in.

Silence hung in the room. He wondered if they were all imagining what it would be like to choke on their own blood, feel the warmth of it filling their lungs. He continued.

'The body was discovered in St Peter's Alley at around three forty yesterday afternoon by school student James Day. Blood splatters on the wall of the alley indicate the murder took place there. The first of the lab results confirm the blood belongs to the victim. There are no street lights through the walkway, making it easier for an attack to take place.' He looked down at his notes, not because he didn't remember every detail of the scene – the glimpse of white bone, the sun setting in the dead woman's eyes – but because the pressure to deliver competently shrouded his mind.

'The fatal injury was a cut to the throat, measuring roughly twenty centimetres long and seven centimetres wide. The weapon severed the right carotid artery, causing the blood loss. There was significant damage to the oesophagus and airways, making it easier for the blood to fill her lungs.

'The injury appears to have been caused by a kitchen knife, a flat blade measuring around twenty-five centimetres long. We know from the way the skin was severed that the blade had started to become blunt from use, and traces of washing-up liquid and food were found in the wound, indicating that the knife was used in a kitchen. The weapon was not found at the scene. Forensics have sent possible DNA findings linking to a third party to the lab and we are awaiting results; however, they have already confirmed traces of latex on the victim's neck, which may indicate the person in question was wearing disposable gloves.'

Lisa nodded. 'The post-mortem was performed last night at my request; there's no time for us to drag our feet on this one. We'll have more information once I meet with Dr Ling this morning.' She took a sip of water. The room was so quiet that Marcus heard it slip down her throat with three hearty gulps. 'As you know, I made a televised statement last night asking for witnesses to come forward. In the meantime, I want all officers on the front line to keep an eye out from here on in – any suspicious behaviour and new faces should be questioned.'

DS Blake Crouch glanced his way. Marcus was a new face. He looked down at his notes.

'Become the community's best friend. Talk to people at every given opportunity; ask them what they've heard. I want all of you to have your ears to the ground. After the Miller fiasco, this case must be solved.'

Marcus looked around the room. Everyone was nodding meaningfully. Another story he didn't know.

'Crouch,' Lisa said, looking down at the detective sergeant. He sat up straighter. 'Obtain any and all CCTV footage near the scene and scan through it for suspicious behaviour and sightings of the victim or a possible attacker around the time of the murder. Talk to the businesses within half a mile of the scene; ask if anyone saw anything out of the ordinary. If my memory serves me, there are flats situated above the shops on the high street that overlook the alley. Ask the occupants if they saw or heard anything that might be useful.' She glanced at a uniformed officer. 'Banks, you can help him.'

'Yes, boss,' Crouch said.

A young uniformed officer nodded. Marcus tried to commit his face and the surname to memory.

'O'Neill,' she said.

Police Staff Investigator Amber O'Neill looked up, blinking her long blonde lashes. From the shadows framing her bloodshot eyes, it was clear she had been up all night. Her golden hair was tied in a bun, with rebellious strands slipping from the band and trailing down the back of her blouse. Marcus had never seen her without make-up before. She looked remarkably young. Too young.

'Go interview the schoolboy; take Hughes with you.'

'At his home, boss?' O'Neill asked.

'Yes. He'll be scared enough as it is without bringing him in.' She scanned the room. 'Campbell.'

Marcus met her eye.

'I want you to look into Cassie Jennings: find out what made her tick, who she liked and disliked, down to what her coffee order was. I want to know everything about her and why someone wanted her dead. A family liaison officer will be assigned to the Jennings family today, and will help gain information from their perspective.'

Marcus looked around the room. These people had lived in the town their whole lives. They would know the victim know far better than he, and he couldn't help but wonder if giving him the task was a way of making him under-deliver. During the two months he had worked for Lisa Elliott, he had begun to question whether she had justice for the victims at heart, or was instead orchestrating each investigation so that she stood out in the eyes of her superior.

'And another thing.' She looked around the room to make sure everyone was paying attention. 'Cassie Jennings was a journalist for the local paper. The press will pick this up and run with it as soon as they catch a whiff – one of their own is dead. They'll want blood. Keep your mouths shut and leave them to me.'

Everyone nodded.

'Questions?' she asked, in such a way that no one dared. 'Good. Dismissed.'

Officers slowly snaked out of the room, barging past Marcus so he couldn't leave his chair. He waited until the path behind his seat was clear, then stood.

'Campbell,' Lisa said. 'Get your coat.'

'Boss?'

'You're coming with me to meet Dr Ling.'

When he hesitated, she eyed him coolly.

'What? You'd rather I ask someone else?'

'Not at all. I'll be ready to leave.'

'Good,' she said, and left the room.

He should be grateful. He had been the one to accompany her to the crime scene, and now he was going with her to learn the full details of the post-mortem. But fear churned in his gut. On the surface, Lisa was helping him develop as a detective, but beneath it there was something rotten. His boss seemed to seek out naivety in others to use to her own advantage.

Marcus would follow her commands, but he vowed to keep a close eye on her. After all, she had his future with the force firmly in her hands.

SIX

Marcus clenched his hands into fists to stop them from shaking. Lisa led the way down the corridor to the examination room, where Cassie Jennings was waiting for them. The thought of seeing her body sewn up like some Frankenstein's monster made his stomach lurch.

Lisa appeared to relish finding weaknesses in her new recruit. He could feel the joy shivering off her, her eyes occasionally darting to his face to catch the fear in his. He would have to learn to hide his emotions from her or she would tear him apart. He had been filled with confidence before taking up the position in Balkerne Heights, but from the moment he began to work beneath Lisa, he felt like a fumbling fool. If other detective sergeants had survived Lisa Elliott, he could too; he just had to keep his head down and get on with the job.

'I bet you a tenner you'll be a vegetarian after this,' Lisa said as she watched him for a reaction. He clenched his jaw briefly and she knew she had got to him. 'We're all the same when it comes down to it. Meat and bone.'

Shut up, he thought. Please shut up.

'Here,' she said as they stopped in the hallway before a scuffed grey door. 'Ladies first.'

She opened the door and held it for him.

He regretted leaving his position in Invicton. It might have been a sleepy town with nothing more than petty crimes and missing cattle that had wandered away from the herd, but he had been respected there, and promoted to detective sergeant. He'd left them in the hope of getting a real case to work on. Now he knew to be careful what he wished for.

He stepped into a small room with white walls. Three plastic chairs faced a large pane of glass, giving a clear view of the examination room.

The body lay on the metal table. It felt wrong to see Cassie Jennings displayed like that, for them to pore over every mole and scar. The sight of her naked body would once have been a sight to earn, but in death it was as simple as looking through glass. The corpse was so pale that he could see blue veins snaking beneath her skin. Her hair had been combed away from her face, giving him a full view of what had once been a beautiful young woman. Someone had loved this body, kissed every inch of skin, cradled her as a child. Now she was a slab of meat with a Y-shaped incision from her collar bones to her pubis, the skin peeled back for strangers' hands to rummage around inside.

He spotted his reflection in the glass and took it all in: the darkness surrounding his eyes, the protruding bones of his skull. Bathed in the stark white light from the examination room, he looked cadaverously pale compared to the dark brown hair swept away from his face. He glanced back at the body; bile stormed in his stomach.

'Morning,' Dr Ling said as she appeared on the other side of the glass, her voice crackling through the speaker on the wall. 'Sleep well?'

He hadn't.

'What've we got?' Lisa asked, standing next to Marcus before the glass partition. Marcus smelt instant coffee on her breath.

'Straight to work, as always,' Dr Ling said.

'Well we aren't here for a cup of tea and a chat, are we?'

Ling forced a smile. Her right cheek quivered with the strain. She looked down at her notes.

'I can confidently say there are no signs of sexual assault. Other than a few abrasions from her fall, the only wound the victim suffered was the fatal cut to the neck.'

She took a small steel instrument from the metal table beside the body and lifted the top lip of the wound. Marcus clenched his teeth. All he had managed that morning was two cups of coffee, and already he could feel them trying to lurch back up.

'The way the skin was cut suggests that it was done with a smooth blade, as I mentioned in the report I sent you last night. The weapon appears to be a kitchen knife of some kind, around twenty-five centimetres, not including the handle.'

'You said something about the killer being nervous,' Lisa interjected.

Ling nodded. 'There seemed to be hesitation before the cut was made, suggesting that the blade was held there for some time, breaking the skin slightly before eventually doing the deed with one quick movement. You can see the shallowness here at the beginning of the cut where the killer paused, as if he was working up the courage, before the eventual depth here, where the blade cut down to the bone.'

She lifted the skin further with the metal instrument, revealing the pink meat of the victim's insides. Marcus clenched his fists until the blood left his knuckles. Dr Ling's voice began to sound tinny and distant.

'The end of the incision clipped the right carotid artery, which as you can see here almost crumbled under the pressure of the blood flow.'

Marcus's legs shook beneath him. He tried to focus on anything but the artery, but Dr Ling's words led him right to it. His eyes fell on the shredded red tube. His stomach clenched and retracted like a beating heart.

'Any fingerprints on the victim's neck?' Lisa asked.

The lights in the examination room flashed bright. Marcus screwed his eyes shut just as the room began to spin.

'Nothing. The person who killed Cassie Jennings was good at cleaning up after himself. Almost as good as—'

'I'm not going to tell you again, Dr Ling. There is no connection between Cassie Jennings and the disappearance of Hayley Miller. Christ, the town will be whispering about it soon enough, I don't need to hear it from you.'

A beat sat between them, but all Marcus could hear was the thrum of blood rushing in his ears.

'Are you all right, Detective Campbell?' Dr Ling asked from the other side of the glass. He tried to look at her, but she was nothing more than a featureless blur against the bright lights.

'I ... I need ...'

He put his hand to the wall and rested his head against the paint. He couldn't be sick in front of Lisa, she would tear him apart, but the back of his throat was going numb and his stomach was beating with his pulse. The room began to spin.

'For Christ's sake,' Lisa said as he vomited black coffee over the floor.

'Sit him down,' Dr Ling said. 'He looks faint. I'll be right there.'

Marcus threw up again, this time down his shirt. He closed his eyes to stop the room from spinning.

'Did you really have to embarrass me like that?' Lisa asked as she guided him to the closest chair. He couldn't answer. He was worried that if he didn't clench his teeth together, more vomit would come.

'Are you all right?'

He opened his eyes. Dr Ling was crouched before him with her hand on his knee.

'Sorry.' It was all he could think to say. His vision was blurred around the edges as the fainting spell began to pass.

'You should have eaten,' Dr Ling said. 'Coffee can't sustain you all morning, not in this job.'

'What? So there would be more mess to clean up?' Lisa said with a dry laugh.

'Why don't you go and get him some tea, Lisa? Lots of sugar. You know where the machine is.'

Lisa's face hardened.

'When you're ready, Campbell, we have a job to do. I'll be in the car.'

With that, she left the room.

Marcus looked down at himself and saw dark brown liquid dripping from the lapels of his jacket and soaking through his shirt.

'Ignore her,' Dr Ling said quietly. 'Lisa was exactly the same when she attended her first autopsy. I saw it with my own eyes. She's just too brave and too foolish to admit it.'

Brave? Marcus thought. Lisa Elliott isn't brave; she's a monster.

SEVEN

Naomi reached into her wardrobe and traced the letters her mother had sewn into the sides of her cotton shirts. She felt a jagged 'W' and yanked the white shirt off the hanger so hard that it cracked. Rain tapped on the window pane like fingertips drumming against the glass.

She had spent the night awake, listening to the sound of the hours ticking away, waiting for the stranger to pound on the door again. Her eyes closed at dawn, and she woke to Max nuzzling her face with his wet nose. She was late. There was no time to go to the cliff. There would be people on the green by now, each of them with the power to stop her from jumping. She wouldn't see them coming until it was too late.

She stepped into her work trousers and tucked her shirt inside. The only thing that kept her going was the thought that it would be the very last time. One last morning, one last shift, and then it would all be over. Her uniform would be found folded in a neat pile at the top of the cliff as her body jolted with the waves below.

Max barked loudly to the sound of the doorbell.

Naomi rushed down the stairs and took the dog by the collar. She put her hand on the handle, then stopped. She remembered the banging on the door, the sound of it quivering with the stranger's blows.

She stood motionlessly with Max fidgeting by her side. The bell rang again. She opened the door with a shaking hand.

'Hey,' Dane said.

Naomi sighed. 'Hi.'

'Can I come in? I'm on a break between shifts.'

'I'm late for work.'

'I can drive you.'

It was the only way she would make it to work on time. She hesitated before replying.

'All right. But I'm late, so I can't stand around talking.'

She stepped aside and let her ex-husband enter the house, steeling herself as he passed. He greeted Max, then kicked off his shoes and sat down on the sofa in the spot that was once his.

Naomi shut the door and ran back upstairs for her bag. It was big enough to store her collapsible cane inside, just in case. After Max's behaviour by the alley, drooling at the taste of the murdered woman in the air, she couldn't take any chances. She made her way downstairs again and shrugged on her coat.

'Got any beers lying around?'

To anyone else, the request for alcohol so early in the morning would have been queer. But Naomi knew that his unusual shift patterns at the hospital had affected his body clock. As the rest of the town slept, he had been working.

'Don't you have another shift today?' she said as she slipped into her shoes.

'One beer won't hurt.'

'It might hurt your patients.'

'I'm a nurse, not a doctor. All I do is hold sick bowls and empty piss pots all day.'

'I told you, I'm late for work. I don't have time.'

'I'm driving you; that knocks fifteen minutes off your journey.'

'Dane, I said no. Max, come.'

Max's claws tapped against the hardwood floor until his fur brushed against her trousers. She strapped the harness around his torso.

'Ready.'

She listened to Dane squeeze into his shoes and walk towards the door. He sounded more tired than usual. His breaths were laboured and his movements slow and heavy, as though he had slept as little as she had. They had always been in sync, before the separation. Her heart drummed against her ribs and her fingers twitched by her sides as she fought the urge to reach out and touch him. Dane and Naomi hadn't fallen out of love; they had been ripped from each other like a ribcage cracked in two.

She opened the door and breathed in silently as he passed, inhaling the clinical smell of the hospital and the scent of shaving foam that seemed to linger on his face from morning to night. She longed for him to touch her, to hold her in his arms just once, but as soon as she breathed out, the pain flooded back into her chest.

He would never forgive me for what I did.

Dane walked down the path towards the car as Naomi locked the door.

'Morning, Naomi,' George said from the other side of the low brick wall. He was out of breath. Heat radiated from him despite the nip in the air.

'Morning, George.'

'Hey, Max.'

George leaned over to stroke the dog. He smelt of fresh sweat.

'You coming?' Dane asked from the car. 'I thought you were late.'

'See you around,' George said.

'Bye,' she replied.

She heard him unlock his front door and walk inside, and wondered what he did in there alone; whether he was as lonely as she was.

Max jumped into the boot of the car. His tail brushed against the wet ground and flicked rainwater into her face. She wiped it away as she shut the boot and headed round to the passenger side, where Dane was waiting for her. She heard the car door open.

'Thanks,' she said, and got inside.

Dane closed the door. Naomi's heart raced as she heard his footsteps move around the car and stop at the driver's door. Even after two years, her body was still claimed by him, reacting to his every word and movement. As he sat behind the wheel, she wondered if he kissed like he used to, or whether Josie had taught him something new. He switched on the engine and turned the heating up high.

'Who's that guy? He didn't live there before.'

'George. Jane is renting the house to him. She lives in the Isle of Wight now.'

Max panted heavily in the back of the car, steaming up the windows. Dane pulled out of the parking spot and drove off down the road.

'Know him well?'

'George? He's my neighbour. It's normal to be on speaking terms.'

'You don't have to get defensive.'

'I'm not.'

She listened to the whine of the engine, the growing revs before each gear change.

'Did you hear about Cassie Jennings?' he asked.

'It's so awful. I can't help but think about Hayley.'

'I'm sure everyone in town is today,' he said. 'Grace all right?'

'I haven't spoken to her. She's angry with me right now.'

'What did you do?'

'Why do you automatically think it's my fault?'

'You said she was angry at you; you must have done something.'

'How's Josie?' she asked.

She listened to the grumble of the engine and the rush of cars on the other side of the road.

'She's fine. Why?'

'I just wondered why you came to see me instead of her.'

'She's at work. What's got you today?'

Naomi sighed. 'Sorry. I find it hard sometimes, this friends thing.'

47

'Just because we aren't married any more doesn't mean we can't be friends.'

'How does Josie feel about you constantly coming to visit your ex-wife?'

'She's fine with it.'

'I doubt that.'

'It doesn't matter. I want to see you. You're my best friend. You've been in my life for over fifteen years.'

'Yeah, and you ruined it.'

'Don't start, Naomi. That's not fair. You're the one who ended it.'

Her hands started to shake. She gripped the sides of the seat.

'What's not fair is you dropping by like everything's fine. You didn't fight for me, because you wanted children. You made that decision. You left me just as much as I left you.'

'You made the decision by refusing to even think about the idea.'

Blood rushed to her face. 'Of course I thought about it! I thought about it for fifteen years. You left because you weren't getting your own way. We were fine as we were.'

'Why are you doing this?' His hands clenched around the steering wheel until the leather squeaked beneath his palms.

'I'm doing the normal thing, the right thing. I'm trying to move on. You come round like everything's fine and rip open old wounds every time they start to heal.'

'Well I'm not leaving things between us on bad terms.'

'That's how divorce works. We're not supposed to be on good terms.'

48

He smacked the dashboard with a heavy fist. 'That's bullshit! You're just trying to push me away.'

Naomi rubbed her face and sighed into her hands. It was only then that she felt the tears. She swiped them away and swallowed down the resentment – he had chosen his desire for children over her. If she weren't still in love with him, she would hate him for the choice he had made.

'I'm sorry,' he said.

'You can't keep coming over pretending that everything is how it used to be. We can't be friends any more. You need to respect that.'

The car came to a stop. Dane lifted the handbrake and turned off the engine.

'I do.'

'You don't though, do you? You'll be round again next week as though this never happened.'

'I miss you sometimes, all right? Am I not allowed to miss my wife?'

Silence fell. The wind curled around the car. Faint raindrops pattered against the glass.

'I'm not your wife any more, Dane.'

'I know.'

She listened to the sounds of his sad, shallow breaths. If only she could surrender herself and give him what he wanted. She knew that she could kiss those lips right there and have him back without a word. But she couldn't give him what he wanted, and he would never forgive her for what she had done. They couldn't surrender to each other when her secret was pushing them apart.

Even though he had Josie, Naomi realised that Dane was as lonely as she was. They had both lost their birth mothers at a young age and struggled through life until they found each other. Now they had to face the world apart.

As she began to get out of the car, she felt his hand on her wrist.

'I still love you, Naomi. I always will.'

She snatched her hand away before what he had said could sink in, but it was too late. She had heard them, the words she had longed for.

She followed the car round to the boot, tracing her hand against its cold exterior until dirt coated her fingertips. Her hands darted to her face and wiped the tears away again, smearing the grime from the car beneath her eyes.

Dane's footsteps crunched on the gravel drive and the boot opened with a faint squeak. Max jumped out with his tail wagging against the body of the car and sniffed the gravel at their feet. She reached for his harness and felt Dane's hand place it in hers. She missed those hands.

She felt him wipe the dirt from her face and shivered beneath his touch.

'Every time you think you miss me, remember Josie and how that would make her feel.'

He went to say something, but swallowed the words down and coughed. His hand slipped from her face.

'Thanks for dropping me. Come on, Max.'

Max led the way round the café towards the back door. A sob rattled Naomi's throat. She swallowed it down and placed her hand on her stomach.

She resented her womb, the empty vessel inside her that society demanded she fill. How could she protect a child when she struggled to protect herself? Why couldn't Dane understand? And she couldn't be a parent, not with her birth mother's blood running through her veins.

She stepped into the utility room and took a deep breath. Max filed in beside her, panting restlessly, and settled down in his basket with a sigh. Old Daisy, her boss's wire-haired terrier, didn't even stir in her bed.

'I'm sorry you didn't get your walk, Max. I'll take you out at lunch, okay?' She rubbed his head and made her way inside.

The kitchen was always hectic, even when there were only a couple of customers. Nick, the young dishwasher, would be standing by the sink waiting to scrub pots older than his years. There had been a second washer until two weeks ago. Nick would be the next to go, leaving Naomi to pick up the extra work, until finally she would have to go too, after more than two decades of walking across the same floorboards, leaving only Peggy and Mitch to run the café until it shut down for good. When they found out that she had committed suicide, maybe they would let Nick stay on as the waiter. Silver lining.

'Hiya, love,' Peggy said from the stove.

'Morning.'

'You hear about Cassie Jennings?' Mitch asked from the breakfast table beneath the window.

'Awful, isn't it?'

'Someone in the offie this mornin' said it was a robbery,' said Peggy.

'Don't be a fool, Peg,' Mitch said, ruffling his newspaper. 'No one slits a girl's throat for 'er purse.'

Naomi took her apron from the hook on the wall and tied it at the back.

'The police said it wasn't being treated as a robbery,' she said, remembering the news footage. 'But I don't understand why else someone would kill an innocent woman.'

'Some people are like that, ain't they,' Mitch said. 'Killin's a thrill for 'em.'

'But why her?'

'She was in the wrong place, wrong time, I say,' Mitch said. 'Cassie didn't seem like the kind of girl to get into trouble, let alone get cut up into strips.'

'Stop it now,' Peggy said. 'I'm feeling sick.'

Peggy was in her fifties, with a voice as thick and sweet as treacle. Even a scalding bath couldn't draw the smell of cooking grease from her skin after all her years of standing at the stove. Naomi loved that smell.

Mitchell had just celebrated his sixtieth birthday. Most of his hair had fallen out over the last twenty years, but he still had a thinning grey ponytail pinching the few remaining strands together at the nape of his neck.

'Can't help thinking about Hayley Miller,' he said, lighting a cigarette.

'That was so long ago, Mitch,' Peggy replied. 'And they never found a body. We don't even know she's dead.'

'Oh there's a body all right,' he said.

'Now stop this talk,' Peggy said, putting a plate on the table. 'Eggs and rashers with hashies.'

'Cheers.'

'Tea for you, love,' Peggy said, and placed a mug in front of Naomi.

'Thanks, Peggy.'

Mitch had the same breakfast every morning. Naomi wondered how he managed it. He stubbed out his cigarette, folded his newspaper and put it beside him, on the left like always.

We're all fools. We've cemented ourselves into our routines and now we're stuck. Move the paper, Mitch. Move the damn paper.

'What do the papers say about the murder?' she asked.

'Sources this, sources that. Why don't they just admit they're making shit up and be done with it?'

'Mitch,' Peggy warned. 'Don't swear in front of Nick.'

Nick was so quiet and reserved that Naomi had forgotten he was in the room.

'It's true, ain't it? And the police won't say much neither. Of course they'll say it's a one-off. They can't have people knowing they're as much in the dark as we are.'

Naomi thought of the person at her door the night before. She parted her lips to tell them, but swallowed down the words.

'You all right, darlin'?' Peggy asked, stroking Naomi's hair. 'You don't look well.'

'I'm just tired, that's all.'

The bell above the front door rang.

'That'll be Derek,' Naomi said.

'At least have a sip of your tea,' Peggy replied.

Naomi took a sip of scalding tea and walked through the kitchen to the diner. She had been working there long enough to know where everything was: nine tables with space to walk between them without tripping even if the place was full, which it hadn't been for years. She took her pen and pad from the pocket of her apron and headed for Derek's favourite table.

'Morning, Derek. Usual?'

She listened to the wind whistle through the gap beneath the front door and press against the window panes.

'Hello?'

The chime above the door danced noisily in the wind.

'Anyone there?'

Naomi thought of herself shivering in the doorway of her house with the stranger standing before her. She stepped back towards the safety of the kitchen.

The window shattered so loudly that she barely heard her own scream. She fell to the floor with her hands out, forcing shards of glass into her palms.

'What the hell's going on in there?' Peggy shouted. 'Naomi! Mitch, get in here!'

She rushed to Naomi's side and rested a hand on her back.

'Are you all right?'

Naomi lifted her hands and felt warm blood trickle down her wrists.

'What happened?' Mitch said.

'Someone threw a brick through the window,' Peggy replied. 'It could have hit Naomi. Look at her hands!'

'Shit.'

'Get the car, Mitch, she'll need stitches.'

'I'm fine, honestly.'

'There are shards of glass deep in your hands, love. You're not fine.'

'Who the hell would do this?' Mitch asked as he walked towards the window, glass crunching beneath his soles. 'Now we'll have to close the damn café!'

'Mitch, the car!'

'All right!'

He stormed back into the kitchen and out the back door, slamming it behind him with such force that the whole building seemed to quiver.

'Come on, love, let's get you up.'

Peggy slipped her hands under Naomi's arms and lifted her to her feet. The wind howled through the broken window.

'Nick, call the police and then start sweeping up this glass.'

'You can't leave him here alone,' Naomi said, her voice noticeably shaking. 'What if the person who did it comes back?'

'I'll take you to the hospital. Mitch can stay here with Nick.'

Peggy led her out the front door and into the cold, blustering day. The wind chime was louder now, screaming in her ears as they passed beneath it and crossed the gravel driveway. The wind sent her hair slanting to the left and cooled the blood streaming down her arms.

'Mitch has pulled the car up out front. I'll open the door for you.'

She heard the laborious purr of the engine. The door opened with a squeal. Peggy rested her hands on Naomi's hips and eased her into the car until she was sitting down, blood dripping onto her lap. Peggy reached over with the seat belt, the smell of Mitch's breakfast stained into her clothes.

'I'm taking her, Mitch. You go in with Nick and wait for the police.'

Mitch got out of the driver's seat and slammed the door behind him.

'There,' Peggy said as she fastened the seat belt. 'Hold your hands up, darlin', and don't clench them like that.'

'But the blood ... your car ...'

'It doesn't matter.'

Naomi heard the door shut and listened to Peggy and Mitch bicker outside the glass. Panicked breaths shook from her lips. She tried to focus on anything but the blood soaking into the sleeves of her shirt and pooling at her elbows.

The brick could have hit her, Peggy had said. The question was, had it been meant to?

EIGHT

No matter how many mints he popped in his mouth, Marcus could still taste bile at the back of his throat. His stomach growled beneath his second shirt of the day. He had tried to eat a sandwich at lunchtime, only to rush to the toilet and spew it back up at the thought of the pink meat inside Cassie Jennings' neck. Maybe he would become a vegetarian.

He sat hunched over his desk and read through the list of people in the town who were known to them for the wrong reasons, searching for a link to the murder. Another task Lisa had given him, almost as if she were punishing him for throwing up.

Marcus always forgot how many people harboured dark secrets until he read over their pasts.

The local butcher, whom he had seen just the day before, had spent eight years in prison for grievous bodily harm. He had beaten a burglar with a leg of lamb, grinding his head into the white-tiled floor until flesh was dangling from the animal's bone. When the police arrived, they hadn't known if it was lamb splattered up the white tiled walls, or whether the meat belonged to the man twitching on the floor, his scalp sliced open and hanging over his eyes.

'Team meeting,' Lisa barked. 'Now.'

She passed through the office and kicked open the door to the incident room. She had come from a meeting with the superintendent. If she was in trouble, so were they. Marcus piled into the incident room with the rest of the team, who looked equally drained.

Amber O'Neill had applied make-up since the briefing that morning, but it had worn away until all that remained was gloops of mascara in the corners of her eyes. The youngest in the team, she looked as haggard as the rest of them. When she noticed Marcus eyeing her hands shaking on the tabletop, she placed them in her lap.

DS Blake Crouch's tie hung a couple of inches below his collar. His eyes were red, with inflamed lines framing the contact lenses that he should have taken out hours ago. Some of the dark hairs on his head had turned grey, which seemed to make him more and more desperate to bag the next promotion. Marcus could almost smell the anxiety leaking through his pores.

'This is horseshit,' Lisa spat as she looked round at her team. 'No witnesses. No statements, thanks to the kid being scared speechless. No CCTV. Nothing. The press is hounding every officer that steps in or out of the station and we have absolutely eff-all to tell them.'

Without the uniformed officers in the room, it became abundantly clear how understaffed they were for a murder investigation.

Lisa rubbed the bridge of her nose and sighed. 'I refuse to be dragged into the superintendent's office again tomorrow without a single lead. Tomorrow we hit this from every angle we have. I want you all in the office by eight o'clock and waiting in this room for my instructions.'

She looked at Blake. 'Any luck with the CCTV from the off-licence?'

'A dummy camera. Hasn't worked in years.'

'Anyone from the flats see or hear anything?'

'Only a few of them were in. I'll try again tomorrow.'

'What about previous convictions?' She turned to Marcus, who immediately sat up straighter. 'Any red flags?'

'Some possible suspects convicted of violence against women, but they were all domestic.'

'Amber,' she said, so quickly that she made the woman jump. Amber had seemed on edge before, but beneath Lisa's glare, she looked ready to shatter. 'Has Dr Ling been in touch with the DNA results from the post-mortem?'

'The only DNA that was found at the scene belonged to the victim.'

'Christ.' She pinched the bridge of her nose, creasing the skin around her eyes. 'What about the phones? What did the records show?'

Marcus was glad that the responsibility had been passed on to Amber. She rearranged the paperwork in front of her, shuffling through for the right document, the pages quivering in her hands. Lisa watched her impatiently with a clenched jaw.

'The smartphone was for personal use. Communication with friends and family, sexting with an ex-boyfriend, group chats with her girlfriends, another group chat with colleagues. She had worked for the local newspaper as a reporter for two years—'

'I know,' Lisa cut in. 'What about the second phone?'

Amber turned the page. Marcus wanted to lean over the desk and tell her to take a deep breath.

'There was only one person she was in contact with using the second phone. There were no texts or voicemails, but lots of logged calls. They started around February this year and stopped the day she died. The number was unlisted.'

'For Christ's sake,' Lisa said, biting down on her bottom lip. 'Nothing? Nothing we can trace?'

Amber shook her head.

Lisa pointed at Blake. 'You'll be following me tomorrow. I can't have my staff vomiting perfectly good coffee.'

Marcus's cheeks burned. He clenched his fists beneath the table.

Blake sniggered under his breath.

'You think this is funny?' Lisa asked. Blake shrank an inch in his chair. 'A woman is dead, and while we play catch-up, the person responsible is out there, potentially gutting another woman as we speak.' She slammed her palm down on the table. All three of them flinched. 'Laugh on your own time. Here, you take the job seriously. Understand?'

Blake nodded quickly before dropping his eyes.

'The press is already trying to tie the murder to the Hayley Miller case. I don't want any of you even thinking her name, let alone speaking it aloud, you hear? We've only just earned back the trust of the town after that shit show. I'm not having anything like that happen again under my command.'

'What happened last time?' Marcus asked, forgetting himself.

'Nothing that relates to this case,' she spat. 'And I don't want to hear another word about it.'

Amber cleared her throat. 'Hayley Miller's mother has been calling all day, asking for the superintendent. I tried to deflect her like you asked, but she keeps—'

'Next time she calls, put her through to me. Now get out of my sight, all of you.'

Marcus stepped out of the incident room and finally breathed. It was only then that he realised he was trembling.

'Are you all right?' Amber asked, looking up at him with large, doe-like eyes. She rested a hand on his arm.

He nodded quickly and headed to the toilets. He bolted the cubicle door behind him and leaned against it with his eyes closed, breathing in the smell of piss.

Fuck her. Fuck all of them.

He took a leak, zipped up his fly and left the cubicle. He stopped at the sight of his reflection in the mirror.

He looked exhausted. The dark circles around his eyes resembled bruises from a fist. He bent over the sink and splashed his face with cold water, then glanced back up at his reflection. Bloodshot eyes stared back at him.

'You can do this,' he whispered. 'Just get to a year, and you can move on.'

He wiped his face with a paper towel and headed back.

Lisa was in her office, her chair turned from the desk and her feet up on the windowsill, her phone pressed to her ear.

Marcus took his suit jacket from the back of his chair and

slung his bag over his shoulder. Just as he was about to leave, he heard Amber and Blake in the kitchen, whispering harshly beneath their breath.

'Tell me what to do,' she was saying. 'Please, just tell me what I should do.'

'Why should I help you? What you did could have destroyed my marriage, my career. I don't owe you anything.'

Blake strode out of the kitchen with Amber pulling at his arm. Tears shimmered on her cheeks.

'Blake, please,' she begged.

They both stopped at the sight of him.

'Night,' Marcus said.

Amber let go of Blake's arm and wiped her cheeks, adjusted her shirt. 'Night.'

'Yeah, night,' Blake echoed.

You couldn't have shagged a younger woman you met in the pub could you, Blake? Marcus thought.

Marcus left the station, took a deep breath of the night air, and decided he would go to the pub before he went home, and drink until the memory of the day became easier to bear.

NINE

Peggy pulled the car to a stop outside the café.

'Mitch used your spare key and took Max home. Let me drop you off, Naomi. You shouldn't be walking alone at night.'

'I need the fresh air,' Naomi replied. She had had enough of the hot, recycled air of the accident and emergency ward.

The hospital was two towns away and severely understaffed. By the time they had been seen and were out of A&E, a road traffic accident had congested every road back to Balkerne Heights. The journey home had taken hours instead of minutes.

She could still hear the screams of the baby with a temperature high enough to scare a nurse into letting mother and infant jump the queue. The sound reminded her why she couldn't be with Dane: she couldn't be that mother holding her screaming baby, worrying if the little life she had created was going to survive the night. She wasn't even sure that she had that amount of love to give. As she had sat in the ward, she had thought of her birth mother. She could have left Naomi in the hospital, in the warmth and safety of others, but instead she had chosen to leave her alone in the dark.

'And how are you going to hold your cane with those hands?'

The glass had been picked out with tweezers; three cuts had needed stitches. Both hands were bound with bandages.

'I'll be fine.'

Peggy sighed. 'Don't come in until you're better, all right?'

'I can't afford the time off, Peggy.'

'It's paid leave, love. We're not going to punish you for getting hurt.'

'Thank you.'

Exhaustion hung from her body. She had to fight to keep her head from lolling back onto the headrest. She could fall apart once she was home. Not before.

'Sorry again about the window.'

'Why are you sorry? You didn't do it.'

Someone was aiming the brick at me.

Peggy left the engine running as she ran inside the café and came back with Naomi's coat. Naomi climbed out of the car. She could hear Mitch locking up the front of the café, the keys jangling in his hand. He called over and asked if she was all right. She nodded in reply and slipped her arms inside the coat. She hugged Peggy tight and headed off down the street.

The top of the cane sat awkwardly in her grip and jabbed at her wounds. She heard Peggy's car turn out of the road and disappear into the night. The thought of home kept her moving. Once the door was locked behind her, she would curl up in the chair by the fire with Max by her feet.

The town was eerily quiet. The shops would have their metal shutters drawn over the windows, the lights turned out, sandwich boards brought inside. The wind whistled through the empty streets and sent dead leaves flying past her ankles. It was only then that she remembered what her mother had said: *don't go out after dark.*

She swept the stick in front of her, feeling for inconsistencies in the path, which came as vibrations up the cane. When the pain got too much, she switched it to her other hand.

A barge horn sounded out at sea and echoed through the empty streets. The clock on the face of the town hall chimed.

Whenever she walked alone, she thought of her mother, who had helped her memorise the town until she had her own map made up of sounds and steps inside her mind. She had taught Naomi as though it was all a game, counting each step from the house to the end of the street like a beat to a song, likening the cobbles down the lanes to the yellow brick road in the land of Oz, swinging Naomi's hand to make her smile. There were five lamp posts from the post office to the bank, and four drain covers to the zebra crossing that would lead her across the road to the bakery. When she thought of the woman who had adopted her and gone out of her way to make her feel safe in the world, she wondered what life might have been like had her real mother not abandoned her in the night. She couldn't imagine that woman spending her day off leading her around the town, walking a few paces behind when it was time for Naomi to try and make it alone with her cane.

Rain began to fall, slowly flattening her hair around her face. She hated the rain; it disguised so many sounds that she needed to hear. By the time she was halfway down the high street, she was soaked through, with rain dripping from her jaw and the hem of her coat.

The smell of marijuana stained the air. A loud burst of laughter echoed down the street. The teens were sitting at the bus stop, smoking and claiming the street for the night.

Naomi tapped her cane against the wall and waited for the end. She could slip down the next side road without being seen.

She turned down the side street, put her hand to the wall, and traced her fingers against bricks until she felt the cool paint of a doorway, then delicately followed the numbers screwed onto the door with her index finger: 15. If she had walked down Straight Lane, as she believed, she was heading the wrong way for home. If she took the next right, she could loop around until she was back on the main road again, out of sight of the teens at the bus stop, who would taunt her like they always did.

She turned right down a narrow footpath, with uneven concrete on the ground. The cane hit the brick walls on either side with every sweep, but she could barely hear its usual scrape along the ground over the pummelling of the rain. The alley smelt of urine and waste, wafting up into the air in a putrid flurry, disturbed by the downpour. The further she went, the louder the sounds grew in the narrow space: her breaths, the beat of her heart, the puddles splashing underfoot.

'No! No, please!'

Naomi froze.

'Hello?'

The rain fell around her and tapped incessantly on her coat. She took a tentative step forward.

'Who's there?'

She listened to the patter of the rain and her own quickening breaths.

A deafening scream ripped through the air.

Naomi jolted and dropped her cane. She held her breath to listen to the night. A dog barked from a distant garden. Wet leaves bunched around her shoes as she tried to find her footing.

Her legs were shaking. She couldn't move.

'Who's there?' she whispered.

She crouched down and felt around for the cane. It had clattered against the wet ground and bounced on impact. The collapsible canes were good for storage, but they were too light. The bandages on her hands soaked up the rainwater as she skirted over puddles. Rotting leaves stuck to her fingers. She found the cane lying in the groove between the brick wall and the ground.

She rose to her feet and tightened her grip; if she dropped the cane a second time, she might not find it again. She had moved and turned in search of it, and now she wasn't sure which way she had come. She stood in the alley listening to the echo of her breaths, trying to remember each turn she had made, listening for breathing that wasn't her own. She raised her hand in front of her, hoping to feel something, anything, that would tell her she had imagined it all.

It's all in your head.

A warm hand enclosed hers. She snatched her hand back, stumbled into the wall and pressed her back against the bricks. She covered her mouth with her hand. The bandage tasted of rain and blood. It was her blood; it had to be. A stitch must have come loose. She dropped her hand and felt the bricks with her fingers.

'Who's there? Who are you?'

Drops of rain flew from her lips with each desperate breath.

'Are ... are you still there?'

She stroked the end of her cane against the ground to get her bearings, her teeth clenched to suppress an approaching sob. As she pushed herself away from the wall and turned right, she longed to give in to the instinct to run, but she had no idea how far she would get or what she might find. The cane hit something heavy in the middle of the path. She stumbled to a stop and raised her hand to feel the air before her. Her fingers grazed something wet and cold. A zip on a coat. The echo of a beating heart vibrated against her fingertips. The stranger's breath exhaled sharply like a laugh and warmed her skin.

She covered her mouth as soon as the sob came, and tasted the blood on the bandages, blood she knew couldn't be hers. She turned back and forced one quivering leg in front of the other. Fear seized her muscles and squeezed her heart into a fleshy fist. The cane thrashed into the wall and cracked.

'Help!'

Blood seeped through the bandage as she tightened her grip on the cane. Heavy footsteps followed behind her in wide strides.

'Someone help me!'

She rushed through the night, raking the cane against the ground in violent thrashes until it hit something with a fleshy thud. She stopped abruptly and stumbled, teetering on tiptoes. Every bone in her body was trembling. She nudged the obstruction with the end of her cane and felt it rock lightly.

She couldn't hear the footsteps any more, just the incessant rush of the rain and the anxious breaths blasting from her lips.

She prodded at the obstruction in the hope of finding a way around it, but it took up the lane. She crouched down and lowered her hand.

Material first. Soaked fabric stuck to something meaty. Her fingertips trailed across the wet mass until they grazed skin. She flinched and fell back on her heels, dropping her cane for her hands to take the brunt. Her palms pressed down onto the wet path and tugged at the stitches. A wet cry flew from her lips and echoed down the alley.

She rested back onto her knees and hovered a hand over the body again, begging herself to stop shaking, to take it all in. She had to know if the person was alive. She lowered her hands and felt hair, skin, an unmoving face, and followed it down towards the neck to feel for a pulse. Her fingers pressed against torn skin and slipped into a deep wound. Her fingernails scraped bone.

She snatched her hand away, covered in something warm and sticky, and cradled it against her heaving chest, smearing the stranger's blood on the breast of her coat. She tried to breathe through the sobs, but the air barely filled her lungs.

A breath caressed the back of her neck and she froze. Rain ran down her face and dripped off her jaw. She could smell excitement on the person's breath, feel their warmth against her back. Hands grabbed at her wrists and dragged her forwards.

'No, please!'

The stranger's gloved fingers laced between hers and pushed her hands down onto the body. Tears ran down her cheeks as pain shot up her arms. Long wet hair tangled around her fingers. She felt breasts beneath the fabric and a stab wound in the stomach. She retched as her fingers slipped into the wound, which felt like a small, toothless mouth in the torso. Tears and snot dripped from her face.

'Enough!' she screamed.

The hands paused, just enough for her to feel the stranger's pulse beating through latex gloves, and released her. Naomi snatched her own hands from the body and instinctively wiped her nose with the back of her hand, smearing blood across the base of her nostrils and the flesh of her top lip. The gloved hand wiped a tear from her cheek.

'Kill me,' she whispered.

She felt one final breath warm her lips. Footsteps splashed through puddles and dissipated down the lane, until it was just her, the body and the rain.

TEN

Marcus followed Lisa down the corridor, focusing purely on keeping his steps in a straight line. He had just finished his third beer when the call came in about the second body. He was still trying to forget the first.

Tension had filled the station in the few short hours that he had been away. Even the usual punters in the cells had been subdued. The latest lead changed everything: they had their first witness.

'I want to talk to her first, while it's still fresh,' Lisa said, her stride hurried. If she could smell the beer on him, she hadn't said. 'I'm not leaving it up to a uniform. We'll go straight from here to the scene. Forensics will have it ready for us by then.'

'Thanks for letting me in on this.'

'Only because Blake didn't pick up his damn phone.' She stopped in the hallway and took a good look at him. He immediately stood straighter. 'You can't freak out on me again, understand?'

He nodded quickly.

If he closed his eyes, he could still see Cassie peering out at him from that musky white skin, her body drained of life and any memory of who she was before.

From the people he had spoken to so far, he had learned that Cassie had been well liked in the town, known as someone who was going places, her name once clawing a smile at the corners of their lips when they talked of her working for one of the big national newspapers one day. But when they heard her name now, the first thing they would remember would be her gruesome end.

'The officers who attended the 999 call said she was pretty shaken up,' he said, conscious of pronouncing every syllable.

'Wouldn't you be?'

Lisa's hair was tied up in a scraggly ponytail, with stray hairs dangling down the nape of her neck. She wore the same clothes from earlier in the day. Marcus wondered if she had been at the station the whole time, or if she had gone home only to step back into her uniform. It was the first time he had seen her ruffled.

'The officers who brought her in said she had bandaged hands,' he said. 'She said someone threw a brick through a window where she works earlier today; she cut her hands on glass or something. It didn't happen at the scene.'

'Sounds like a pretty shit day,' Lisa said.

They stopped outside the interview room door, just as Lisa's phone began to vibrate in her pocket. She looked at the screen and cut the call. It began buzzing again before she had even put it back in her pocket. She sighed and turned it off.

'I'll lead, you chip in if I forget anything.'

Marcus nodded and gulped down his resentment, hoping it hadn't shown in his face.

Lisa opened the door.

'Hello, Naomi, my name is Detective Inspector Lisa Elliott, and this is my colleague, Detective Sergeant Marcus Campbell.'

The woman stared ahead as if she was lost in a memory. As Marcus looked closer, he saw that her whole body was shaking, sending tremors through the blanket draped over her shoulders.

They sat down on the opposite side of the table. Naomi's eyes didn't move. Her hands were wrapped around a cup of milky tea. She had full lips, deep brown eyes that, on closer inspection, seemed to flicker minutely, and jet-black hair that surrounded her face in a wavy mass, still damp from the rain. Marcus could see the absolute fear in her gaze, but there was something else there too. It took him a moment to realise that their witness was blind.

Lisa noticed too. They shared a look.

'Naomi, are you blind?'

The woman nodded.

Lisa leaned back in her chair and rubbed her eyelids, her jaw clenching beneath the skin.

The uniformed officers should have told them about this. Marcus thought they probably would have if Lisa had been more agreeable with her colleagues, and wondered if she would make the same connection.

'We have a few questions for you about what happened earlier this evening,' Marcus said. 'I'll be writing down what's said in our chat, and you'll have a copy to take home with you.'

Give the blind woman some light reading. Good thinking.

'Or we can get you a copy of the recording,' he said, his cheeks burning. 'If that's easier.'

'Okay,' she said quietly.

Marcus pressed play on the recorder and introduced everyone in the room for the tape. Most stations had moved on and integrated the recording equipment within the room like a fly on the wall, but Balkerne Heights was stuck in the past, with such a small budget that even the coffee supply was rationed to three cups per head, per day. They got through their allowance before noon.

'Please tell us what happened this evening, in your own words.'

Naomi took a sip of tea. Drops of beige liquid ran down the side of the cup and dribbled over her fingers.

'I ... I was walking home from work, and—'

'Where do you work?' Lisa interjected.

'The Orchard Café. My bosses are Mitchell and Peggy Delaware.'

Marcus knew the name Mitchell Delaware. He thought back to the files he had read that day, the crimes that had been committed in the neighbouring streets, and remembered.

Mitchell had been found in a local brothel during a raid in 1999, a small terraced house on the worst street in town, filled with young foreign women who had been promised a better life, only to be forced to share a bed with dozens of men each day to pay back their debts. He had only been given a slap on the wrist the first time. Marcus wondered if the man's wife knew about the secrets that lay between them in bed each night.

'Continue,' Lisa said.

'I was walking down the high street and took a different route; I wanted to avoid some teenagers sitting at the bus stop. I've memorised most of the town's roads, but not all. I wasn't sure where I was and took another right, hoping to loop back round onto the high street. That was when I heard someone in the alley with me. She ... she was begging for her life. And then I heard her scream.'

'The victim?'

Naomi nodded and knocked a tear from her eye. She quickly wiped it away with the back of her bandaged hand. Her eyes were restless, twitching from side to side.

'I called out, but nothing happened. I turned to leave the way I came, but someone blocked the path.'

'Who?' Lisa asked.

'I think it was the ...' She couldn't seem to form her lips around the word. 'The ... killer. Whoever it was followed me down the alley until I found ...'

She took a sip of tea and closed her eyes as steam rose from the cup.

'The body,' Lisa said.

Naomi nodded.

'For the purposes of the tape, Naomi nodded her head in agreement.' Marcus wondered if she could smell the beer on his breath.

'What happened next?' Lisa asked.

'The person who killed her came up behind me.'

'You think it was the killer, or you know?'

'Well, whoever it was came up behind me and took my hands and ...'

Another tear fell, but this time she didn't wipe it away. She wasn't in the room any more; she was back in the alley.

'The stranger's hands dragged mine up and down the body, made me feel it. It was still warm. I felt a stab wound in her torso and a cut on her neck.'

The uniformed officers who had responded to her 999 call and brought her to the station had cleaned Naomi up pretty well: the blood had been washed from her face, and she wore a plain grey tracksuit given to civilians in custody; her hands had been scrubbed clean and wrapped in fresh bandages, though crimson stains still lurked under her fingernails, the blood that had once flowed through a living body now stuck within the crevices of another. The officer who had called it in said Naomi had been found with the dead woman's hair tangled around the base of her fingers.

'Were the hands small? Large?'

'Medium. Gloved.'

'In what? Wool, leather, latex?'

'Latex, I think, or something similar.'

'You think.'

Lisa was struggling. Usually she would stare into a person's eyes until they told her everything she wanted to hear, but Naomi was immune to her penetrative glare.

'I begged for them to stop. And then I felt a hand stroke my face.'

'Stroke?' Marcus asked.

'Yes. It wiped a tear off my cheek.'

'Why didn't he kill you too?'

Marcus shot a look at Lisa; she was leaning in as though she wanted Naomi to feel the heat of her words.

'I ... I don't know.'

'Why would this person kill a woman and then give you a tender stroke? What makes you so special?'

'I don't know. Pity?'

'Because you're blind?'

'Maybe I wasn't a threat because I couldn't see their face.'

'Can you describe the person to me?'

'Medium build, I think. Like I said, average-size hands.'

'A man or a woman? Cologne or perfume?'

'I don't know. The rain, it throws me off.'

'Aren't your other senses supposed to be heightened or something?'

Marcus bit down on his bottom lip.

'All I could smell was blood.'

Lisa shook her head. 'Well, thank you for coming in, Ms Hannah, you've been very helpful. DS Campbell will show you out.' She pushed her chair back, the legs screeching against the floor, and headed for the door.

'One moment, please,' Marcus said to Naomi, and followed Lisa out of the room.

'What the hell was that?' he called after her as she headed down the corridor. She stopped and turned back.

'Are you kidding? The woman's blind. She couldn't tell us anything of value.'

'You haven't even given her a chance.'

'Out of all those questions we asked her, the only answers we got were that she gets lost easily and the killer was wearing gloves. A dog could have told us more. We haven't got time for this.'

'Perhaps you're forgetting she's a victim herself. She found a body today.'

Lisa approached him, only stopping when her face was inches from his. 'Perhaps *you're* forgetting who you're talking to.'

He held his breath and clenched his teeth until his jaw clicked.

'Sorry, boss.'

Both of them noticed the insincerity in his voice.

'Get a uniform to drop her home. Meet me at the car in ten.'

Lisa turned and headed back down the hallway, her ponytail swishing left and right.

Marcus sighed and returned to the room.

Naomi was still sitting at the table with the cup of tea in her hands, with her head tilted to the right to listen as he entered. He couldn't imagine living her life, trapped in the darkness with the taunts of a busy, vibrant world right before her eyes. He wondered if she got lonely in the dark.

'I'm sorry about that,' he said. 'My boss, she's ...'

'She doesn't think I'm a credible witness because I'm blind.'

Marcus hesitated. 'Yes.'

Naomi rested her hands in her lap and sucked on her bottom lip.

'Can I do anything?'

'Can someone take me home?'

'Of course, and here,' Marcus took a card from his wallet and put it on the table before realising how thoughtless the act was. He tried to prise it from the tabletop, picking at the edge with his fingernails, before placing it in her bandaged palm. 'My card, in case you need anything.'

When she didn't say anything, it dawned on him that she wouldn't be able to read it.

'Is there someone who could read the number to you, perhaps?' He hadn't wanted to sound condescending, but he could hear it in his tone. He cleared his throat. 'Or I could put it in your phone for you.'

'That's all right.'

She picked up her cane and stood, leaving the blanket on the back of the chair. The cane looked bent, and he spotted the crack in the middle, like a break in a bone.

'Detective …'

'Call me Marcus.'

'Marcus, am I in danger?'

The truth was, he had no idea. Lisa had just walked off and abandoned their one and only witness. Could they protect her? Did they need to?

'I don't think so.'

Way to instil confidence in a witness, you dick.

He cleared his throat again. 'I'm confident there won't be any repercussions, but if you're ever worried about your safety, call me.'

Naomi nodded languidly. It was clear she didn't believe him.

Marcus led her through the station and arranged for PC Kate Finch to take her home. He handed Naomi a flyer for a counselling service and guided her to the car park, at a loss what to say to a woman who had felt death with her own hands. They stood in the cold waiting for Kate to bring the car around.

When the car pulled up, Marcus opened the door, then shut it behind her. Naomi stared ahead, clutching the flyer in shaking hands, and he wondered how long it would take for her to trust the world again. He nodded at Kate in the driver's seat and watched the car draw away.

'Marcus.'

He turned. Lisa stood in the doorway with her face drained of colour and a fist curled tightly around her phone.

'The murdered woman the witness found ...'

'Yeah?'

She hesitated, swallowed so hard he saw her throat move. 'It was Amber.'

ELEVEN

The crime scene was different this time. It wasn't just the additional personnel, it was the grim silence that hung over them, pressing down on every pair of shoulders. This victim was one of their own.

Officer Amber O'Neill was lying on her back in a dark pool of blood and rain. Her head had fallen to the right. Her eyes peered down the alley and watched every officer arrive, giving everyone a good look at the open wound in her neck. Her coat had been yanked from her body and discarded further down the alley, and the white shirt on her torso was askew, with the collar resting on the middle of her back, and half of the buttons pulled clean off, exposing her bra and the tender white flesh on her chest. Someone had stolen her life and taken her dignity with it. Marcus remembered the touch of her hand on his arm just hours before, how warm and alive it had been. Now the girl was dead at his feet.

Lisa was staring down at the body. Her jaw clenched until the bones moved beneath the skin.

Marcus was quiet too, but not just because the only member of the team he had actually liked had died. Superintendent

Matthew Cunningham stood between them, taking in the sight. The superintendent was another member of staff who Marcus had only met the once, on his second day on the job. Cunningham was often out of the office, working from different locations. But since the first murder, he had been working from the station and going in and out without being seen by anyone but Lisa. Until now.

Dr Ling was examining the body to the flash of the camera blasting white light over the rain, the blood, the flesh. The flash filled Marcus's eyes until all he saw was white blots in his vision, which followed him every time he tried to look away. The tarpaulin tent protecting the body flapped and whined with the wind.

'Explain this fucking mess.'

The superintendent was a man of few words, but each of them hit Marcus in his chest like a finger jabbing at his ribcage.

'I believe—'

'Not you,' he said to Dr Ling. 'Her.'

For a mere second, Marcus saw fear in Lisa's eyes. He would have to relish it later.

'It appears to be the same killer. The body—'

'Amber O'Neill's body,' Cunningham spat. 'An *officer's* body.'

'Amber is similar in age to the first victim, same ethnicity and build; her throat was cut in the same fashion, and her body was found in an alley, a place in which the killer likes to attack. Whether consciously or not, the killer is following a pattern.'

'I could have told you that,' he said.

Marcus tried to appear unfazed by the superintendent's

intimidating presence, and hid his shaking hands in his pockets. Cunningham reminded him of his father, a man who was prone to shouting and always ready to use his fists. Marcus felt every punch his father had thrown as if the bruises were rising back up to the surface.

'We are looking for a link between the victims to see if they are meaningful attacks or random selection within the killer's preference.'

'A police officer is dead, Elliott. This isn't just some random girl; it's bigger than that now. We don't have time to stroll our way through this.'

'I know, sir.'

'I fucking hope you do.'

Cunningham sighed and looked over his shoulder to check the uniformed officers were still manning the entrance to the alley. Marcus knew he wasn't thinking about Amber. He was thinking about the press and the answers he would have to give.

'Why was she walking home?'

'She didn't own a car.'

'And no one offered her a lift?'

'With all due respect, sir, I'm her boss, not her mum.'

Cunningham stared at her until she looked away. Her eyes landed on the body, revealing a flash of grief as they settled on Amber's sliced neck.

'You,' he said to Marcus. 'Tell me about the witness.'

'Naomi Hannah, thirty-six years old, blind.' He could hear his voice shaking slightly in the man's presence.

'What did she have to say?' he asked.

'She's not a reliable—'

'I'm not talking to you, Elliott.'

'She described the suspect as of medium build, and believes he was wearing latex gloves, or something with a similar consistency.'

'Anything else?'

'He seemed to ...' Lisa watched him, as though every word he spoke was a betrayal, 'play with her. I think the killer enjoyed her disability; it added to the fun of it. He blocked her path in the alley so she would have to turn back towards the body, and then made her interact with it.'

Marcus knew he was in for it the second the superintendent left, but he had to speak his mind. Lisa wouldn't listen to him any other way.

'Did the killer try to harm her too?'

'Not physically.'

'Interesting. Lisa, work on this.'

'She isn't important in finding—'

'I told you to work on it, not debate it. The way the killer interacted with the witness could be key to finding out who this fucker is.'

'Yes, sir.'

Cunningham looked at his watch. 'I want the scene report on my desk first thing, and the follow-up routes you're taking. It won't be long before the press hears about this and I want to be ready. This cannot turn out like Hayley Miller's case, understand? We can't close another high-profile case unsolved. Nail this fucker.' He took one final look at Amber's body; his right eyelid twitched at the sight. 'And for God's sake, someone tell the girl's family.'

'Sir,' they said as he turned and made his way down the alley, lighting a cigarette in a cupped hand. Smoke curled over his shoulder.

Lisa and Marcus stood before the body in silence. Dr Ling spoke to her colleague in whispers. The smell of cigarette smoke had just begun to fill Marcus's nostrils when Lisa squared up to him, pushing herself onto the balls of her feet.

'Never show me up like that again.'

'He asked me what I thought, so I told him.'

'You went behind my back. I told you the blind woman wasn't important, because it's true. She's nothing to this investigation, and nothing to the killer, otherwise she'd be dead. My word is to be sacred from now on, you hear? If anyone asks for your thoughts, you tell them mine. I run this team, I run this investigation, and I run you. Understand?'

He nodded, tightening his fists in his pockets.

'We're a woman down, so you and Blake need to step it up. No bitching at each other, no stepping out of line. Be in the office by eight sharp. It's going to be a long day.'

Marcus nodded and turned back towards the mouth of the alley, submerging himself in the darkness of the night before he dared to take a deep breath.

Lisa didn't trust his judgement; she would rather send him home and get all the work, and the credit, for herself.

'Lisa,' Dr Ling said behind him. 'Amber had two phones. Just like Cassie Jennings.'

He stopped mid-step.

'You're sure?' Lisa said.

'Look.'

Marcus walked back up the alley and stood beside her. Two mobile phones were nestled in Amber's bag.

'Same make as the first victim's,' Dr Ling said, pointing to the pay-as-you-go model.

The phone was indeed the same as Cassie's, a knock-off designed to look like a touch-screen smartphone but for an eighth of the price.

'Shit!' Lisa stood back and paced up and down with her hands on her head. 'We can't know for sure they were in contact with each other, not until we link the calls from each of the phones.'

'What were they doing that meant they needed untraceable phones?' Marcus asked.

'Right now, I don't even want to know.' She rubbed the skin on her face and released a hot sigh into her hands. 'We're fucked if Amber was doing something she shouldn't have.'

She closed her eyes and sighed.

'Go home. I need you fresh and alert tomorrow.'

Marcus turned away again without a word and clenched and unclenched his hands, trying to bring the blood back into them.

He thought back to the argument he'd overheard between Amber and Blake at the office, the tears shimmering on her face and the desperation in her eyes.

Tell me what to do. Please, just tell me what I should do.

Why should I help you? What you did could have destroyed my marriage, my career. I don't owe you anything.

What did you do, Amber? he thought to himself. What did you do that could have affected Blake?

He fished his car keys from his pocket. Lisa had decided not to drive him to the scene after all. She'd told him she needed time to think. He wondered if she had been coming up with her next statement for the press. Whatever the reason, she had made it very clear: she preferred to work alone.

He thought of Blake and the anger that had radiated off him as he emerged from the kitchen. Whatever had happened between them could link to Amber's murder. She had needed help. But it was too late. He would talk to Blake tomorrow and find out what he knew.

He sat behind the wheel of his car and rested his forehead on the steering wheel, unfurling a hot sigh into his lap. He thought about what the superintendent had said about the Hayley Miller case. She was like a ghost stalking everyone in the town. Everyone seemed to know about her but him. Their eagerness to keep the case in the dark only made him want to bring it to light. He had to find out what had happened to her.

As he turned the key in the ignition, he noticed his hand was shaking, and only then did he realise it wasn't hunger churning in his stomach, but fear.

TWELVE

Naomi knew it was her own blood coating her fingers, but she couldn't shake the thought that it belonged to the murdered woman.

The police officer had taken her to the hospital to get her stitches redone after she'd spotted fresh blood seeping through the bandages. Kate, her name was. She had sat with her for over an hour as they waited for a nurse to come, needle in hand, ready to sew her back together again. It would take more than a few stitches to fix her.

Stop moving, the nurse had said curtly. But Naomi couldn't stop her hands from shaking. In the end, the woman had pressed the backs of her hands against the top of the metal table.

It's not her blood.

She could still feel the woman's hair tangled around her fingers and the blood packed beneath her nails. She couldn't see that the water in the sink was running red with her own blood.

Max lay by her feet, dozing lightly.

Once more and then I'll go to sleep.

She couldn't bear the thought of closing her eyes. The memories would be waiting for her.

The brush jabbed beneath her fingernail. She dropped it into the sink and shoved the finger in her mouth, massaging the wound with her tongue. The taste reminded her of the alley, breathing in that metallic scent of death. She sat on the side of the bath and sucked at the wound until the pain ceased.

Max barked and chased the sound of the doorbell. Naomi jolted and bit down on her finger.

She longed to avoid whoever was waiting at her front door, but she couldn't face going to sleep. Closing her eyes meant lowering her guard. She was too easy to catch when she was awake; she couldn't risk sleep. Not yet.

She crept down the stairs, listening to Max shuffling impatiently before the door. She wiped her finger on her top and took the handle.

'Naomi, what's wrong?' Dane asked. 'Why are you crying?'

She patted her cheeks and felt the tears.

'Naomi? What's happened?'

He stepped into the doorway and guided her back inside; shut the door behind him. She could smell the aftershave lathered on his neck and fought the urge to sit him down, crawl up onto his lap and breathe it all in.

'Your hands! What the hell happened to you?'

His shock made it all real. The words caught in her throat.

'Naomi?'

He held her arm and she crumpled. She fell into his chest, wetting his work tunic with her tears.

'Who did this to you?'

'I ... I don't know.'

'We should call the police.'

'I have!' She was going to tell him, but he was too quick.

'Naomi ...'

She kissed his lips and pulled at him until their bodies were pressed together, ribs to ribs. She felt the hammering of his heart against her chest.

'Are you sure?' he whispered, his words warming her tears.

She drew his lips to her again, tasting him, needing every part of him, and let him take her in his arms and carry her up the stairs.

She needed to feel safe.

She needed to forget.

THIRTEEN

Marcus slipped into the archives room and closed the door quietly behind him. He checked the clock on the wall. There was no telling how long Lisa and Blake would be in their meeting. He had to move quickly.

The windowless room smelt of dust. Damp speckled the walls. The room doubled as a supply closet, with jars of coffee, boxes of tea bags and toilet rolls stacked on top of the filing cabinets lining the walls, each of which was filled with blood and murder, rape and domestic violence, petty crimes and parking ticket receipts. Every crime that had happened in Balkerne Heights had been shoved into the drawers, hidden away in the dark depths of the station to collect dust and grow yellow with age. But the town remembered, and Marcus was ready to claw the past back up again. If there was a connection between Hayley Miller's disappearance and the recent killings, he would find it.

He scanned the labels on the cabinets, arranged by year, and thought back to the scene of Cassie Jennings' murder, the first time he had heard the mention of the past.

Do you think this could be the same attacker as …

Not a chance. That was twenty years ago.

He turned the skeleton key in the lock for cases from 1997 and pulled open the first drawer. The cabinet's musky breath billowed up into his face.

Inside were wads of paperwork wrapped in brown slip files. He skimmed through them, scanning the dates, the crimes, the pain and suffering moving beneath his fingers.

He glanced at the closed door as he heard footsteps from the hallway. He held his breath and listened, frozen to the spot, until he realised it wasn't footsteps but the rapid beat of his heart.

He slammed the drawer shut and opened the next, holding his breath against the dust as it drifted up. He skimmed through, wiping his brow as a drop of sweat fell into the drawer and soaked into a rape case from March 1997. He stopped when he noticed the large file hidden at the back of the drawer. Pages bulged from it as though they were ready to burst out. He pulled the rest of the paperwork forward and eased the file out, scraping his knuckles against the metal slider on the inside of the drawer. He licked at the blood and opened the cover.

Hayley Miller.

The file was quivering in his hands, stained with a small swipe of his blood. He licked his finger and tried to wipe it away, but only succeeded in rubbing it into a swirling red cloud.

He couldn't read it all there in the archives room; there were over a hundred pages in his hands. He would have to make his own copy during the day and return the file before anyone noticed.

He quickly skimmed through it, watching black words and photos whip past in a blur. He stopped as a familiar name stared up at him.

Interrogation of Dane Hannah in relation to case 99367, 1900 hours, 5 April 1997.

He flipped the file shut and checked the name on the front again. It was definitely the file on Hayley Miller's disappearance. This Dane shared the same surname as their witness.

The door handle snapped downwards with a heavy hand and the door knocked into the open drawer of the filing cabinet. Lisa stood in the doorway, looking at the file in his hands.

'What's that?'

A drop of sweat snaked down his back.

'I'm checking past cases, the ones I was telling you about, crimes against women. I was looking for the file on –' he closed his eyes and clicked his fingers to summon a name – 'John Wilkes, the guy who attacked his female colleague.'

'That happened seven years ago; you won't find it in the 1997 files.'

'Oh.'

He closed the cabinet drawer with his foot.

'Put that file back then,' she said. 'We haven't got Amber around to sort this place out if we make a mess of it.'

'Oh, this?' He looked at the file in his hands, the back of it blank, Hayley Miller's name pressed against his chest. 'It's a case from 2010. I'll put it back when I'm done.'

Lisa eyed him coolly, glanced at the case file vibrating in his grasp, and back to his eyes. She took a jar of coffee from the top of the filing cabinet and turned to leave.

'Marcus ...' she said, turning back.

'Yeah?' His shirt was sticking to his back, drinking in the sweat.

'Look into Cassie Jennings' family. I'm sure we have case files on every single one of them. Her father was always in and out of the station, and her brothers have spent time in prison over the years. Might find something there.'

'Good thinking. Thanks.'

She studied him for a beat, as if searching for something in his eyes, and left the room.

He only breathed out when he heard her turn in the bend of the hallway.

FOURTEEN

Naomi woke up to the warmth of the sun on her face. The room smelt of fresh sweat; she could taste the saltiness of it on her tongue with each breath. It wasn't long before the memories came hurtling back.

Brick. Glass. Body. Killer. Police.

The mattress moved beneath her. A sigh unfurled from the other side of the bed.

Dane.

She still tingled where his lips had been, the memory of them scorched into her skin. She reached out and stroked his back. The beat of his heart buzzed beneath her fingertips. So many nights she would wake up from a nightmare and feel the bed for him. Now that he was there beside her, she couldn't wait to get rid of him and the guilt.

It could be like this again. If only one of us would make the sacrifice.

'Afternoon,' he said, his words blooming sleepily. He was on his side of the bed and she on hers. It was like he'd never left.

She smiled weakly, guilt pulling at the corners of her mouth. 'You feeling okay?'

'This was a mistake.' She pulled up the duvet to cover her chest.

'It wasn't and you know it.'

'We can't go back to how it used to be.'

'Why can't we?'

'You want a baby. I don't.'

'We could adopt a kid, a grown-up one.'

'Christ, Dane.' She threw back the duvet and got up. 'How many times do I have to tell you that I don't want to be a mother?'

She went into the en suite and shut the door behind her. They weren't just hurting each other now; there was another heart they were breaking.

'Let's talk this through,' he said from the other side of the door.

'Get dressed, Dane.'

She sat on the toilet and covered her face with her hands. Two years of staying strong, and with one moment of weakness she had given in and ruined it all. She would have to start all over again.

She flushed the toilet and returned to the bedroom. Dane was pulling on his trousers.

'What's changed from this morning? You initiated it.'

'I'm sorry. I was scared. I needed to feel safe. This is my fault.'

'I'll leave Josie, I'll end it with her.'

'I don't want you to.'

'Why?'

'Because she can give you what I can't!'

They were back there, in the very same place that had torn them apart. Head to head, heart to heart. He was quiet for too long. She instinctively put her hands behind her back.

'What happened to your hands, Naomi? Did you do that to yourself?'

'No.' It wasn't a lie, but the word shook, betrayed by her own lips.

'Are you trying to hurt yourself again?'

He came towards her. She stepped back.

'No!'

'Show me.'

'You don't believe me?'

'No, I don't.'

'Well, I'm not your concern.'

'Show me your hands.' He snatched them from behind her back.

'I said no!'

He pulled at the bandage on her right hand. Pain shot up her arm as though he was slicing her muscles into ribbons. She tried to get away from him, but he snatched her back. The bandage flittered to the floor.

'What's wrong with you?' he yelled, and shook her roughly. 'Why do you do this to yourself?'

'Get off, you're hurting me!'

The doorbell rang. They stood in silence. Dane slowly loosened his grip on her arms.

'You need to leave. Out the back.'

'We need to talk about this. I want to help you.'

'Dane, please.'

She headed for the stairs with his feet clipping the backs of her heels.

'You can't keep running away from your problems. I can't leave knowing you're going to hurt yourself again.'

'I won't.'

As they reached the bottom of the stairs, he took her by the arms and turned her towards him.

'How do I know that? How can I believe you? Look how we met, for Christ's sake.'

The doorbell rang again. Max barked and rushed between them, his tail knocking against their legs.

'Ignore it.'

'They'll know I'm in. I wouldn't leave the house without Max.'

She walked towards the kitchen and unlocked the back door.

'Please, Dane.'

Dane walked through the doorway and their arms brushed, a brief reminder of what they had done. She thought of him on top of her and the way his weight had pressed her down into the bed. He hadn't even left yet and she already missed him. She had to fight the urge to claw him back.

He went to speak, words forming and dying in his mouth.

She shut the door and locked it. The doorbell rang for the third time.

'I'm coming!'

She rushed towards the front of the house and opened the door.

'You didn't forget, did you?' Rachel asked as she walked inside. 'I was about to use my key.'

'No, Mum, I didn't forget. I was in the bathroom.'

The gasp cut Naomi's response in two.

'What happened?'

The bandage from her right hand was still unravelled on the bedroom floor.

'Naomi?' Rachel pulled her into a hug. 'You're so special to me, I can't bear it.' Her voice crackled in Naomi's ear.

'I'm okay, Mum.'

'Did you have an accident at work? Christ, are you still able to go in? I can give you more money if you need it. I still have some equity in the house.'

'Mum, you've done enough for me. You've kept this roof over my head. Just sit down and I'll tell you.'

Her mother reluctantly pulled away. They sat on the sofa and Naomi took a deep breath.

'Last night—'

The doorbell rang again.

'That'll be your sister. I'll get it.'

Naomi sighed inwardly and closed her eyes.

How do I tell them? How could they possibly believe me?

'Hi, Mum,' Grace said. 'Naomi.'

'Hey.'

'Sit down. Something's happened to your sister and she was just about to tell me.'

'Hang on,' Grace said, and shut the door.

'Sit down Grace, please.'

'Christ, Mum, give me a minute to take off my coat.'

Rachel sat beside Naomi again and stroked the tender skin on her wrist with her nails, the way Naomi liked.

Grace sat down heavily on the armchair with a sigh.

'Right then, what's happened?'

Naomi paused, unable to decide where to start.

Grace was strong. Naomi knew her sister could handle the truth, but their mother?

Someone threw a brick at me through the window of the café and I had to go to hospital, and then on my way home I stumbled across a dead body with the killer still at the scene before spending two hours in the police station, followed by another trip to the hospital, and wound up in bed with my ex-husband because I have no impulse control and no self-respect, and every time I try to kill myself I fail.

'I ... I fell over in the garden, landed on some bark in the flower bed.'

'That's it?' Grace asked.

'I told you it was a bad idea you living alone after Dane left,' Rachel said. 'It was an accident waiting to happen.'

'I didn't fall because I'm blind; I fell because I wasn't paying attention.'

'What if you had hit your head? Who would have known?'

'Don't get carried away, Mum,' Grace said. 'She's fine. People get injuries all the time. Craig tripped over one of the kids last week and nearly lost an eye on one of the kitchen corners. It happens.'

'I'm not overreacting, Grace. I'm worried about my daughter.'

'Mum, I'm fine. Honestly.'

'See? She's fine.'

'She's saying that because she doesn't want me to worry.'

'Mum, she's nearly forty years old, she can look after herself.'

'It doesn't matter how old either of you are, I will always worry about you.'

'Look,' Naomi said. 'I know you care, and it's lovely of you, but I'm fine. I've had one minor accident in thirty-six years; I don't think that's too bad.'

'All right,' Rachel said. 'But for Christ's sake tell me these things when they happen.'

'I will.'

'Thanks for calling to apologise about missing the party, by the way.'

'Grace, don't spoil it. She didn't mean to miss it, did you, darling?'

'I'm sorry, Grace. I'll make it up to the twins. I still have their presents ...'

'It isn't about the bloody presents. It's about you showing up and being their auntie.'

'She said she's sorry.'

The room fell silent. After a while, Naomi heard the sniffle of tears.

'What's the matter, sweetheart?' Rachel asked.

'I'm sorry,' Grace said between breaths. 'It's the murder. It's bringing it all back up again. I have to be so strong at home, but all I want to do is cry.'

'Let it out, darling, you can with us.'

Naomi sat silently on the sofa as Rachel comforted her sister, rummaging in her handbag for a tissue. The two of them had been close as children, but Grace's secret had forced them so far apart that neither of them knew how to cross the gulf that had opened up between them.

Something had happened between Grace and Hayley the night before she disappeared. Grace never told Naomi what it was. All she had said was that she and Hayley weren't friends any more, and the next day, when Hayley was reported missing, she had begged Naomi not to say anything about their falling-out. But something had changed. Grace walked out of a room when Naomi entered, and only spoke to her when she had to, with a new chill to her voice. Even after all these years, the secret still sat between them, pushing them apart.

Whatever Grace had done, it had changed their family for ever.

FIFTEEN

Naomi stood at the platform edge, behind the bumps on the tiles, and waited for the train.

She wouldn't see it coming. She would hear it rattling along the tracks in the distance until it was so close she could smell it. That was when she would jump, when the driver had no time to slow down.

It was late. The air was crisp and cold in her lungs. A vixen was yelping further along the tracks.

With the platform empty, she let the tears fall. It would hurt, but only for a few seconds. Once she jumped, she wouldn't be alone in the darkness any more; she wouldn't be overlooked by men like she was another woman's shadow, or turned down at job interviews; she wouldn't have to live at home with her mum for the rest of her life as everyone else around her evolved, loved, reproduced, succeeded – lived. At twenty-one years old, she should feel invincible, but instead she was lost in an existence that refused to move forward. All she had ever wanted was a normal life.

The suicide note was in her coat pocket. She would slip out of her coat and leave it on the platform just before she jumped.

Her mother deserved to know why, that it was nothing to do with her. She was the only person who had truly ever wanted Naomi, but it wasn't enough. It couldn't substitute for a tender first kiss, or the loneliness latched around her heart, the desperate yearning to be touched, or her hunger for a life that left her to starve.

The train was coming.

Muscles twitched in her legs. She forced her feet into the ground. The tears on her cheeks had chilled with the night air; she instinctively went to wipe them away, but stopped herself. The slightest sign of distress could ruin everything. So many opportunities had been taken from her; she wouldn't let this one slip away.

She thought of her birth mother leaving her at the bus stop never to return; she heard the voices of every interviewer as they told her why they weren't hiring her, always skirting around her blindness. She thought of her virginal, untouched body, and of all the kisses she imagined pressing lightly against her lips, over the skin on her neck and breasts, down across her stomach towards the nerve endings between her legs. She would die with an unloved body ripped to shreds.

The rhythm of the train's wheels resonated in her ears.

'Stand back from the platform edge. The next train at Platform Three does not stop here.'

She slipped out of her coat. Two small steps and she was at the platform edge.

Don't give in to the fear, she told herself. It will only hurt for a second, and then you will be free.

The train was close. It was so loud that she could barely hear her own thoughts.

'I'm sorry, Mum!' she shouted over the sound of the engine hurtling towards her. She raised her foot to step off the edge.

The train whooshed past, clattering against the tracks again and again as each carriage zoomed by, its speed sucking the air from her lungs and cooling the tears on her cheeks.

'Don't,' he said with his hand still in hers, the hand that had pulled her back just as she had begun to lean into the fall.

The train was gone, rattling away into the distance until it was nothing but a low, fading grumble.

'Tell me your name,' he said.

'Naomi,' she whispered.

'I'm Dane,' he said.

SIXTEEN

Hayley Miller was just eighteen when she disappeared from Balkerne Heights. Marcus had devoured over fifty pages of her past, scanned every inch of the crime-scene photos, images of her blood splattered on the grass at the top of the cliff, dried to a crisp in the morning sun. There was enough of it to assume they were looking for a body, not a missing girl waiting to be found.

The amount of blood meant it had come from a main artery, such as the carotid in her neck. Just like the deaths of Cassie Jennings and Amber O'Neill. He couldn't make assumptions, but the similarity between the findings and the recent attacks couldn't be ignored.

He glanced up from the file and looked around the office that he would never see in the same light again. It looked smaller with the night pressing against the windows, and empty offices glaring back at him from behind the glass partitions. He wondered if it was the detectives in those very offices who had decided to bury the secrets back in 1997, or whether the decision had come from higher up.

When Lisa had been reluctant to discuss the case, Marcus thought she was trying to keep the team from feeding into the town's paranoia, to keep control of the investigation before the locals snatched it from her grasp and turned it into something untameable. He'd had no idea she was protecting the force from being dragged into the limelight, after the public became aware of police corruption within the case.

As Hayley had left her house for the last time, she'd told her mother she was meeting a boy for a date. *Another boy?* her mother had asked, before her daughter slammed the door in her face. Hayley had earned a reputation for being promiscuous, something that would taint her disappearance. The town blamed her for opening her legs. They blamed her mother for failing to raise her right and reel her in when she misbehaved. Marcus noticed that the neighbours who gave character statements never blamed the boys who had climbed on top of her, or the parents who raised *them*.

Now Marcus had a name. The boy Hayley had planned to meet the night she disappeared was Dane Hannah. Naomi's ex-husband.

But he couldn't bring himself to read the transcript of his interrogation yet, not when another name stared at him from the stark white paper.

Blake Crouch.

Back in 1997, Blake's father, Superintendent Nathan Crouch, had been running the police force in Balkerne Heights for over seventeen years. When his son's name was listed as a person of interest in the disappearance of Hayley Miller, evidence supposedly went missing. What evidence, the file didn't state. Superintendent Crouch himself dismissed the accusation as a groundless attempt to undermine the police force during their search for the truth of the girl's disappearance.

But with Lisa's eagerness to bury the case, Marcus didn't know what, or who, to believe. If the current case was connected to the disappearance of Hayley Miller, would Lisa follow it through to discover the truth? Or would she bury it further to protect Blake, her job, and her future in the force, even if it meant failing the town she had been employed to protect? With Superintendent Matthew Cunningham also named in the file as a detective on the case, Marcus knew that if Lisa wanted it buried, the Superintendent did too.

Marcus couldn't trust Blake; he had known that the second his eyes changed after Marcus asked what had happened between him and Amber the night of her murder.

'She made another fuck-up on the system,' Blake said. 'Wanted me to hack into the server to correct it. Last time I helped her out I got cautioned for it. I wasn't going to do it again.'

'And that would destroy your marriage?'

'What's my marriage got to do with you?' he'd spat, as he squared up to Marcus in the small kitchen. 'You like snooping around, listening to other people's private conversations?'

Marcus walked away knowing that if he was going to find out the truth about Hayley Miller and how the case linked to the recent killings, he would have to work alone.

The clock chimed as it hit eight o'clock. He closed his copy of the case file and slipped it into his bag. He was heading home, but he wasn't finished yet. He had some more reading to do.

SEVENTEEN

Dane sat in the interrogation room with his eyes closed and tried to calm his racing heart. The room was small with windowless walls. The only way in or out was through the single door, and he was the furthest from it.

'Here,' his solicitor said.

Dane opened his eyes and saw a tissue in the man's hand.

'For the sweat,' he said.

'Oh.'

He took it and dabbed at the sweat on his forehead and above his lip.

The lawyer, a grey-haired man with leathery skin and yellow teeth, had told him to keep quiet about his secret. They wouldn't find out unless they found Hayley's body. Better to keep his cards to himself until they needed to be dealt, he said.

The door opened and two men walked in, both dressed in black suits and white shirts, ties tightened around their collars like nooses around their necks. The door clicked shut and the two men sat on the opposite side of the desk.

'Dane, my name is Detective Inspector Carl Roster, and this

is my colleague Detective Sergeant Matthew Cunningham. You understand why you're here?'

Dane glanced at his solicitor, who nodded.

'Yes.'

'Good.'

DI Roster turned on the tape recorder and reeled off information about the date and time. He asked Dane to confirm he had been read his rights. Dane said yes. The word scratched in his throat.

'You're not under arrest,' DI Roster said. 'You're here voluntarily and can leave at any time.'

Dane looked at the windowless walls and the closed door. It didn't seem that way.

'But it would be in your best interest to clear your name so we can find the person who is involved in hurting Hayley. Do you understand?'

Dane wanted to run towards the door, but he couldn't trust his legs to carry him.

'Dane?' his solicitor prompted. He looked Dane dead in the eye, as though he could see every terrified thought. He was telling him to stick to the script.

'Yes.'

'You're here because of your relationship with Hayley Miller. I understand you were intimate friends in college. You just graduated, right?'

Dane nodded, and realised it could be in response to either question. Every word the detective spoke felt like a hurdle he had to jump to make it into the clear.

'Yes, I just graduated.'

'Twenty is a bit late to finish college, isn't it?' DS Cunningham asked.

'I didn't decide to study nursing until after I'd finished sixth form.'

DS Cunningham smirked down at his paperwork.

'There's nothing wrong with a man being a nurse,' Dane said, clenching his hands into fists between his legs.

'You'll see a lot, being a nurse,' DI Roster said. 'You're not squeamish?'

'I wouldn't make a very good nurse if I were.'

'So you're okay with the sight of blood? It doesn't frighten you?'

'No.'

'It's a very admirable vocation. Let's put your knowledge to the test.'

'Test?' Dane asked, and glanced at his solicitor, who looked equally confused.

'For fun,' DI Roster replied, leaning back in his chair. 'You're a young guy; you like fun, don't you?'

Dane nodded.

'Good. Let's get started.' He picked up a notepad, read something on the page. 'What's the largest bone in the human foot?'

Dane looked at his solicitor again. They mirrored each other's frowns.

'The calcaneus. The heel bone.'

'Correct,' DI Roster said. 'Impressive. How many pints of blood are there in the human body?'

'Eight, on average. I don't understand why—'

'We're having fun, aren't we?' DI Roster asked. His lips were turned up in a smile, but his eyes were serious. He looked down at his notepad. 'How much does the human heart weigh?'

Dane had to think. He stared down at his clenched fist, the same size as his heart. He wanted to get out of the room. If he played along, he might get out faster.

'Ten ounces, I think.'

'Close. Eleven. Where are the carotid arteries located?'

He pointed to both sides of his neck, just as his solicitor gestured for him not to. DI Roster smirked, his eyes never leaving Dane's. Dane looked at the lawyer and then the detective, wondering what he had done.

'So, we know you're aware of the location of the carotid arteries, the major vessels transporting blood to the brain, and that if they were cut, the brain would die. You would know where to cut, wouldn't you, Dane, if you wanted to end somebody's life?'

'Don't answer that,' his solicitor said.

'Hayley lost a lot of blood before she went missing. Someone had to know where to cut her to make her lose that much blood.'

Dane felt a drop of sweat slip down his neck. The room was too hot. He needed to get out.

'Why did you hurt Hayley, Dane? Was it because she broke up with you? Slept around behind your back?'

'My client doesn't need to answer these ludicrous questions, DI Roster.'

'She got through a lot of guys in college, didn't she? You

116

couldn't have liked that, knowing that half the guys in your year had shagged your girlfriend.'

'DI Roster,' the lawyer warned.

'She slept with your friends, too. Did that make you see red? Did you decide to stop her before she humiliated you any further?'

'I ...'

'She met you the night she disappeared, didn't she, Dane?'

'She never showed,' he replied, licking the sweat from his top lip.

'Dane, stop talking,' his solicitor said.

'You sure?' asked DI Roster. 'Can anyone verify that?'

'We were meant to meet at the beach to talk, but she didn't turn up.'

'Why would you be meeting up to talk, Dane? You'd broken up months before, hadn't you?'

'We were still friends.'

'That's not what I've heard,' DI Roster said. 'Hayley's friends seem to think that the two of you despised each other. So what was there to talk about?'

'I ...'

'Yes, Dane? What have you got to say?'

'I want to go home now.'

'This is over,' his solicitor said. 'If you want to speak with my client again, you'll need sufficient evidence. You won't waste any more of our time with your speculations and fabrications.'

DI Roster's eyes never left Dane's. Dane blinked and looked away. His legs quivered under his weight as he stood. His head felt light.

'When you're ready to start talking, Dane, we'll be here. It would be better for you to tell us before we find out the truth.'

The truth burned inside him as though it had set fire to his lungs.

His solicitor stood up and guided him out of the room with a hand on his back. He wiped the sweat on his trousers.

'They haven't got anything, Dane,' he said. 'Just stay low and you'll be fine.'

'Unless they find the body,' he whispered.

EIGHTEEN

I can't believe it,' Rachel said.

'I can't either,' Naomi replied. 'It's been a week, and ...' She could still feel the murdered woman's hair tangled around her fingers, but she couldn't tell her mother that. 'And I'm struggling to come to terms with it.'

In the end, she had decided to tell Rachel what had happened. It wouldn't have taken her long to discover the truth. Rachel had a way of worming things out of her daughters; she had always told them there shouldn't be secrets between them. If only she knew.

'I told you ...' Rachel cleared her throat. 'I told you not to go out after dark.'

'I'm sorry, Mum.' Naomi took her mother's hand.

'Why would someone do such a thing?' Rachel asked as she rummaged in her bag for a tissue. 'Harm women like that?'

'I don't know.'

'You could have died. I could have lost you.' She pulled Naomi into a tight hug. Her tears were wet on Naomi's cheek.

'I'm okay, Mum.'

'Are the police protecting you?' she asked as she pulled away.

'They don't think I'm in danger.'

'Of course you're in danger. The attacker knows what you look like and will know you went to the police.'

'Whoever it was, whoever killed that woman, didn't kill me, so they must think I'm safe.'

'They're risking your life on a hunch.' Rachel stood up. 'I'm going in to speak with the detective. I won't let them leave you in danger like this.'

'Mum, I'm fine, sit down.' Naomi felt the air for her mother's hand. When her mother didn't reach out, she lowered her own hand back down to her lap. 'It's been a week and nothing's happened to me.'

'That's because you haven't left the house. You're too scared to go out, aren't you?'

Naomi picked at a thread in her jeans and wrapped it around her finger until the tip swelled.

'I'm going to go down there and demand they do something. I'm not having your life at risk so they can save a few pennies. I know the superintendent's mother; I'll make sure something is done. They have to treat you just like anyone else.'

Naomi knew she wasn't talking about her blindness. She was referring to the colour of her skin.

'Mum, please don't. They will get in contact when they know something, I'm sure.'

'They haven't contacted you? They can't leave you in the dark like this. I'm going to talk to them.'

'Mum—'

'You can't stop me, Naomi.'

Naomi sighed. There was nothing she could do or say. When

her mother was set on something, the best thing to do was to get out of her way.

'I love you, Mum,' she said.

She heard her mother sniffle back tears.

'I love you so much, Naomi. I can't lose you.'

'You won't.' Naomi stood up, and Rachel pulled her close and wrapped her arms around her.

'Promise me you'll fight this.'

Naomi was sure Rachel was talking about any repercussions from her discovery of the body, but deep down she wondered if she knew about her suicide attempts. She let her mother hold her and listened to her tears, the beat of her heart.

'I promise, Mum.'

It was only then that she understood how selfish she had been trying to take her own life. As she stood on the cliff, she had told herself it was her decision whether to live or die, but as her mother's tears soaked through her blouse, she realised how much pain she would cause. If she committed suicide, it wouldn't just be her own life she would destroy.

Rachel pulled away. 'I know you don't need mirrors, but you could at least have one up on the wall for your emotional mother. I have mascara all over my face!'

Naomi forced a laugh. 'There's a small mirror in the bathroom, I think. I can't remember if Dane took it with him.'

'I have a pocket mirror in my bag,' Rachel said. 'I'll go and sort myself out and then go to the police station.'

She squeezed Naomi's hand and made her way upstairs.

Naomi couldn't stop her mother from going to the station, but she didn't have to tell her that the detectives wouldn't be there. Amber O'Neill's funeral was being held at noon, and every officer in Balkerne Heights would be attending the service. And so would she.

Naomi had made a mistake. It was wrong for her to be there, surrounded by Amber O'Neill's family and colleagues, as her coffin was lowered into the ground. The mourners had their own special memories of the young woman: her first steps, her first wobbly tooth, her first promotion. All Naomi had was the memory of her corpse cooling beneath her fingertips.

She leaned against the tree and tried to hear the vicar's speech over the sound of the rain pattering against the leaves and dripping onto her shoulders.

She had chosen her spot an hour before the service, led to the grave by the vicar himself, and waited for the mourners to arrive. She didn't want to intrude, but she needed closure as much as the rest of them. She had thought being here would give her that, help her forget the feel of the cooling flesh beneath her hands, but as she stood behind the tree, listening to the incessant squeak of the device lowering the coffin into the ground, she wished she had stayed at home.

People cried at the graveside. Raindrops rapped loudly against the army of umbrellas and slithered down Naomi's skin, reminding her of the alley. When she thought of the attacker breathing on her, her neck warmed with the memory, as though she was back there with the body cooling at her feet. She swallowed the memory down.

The service ended and a heavy silence hung over the crowd as the rain calmed to mere spittle and sunlight pierced through the clouds. Naomi pressed herself against the tree and held her breath as the mourners made their way towards the church hall for the wake, weaving between graves with the dead at their feet. Birds sang in the treetops, oblivious to the pain of those beneath.

Once the sound of footsteps had dissipated, Naomi walked in the opposite direction, her cane knocking raindrops from the grass.

'Naomi!'

She froze, blinking away the rain. Whoever it was, they wouldn't want her there. She was a physical embodiment of Amber's death – she had been there and felt the body with her own two hands.

She walked on with her head down.

'Naomi!' The man was closing in. Naomi recognised his voice and stopped.

'Detective?'

'I thought it was you,' Marcus said, out of breath. 'Are you all right?'

'I shouldn't have come. I just thought that if I did, I might get some closure. It was selfish of me. I'm sorry.'

'Don't be sorry,' he replied. 'I understand completely. Do you want to come to the wake? I'm sure it wouldn't be a problem.'

'No, no. I've intruded enough.'

They stood in an awkward silence as the rain began to thin.

'I still haven't heard anything,' Naomi said. 'This is the first time I've left my house since it happened.'

'We're working hard on the case, Naomi. As soon as we have answers, I will call you personally.'

'And what am I supposed to do in the meantime? Sit at home and hope the killer doesn't come for me?'

'I can't discuss the case, but please trust me. I promise I will make sure no one else is hurt.'

Thunder rumbled above their heads.

'Are you allowed to do that?' she asked.

'Do what?'

'Make promises.'

'It can be our little secret.'

Naomi didn't think she could bear to keep any more secrets.

'You'd best head inside,' she said. 'For the wake.'

'Are you sure you don't want to come in for a while, just to get out of the rain?'

'No, I'm fine.'

'Well, I'll be in touch.'

Naomi listened to him walk away and sighed.

She trusted Marcus when he said he wanted to help her, but she couldn't believe that he could guarantee her safety. However hard he worked, she couldn't escape the feeling that she was on her own, and that whoever was responsible for the murders wasn't done with her yet.

NINETEEN

Naomi walked along the beach as Max jumped through the waves rolling towards the shore.

It had been a week since she slept with Dane and she could still feel his lips against her neck, his warm tongue tasting the skin on her thighs. The guilt hadn't dissipated; it had sunk into her bones. But for those few short hours that they'd been together, all the pain she felt inside had evaporated with his tenderness, and she had been made whole again.

The emptiness inside her had been her companion longer than anyone else: Max, her family, her ex-husband. It had appeared the night she woke in the corner of the bus shelter. As she'd walked home from Amber's funeral, she'd wondered whether her blood mother was dead or alive. Was she buried in the very same graveyard? Had Naomi unknowingly passed her tombstone? Or was she still out there, searching for veins between her toes to inject the substance that she loved more than her own flesh and blood?

Naomi's first memory was of her mother slapping a used syringe from her mouth. She had been sucking on the needle, rolling her tongue around it, tasting the metal. It was the only way she could identify objects in her small, dark world. As her mother slept on the sofa with heroin swimming through her veins and strangers comatose in other parts of the room, Naomi would crawl across the dirty carpet popping things in her mouth, remembering the shapes of them with her tongue and lips. She could still recall the sound of her mother's belligerent scolding, and the feel of rough hands snatching her up from the ground, with a grip so tight it pinched at her skin. The memory always ended with the sound of the bolt sliding across the other side of the bedroom door, and her own infant cries bouncing off the walls.

She shook away the memory. It didn't matter if her mother was dead or alive – she was dead to Naomi. Her real mother was Rachel, the woman who loved her and had taught her everything she knew.

'Max! Come, boy!'

Max followed the waves in towards the sand and shook salty water from his fur. He padded towards her and panted against her jeans. Naomi leaned down and secured his harness with the tips of her fingers, trying to keep the bandages dry.

They walked back the way they'd come. Max would lead her towards the concrete steps by the sea barrier, and it wouldn't be long before they were at home by the fire, drying off and dozing. The more she slept, the more days were put between her and the night in the alley. It wouldn't be long before it was just another dark part of her past.

Max stopped in front of her and let out a slow growl.

'Max? What's wrong?'

He barked in a way she hadn't heard before, his jaws snapping at the air.

'Hello?' she said.

The wind whistled around them and whipped a lock of hair across the bridge of her nose. She swiped it away and tucked it behind her ear.

Max growled again and pulled against the harness, the sand moving beneath his paws.

'Who's there?'

She listened to the howl of the wind. Someone was blocking their path, breathing the same excited breaths as the person who had stood at her front door. And the stranger in the alley.

She tried to turn back, but Max wouldn't move.

'Max, come!'

He growled through bared teeth as she eventually managed to drag him away and headed up the beach.

'Quickly now,' she whispered.

She listened to the heavy breathing behind her and the sound of trouser legs rubbing against one another with wide strides.

Her nose hit the beach first. Sand filled her mouth and coated her eyes.

She lifted herself up with her arms, the stranger's touch pulsing on her back where she had been pushed. She spat sand from her mouth. Max growled and leapt. A man's cry echoed along the beach.

'Max, no!'

Her eyes streamed as the sand scratched with every blink and burrowed beneath her eyelids.

Max's growls were muffled; his teeth had sunk into fabric or flesh. Feet shuffled in the sand and kicked it into the wind until it was darting into Naomi's face and hitting the back of her throat. Max let out a yelp.

She choked on sand and swallowed it down.

'Don't hurt him! Please!'

She crawled along the beach and clawed at the air with one hand. Max's cries reverberated along the shore.

'Please stop!'

Sandy tears slipped down her face. As she came closer, she heard the impact of what sounded like punches against Max's ribcage, knuckles against bone.

'Stop it!'

She reached out and found the stranger's leg. She slipped her fingers beneath the hem of the trousers and dug her nails into the skin. Something warm and wet splashed against her face. Blood. Max's blood.

'No! Don't hurt him!'

Wet hands snatched her coat and dragged her to her feet. She could smell the blood and feel the heat of the stranger's breath against her tears. She remembered the night in the alley, the hot breath that had escaped as a laugh. It was him. The man holding her by the scruff of her coat was the man who had killed Amber O'Neill.

He pulled her up until her feet were off the ground, kicking helplessly in the air, and launched her aside. Sand billowed up around her as she landed on the beach, her head slamming against a protruding rock.

Everything began to spin. Sand blew across her with the wind. The sound of the sea was muffled now, but she could still hear Max's pain-filled yelps, and the faint pleas slipping from her own mouth. *No. Please stop. Not him. Kill me instead.*

Naomi came to with fistfuls of damp sand squeezing between her fingers. Her shoes and jeans were soaked through. The sea was lapping up over her, tucking her in. She could barely open her eyes. She clenched them shut and turned towards the waves, splashing water into her face and washing the sand from her eyes.

Night had fallen. There was a sharp chill in the air and her whole body was frozen. She was alone on the beach, hidden in the dark.

The water felt like ice against her skin, but she welcomed it as she scooped it up again and again. Her head was throbbing, mimicking the beat of her heart. The bandages on her hands were soaked through and lined with sand.

Max.

'Max?'

Her voice was lost amongst the rush of the waves. The wind howled in from the sea and crept up the cliff face.

'Max?'

She scrambled up from the water and tried to stand, but lost her footing. She fell to her hands and knees and crawled, feeling the beach beneath her fingers. Seawater dripped from her jaw and slanted down her neck with the wind. She snatched at the sand, packing it under her fingernails, and called out his name until she felt his paw.

'Max!'

He was cold and wet, sand embedded in his fur like mites. She traced the top of his back and then his ribs towards his stomach, and felt the cuts between the bones.

'No ...'

Tears streamed down her cheeks as she lay beside him and pulled him close.

'Don't leave me,' she whispered.

She sat up and snatched blindly at her pocket for her phone. It dripped in her hands, soaked from the sea. She threw it to the ground, then lay back down beside him and buried her face in his fur.

Something moved beneath his coat. She darted her head towards his chest and pressed her ear against it, breathing in the scents of sea and blood, the fumes so potent it was like heaving in gulps of kerosene.

A heartbeat.

TWENTY

Marcus's tie lay beside the computer mouse, stained with blotches of black coffee. His shirt was untucked beneath the desk. The funeral had taken it out of him. Lisa had made sure he returned to work while the rest of them drank, ate, and tried to forget that one of their own had been murdered.

Marcus hadn't known Amber long, so it had made sense for him to go back to the office and continue with the case, but coming from Lisa, it felt vindictive. She wanted him excluded, with nothing but the tick of the clock for company.

He rubbed his eyes. The paperwork on his desk was blurry. He blinked furiously until the words came into focus again. He picked up the call logs from Amber's disposable phone. The phone she had used to contact Cassie Jennings.

Their victims had known each other.

More importantly, their victims had known something dark enough for the killer to hunt them down and slash their necks like cattle in an abattoir.

The phone on his desk rang out and made him jump. He had been sitting in silence for hours. He snatched the phone up and spoke quickly.

'Detective Sergeant Marcus Campbell.'

'Hi, son, it's Carl Roster returning your call. I got your voicemail.'

Even though he was alone, Marcus glanced around the office to make sure he wouldn't be overheard.

'Detective, thank you for calling me back.'

'I'm not a detective any more, son, I'm an OAP.' He laughed on the other end of the line, then coughed. 'You said in your message that you were looking into the Hayley Miller case?'

'That's right,' Marcus said. 'I have reason to believe it may be linked to new attacks.'

'You mean those murdered women?'

Marcus's instinct was to deflect, but he remembered that Roster had been a detective many more years than he had. If he wanted Roster to share his thoughts on the case, Marcus would have to share too.

'Yes, sir.'

Roster sighed. 'It was a messy case, that one. What makes you think it's connected to the recent attacks?'

'The crime scenes seem similar to the one described in Miller's case file, but the main reason is ...'

He wondered where Roster would stand on what he was about to tell him. Had he been a part of the cover-up?

'Yes, son?'

Marcus took a deep breath.

'I believe my superiors are burying the Miller case to keep the corruption scandal in the dark, when there is reason to believe the two are related.'

He listened to the man breathing down the phone.

'That's dark water you're getting yourself into, son.'

'I know.'

Roster was quiet again.

Being called 'son' did something to Marcus. It made him wonder if Roster was a father, and a good one, compared to his own.

'Talk to Miller's mother,' the older man said eventually. 'She had her own theories, but they weren't followed up.'

'Thanks, sir. I owe you one.'

'If you get anywhere with the case, let me know. It's stuck with me, that missing girl.'

'I will, sir.'

'And son?'

'Yes, sir?'

'Be careful digging up this case. If your bosses want it buried, they're likely to bury you too if they find you with the spade, you understand?'

'I do. Thanks, Detective.'

Marcus replaced the phone and rubbed his face. If Roster *was* part of the cover-up, all he could do now was wait for repercussions. If he wasn't reprimanded in the next few days, he would continue digging and contact Hayley Miller's mother.

His mobile phone vibrated against the desk. It was only when he checked the screen that he realised how late it was. Natalie was calling.

'I'm sorry, I didn't notice the time.'

'I've been waiting for you to come home for over two hours, Marcus.'

He thought of her sitting at the small table in their flat, looking across at his plate of food as it cooled. Her long black hair would be straightened, her make-up fresh, her clothes chosen especially, her brown eyes slowly filling with tears.

'I'm sorry, it's been a long day.'

'I have a job too, Marcus.'

'I know, I know. I'm sorry.'

'So are you coming home any time soon? Or should I finish off this bottle of wine and get an early night?'

PC Tanya Earnhart appeared in the doorway of the office, alarm and excitement in her eyes. Marcus covered the mouthpiece.

'A blind woman has been found wandering along the beach. She was attacked and her dog was stabbed. Is that your witness from Amber's case?'

Marcus thought of the scene, blood smeared on the wet sand and turning the white foam of the broken waves a light pink. If they wanted to find out who had done this, he had to act fast.

'Shit. Hold on.'

He uncovered the mouthpiece and heard a gulp of wine slide down Natalie's throat.

'I'm really sorry, Nat, but I have to—'

'Oh, save it.'

He listened to her hang up, then pocketed his phone and rushed for the door.

TWENTY-ONE

The station smelt of salt from the sea. Marcus knew he shouldn't think of Naomi as anything more than a witness, but as he made his way to the interview room, his heart raced at the thought of seeing her again.

He reached the door to the room and took a deep breath before turning the handle and stepping inside.

Naomi was visibly shaking. Her hair was riddled with sand, and traces of splattered blood still stained her forehead. She was wrapped in the same blanket as before, her freshly bandaged hands holding another cup of steaming tea. It was like stepping into the past.

She had been found calling for help, her dog bleeding in her arms, her legs buckling with the weight of him. She had walked for hours up and down the beach, waiting for someone to find her.

'Naomi.'

'Hello, Detective.' Her voice was solemn, hoarse from hours of screaming for help. Marcus imagined her stumbling up the beach, crying out again and again.

'I'm sorry to have to see you like this again,' he said, sitting opposite her. He was glad Lisa wasn't here. Doing this alone meant actually getting some help for the woman. Lisa had been drinking at the wake, and Marcus didn't want to know how cruel she could get during an interview with wine in her veins.

'Me too.'

He pressed play on the recorder.

'I'll be recording our conversation again. Are you okay with that?'

She nodded.

'For the purpose of the tape, Naomi Hannah nodded her head.' He reeled off the formality of information for the tape, and then focused his attention on the broken woman before him.

'Naomi, can you tell me what happened tonight?'

She closed her eyes and took a deep breath, bracing herself.

'Is Max still alive?' she asked.

'As far as I know.'

Her shoulders visibly relaxed.

'He will be in surgery for some time. Likely for most of the night. What happened to him? To you?'

'We were walking on the beach. We must have been down there for over an hour. When it got colder, we began to walk home. Max started growling. Someone was there in front of us.'

Tears filled her bloodshot eyes as they jittered from left to right, searching for the memory. Marcus half expected the tears to run red.

'I turned back. I only managed a few steps before he pushed me to the ground.'

'He?'

'While I was getting up, Max attacked him and I heard a man's cry. It was definitely a man.'

'You're sure?'

She nodded. A tear plummeted towards her jaw.

'Max bit him, I'm not sure where, but I could hear it. He was growling, with something in his mouth. But then he ...'

She covered her face with bandaged hands.

'It's okay. Take your time.'

She stayed shielded behind her hands for a moment.

'Would you like a tissue?'

She nodded and wiped her nose with the back of her hand, soiling the fresh bandage. Marcus hovered a tissue above her hand and let the tip brush against her fingertip to let her know it was there.

'Thanks.'

She wiped her cheeks, blew her nose.

'What happened next, Naomi?'

'Max started yelping. I took hold of the attacker's leg and dug my nails into it. I could hear the strength that was being put into those punches, Detective. This person ... this person was filled with hate. Well, I thought they were punches until later, when I felt the cuts.'

Marcus stayed silent, conscious of letting her tell him in her own way.

It felt wrong to admire her beauty without her consent. She had no idea that he was eyeing her lips, the shape of her eyes, the smooth skin on her cheeks. It felt wrong, but he couldn't help it. She was beautiful.

He looked down at her fingernails and hoped his colleagues

might have found deposits of skin and blood nestled beneath them.

'The attacker picked me up and threw me aside like I weighed nothing. I hit my head on a rock and didn't wake up until some time later. The tide had started to come in. That's when I found him.'

Silence fell between them. Naomi wrung her hands in her lap. Marcus cleared his throat.

'Other than the incident in the alleyway, do you know anyone who might want to cause you or Max harm?'

She thought about it, but eventually shook her head.

'What about your past?' He looked down at her bare wedding finger. 'Any former partners?'

'I have an ex-husband. It's complicated, but he would never want to hurt Max or me. Max was his dog too, in many ways.'

'How is it complicated?'

'We're friends.'

'And that's complicated?'

'I think so. Dane doesn't understand that I need to detach myself from our relationship. He is adamant that we should stay friends, even after two years.'

Dane Hannah. The same name from Amber's case file. Naomi's ex-husband had been questioned in her disappearance.

'Has he remarried?'

'No. He has a girlfriend, though. Josie. Blonde and pretty, I'm told. Younger.'

Marcus looked at his notes from the first interview.

'And what about your workplace? Do you have good relationships with your bosses? Co-workers?'

'I've worked for Mitchell and Peggy for twenty years, and Nick is only young. Nice kid. Doesn't say much.'

The normal chatter allowed some colour to return to her cheeks.

'Are all the customers nice people?'

She nodded, rubbing her thumb up and down the side of the cup.

'What about your family?'

The colour seemed to vanish again. There was something to be told there, but he knew he had to ease the information out of her. He didn't want her to shut down.

'I'm close to my mother and sister. My sister, Grace Kennedy, has two kids and a stay-at-home husband, Craig. She works from home two days a week, comes over on Wednesdays with my mum.'

'And your father?'

She swallowed and began ripping the tissue. 'I never knew my father.'

He let the conversation fall so she would fill the silence.

'My ... my biological mother left me at a bus stop when I was three. Rachel found me and adopted me. She's my mother, has been since that day.'

'Have you ever spoken to your biological mother?'

She shook her head.

'So there is no one in your life who might want to see you harmed?'

'No.' She sighed. 'But ... something happened before.'

'What do you mean?'

'Just before this all started, before Amber, someone banged

on my front door but wouldn't respond when I answered. But I knew they were there, I could feel it. I could hear someone breathing. I wasn't hurt, just rattled.'

He measured his tone to seem interested rather than frustrated. 'Why didn't you mention this before?'

'It seemed so small compared to what happened the night I found Amber. It didn't even enter my mind. So much has happened since then.'

Her fingertips pulled at the tissue until small pieces littered the table.

'Do you think the person who did this might have been the person in the alley?' she asked, her blank gaze resting on his neck.

'That's certainly something we'll be looking into.'

He took a deep breath.

'Naomi, did you know Hayley Miller?'

'Everyone knew Hayley Miller,' she said. 'She was my sister's best friend. Why?'

He wrote down the relationship on his notepad.

'What is happening to you may not be connected, but I'm looking into every possibility.'

'I didn't know her very well. I kept to myself as a kid. But she and my sister were close, more like sisters than we were.'

He heard the hurt in her voice, watched her pick apart the tissue until it was gone from her hands.

'You promised no one else would get hurt,' she said. 'You said you didn't think I was in danger, and now Max has been ...' She couldn't finish. Tears welled in her eyes. He wasn't sure if they were tears of sadness or anger. 'You promised me.'

'I'm sorry,' he said, unsure what else he could say. He had let her down, broken a promise he should never have made.

'Do you ... do you think my life is in danger now?'

He knew that once a victim thought they were in danger, they expected answers and fast. Lisa didn't believe Naomi was at risk, and if he told Naomi what he thought, he would have two women to convince. He looked into her wandering eyes.

'Yes,' he said finally. 'I do.'

Lisa entered the office, bringing in the cold night with her, and shrugged off her coat.

'Anything?' she asked.

'Not yet,' Blake replied as his eyes continued to scan the CCTV footage that they had acquired from the beach shop on the seafront. He looked noticeably haggard beneath the strip lighting.

Marcus couldn't help but look at Blake differently after reading Hayley Miller's file. The corruption. The buried secrets. Blake was hiding something, not just from them, but from the investigation. If the cases were linked, he was a suspect. Marcus wondered how far Blake would go to protect his secret from emerging. He had already lied about his argument with Amber before her murder. What else did he have to hide?

'Naomi dug her nails into the attacker's ankle,' Marcus said. 'Swabs have been taken for possible DNA and sent off for analysis.'

'Good,' Lisa said.

'Naomi said something ominous like this has happened to her before.'

Lisa scoffed as she hung up her coat. 'Have another dog, did she?'

'Someone knocked on her door but wouldn't speak when she asked who was there.'

'So some kids were playing a prank.'

'She didn't believe it was kids.'

'Well, how would she know?'

He clenched his jaw.

'This could be completely unrelated,' she said. 'The killer likes women, not dogs.'

'And one of those women was the owner of the dog.'

She stared him down until his right eyelid began to twitch.

'Those killings weren't personal. This attack was. You don't try to kill a blind person's dog and leave them to live unless you want them to suffer. The person who killed Amber and Cassie Jennings didn't taunt them – he executed them. Different motives. Different killers. And you know killers like this choose victims within their own ethnicity group. Naomi doesn't fit his preference.'

'Naomi confirmed that the person who attacked her dog was a man. The dog bit him and he yelled.'

'Maybe the next time she's attacked we'll get a little bit more detail. She likes to ration out the information, doesn't she?'

'I believe she is in danger and needs police protection.'

Lisa laughed. She was enjoying it.

'For an attack on a dog? Not a chance. We haven't got the

resources to pass out officers like Tic Tacs.'

'You said the attack on her dog was personal. Doesn't that qualify her for protection? Someone wants her to suffer, and is unlikely to stop until she's hurt too.'

'I'm not authorising it, Marcus. You might want to remember that one of our own was buried yesterday.'

'Lisa,' Blake said, looking up from his screen with bloodshot eyes. 'I might have found something.'

They both made their way to his desk and peered down at the screen. As Blake talked, Marcus wondered what he had looked like when he was younger, when he was a suspect in Hayley Miller's disappearance.

'This CCTV footage from the shop on the beachfront recorded Naomi and her dog walking down the beach. Ten minutes later, a blonde woman walked the same way.'

'Show me.'

They all watched as he rewound the footage. Cars reversed up and down the street, before a blonde woman emerged from the beachfront steps and walked backwards across the road and out of the shot, followed by Naomi and her dog. Blake pressed play and let the footage roll. Marcus eyed his colleague's reflection in the computer screen. The shadows around his eyes made them look like they were sinking into his skull.

Naomi and the dog crossed the street. The digital clock in the right-hand corner of the screen said 16:39.

'It takes a few minutes for Blondie to show up.'

'Fast forward,' Lisa said.

Blake forwarded the footage until the blonde woman appeared from the same spot. She crossed the street, peering cautiously behind her, before reaching the stone steps and making her way down towards the beach. The time stamp in the corner said 16:41. Two minutes behind Naomi.

'She comes up about an hour and twenty minutes later.'

Naomi hadn't returned up the steps; she couldn't find them. She had wandered over a mile down the coast before being found. Marcus thought of her carrying her dog along the beach as night fell, his blood the only thing keeping her warm.

'Find out who she is, and make a copy of that tape and put it on my desk.'

Blonde woman. What was it Naomi had said? *Ex-husband. New girlfriend. Blonde. Josie.*

'Lisa, I have an idea who she might be.'

TWENTY-TWO

Naomi closed the front door behind her and let the silence fill her ears. The house was empty without Max, who would have been panting after his walk and shedding sand across the floorboards. She was all on her own now.

She had tried to clean herself up in the bathroom at the police station, but she had simply moved the sand up and down her body. Flecks of blood lingered on her hands and face, but she couldn't bring herself to wash it away; it might be all she had left of him.

She stripped off the clothes she had been given at the police station and listened to the sand fall to the floor. She left the garments and her underwear in a heap at the bottom of the stairs and climbed up towards the bathroom.

She turned on the shower above the bath and sat on the edge. Her hands were shaking, but she managed to peel off the bandages and lift herself into the tub. As the spray washed away the sand, the blood, the dried tears stuck to her cheeks, she waited for the pain to stop.

Max is alive. He'll be okay. You'll be okay. You have to be.

She sat there until the water ran cold and her fingertips wrinkled. Sand collected around her buttocks and hid beneath her feet.

I can't deal with this now, she told herself as she stepped out of the bath and dried herself. I'll face it tomorrow.

She crawled across her unmade bed and pressed the play button on the answering machine.

'Naomi, it's Dane. I'm sorry if I—'

'Message deleted.'

'Naomi, pick up. I just want to know you're—'

'Message deleted.'

'Naomi, pick up the damn phone. I—'

'Message deleted.'

'Hi, darling, it's Mum. I was just calling to see—'

'Message deleted. You have no new messages.'

Naomi crawled beneath the sheets and listened to the noises of the empty house. The windows clicked in their frames. Water dripped from the shower head. Her heart kept on beating, even though it had been ripped in two.

Tomorrow. I'll face it all tomorrow.

TWENTY-THREE

Josie Callaghan was in her mid- to late twenties, younger than Marcus had expected. She sat before Marcus and Lisa with her arms crossed, the usual stance of someone ready to defend themselves. Her skin was decorated with faint freckles that were just visible through her make-up. Even though she was aesthetically beautiful, there was something sour in her eyes.

Marcus and Lisa sat next to each other but with as much distance between them as possible. They had barely talked all morning. Lisa had been in a foul mood ever since the superintendent had heard of the attack on Naomi's dog and ordered police surveillance to drive past her property every hour for the next few days. She didn't like to be proved wrong.

Although Marcus was pleased that the superintendent was taking the matter seriously, he hadn't enjoyed it much either: the sound of the superintendent's raised voice booming from behind the door of his office had reminded him of all of those sleepless nights as a child, listening to his father berate his mother moments before he hit her, warming up his fists before he came into Marcus's room, when the real show began. He could still remember the thick skin on his father's knuckles, hardened over the years to protect the bones beneath. As he and his mother had grown weaker, his father had only grown stronger.

'Why am I here?' Josie Callaghan sounded impatient, confident. Something Lisa was likely to rip away.

'I'm sure you know why,' Lisa replied.

Josie shrugged.

'Do you know this woman?' Lisa slid a photo of Naomi Hannah across the table, a still taken from the CCTV footage that captured her walk to the beach. Recognition sparked in Josie's face. Marcus noticed the flash in her eyes and a twitch in a muscle beside her mouth, but she swallowed it down.

'No. Should I?'

'It's in your best interest to tell the truth, Josie.'

'I am.'

'So you didn't see her at the beach last night?'

'No.'

'What if I told you I could prove that you're lying?'

Doubt shimmered in her eyes.

'Well can you?'

'Do you walk along the beach often? Or did you go there purely to follow Naomi?'

Lisa removed the next CCTV still from the file of Josie walking towards the beach, with the time stamp in the corner showing that they were just two minutes apart. Lisa slid it across the table.

'How do you know that's me?'

'We couldn't be sure at first,' Lisa replied. 'There are plenty of other blonde women in Balkerne Heights. So we looked at CCTV footage closer to your house, and saw you making your way to Naomi's and then following her down to the beach. Pretty incriminating.'

Josie tightened the knit of her arms across her chest, an unconscious move to make her feel safer. She exhaled sharply and stared into Lisa's eyes.

'I live near the beach. Of course I'm going to go down there. That's the way I walk.'

'You live quite far from Naomi's house, though,' Marcus pointed out.

'I didn't always. I like to follow routes I'm familiar with. You should know it's frightening for a woman to walk alone, especially with what's happening.'

Marcus didn't believe Josie was scared of anything.

'So now you're telling us you *were* at the beach last night, when just a moment ago you denied seeing Naomi there?'

Josie hesitated, swallowed until her throat bobbed beneath her skin. Marcus couldn't look at throats any more without imagining how they would appear sliced open.

'Shouldn't I have a solicitor?'

'If you think you need one, we can get that set up for you, as we mentioned when we got in touch with you. But you didn't think you had something to hide then. What's changed?'

Marcus had to commend Lisa for her interrogation skills. Waiting for an assigned lawyer could take days in such a small town. The implication that needing a lawyer was incriminating often led to the suspect waiving their right to prove their innocence.

'I don't have anything to hide.'

'Good. Then we'll all promise to be honest with each other. My colleague and I will forget that you lied before. Clean slate, okay?' She smiled briefly, a patronising grin that dropped almost as quickly as it appeared. 'Why did you follow Naomi down to the beach last night?'

'I wasn't following her. I was simply going to the beach.'

'I thought we promised not to lie to each other,' Lisa said. 'We need the facts to rule you out of what happened on the beach last night. You're helping yourself, not us.'

Marcus had been on the receiving end of Lisa's glare and knew how Josie would be starting to sweat beneath her clothes.

'She's my boyfriend's ex-wife.'

Lisa stayed quiet, her eyes never leaving Josie's.

'They still see each other.'

'Romantically?'

'Yes.'

'You're sure?'

Josie nodded.

'How do you know?'

'I just do.'

'So what, you followed her to beat her up?'

'Of course not. I followed her to tell her to back off.'

'And she didn't.'

'No ... I didn't get the chance.'

'You were on that beach for well over an hour, Miss Callaghan. You had plenty of time.'

'You don't know how hard it is to build up the courage to tell someone to stay away from the love of your life. She 'doesn't deserve him; he's not hers any more.'

'Did you go to her house last week?' Marcus asked. 'Naomi said someone stood outside her door.'

'What does that have to do with what happened at the beach?'

So you did go and see her, Marcus thought. You couldn't summon the courage to speak out, to tell her to back off, so you decided to try again and followed her down to the beach.

'Following someone like that can be harassment, you're aware of that?' he asked.

Josie looked him in the eyes. 'Charge me with whatever you like. It won't stick.'

'So you know what happened on the beach?' Lisa asked.

'I saw him, what he did.'

'He?'

'He came down the steps on the sea wall and walked towards her. I didn't see his face.'

He, Marcus thought. Just like Naomi said.

'I hung back so he wouldn't see me and watched him approach her and the dog. He blocked her path. I thought he was going to rob her. The dog started barking and Naomi turned around. Then he pushed her down.'

'What did you do then?' Lisa asked.

'I stayed back, started to walk away. I was scared, all right? The dog was attacking the man when I turned and ran.'

'The dog was stabbed six times, Josie.'

Her eyes widened, but immediately she steeled herself again. Marcus wondered what she had been through herself to learn how to harden so easily.

'Who would want to hurt Naomi and her dog?'

'I don't know.'

'You would, wouldn't you?'

'I didn't.'

'You mean you didn't get the chance. Someone else got there before you had time to build up the courage.'

'It's not like that.'

'Isn't it? You hate her, right? She had her chance with your boyfriend and yet she's still screwing him. I know I wouldn't put up with it.'

'I wanted to talk to her, not hurt her.'

'But I bet you've thought about it.'

Josie went quiet, picked at the skin around her nails.

'You've been through a lot, Josie. No one would blame you for fighting for what's yours.'

'Don't bring her into this,' Josie said.

Marcus looked between the two women. They knew something he didn't.

'Trying to find out who you are, to make a life for yourself ... It had to be hard, living in your sister's shadow. You've finally found someone to love, and Naomi threatens to bring it tumbling down. No wonder you want her out of the way.'

'I told you, this isn't about Hayley.'

Marcus's throat dried up. 'Hayley Miller was your sister?' he asked. 'But your surname ...'

'Mum remarried. Is this relevant?'

He had read in Hayley's missing persons file that she had a sister called Josie, but had failed to connect the two because of the difference in surnames. As the two women

152

continued to talk, he quietly scolded himself for the oversight.

'Why didn't you report the attack?' Lisa asked. 'Naomi was knocked unconscious as the tide was coming in. She could have drowned. Her dog nearly died.'

Hayley Miller was Josie's sister.

'I wasn't thinking straight. My only thought was getting home, being safe.'

'But when you got home, when you *were* safe?'

'And let Dane figure out why I was down there? I haven't confronted him yet, I wasn't going to let him find out that way.'

'So you left her there to die.'

She sighed deeply and shrugged her shoulders. 'Karma's a bitch. That was hers.'

'Sorry,' Marcus said and raised his hand. 'You're dating a man who was questioned in the disappearance of your sister?'

'He wasn't arrested,' Josie spat.

'But they had a relationship, didn't they? Dane and your sister?'

'My sister fucked half the town. If I tried to avoid every bloke she slept with, I'd still be a virgin. She was a slut. Everyone knew that.'

Marcus looked down, blinked quickly. His head was swimming. Naomi's ex-husband had dated Hayley, who was Josie's sister; Marcus's colleague had been questioned about Hayley's disappearance before it was covered up, and Naomi's sister had been Hayley's best friend. They were all connected to Hayley Miller, who might have died in the same way as Cassie Jennings and Amber O'Neill.

'I think you're lying about the attacker on the beach,' Lisa said.

'Think what you want. I know what I saw.'

'Why should we believe you? You didn't report what you saw to the police, and you lied your way through the first part of this interview. Why should we trust you?'

'I don't care what you think. I know what I saw.'

'Can you prove it?'

She hesitated. 'No.' Then her face changed. The confidence seeped back into her eyes. 'Can you prove that I'm lying?'

'Actually, I can,' Lisa said. She got to her feet. Josie shrank in her chair. 'Stand up, please, Miss Callaghan.'

'Why?'

'I need to check your ankles.'

Josie stared at her. 'What for?'

'Naomi fought the attacker as best she could. She dug her nails into the person's ankle, which would have left abrasions.'

Josie smirked, amused by Lisa's demand. She stood up, bent down to her left ankle and rolled up her jeans to the middle of her calf. No cuts or scratches, just a tattoo of a butterfly.

'Turn your foot to the left.'

Josie followed her orders, revealing nothing but pearly white flesh on the inside of her ankle.

'Right ankle, please.'

She bent down and rolled up the other leg. She turned her foot without being asked. No scratches. No bruising. She rolled down her jeans.

Lisa's face was blank.

'I think I'll be going now,' Josie said. She took her coat off the back of the chair and walked to the door, a grin plastered across her face.

'What did the attacker look like, Josie?' Marcus asked.

'I didn't see his face. It was getting dark. I guess you'll have to do your job, instead of relying on people like me to do it for you.'

She smirked again and shut the door behind her.

TWENTY-FOUR

Naomi sat in the chair by the fire and tried to focus on the crackle of flames, but it was no use: the memory of Max's yelps echoing along the shore bled into her ears. A lot of things had happened in her life that she struggled to forget, but the sound of Max's pain was sure to stay with her until the end. She picked up the iron poker and shuffled the wood around.

Except for the glow of flames, the house was in total darkness. She had only ever turned on the lights for Max. She had lived in darkness her whole life. Finally the outside world matched her own.

The house was nothing without him. It was like sitting in a room stripped of every bit of familiarity: no furniture, no curtains, no cushions, no carpets, just a shell that echoed her every lonely breath.

The tears wouldn't stop.

Every time she closed her eyes she could hear Max yelping with the impact of the knife, feel the weight of him in her arms as she carried him up the beach. She still couldn't raise her arms above her chest.

She put the glass to her lips and drank the rest of the brandy in two large gulps.

She thought back to the first time she had met Max. He had been just two years old and fresh from training, and he still had that distinct puppy breath. She had let him sleep on the bed with her and Dane for the first few nights, before he found his spot on the floor beside her. They had a bond that couldn't rival any other. When she had trekked to the cliff that morning she had wanted to die to put an end to the loneliness, but it was only now that Max was gone that she realised: she was truly alone for the first time since waking up at the bus stop.

She thought back to the killer in the alley. She could still feel the stranger's hands on top of hers, moving them over Amber's mutilated body. It was important for her to use her name; Amber wasn't just a body, she had been a person who had lived and breathed.

She tried to match the stranger's touch and sounds to those on the beach. The hands that had lifted her off the ground had been the same pair that had forced her to feel Amber's body, the same ones that had wiped a tear from her cheek. The police were wrong, she wasn't safe or immune, and it had taken the attack on Max for them all to realise.

The doorbell rang, slicing through the silence in the room. She sat rooted to the chair; life couldn't hurt her if she refused to open the door and let it in.

It could be her mother, or Dane, maybe even George, but she couldn't bring herself to tell them that Max had almost died right in front of her and she had done so little to save him.

Knuckles rapped against the door. She didn't know the

person standing on the other side, or at least not well enough to distinguish their knock from another. Her mother knocked delicately. Her sister's was fast and short, like she wanted to get her visit over with as quickly as possible. There was a hardness to Dane's. She hadn't learned George's yet, but it didn't sound as though it belonged to him. It was fast and persistent, like a delicate hand imitating strength.

It could be the police; maybe they had found the person who had hurt Max and wanted to tell her in person. She put down her glass and went to the door. Her clothes were still piled at the bottom of the stairs, stained with the potent scent of the sea. Grains of sand stuck to the soles of her feet.

'Hello?' she said behind the door. She cleared her throat, spoke louder. 'Hello?'

She waited for a reply. Nothing came.

She turned the key in the lock, took a deep breath and opened the door.

'Don't say a word,' a woman's voice said, and something hard pressed against Naomi's head. 'Or I'll smash your fucking brains in.'

Naomi quivered against the cricket bat pressed against her temple. The cold night air drifted in through the open door.

'Who are you?'

'You know who I am. Come with me.'

'Not until you tell me who you are.'

'You could say I'm your dose of karma.'

Josie was the only person she had wronged. Dane must have told her. He had said he would leave Josie for her; perhaps he thought that if he went through with it, Naomi would have him back. She gnawed at the inside of her lip.

'This has nothing to do with me, Josie. You need to speak to Dane.'

'This has everything to do with you. Are you going to come quietly, or do I have to drag you?'

Naomi considered screaming for help and wondered how long it would take for the bat to rise and crack down on the top of her head. Josie was reckless, that much was clear. She had made her way to Naomi's house armed with a cricket bat. Whatever she planned to do, it was obvious she didn't care about the consequences. Her reason for being there mattered more.

'Well?'

She could slam the door shut, scream until her neighbours peeked from behind the curtains. Josie placed her foot on the step to block the door, as though Naomi had thought aloud.

The path was cold beneath her bare feet. The door clicked shut behind her.

Josie ushered her forward with the end of the bat. Naomi felt the air before her, stepped forward hesitantly, and kicked the iron gate with a misguided step. The gate screeched open and banged against the brick wall.

Please, George, look out of the window.

'Turn right and keep walking until I tell you to stop,' Josie said.

Naomi stepped out onto the path and turned right. The bottoms of her feet were already numb against the wet path, and her right foot throbbed from the impact with the gate.

The street was quiet. Curtains would be drawn. Doors would be locked. No one would see her pass before their windows, lit only by the street lights that buzzed above their heads, led by a deranged woman wielding a cricket bat.

'I don't want Dane. I've been telling him that for two years.'

'Then why are you sleeping with him?'

'I'm not.'

She had never felt so lost before, walking without Max or her cane. Her knowledge of the town wouldn't come; the fear was like fog trapped inside her skull. She held her hands out to feel her way forwards. A snail shell crunched beneath her foot.

'He came home smelling of you.'

'How do you know it was me?'

The bat pressed harder into the middle of her spine.

'Turn right.'

The cold air slipped through her hands. Stones dug into the soles of her feet. If she wanted to survive, she had to give Josie what she wanted. There was no way she could run without knowing what lay in front of her. She was totally at the woman's mercy.

'It happened once,' she said, and stepped away from the kerb as she veered to the left. The bat dug between two vertebrae. 'I told him it was a mistake.'

'You're a liar. You want him to keep coming back.'

'I don't, Josie. I've told him a thousand times.'

'Well, that isn't working. It's time we tried something new. Turn left.'

Where are you taking me, Josie? What are you going to do?

Mud squelched between her toes. Grass tickled the sides of her feet. The wind rushed at her from the west. They were walking across an open field. No street lights. No witnesses. Just darkness. The chime of the town's clock tower stalked the wind.

All this was a scare tactic. No one would resort to such violence. But Naomi didn't know Josie at all. She had no idea what she was capable of.

Her hands fumbled against a wooden gate, soft from the rain and coated in algae.

The woods.

Suddenly she could smell the tree sap on the breeze, the musk of rotting bark.

'Why have you brought me here?'

'I don't want anyone bothering us.' Josie jabbed the bat into Naomi's spine and thrust her into the gate.

Pain shot up her arms and she bit her lip: she refused to let Josie hear her scream. The wind whistled between the trees. She stumbled on with her arms outstretched, her hands dusted with algae.

'How far?'

'As far as I tell you.'

She fanned out her fingers, desperate to feel something other than the thin night air. It felt like she was falling, waiting to hit the ground.

'I never understood what Dane saw in you.'

Naomi stumbled on a rock and Josie snatched at her T-shirt and yanked her upright. She could feel hot blood pooling around the nail on her big toe.

'I think it's because you need him. Men like to be needed. Well, I need him too. Hurry up!'

Josie jabbed the bat into Naomi's right shoulder blade. Pain reverberated down her arm and sparked in her fingertips. This time she did scream, but Josie didn't tell her to stop: they were deep enough in the woods that she didn't have to worry about being heard.

No one will hear me scream.

'Dane and I were married for fifteen years, Josie. It takes longer than two years to forget something like that. We've spent most of our adult lives together.'

'Well now you're on your own. Dane's not here to protect you tonight, is he?'

Naomi kept walking, listening to the sounds of the woods. Nocturnal animals scuffled under shrubs on the woodland floor, and twigs snapped beneath her feet. The tops of the trees thrashed together with the force of the wind. However loudly she screamed, she would never be heard.

'I was dragged into the police station today because of you. Do you want me to lose my job as well as my boyfriend? Can't you let me have one thing?'

'I didn't say anything about you. I don't know what you're talking about!'

'You're so full of shit.'

Josie shoved her hard. Naomi toppled to her knees, and stones bit through the bandages on her hands.

'Tonight is a warning. If you don't stay away from Dane, I'll kill you next time.' She stamped on Naomi's left hand. Naomi's scream echoed between the trees and sent birds flocking from the treetops. The sole of Josie's shoe squeaked as it worked her fingers into the ground. Tears streamed from her eyes as she felt the bones bend and twist.

When Josie stepped back, Naomi snatched her hand away and cradled it to her chest. Her fingers thrummed with her pulse.

'Remember this pain,' Josie said. 'And remind yourself how much worse it will be if you see Dane again.'

Cold tears dripped from Naomi's jaw. She shivered and rocked against the wind.

'You know, I almost felt sorry for you when I saw you up close for the first time, standing there in the doorway. I could've waved my hand in front of your face and you wouldn't have had a clue.'

'What ... what are you going to do?' Naomi asked.

'I'm going to leave you here.'

'You can't! I'll never get home!'

Josie scoffed. 'That's sort of the point.'

'Josie, please.' Naomi reached up and felt the hem of her coat. She tugged and pleaded. She couldn't ignore the fact that her fate rested in Josie's hands.

'Don't touch me!' Josie shoved her to the ground.

'Please don't leave me here. Please!'

'You're pathetic,' Josie spat. She leaned down and gripped Naomi's jaw. 'Stay well away from Dane, or I swear I'll make sure you—'

Josie was yanked upwards with a rush of air, and hot liquid sprayed down on Naomi's face and hair, as though the sky was raining blood. She heard Josie fall to the ground and thrash wildly on the woodland floor, blood gargling in her throat.

Naomi staggered to her feet and stumbled, blinking away the blood as it snaked down her face. She had no idea where she was going or what might lie ahead. She lurched to the left until the bark of a tree snagged beneath her fingernails. If she wanted to survive, she had to hide. She weaved between the trees, stumbling from trunk to trunk, biting down on her bottom lip to suppress a sob. The uneven ground was smothered in layers of rotting leaves and fallen twigs that snapped underfoot. She had to fight the instinct to freeze with fear. Each step took courage. She swung her arms out in front of her, flinching when her hands scraped against bark.

Once she was deep enough in the woods, she hid behind a tree trunk and clasped her hands over her nose and mouth, listening to the wind drift between the trees, and the wild thump of her own heart.

A twig cracked. Dead leaves moved on the woodland floor with approaching footsteps. Someone else was out there, breathing the same air, feeling the same chill. The footsteps whispered around the right of the tree and stopped so close that she could feel the heat from the stranger's body.

It's dark. He might not see me in the dark.

He was listening for her. If she was caught now, it was all over. Her pulse pounded in her ears.

The footsteps moved on, deeper into the woods, stopping and starting, the unknown person listening for the slightest sound. She couldn't hold her breath any longer; veins were snaking up her neck and swelling at her temples.

She exhaled loudly, heaved in fresh air, and clamped her hand over her lips again with a loud slap.

Silence. Deafening, torturous silence. Naomi pressed her back into the tree until her pulse vibrated against the bark. Tears snaked from her eyes and ran down the seal of her hand.

The bushes began to rustle again. He was coming back.

Sobbing, she pushed away from the tree and stumbled forward. Branches clawed at her clothes and skin. She was too slow. She tried to pick up speed and walked into a large fallen branch. She scurried beneath it and scratched her face on something sharp. Her hands thrashed wildly through the air, scraping against bark until her nails cracked and bled. She lurched onto the path again and forced herself to run, to ignore the terror of not knowing what lay ahead. Stones dug into the soles of her feet with every misguided step as she anticipated a hard knock from a tree trunk or the quick snatch of the killer's hand in her hair. She stumbled over something solid and fell to the ground. Dirt coated her teeth and framed her nostrils.

A hand snatched at her ankle. Blood was still gargling in Josie's throat as she tried to speak.

'I'm sorry,' Naomi whispered, and yanked her leg free from Josie's grasp. She scrambled to her feet and turned blindly from the path until she was back between the trees again. She hoped she was walking deeper into the woods, but for all she knew, she could be stumbling around in circles.

She staggered along blindly, with leaves bundling around her feet and branches snagging her clothes, until she slammed into a tree and landed on the ground in a cloud of dry mud. One foot was dangling over some sort of drop. She examined the dip in the earth with her hands, moving downwards with the ditch until she slipped onto dry and rotting leaves. She pulled her knees up to her chest and lay still.

It was only then that the pain crept in, pulsing at the bottoms of her feet and in her mutilated fingers. Her skin itched with Josie's blood. She clenched her eyes shut and listened to the night.

Something small crept amongst the leaves beside her feet. The ditch smelt of animal excrement.

She lay in the dark with her hands over her mouth to disguise her laborious breaths, shivering so hard that the leaves rustled around her. Sweat dripped down from her forehead and into her eyes. She couldn't be found now – she was too exhausted to run again. A single tear ran down her cheek and tapped onto the leafy bed.

And then she heard him, no more than ten feet away from her.

It had to be the man who had dragged her hands across Amber's body, the man who had hurt Max. He was breathing heavily into the night, standing motionless as though he was trying to spot her silhouette in the dark.

She tried to remember what clothes she had put on that morning, and feared she was wearing colours that clashed against the palette of the wilderness.

The man sighed heavily. Shoes scuffed against mud and leaves until at last the wood quietened and the cold night fell around her like a blanket.

Naomi stayed in the ditch until the birds began to sing with the dawn.

TWENTY-SIX

Marcus woke abruptly to the sound of his phone vibrating on the bedside table. He'd been dreaming of Naomi.

Stop. You have to stop.

He opened his eyes. Natalie lay beside him, looking at him as if she knew exactly what had been playing on his mind as he slept. Was it cheating when it was just a dream? When you knew deep down that it would never happen? His cheeks burned at the thought of her knowing his thoughts, his desires. But that was the thing with Natalie: she never let him have anything all to himself; she had to have a piece of it.

'What day is it?' he asked gruffly.

'Saturday. We're meant to be spending the day together.'

He sighed and picked up the phone.

'Hello?' he said, cleared his throat.

'It's me,' Lisa said, wide awake. 'I'm with your girlfriend.'

'What?' He looked at Natalie to check if she'd heard.

'Naomi Hannah was found in the woods this morning.' Lisa waited a beat. 'Alive.'

Marcus sat up and swung his legs off the side of the bed,

rubbing his left eye with his free hand. Natalie watched him in the mirror.

'I thought the uniforms were keeping an eye on her?'

'When they knocked around ten p.m., there was no answer. Assumed she'd gone to sleep. They're hardly going to kick down the door just to tuck her in.' She sighed into the phone. 'Naomi's in hospital, and Josie Callaghan was found with her throat cut.'

'Shit.' He stood up and ran to his wardrobe, balancing the phone between his ear and shoulder as he pulled out a white shirt and black suit.

'We're supposed to be spending the day together!' Natalie shouted.

'Lovers' quarrel?' Lisa asked.

'No.'

'What do you mean, no?' Natalie asked.

'Not you! I'm on the phone, Natalie.'

'Should I call Blake instead? You sound as though you have your hands full over there.'

'No, I'm coming.'

'You're a real prick, Marcus,' Natalie spat. She clambered out of bed, naked except for her knickers, and barged her shoulder into his. The bathroom door slammed behind her.

'Meet me at Naomi's house at ten. The scene's not far from there. Not much I can do here at the hospital while she's out for the count.'

Lisa hung up. Marcus looked at the bathroom door and listened to Natalie's sobs and the clatter of toiletries falling into the sink.

172

Lisa was waiting for him when he pulled up outside Naomi's house. He was ten minutes late, and she didn't look impressed.

'You look like shit,' she said, glancing at him as he climbed out of the car.

So do you, he thought. Dark circles stalked Lisa's eyes, livid against the chalky skin on her face.

'Did you forget to brush your teeth?' she asked.

Shit. Natalie had locked herself in the bathroom, screaming at him from the other side of the door.

Lisa turned and walked down the road.

'What happened to Naomi?' Marcus asked as he tried to angle his breaths down towards his chest.

Lisa pulled a pack of mints out of her jacket pocket.

'Thanks.'

'It's not for your benefit,' she replied.

He took a mint and passed the pack back to her, their fingers grazing for a brief second, enough to make him squirm.

'Uniforms said she was found by a dog walker, wandering around the woods covered in blood. She was disorientated; thought it was her guide dog and latched onto it, hysterical. The dog bit her.'

'Why was she in the woods?'

'She hasn't spoken yet. She's been asleep since being admitted. Once we've wrapped up here, I want you to go to the hospital and wait for her to wake up. I don't want her telling her story to a nurse.'

They walked to the end of the road without a word. Marcus's teeth ground against the mint until it became mush and slipped down his throat. He rubbed at the crust in the corners of his eyes with his fingertips.

'When was Josie found?'

'Just after six, by a homeless man.'

The woodland came into sight around the bend, a wall of greenery that hid what the night had left in its wake. Naomi had been in there, stumbling around in the dark as the rest of them slept. He had spent the night dreaming of her while she was stuck in a nightmare.

'Thanks for calling me.'

'You pick up the phone when I call. Blake doesn't.'

Lisa led him towards the woods and through the gate, past two uniformed police officers. Crime-scene tape fluttered in the wind.

'You don't need to watch where you step,' Lisa said, ducking under the tape. 'Forensics have searched the path already.'

Marcus followed her. Other than the dead leaves crunching beneath their feet, the place was quiet, almost tranquil. That would all change when they saw the blood. Yellow markers were dotted along the path where evidence had been found: a footprint, a drop of blood, a human hair.

'Do you think the person who killed Josie could have been the same person responsible for the disappearance of her sister?'

Lisa stopped abruptly. 'I told you not to talk about Hayley fucking Miller, Campbell.'

'But it's not every day that two sisters are attacked like this.'

'If you're going to keep this up, you can turn around and go on home.'

Lisa headed on. He followed obediently.

Marcus spotted the white tent ahead of them. Camera flashes escaped from within and cast the shadows of the moving bodies against the tarpaulin walls. They seemed to be crouching over the body like a pack of wolves hunched over their prey.

Lisa walked into the tent as though she was strolling into the office. She didn't need to look down at the body – she would have seen it before Marcus arrived – but to him it was fresh.

Josie was lying face down in the mud. Her blonde hair was stained crimson, and her arms were stretched out before her as though she had died trying to crawl to safety, her nails dug deep into the dirt. Blood had stained the skin on her hands and wrists and dripped down her elbows as she had tried to stop it from gushing out of her neck.

'Anything?' Lisa asked Dr Ling, who was watching over her colleague as he took photos of the body.

'Same MO as with Amber and Cassie. Throat slashed and left to drain out.'

'I meant any evidence.'

'There are some fingerprints and loose hairs, but they could be hers or Naomi's.'

'Any sign she fought back?'

'There might be some skin tissue under her nails.'

'Her hair,' Marcus said. 'She's the third victim. All of them had blonde hair.'

'He obviously has a type,' Lisa replied.

'Dr Ling,' someone called from outside the tent, the words echoing through the woodland.

'One moment, please.'

Dr Ling stepped out of the tent. Lisa followed her quickly. If they had found something, Lisa wouldn't be told when she could take a look.

Ling weaved through the undergrowth towards a man dressed in white waving his hand. Branches clawed at Marcus's trouser legs. Lisa was right behind the pathologist, almost stepping on her heels.

'What is it?'

'A watch.'

Dr Ling stopped and looked down as Lisa pushed in and stood beside her. Marcus peered over their heads to where the man was holding back a branch, revealing a silver watch resting in the dirt. The strap was metal too, made of small silver rectangles, like a row of steel teeth.

'Is that blood splattered on the face?' Lisa asked.

'Looks like it,' Dr Ling replied. 'We'll know more once it's tested.'

'There'll be hairs trapped in the strap too.'

'Here's hoping,' Ling replied. 'Take photos and bag it, Sam.'

'Do you think it belongs to the killer?' Marcus asked as Lisa headed back towards the path.

'It looks too clean to have been out here for long. And the blood speaks for itself.' She looked behind him towards Dr Ling. 'When will we know?'

'I'll have them test it first and get back to you.'

'When will you be ready for the autopsy?'

'I'll do it today. No point making her wait in the fridge until Monday.'

'Call me when it's done and I'll head over.'

'Me too,' Marcus said.

'Only if you've got the story from Naomi. You'd best get going. Call me once she's awake.'

A scream ripped through the trees. The white tent began to squirm as bodies writhed inside, clawing at the walls to get out.

'Dr Ling!' a voice cried from the tent. 'Dr Ling, come quickly!'

Ling ran towards the tent, following the urgency in her colleague's voice, Lisa and Marcus following her, dodging tree roots and branches.

Something was happening inside the tent. A struggle of bodies, moving the tent from side to side. Limbs pressed against the walls like feet kicking out from a womb.

The pathologist burst inside and gasped. Marcus squeezed in beside her and looked down.

Josie had been turned onto her back and was staring lifelessly at the ceiling of the tent. The cut in her throat was packed with mud, which also filled her nose and mouth and hid within the grooves of her teeth.

Marcus couldn't tell what he was supposed to be looking at – she was just as dead at the front as she was at the back – until suddenly he noticed and the blood drained from his head.

Josie Callaghan blinked.

TWENTY-SEVEN

The nurse came to check Naomi's stats every hour, and every time she looked surprised to find Marcus still sitting there. He wasn't going to leave, not until Naomi woke up.

Angry scratches covered the right side of her face. The fingers of her left hand were straightened in small splints. He wouldn't know how much had been broken inside until she opened her eyes. He sighed into his hands.

The heart monitor began to race. Naomi was feeling the bed sheets with her hands with quickening breaths and wide eyes.

'Naomi, you're okay.'

She flinched and stared in his direction.

'It's Marcus. Detective Sergeant Marcus Campbell.'

She sank back towards the bed, but continued to twist the sheets with her free hand.

'You're in hospital, but you're doing fine.'

He watched the memory of the night flood her eyes.

'Can you tell me what happened?'

'I ...' Her voice was timid, barely a whisper. 'I'm going to die, aren't I?'

We could have done so much more to protect you.

'You are not going to die, Naomi. I will make sure that doesn't happen.'

'You can't be there all the time. It seems he's always watching.'

'What happened?' He leaned in, waiting to hear every faint word that slipped from her lips. She quivered in the bed, tears snaking silently from her eyes, which glazed over as she returned to the woods. Marcus began to wonder if she was still disorientated. 'You can trust me, Naomi. What happened to you?'

Her face tightened and her voice deepened as she said her name.

'Josie.'

A memory flashed in his eyes. Josie lying on her back, the mud packed in her throat moving with her breaths.

'She came to my door and put a cricket bat against my head.' Naomi stroked her temple as though she could still feel the wood pressing against her skull. 'She said I had to go with her.'

'Go where?'

'She led me into the woods,' she said, clenching the sheet in a fist. 'She was talking about my relationship with my husband.' Her face creased and she shook her head. 'Ex-husband.'

She licked her cracked lips. Sighed.

'She told me it was a warning. If I didn't stop seeing Dane, it would be worse next time. She planned to leave me there alone in the woods. And then ... blood. Hot blood rained down on me.' She wiped her palms along the sheets as if removing the blood from her hands. 'Someone had hurt her. She couldn't speak. I managed to run away and hide behind a tree. Someone was chasing me, spotted me when I couldn't hold my breath any longer.'

She was speaking faster as the intensity of the memory grew.

'I just remember running. Running as fast as I could with my hands out in front of me. I fell down by a ditch and hid there.'

She stared into the distance. She was back there in the woods, hiding in the dark.

'I stayed there for hours,' she whispered, the words cracking with her tears. 'My skin was wet. I felt insects crawling under my clothes. It was so cold.'

She's broken. The killer has finally broken her.

'I don't remember much after that.'

'You were confused,' Marcus said gently. 'A dog walker found you, and you thought—'

'Max ...'

'It wasn't Max, Naomi.'

'He bit me.'

'She. A German shepherd called Penelope.'

'I must have scared her.'

'You weren't yourself. You were close to hypothermic. You were out in the woods all night.'

'How long have I been here?'

'Since around eight this morning.'

'What time is it now?'

'Gone three.'

His phone began to vibrate in his pocket. He ignored it.

'I have to ask you a question, and it might sound unkind.'

She nodded, wiping the tears from her cheeks with scratched hands.

'Why does the killer let you live?'

She was silent for a while.

'I don't know. But I'm starting to wish he didn't.'

'We'll find him, Naomi. I promise you that.'

'You've made promises before, Detective. But that's all you've done. I've been left in the dark this whole time, and all I can do is hope to survive.'

Marcus went to speak.

'Find him, Marcus. I don't know how much more I can take.'

'I will,' he said.

She rested her head back against the pillow, and they sat listening to the beep of the heart monitor. Rain tapped against the window pane behind Marcus's head.

'Why did you ask me about Hayley Miller?' she asked. 'After the attack on the beach. You asked if I knew her.'

His investigation into Hayley Miller's disappearance had to be kept a secret or Lisa would bury it so deep he would never find it again. But he needed to speak his thoughts aloud. He needed someone to be on his side.

'I'm looking into the possibility of a connection between the recent murders and Hayley's disappearance.'

'She was my sister's friend, not mine. I barely knew her.'

'But so many people in your life did. Your sister was her best friend. Josie was her sister. Dane ...'

'Dane?' Her eyes twitched minutely, left and right.

She doesn't know.

'It may not be connected. I just want to make sure.'

'What about Dane?' she asked, and sat up. 'How did he know Hayley?'

Marcus sighed silently. It was as though she didn't know who to trust. She had no idea how few of them there were.

'He was questioned when she disappeared. They had dated, and she was supposed to meet him the night she vanished.'

'Dane? My Dane?'

'Yes.'

'But I would have known ...'

'Only if he told you.'

'But my sister, my mum, surely they would have said something ...'

'It wasn't common knowledge that he was questioned. The police tried to conceal as much as possible. The town was already talking, making up its own mind about what happened.'

'But someone would have told me they'd dated.'

'Hayley dated a lot of people. She was known for her promiscuity. They might not even have known.'

A tear slipped down her cheek. She wiped it away with an aggressive hand.

'And you think her disappearance could be connected to what's happening to me?'

'I don't know, Naomi. I'm looking into every possibility here. It's a hunch, but I believe there's more to it than that.'

A rumble of thunder rolled across the sky behind the window pane.

'Get some rest,' he said. 'Call me if you need anything, or if you have any questions. Is there anyone you want us to contact for you?'

She hesitated before answering, as though she was thinking

of the people in her life, and who she had left to trust. It took her a while.

'My mum.'

She gave him the number and he typed it into his phone.

'I'll speak to the nurse and ask her to give your mum a call.'

She turned over and lay with her back to him. As Marcus walked around the bed to leave, he took one last look. Her eyes were open, staring out at the room as a tear spilled over the bridge of her nose.

He had promised to protect her and he had let her down at every turn. He vowed that he would never make promises again.

TWENTY-EIGHT

Even with the painkillers, Naomi still felt the tenderness all over her body. The muscles in her legs were weak from running through the woods. Her fingers were hot and throbbed in time with her heart. She leaned on her mother's arm as they walked through the front door.

'We should get you cleaned up,' Rachel said.

'I just want to rest.'

'Bath first, then you can rest.'

Her mother took her hand and led her to the banister. 'I'll be right behind you.'

Naomi took a deep breath and put her foot on the first step.

'That's it,' Rachel said, and pressed her hands into Naomi's back to keep her upright.

When they reached the bathroom, Naomi sat on the toilet seat and let her mother undress her as though she were a child again. With Rachel and Grace choosing her clothes and food, and so many other aspects of her life controlled by others, she had often felt like she had never grown up at all; that she was still the little girl huddled in the corner of the bus shelter.

Rachel turned on the taps and placed a folded towel at the

foot of the bath. Naomi listened to her swishing her hands through the water. The pain dulled the embarrassment of exposing her naked body.

'Here we are.'

She put her hands in her mother's and rose from the seat, placing one foot in the water and then the other.

'Easy now,' Rachel said.

The water lapped past her navel and swam over her breasts. Rachel rested her hand at the nape of Naomi's neck and lowered her head to the rim of the bath. The hot water stung the scratches littering her body.

'You relax, I'm going to change your bedding.'

She sank lower in the bath until the water was up against her chin.

'I'll be back soon,' Rachel said.

Naomi lay in the bath and inhaled the steam, listening to her mother open and close the door to the linen closet; the creak of the floorboards under her weight as she circled the bed. She submerged herself under the water.

Bubbles popped as they made their way to the surface, rising from her body and tickling her skin. Beneath the water, she was away from the fear, the danger. It had been weeks since she had felt so safe. She stayed there listening to her heartbeat thud against the base of the bath, even when her lungs began to spasm. Small bubbles crept from her nostrils. She closed her eyes.

Hands burst through the surface and snatched at her arms. Water splashed over the edge of the bath as Naomi was hauled upright, gasping for air.

'What were you doing?' Rachel yelled.

'I was resting.'

'You nearly gave me a heart attack. I thought you'd drowned.'

Naomi wiped the water from her eyes and coughed up the rest of the water.

Her mother sighed and rested back on her heels, her knees clicking.

'Sit up. Let me wash your hair.'

Naomi sat up straight and let her mother pour hot water over her hair and delicately massage it with shampoo. Foam ran down her back and stung the small cuts on her skin.

'This reminds me of the first time I gave you a bath,' Rachel said through a smile. 'You were so frightened in broke my heart.'

She could have known about Dane and Hayley and didn't tell me.

'Bt luckily you learnt quickly,' she said with a laugh. 'I couldn't let you start nursery with matted hair.'

Naomi tensed her muscles against her mother's touch.

'It took a long time to earn your trust. I suppose you don't remember much of that time. They were the hardest yet most rewarding years of my life.'

Naomi listened to the sound of the water trickling down her back. The loofah slid up and down her body, scraping against her wounds.

She sat there as the water drained away, too nervous to stand without slipping, then took her mother's hands to step out onto the bath mat. Rachel rubbed her down with the towel as Naomi stood there naked and numb.

Rachel led her into the bedroom. The clean sheets were so soft, she could have slept instantly. She sank down onto the bed.

'Tablets,' Rachel said, and passed her three pills and a glass of water. 'Two for sleep, one for pain.'

Naomi nodded and gulped them down, then laid her head on the pillow. She closed her eyes as her mother stroked her hair, listening to Rachel's regular breaths curling in and out of her nostrils. She breathed in the scent of her mother's perfume and sank against the mattress.

'Why won't you talk to me? Tell me what you're thinking?' her mother whispered, her hand caressing her hair as Naomi slipped into the depths of sleep. 'Why won't you let me in?'

I can't trust you, Naomi thought to herself. I can't trust anyone.

Naomi woke from the nightmare with a jolt. She had been back in the woods, only this time Josie had used the bat she had threatened her with. It came down again and again as the killer watched from behind the trees, telling Josie where to hit her and how hard, until the last swipe knocked her awake. She had heard her bones crack, felt blood running into her eyes. It had seemed so real that she patted the duvet, checking for the woodland floor beneath her palms.

Her skin was numb from the painkillers, but she could still feel the pain squirming in her fingers, waiting to rise.

Someone was sitting at the end of the bed, pinning her down with their weight.

'You should have called me,' Grace said.

'How long have you been here?'

'Mum needed to get some rest. She's too old to be doing all this. What if you'd fallen down the stairs and taken her with you? You might be able to get back up again, but it isn't that easy for her.'

'I knew you'd be working, I didn't want to—'

'None of this is exactly ideal, but if it means keeping Mum safe, I'll do what I need to do.'

'You have the kids to worry about.'

'Craig's the stay-at-home parent. I can come if you need me.'

'I'm sorry.'

Grace sighed. Naomi felt the heat of her breath.

'What happened to you out there?'

'I don't want to talk about it.'

They fell quiet again. Clicking sounds came from her sister's mouth as words started to form before they were pushed back down.

'What's going on with you?' she asked finally.

'I don't know. Someone wants to hurt me.'

'Why?'

'How should I know?'

'Mum can't stay here if it's not safe. You know that.'

'I know.'

They listened to each other breathing. It was monotonous enough to make Naomi's eyelids flicker again as the pills began to coax her under.

'Did you know that Dane and Hayley dated?' she asked.

'How did you hear about that?'

'So you knew?'

'Of course I knew. She was my best friend.'

'You never said anything.'

'You'd finally found someone who made you happy. Mum would never have forgiven me if I told you.'

'He was questioned when she disappeared, did you know that?'

'Half the town was questioned. Hayley was ... friendly with a lot of people.'

Naomi's depression had kept her in the dark. There had been secrets in her own home and she hadn't even realised.

'Were *you*? Questioned, I mean?'

'Why are you asking about Hayley all of a sudden?'

'The police think that what's happening to me might have something to do with her disappearance.'

Grace didn't reply, but Naomi could hear each breath coming quicker than the last.

'Grace, I said—'

'I heard what you said.'

They both fell quiet again. A car crept up the road. A bird sang from one of the trees lining the street. Naomi took a deep breath.

'What happened between you two, before she went missing?'

'It was a long time ago,' Grace replied dismissively.

'But if what happened to Hayley is connected—'

'You said you'd never tell.'

'I won't. I haven't got anything to tell. You won't talk to me. You've been pushing me away ever since.'

Grace sighed heavily.

'Have you ever thought that I'm protecting you?'

'But I'm your sister, you can confide in me.'

'There's nothing to confide, all right? It was a long time ago.'

'But we've never been the same since. I miss you.'

Grace straightened out imaginary creases in the duvet. 'Get some rest,' she said, pulling it up below Naomi's chin. Her hands were shaking. 'Call me if you need anything, not Mum. It will only worry her.'

Naomi nodded.

'Goodnight, Naomi,' Grace said from the door.

'Goodnight.'

Naomi stared into the darkness and listened as Grace went down the stairs and closed the front door behind her. Silence rang through the house. She was alone again.

All these years she had thought her sister had asked her to keep her secret because she was ashamed of the fight she and Hayley had had. But it was clear to her now that something bad had happened ... something Grace was protecting her from.

TWENTY-NINE

Grace sat deep in the corner of the sofa in the living room with her hair covering her face in thin strands. She was wearing the dress Hayley had given her before they stopped talking; she hadn't taken it off for three days. The fabric didn't smell of Hayley any more but of her own sweat, the musky scent of misery wafting from her whenever she moved.

The detectives watched her closely, eyeing every scratch and bruise on her skin.

The room felt too small for the four of them: the detectives, her mother and her.

Her mother tried to take her hand. Grace moved it away.

The detectives sat on the sofa opposite, drinking the tea her mother had insisted on making, brought in on a tray with a sugar bowl and a jug of milk, as though they were guests, not police officers preparing to pick her daughter apart. Her mother sat beside her with her hands jittering in her lap. She leant over the coffee table and moved the milk jug until it was in line with the sugar bowl. Mum was a fixer, but she couldn't fix this.

'You know Hayley better than anyone, Grace,' DI Roster said. 'Do you know of anyone who would want to harm her?'

She shook her head and thought of the hands that had given her the bruises, scratched her, pulled her hair, dragged her away from Hayley. She swallowed down the tears. It was all her fault.

'The more we know, the more chance we have of finding her,' DS Cunningham said.

'Mrs Miller said that the two of you had a disagreement,' DI Roster added. 'What was that about?'

'It doesn't matter now,' Grace whispered.

'Is the tea all right?' her mother asked. 'I can make coffee if you prefer. I should have asked.'

'Tea is fine, thank you,' DI Roster replied. His eyes never left Grace. 'Hayley's mother thinks you fell out over a boy,'

'Her mother barely knew her. No one did.'

'Except you, right?'

Grace lowered her head and eyed the detectives through her hair, which moved with her breaths.

'You may be the only person who can help us find her, Grace.'

Her cheeks burned under DI Roster's scrutiny. She had promised Hayley that she would never tell; she had learned the hard way that she couldn't trust anyone enough to tell them the truth – especially the police.

'What happened between the two of you?'

Tears burned in her eyes and filled them to the brim.

'Are you keeping a secret for her? Is that it? You aren't

helping her by keeping it to yourself. You're stopping us from finding her.'

Her whole body shook. Tears slipped down her cheeks and quivered on her jawline.

'You like to dress like Hayley, don't you? Style your hair the same way, wear the same perfume. You admired her a lot, didn't you, until she began sleeping around?'

'They didn't deserve her,' she whispered.

'What was that?'

'I said they didn't deserve her. They used her. She was destroying herself.'

'She was destroying the image you had of her, wasn't she?' DI Roster said. 'You realised she wasn't perfect after all.'

'I knew she wasn't perfect. I just wanted to protect her.'

'And you ended up pushing her away.'

She shot up in the chair, spit flying from her mouth. 'You don't know anything!'

'Grace, calm down,' her mother said, and reached for her hand. She noticed the tears streaking down her daughter's face. 'Oh Grace. I'll get you a tissue.'

'Would you ever have hurt Hayley? She hurt you, didn't she? Did she make those scratches on your arms? Give you the bruises?'

'You don't know what you're talking about!'

'Then help us understand, Grace.'

The room fell silent. Her legs quivered. She listened to the rush of her heart and tasted the salt in her tears. She wiped her palms on her dress.

'That's Hayley's dress, isn't it?' DS Cunningham asked.

'She's wearing it in this photo.' He held up the photo that had been splashed across every newspaper, every missing poster. Hayley smiled for the camera. The dress fitted her perfectly. On Grace, it hugged her thighs and pulled taut over her stomach.

A memory flashed in her mind: Hayley's eyes rolled back into her head. Saliva dribbling between her lips, followed by moans of confusion and fear. Grace caught the sob in her throat and ran from the room.

'I'm so sorry,' her mother said. 'She's distraught. Hayley is her best friend.'

Grace bounded up the stairs, pushed open her bedroom door, and crept into bed.

She wanted to tell them what had happened to Hayley, but she couldn't trust them. If she told them, they might arrest her too. The words filled her mouth, begged to be let out, but Hayley's words echoed inside her head, the last words she had ever said to her, calling down the street as Grace stormed away.

Please don't tell them. They can't know. You know what will happen to me if they find out.

Grace sobbed into the pillow until she was exhausted enough to close her eyes.

THIRTY

'The blood splatters on the watch face belong to Josie,' Lisa said as she glanced down at her phone. 'But they didn't find any hairs in the strap.'

Marcus thought back to the woods that morning, the way the sun had peered through the tops of the trees and shone in the links of the watch. He imagined faint arm hairs caught between them like tiny bones being gnawed by metal teeth. Someone had taken care to remove any traces of the owner.

'How long will it take to check the different blood types found at the scene?' he asked.

'Ling said she'd have the results by morning. Guess her team is working overtime this weekend.'

Like us, Marcus thought.

'I want samples from immediate family, friends, lovers, in case nothing shows on the system.'

He looked at her and wondered what she did all day after she'd delegated everything to those below her. She looked up and met his eye.

'You going to go faint on me again?'

'No.' He looked through the glass partition into Josie's hospital room and eyed the stitches in the woman's neck. 'What did Ling say about the attack on Josie?'

'Due to the difference in the skin tears, she can't confirm that her throat was cut with the same weapon as the others,' Lisa said with her eyes on the window. 'But the hesitation the killer initially showed is gone, which could be why the cut was made differently to the others. His confidence is growing the more the bodies pile up.'

She sighed and put her phone back in her pocket.

'I want to know why he wants Naomi alive. Why would he want to ruin someone's life to such a degree but let them live? He clearly enjoys the kill. Perhaps it's fun for him, like a cat playing with its prey.'

'Cats don't do that for fun,' Marcus replied. 'They play with their prey to wear them out, so that when they finally make the fatal bite to the neck, the prey is too tired to defend itself.'

'You need to get a life.'

With this job?

They both glanced back through the glass.

He thought about Naomi's sister Grace and the report he had read on her interview during the search for Hayley Miller. He thought of the cuts and bruises that had littered Grace's skin, and wondered if someone had hurt her to keep her from talking. It seemed to him that everyone but him had a secret to hide.

'You'd think Naomi would be an easy catch,' Lisa said. 'She'd never see him coming.'

'Maybe that's the point,' Marcus replied. 'The statistics speak for themselves. The majority of homicides are committed by someone known to the victim.'

'Statistics,' she scoffed under her breath.

'All I know is that I don't want to see Naomi on Dr Ling's cutting table. I won't let that happen.'

'Don't make promises you can't keep,' Lisa replied.

The heart monitor beeped on the other side of the glass. Marcus thought back to the forensic team jumping back from Josie as she blinked at their feet. Lisa had been thinking of it too.

'I can't believe they didn't know she was alive,' she said. 'They were working around her for hours.'

'Sam said he couldn't find a pulse. It had been too faint.'

He thought of the man's face draining of blood. *There ... there wasn't a pu-pulse. I promise. I promise.*

'She could have died right at their feet, Marcus. They won't get off easy. Someone will lose their job when I'm done with them.'

Marcus looked through the glass at Josie. The only movement was the rise and fall of her chest.

'When can we arrest her?' he asked.

'We don't know if she's guilty yet.'

'Of course she is. Naomi said—'

'I know what Naomi said, but she isn't the one with her throat cut, is she? I want to hear what Josie has to say.'

'You don't trust Naomi?' he asked.

'I don't trust anyone who comes across as helpless as she does, and you'd be stupid to fall for it.'

You don't trust anyone, full stop.

He could feel her watching him. The heat of her gaze burned against his cheek.

'You've been reading up on the Hayley Miller case, haven't you?'

He looked at her and saw the distrust in her eyes.

'You knew an awful lot when we interviewed Josie. Before that, you didn't even know Hayley's name.'

'I can't ignore the similarities, boss. Josie was her sister, and now she's lying in a hospital bed. Dane was questioned about her disappearance, as was Grace, Naomi's own sister. And Blake—'

'Why do you think I'm not looking into it, Marcus, huh? Can you use your brain for a second? The superintendent wants it buried. The corruption scandal nearly destroyed us and we've only just earned the town's trust back. We can't afford to lose it again.'

'But if it's connected, you could solve Hayley's disappearance for good.'

'Or have two unsolved cases for the town to hold against us. I told you not to pursue this, Marcus.'

'I'm just doing my job.'

'You want to keep it?' She glared at him, but this time he refused to look away.

Her phone vibrated in her pocket. She glanced down and sighed at the screen.

'I'm going home. You should too. Early start tomorrow.'

'I'm going to stay.'

'Suit yourself, but you'll be getting the bus.'

She left without saying goodbye, strolling past the nurses' station in silence, even when the nurse on shift wished her goodnight.

Marcus waited until she was out of sight before entering Josie's room. Her chest moved up and down faintly, fed by the air creeping through the tube filling her mouth. He sat down beside her and studied her wound.

Her throat was stained with dark bruises. Stitches lined the wound, which was red and inflamed. But even beneath the bruises and the swelling, the resemblance to Hayley Miller was striking. He thought back to the missing persons photo at the front of the file. They had the same blonde hair and ice-blue eyes, their lips formed from the same mould. Marcus wondered if Josie's malicious nature was born of the life she had led, or whether it was something else she and Hayley had shared, woven within their DNA.

Dane Hannah had had a relationship with Hayley Miller, and now he was dating her younger sister. Was that by chance? Or had he chosen her because of the likeness they shared? He looked at Josie's chest rising and falling with the machine, her eyes moving gently behind her eyelids.

'No one has come to see you,' he whispered. 'Is Dane all you've got? Is that why you hate Naomi so much?'

The door opened and the overhead light flicked on.

'Who the hell are you?'

The man was tall, with a shaved head and tattoos up both arms. His skin was tanned and leathery. But Marcus could see the similarities between him and Josie. They had the same blue eyes, just like Hayley.

'Detective Sergeant Marcus Campbell. I was just leaving.'

'Good. I ain't sharing a room with no pig.'

Marcus stood and took one final look at Josie lying in the bed. She looked almost angelic beneath the wounds.

The man stayed in the doorway, tensing his muscles and puffing out his chest so it was difficult for Marcus to slip by. He smelt of stale sweat and cigarettes.

Marcus made his way down the corridor with a quick stride. He was certain that when Josie woke up, she would lie about what had happened. He had to find out the truth before then.

THIRTY-ONE

Naomi woke up to loud bangs that had infiltrated her dream. She had been back in the woods. Josie had a fistful of her hair and was thrusting her head into the woodland floor, knocking the teeth from her gums until blood exploded from her lips in a hot red mist.

She shot up in bed, smoothing down her hair where Josie's fist had been, and listened to the sound reverberating through the house.

Bang. Bang. Bang.

She peeled back the sheets and moaned as the pain woke.

Bang. Bang. Bang.

She hobbled to the door, wrapped herself in her dressing gown, and stood on the landing and listened.

She longed to hear Max's claws tapping against the hardwood floor and his tail knocking against the banister. But instead she was alone, shivering at the top of the stairs as she tried to find the courage to open her own front door.

Bang. Bang. Bang.

The stairs creaked under her feet. Her heartbeat echoed in her throat.

She crept towards the sideboard and felt along the top for the keys. Even with the key poised and shaking before the lock, her hand refused to grasp the handle.

She imagined a variety of people behind the door. Josie with her neck still cut open, pulling at her leg like she had from the woodland floor. Detective Sergeant Marcus Campbell, bringing bad news of Max after one of his numerous operations. Max wouldn't be coming back to her – he would be retired from his duties once he recovered, and would be found a home with a foster family who could care for him and his needs – but she still longed to see him one last time, and hear of his progress. But the most vivid thought was of the person who was set on destroying her. Maybe whoever was harassing her had finally decided to end it. It wouldn't be the first time she had been confronted at her own front door.

Beneath the fear, she decided that she couldn't be so passive any more. If someone wanted to destroy her, she would fight. Fight until the end.

She unlocked the door, then slipped the key from the lock and placed it between her fingers, her hand clenched around it, the metal poking out like a spike. If it was someone who wanted to harm her, all she had to do was give one good punch to the stranger's eye or throat. If the person spoke, she would aim for the direction of their voice. If she opened the door to silence, she would wait.

The door swung back with a creak. The cold night nipped at her bare legs.

'Hello?'

Someone sniffed back tears. Naomi clenched her fist around the key.

'Why didn't you tell me?'

She breathed out and placed the keys on the sideboard with a shaking hand. She wasn't sure if the relief she felt was because it was Dane, or because she didn't have to hurt anyone. It took a certain person to commit bodily harm, and even when the time came, she wasn't sure she was capable of it.

Dane spoke in a whisper. 'Two police officers came to the flat and told me. It would have been easier coming from you.' He was slurring. Naomi could smell whisky on his breath.

'Your girlfriend was going to leave me out there in the woods, Dane.'

'She nearly died.'

'We both could have. But we wouldn't have been there if it weren't for her.'

He sighed and leaned against the door frame. The smell of whisky was so strong that it made her eyes water.

'Can I come in?'

'No.'

George's front door opened.

'Is everything all right?'

'This has nothing to do with you,' Dane spat.

'Is he bothering you, Naomi?'

'Oh fuck off,' Dane said.

'I'm okay, George.'

'I won't leave until he does.'

'I'll make you leave,' Dane said.

'Dane, stop. It's late, and you've woken us all up.'

'I don't give a damn that it's late!' His words echoed down the street.

'*Shut up!*' a neighbour shouted.

'You need to leave,' George said.

'I'm not going anywhere until Naomi talks to me.'

'She won't—'

'Come inside,' Naomi said.

George fell silent.

'Damn it, Dane, I said come inside. You're waking up the whole street.'

Dane stumbled into the house. The soles of his shoes squeaked against the floor. He slumped down on the sofa.

She used to hear him in the house even when he wasn't there. She would hear the springs in the sofa where he used to sit; she heard him singing in the bath, the tune bouncing off the tiled walls. Once, when she woke in the middle of the night, she heard him on the other side of the bathroom door. She had stumbled sleepily across the room and opened the door, cutting the sound dead. It had all been in her head.

'I'm okay, George,' she said into the night.

'If you need me, I'll be in my living room. Shout for me and I'll hear you.'

Naomi shut the door and sighed.

'Your girlfriend almost got me killed, Dane. What makes you think I want you here?'

'I'm sorry.' He was crying. 'I didn't know she would ... that she could ... Hell, I hardly knew her at all. I barely listened to her. We just ... existed beside each other. I never let her in. I've never stopped loving you. You love me too, I know it.'

Her legs were shaking. She longed to sit, but she couldn't relax with him there. If she wanted to survive, she had to keep herself together.

'I don't need to have children, all right? I just want you.'

She had longed to hear those words for years. Her chest tightened.

'It's too late for that.'

He got up from the sofa and came to her. She breathed in the smell of whisky.

It wasn't enough that he had broken her heart and pushed her to the brink, or that his girlfriend had put her life in danger; he had to keep pulling her in.

Dane was the only man Naomi had ever loved. Ever since waking at the bus stop, she had felt afraid of the world and found it impossible to trust anyone in it. But Dane had taught her to love with all her heart, and she had given in despite every instinct inside her begging her to flee. She had given him everything, and now she had to take some of herself back. Her love for him could get her killed. If she didn't pull away, she would continue to put herself in harm's way.

She stepped closer, and as Dane reached to touch her face, her finger prodded at his chest and pushed him away.

'I told you to leave me alone, to stop coming to my house, but you wouldn't listen. You *never* listen. For once, Dane, this isn't about you. I'm not safe with you in my life.'

She turned for the door. Dane grabbed her shoulders and brought her back.

'What the hell does that mean?'

'It means that I can't keep myself together when you're

around. When I think of you, I forget everything else. I forget to keep my guard up, and right now, I need that guard to survive.'

'I can help you. I can protect you.'

'I don't need you to protect me.'

'Well, you're not doing a great job on your own, are you? Look at you, for Christ's sake.'

The pills had worn off and the pain in her fingers was rising by the minute, blinking its eyes and stretching its limbs. She wrapped a hand around her fingers and felt them throb in her palm.

'I need you. I'm sorry, I'm sorry for everything. We can go back to how it was, I promise.'

'Too much has happened, Dane. I need to be alone.'

'So you can screw your neighbour?'

Naomi pulled away from his grasp and stepped towards the front door.

'Leave, and don't come back. If you do, I'll call the police.'

Dane followed her to the door and stopped in front of her.

'What happened to you? Where has the woman I love gone?'

'You. You happened to me.'

Naomi could smell his cologne, the scent she had to have on her pillow to fall asleep at night. She backed up against the wall.

'You might hate me, but I could never hate you. I won't give up on us, Naomi. I can't. These two years have been the worst years of my life. I need you, and I know you need me too.'

She listened to his voice, the voice she had loved for fifteen years, and wondered how many times he had lied to her. He had dated Hayley Miller before she disappeared. He had been sleeping with Hayley's sister. Naomi asked herself if she had ever known him at all. Yet even with all her doubts and fears, was there anything he could do that would make her stop loving him? She had to be strong, and she had to know the truth.

'What happened to Hayley Miller, Dane? You've kept the secret from me long enough. I deserve to know.'

For the first time, Dane fell silent.

'What do you know?' he said eventually. His voice had changed. She could hear his paranoia, as though it dripped from every word. In all the years she had known and loved him, she had never heard him sound like that.

'Tell me the truth.'

Dane came towards her. She felt the heat of him against her body.

'I didn't kill her.'

'I never said you did. I asked for the truth. Something had to have happened for you to lie to me for all these years.'

'I never lied to you, Naomi.'

'You kept secrets. The two are synonymous. They both involve deceit.'

She could almost hear his thoughts ticking over as he gambled with what and what not to tell her. Finally he gave a rattling sigh.

'Hayley was pregnant.'

Naomi closed her eyes. She thought she had been ready to hear what he had to say, but not that. Anything but that.

'She didn't know for certain whose it was, but she thought it was mine. She was terrified what her family would think and made me promise not to tell them until she was ready. I would have looked after them, her and the baby. I would have done it.

We were going to talk it through, but she never showed. That was the night she died, and I've kept her secret ever since.'

Naomi blinked away tears. Dane had been obsessed with having children, and finally she knew why. He had been denied a child when Hayley disappeared, and he had longed to try again ever since. He didn't want *her* child; he wanted the child he had lost.

'I can't be blamed for what happened to her, Naomi. I can't. Please believe me. You know me.'

'I don't know you, Dane. You have a whole other life I don't know about.'

She flinched as she felt the heat of his hand creeping towards her face.

'Get out.'

'Naomi, please ...'

'Get out!'

He stumbled towards the door and yanked it open violently. The door slammed shut behind him.

Naomi locked it and rested her back against it, breathing heavily.

She couldn't trust him any more. She couldn't trust anyone connected to Hayley Miller.

THIRTY-TWO

Marcus sat down on the sofa and smiled politely as he looked around the room.

The net curtains at the window were yellow with nicotine. Dead flies lay on their backs on the windowsill. The furniture and decor dated back to the eighties. Judging by the dust coating the mantelpiece, the room hadn't been cleaned since then either. The surface of the coffee table was tacky from old spills. Marcus prised his mug from the sticky surface and splashed coffee on the table.

'Leave it,' Anita Callaghan said. 'No bother.'

Marcus gave her another polite smile and stifled a yawn. He had been up all night working on the questions he planned to ask her, but as he sat before her in the smoke-hazed room, he wished he hadn't bothered. He could see by the state of her that she wouldn't have any new information to share. She had given up hope. It was a dead end.

Anita Callaghan sat on the other side of the coffee table in a bathrobe. Remnants of mascara rested beneath her eyes, and her hair was ruffled from sleep. Wrinkles creased the corners of her eyes and etched her cheeks, with deep smile lines around her mouth. She had been happy once.

She lit a cigarette and took a long drag, giving him a glimpse of stained teeth. When Marcus couldn't hold his breath any longer, he inhaled the smoke.

'Thank you for talking to me.'

'I've got to get to the hospital for ten,' she said. 'See my girl.'

'I understand. I won't take up much of your time.'

'I ain't had much luck, have I? One daughter missing, another attacked. Boys in and out of the nick. Two failed marriages. I'm starting to think I'm cursed or something.'

She tapped ash into an overflowing ashtray sprouting cigarette butts stained with red lipstick.

'I don't know what she did to deserve that, Officer. She's usually a good girl.'

Her cavalier tone was startling. Someone had tried to kill her daughter and she acted as though Josie had been caught up in some minor felony.

'Karma comes to people in different ways, I guess. You mind?' She took a hip flask from a pocket in her bathrobe and held it up.

Marcus shook his head.

With the cigarette dangling between her lips, she poured dark alcohol from the flask into her black coffee.

'Karma, Mrs Callaghan?'

'Anita. Call me Anita.'

'Karma, Anita?'

'Well, she was always in and out of trouble as a kid. Not serious or nothin', but we all get our comeuppance in the end.'

It was difficult to remember that the woman was talking

about her own daughter. It was clear that she had adored Hayley. Every frame in the room held a photo of her. Marcus had yet to spot a picture of Josie or her brothers. He had heard of parents resenting their living children after another had died, but he hadn't witnessed it until now. The room suddenly turned cold.

Anita gulped at her coffee and savoured the taste, but he suspected it wasn't the caffeine she was enjoying.

'This is to do with what happened to Josie the other night, ain't it?'

She took one last drag on the cigarette and screwed it into the ashtray. Her eyes never left him. Smoke curled towards the ceiling.

'Ain't it?'

Marcus noticed the hope in her eyes. It was clear that she wanted to discuss her elder daughter. Parents really did have favourites.

'As a formality,' he stated, 'I'm looking over Hayley's missing persons case.'

'Oh, thank God,' she said. She grinned at the ceiling before returning her eyes to him. She covered her smile with a trembling hand.

She looked like a completely different woman. When she spoke of Josie, her face had remained cold and hard, but the mere mention of Hayley had her beaming. A sparkle had returned to her eyes.

'Mrs Callaghan, I want to clarify that this is just a formality. It may not come to anything.'

The smile dropped from her face.

'But you'll try, won't ya?'

'Do you mind if I ask you some questions?' he asked, desperately trying to deflect her intensity.

'Will you? Will you try?'

He looked her in the eye but longed to break away. She homed in on him, unblinking. The pain in her gaze was hypnotic.

'I'll try.'

'Oh thank you ... thank you.' She chuckled to herself behind closed lips. 'I knew one of ya would do something in the end. That Elliott bitch wouldn't even let me talk.' She put another cigarette in her mouth and froze as she lifted the lighter to the tip. 'Sorry if she's your mate,' she mumbled.

She isn't.

'I know it's been a long time since Hayley went missing, so I understand if things are a little hazy, but I want to ask you some questions. You might remember something now that you didn't back then. Investigations can be hectic: lots of information to process in a short amount of time. Something that might have seemed insignificant at the time could be really important now.'

'Ask whatever you want.' She swigged from the flask, seemingly forgetting her spiked coffee cooling on the table.

'Is there anyone you suspected in Hayley's disappearance that we might have overlooked?'

'I always thought her teacher was a perv, that Mr –' she clicked her fingers – 'Jefferies, I think. Yeah, Mr Jefferies.'

'What makes you think that? Did Hayley say something about him?'

'Didn't need to,' she said. Smoke billowed from her nostrils. 'I got eyes in my head, ain't I? I saw the way he looked at her.

When I went to the parent-teacher meeting, he smiled at her in a way that made me wonder. But Hayley always got that; she was a beauty. Can't help that, I guess.'

Marcus remembered the teacher's name from the file. He'd been questioned, but had an airtight alibi.

'Anyone else? Anyone you think the police overlooked?'

'Well they never nicked that cop's son, did they? Didn't even question him once his old man got involved. I've never felt right about that, even if I did know the kid's dad from way back.'

'Were there any particular boys in Hayley's life that you suspected?'

Anita froze and eyed him coolly from the other side of the coffee table. Smoke curled up from her cigarette.

'You heard the rumours, I take it, about my girl being easy. Well she weren't.'

'I wasn't insinuating anything, Anita. As a detective, I don't condemn people because of rumours.'

'Good, because people in this town talk a load of shite. Hayley was a good girl.'

She ground the cigarette into the ashtray and eyed the packet on the coffee table. Disappointment flashed in her eyes when she saw it was empty. Given the number of cigarettes she had smoked during their brief meeting, Marcus wouldn't have been surprised if she had only opened the packet that morning.

'So there weren't any particular male friends of Hayley's that you had suspicions about?'

'I never understood the pigs going after ...' She blushed. 'Sorry. Don't mean nothin' by it.'

'It's fine.'

'I never understood why the coppers went after Dane. He was a sweet lad, treated Hayley right.'

Marcus realised he was wasting his time. She didn't know anything. He gave a quick glance at his watch.

'There was a kid that hung around for a while, but he was a skinny, shy little fella.'

'Do you remember his name?'

'Hang on.'

She got up and left the room, returning with a scrapbook. She sat back down with a sigh and flicked through the pages, each covered with newspaper articles. Suddenly she stopped, squinting at a black-and-white photo above a news story, then passed the scrapbook across to Marcus.

The image was grainy. It was a close-up of Hayley in a class photo, with a fresh-faced boy by her side. The caption gave Hayley's name, as well as the boy's: Craig Kennedy.

'Only person I can think of that weren't looked into. They were in the same class, I think. You know him?'

Craig. Naomi's sister Grace was married to a man called Craig Kennedy.

Yes, Marcus thought. *I do.*

THIRTY-THREE

Naomi woke with a groan as the pain hit her. Her wounds burned as they scabbed over and began to stitch her back together. She got up and hobbled to the bathroom.

It had been weeks since she'd found Amber's body and she was still without answers. Amber would be starting to rot by now, her veins drying up and snapping like vines. Naomi wondered how long it would take for it to decompose until it was nothing but bones, and if she would have answers by then.

She sat down on the toilet seat and buried her face in her hands.

Her mind drifted to Josie, the woman who had almost got her killed in the woods, lying in a hospital bed, her throat stitched from ear to ear.

Josie, Hayley Miller's flesh and blood, had been the one who had stood silently outside her door, who had likely thrown the brick through the window, who had followed her down to the beach, who had dragged her into the woods. And yet her stomach wouldn't stop churning. The person who had been in the alley and on the beach, the same person who had slashed Josie's throat and chased Naomi through the woods, was still out there.

She flushed the toilet and rubbed her arms until the shivers stopped.

She left the en suite and passed through her bedroom to the top of the stairs, listening to the house and the silence. She had shared so many happy memories there with Dane, with Max, and now it was just her and the bricks and mortar, the past bleeding from the walls.

The windows clicked in their frames as the wind blew against them and curled around the house. The stairs creaked beneath her in lethargic whines. She reached the last step and kicked something hard.

Something was blocking her way.

She held her toes with one hand and felt the obstruction with the other.

The sofa.

She ran her hands across the back of it and clambered over, landing on the seat cushions. Her kneecaps slammed against the front door.

'What the hell?'

She crawled along the sofa and climbed over the arm, feeling for the rest of the room.

Bang.

Her knees smacked into something hard and low. It toppled to the ground with a loud crash. Objects flew off the top and scattered across the floor.

Someone had been inside her house while she slept and changed the layout. While she had been dreaming of the killer, he had been here below her.

Walk to the kitchen, reach the sink beneath the window and get your bearings.

She followed the map inside her head, feeling for where things should have been, waiting to pass the edge of the rug in the living room, the coat rack, the cupboard under the stairs.

The pain was instant, like teeth plunging into her skin. Her whole body rattled as she hit the ground. She ran her fingertips along the bottom of her feet and felt shards of glass poking out.

Her hands searched wildly to find where she was in the room, and felt the fire poker clink against its holder. She took it in her hand and sat up, swiped it through the air until it knocked something over with a crash.

'WHAT DO YOU WANT?'

Her words filled the house and echoed in the empty rooms. She sat there with the poker shaking in her hands. Blood oozed from her feet and dripped between the floorboards.

Someone wanted her to be lost in her own home, the only place she felt safe. Someone wanted her to know that she had nowhere to hide.

The doorbell rang. Naomi sat on the floor as the sound ricocheted off the walls, thinking of where the door would be. She rose to her knees and felt around, shards of glass moving beneath her palms.

Knuckles rapped against the other side of the door.

Up to her feet and pressing down into the glass, she hobbled forward, tapping the poker on the floor like her cane and moving obstructions from her path with her free hand.

When she reached the foot of the stairs, she dropped the

poker with a clang and pushed the sofa out of the way. She pressed her palms against the wall and felt her way towards the door, unknowingly smearing blood against the paint. Her hot, anxious breaths bounced back at her. Voices whispered on the other side of the door.

The key was cold, a lingering reminder of the night. She turned it in the lock and opened the door, squinting as the wind blew into her eyes and chilled the skin on her cheeks.

'Hello?'

Her voice sounded quiet compared to the sounds of the day outside: a car whooshing down the road, a plane rumbling in the sky, leaves rustling on the trees lining the street.

'Naomi Hannah, this is Detective Inspector Lisa Elliott and Detective Sergeant Blake Crouch, with two uniformed colleagues.'

'I'm so glad you're here—'

'You are under arrest on suspicion of assisting in the attempted murder of Josie Callaghan. You do not have to say anything, but it may harm your defence if you do not mention when questioned something which you later rely on in court. Anything you do say may be given in evidence.'

Hands landed on Naomi's shoulders and turned her roughly, twisting the glass in her feet like screws. Everything was happening so fast: her thoughts, her heart, the handcuffs biting at the skin on her wrists, chinking against the bones. Someone reached past her and began putting shoes on her feet as she waited with bloody hands behind her back.

I should have jumped, she thought. I should have freed myself when I had the chance.

PART II

THIRTY-FOUR

Something was happening around Marcus. He could feel it buzzing in the air. The office was empty when he arrived after meeting Anita Callaghan before his shift, and an hour later, Dane was brought into the station in handcuffs. A lawyer followed soon afterwards, and they were shut away in one of the interview rooms.

He called Lisa, who disconnected the call after three rings.

He drummed his fingers on his desk and listened to the tick of the clock. He watched the second hand travel around the face. Lisa would be back soon.

He looked up to the sound of voices along the corridor. A uniformed officer was showing a smartly dressed man into an interview room. Something was definitely going on.

'Hey!' Marcus got to his feet and bounded through the door, catching up with the officer. It was the female officer who had questioned him in the first case briefing. He still didn't know her name. 'Who's he? What's he doing here?'

'He's a solicitor for one of your cases. You should know, right?'

'Well, I don't.'

Marcus reached for the door handle to the interview room.

'If Lisa hasn't told you what's going on, I'd wait.'

Marcus barged past her and marched into the room.

'I'm Detective Sergeant Marcus Campbell.'

The solicitor looked him up and down with beady eyes. The man was short and plump, with a horseshoe of hair thinning around his head and a thick neck dangling beneath his jaw.

'Jeremy Winer,' he said nasally.

'Who are you here to represent?'

Winer pulled a file out of his briefcase, rested his reading glasses on the end of his nose, then pushed them to the bridge with a chubby finger. He had to squint to read the name on the top of the page.

'Ms Naomi Hannah.'

Beads of sweat broke out on Marcus's forehead.

'And why does she need a lawyer?'

The solicitor sighed and peered at the file again.

'She is suspected of assisting in the attempted murder of a Ms Josie Callaghan.'

'That's bullshit!' Marcus exploded.

The solicitor jolted in his seat and his reading glasses slipped towards the tip of his nose. He pushed them back up again.

'I'm here to defend her, DS Campbell.'

'I know, I know. I'm sorry,' Marcus said.

He backed out of the room and marched towards the office. He paced from wall to wall.

'She can't ... she can't do this ...' he muttered under his breath.

Voices echoed up the corridor. Marcus stopped and listened to the pounding footsteps. He marched to the door and got there just in time to see two uniformed officers escorting Naomi towards the interview room.

She looked a shell of who she used to be. Her face was thin. She wore pyjamas and a well-worn dressing gown, with shoes on her bare feet. She was ushered into the interview room. The door clicked shut behind her.

Lisa walked towards the office with her head down. When she looked up, their eyes met.

'What's going on?'

'Move aside.'

Marcus stepped out of the doorway and watched her head for her office. He followed her.

'What the hell are you doing?' he asked.

'My job, Campbell. You should try it.' She swung her bag on top of her desk, then turned to him with a smirk on her face.

'That's it? That's all you have to say?' His whole body was trembling.

'Outside,' she said, as she zipped up her coat and grabbed a pack of cigarettes from her pocket.

She had lit up before they had even reached the fire exit to the alley. It was like she was marking the office as hers, like a dog cocking its leg and pissing up the wall.

They walked through the rain and stooped under the bike shed. Smoke billowed out of Lisa's mouth and disintegrated in the rain.

'Get it out of your system,' she said.

'What?'

'Say what you have to say. You're clearly struggling to keep it in.'

'Okay. You're wrong. Naomi isn't a killer, or an accomplice. She's an innocent woman and you're only making her life worse.'

'Dane is the killer, Marcus.'

He stared at her, words forming and dying in the back of his throat.

'It was his watch at the scene of Josie's murder, and witnesses have attested that he had sexual encounters with both Cassie and Amber after the breakdown of his marriage, which phone records confirm.'

'Why didn't I know about this?'

'Because you've become a liability. You see what you want to see. You want Naomi to be innocent, so you won't let anything get in the way of that, even when the truth is staring you right in the face. She is in a sexual relationship with her ex-husband, and she survived the night in the woods when Josie barely made it out alive. She was supposed to be there. She led Josie into the woods, not the other way around. She stood by while her ex-husband attempted to kill his lover. She facilitated the whole thing.'

'You can't know that for sure.'

'Well, it seems to me that she is manipulating him into getting Josie out of the way so they can be together again. Josie wasn't going to let him go without a fight, so they gave her one.'

'That's an accusation, not a fact.'

'Female killers work differently, Marcus. They manipulate people into acting for them. Look at Lizzie Borden and the family maid, Myra Hindley and Ian Brady, Rosemary West and her husband Fred. They had accomplices besotted with them, ready to follow any orders sent their way. It's time you looked at Naomi for who she really is.'

'You didn't have to handcuff her; she wasn't a threat.'

Marcus was shaking, but it wasn't from the cold. He hated Lisa. He hated everything about her: the smug slant of her lips, every freckle on her nose. She couldn't see that her description of him as a detective unable to see past his own opinions and desire to make them fit would perfectly describe her too. She couldn't find out the truth so she ran with a lie, anything to settle the case and move on, even if it meant tormenting a disabled woman. She didn't want justice – all she wanted was prestige and pats on the back, and she didn't care how she got them.

'She needs to understand how serious this is,' Lisa said. 'She needs to be scared into telling us the truth.'

'Don't you think she's scared enough already, with everything that's happened?'

'You need to stop seeing her as the helpless damsel, Marcus. She's just as much of a killer as her ex-husband is.'

'What about Amber and Cassie? You think Naomi is responsible for their murders too?'

'She's capable of it.'

'What motive would she have?'

'Her ex-husband had sexual relations with both of them.'

'So that gives her a reason to kill them?'

'We'll find out.'

'You're pinning murders on a woman who is a victim herself!'

'Lower your voice, Campbell,' she said sternly.

He clenched his teeth and looked away. Lisa sighed.

'One of my first cases when I was with the Met was the murder of a couple who'd been locked inside a house that was then burned to the ground. The perpetrator was never found. They were survived by their fourteen-year-old daughter, Rebecca. The girl was obviously distraught at losing both parents. Four years later, after Rebecca had won a scholarship to university, she killed her boyfriend in the halls of residence by stabbing him twenty-two times and setting him on fire while he was still alive. Why? Jealousy.'

She took a long drag on the cigarette.

'We overlooked Rebecca because we didn't look past the facade. She played up to the image of a young girl incapable of anything more than tantrums and acne, and we let her kill again. I won't let Naomi pass me by without being sure she isn't involved.'

'But you have no evidence to convict—'

'Yet. We got a warrant to enter her home. Blake is orchestrating the search as we speak.'

'But you can't arrest her without evidence.'

'One day you'll understand that this job can't always run on what the rulebook allows us to do.'

The words *I quit* squirmed at the back of his throat, but Naomi needed him. If he wanted her to get the justice she deserved, he had to stay.

'Are you going to help me bring this killer to justice? Amber deserves it. Cassie deserves it. Josie deserves it.' Lisa looked at him intently, and Marcus realised that she truly believed she was right. If he wanted to protect Naomi, he would have to play along.

'I'll try,' he lied.

'I need more than that, Marcus.'

'I will.'

I will unearth the truth.

'Good.'

She dropped the cigarette butt into a puddle and started back towards the door, coughing into her hand. Marcus marched behind her through the rain, his hands clenched into fists inside his pockets.

'Dane is in Interview Room Two,' she said, turning back to him as he shut the door. 'I need you on my side in there.' She eyed him for a beat, searched his eyes for submission, before heading towards the interview room.

Dane was waiting.

THIRTY-FIVE

Dane was a handsome man beneath the fear, but Marcus struggled to see him with Naomi. His muddy blonde hair was thinning and the hairline was slowly creeping from his forehead, making his face out of proportion. He stank of stale whisky, exuding from his skin in nervous sweat. His right leg was jittering, a jumpy response to distract himself. Marcus had seen it all before. He had to fight the urge to wince at the thought of Dane on top of Naomi, grunting, sweating, thrusting into one of the most beautiful women he had ever seen. Dane must have felt like the luckiest man alive when he was with her, before the divorce, before the murders.

'Dane,' Lisa said. 'I'm not here to bully you. I'm here to find out the truth about what happened to Josie. If you're innocent, you have nothing to worry about. The truth should clear all this up.'

Dane glanced at his solicitor, a tight-faced woman with permanently puckered lips, and frown lines that never left her face. 'I am innocent,' he said.

'Of what, exactly? Because I believe you're responsible for more than just the attack on Josie Callaghan.'

Dane's Adam's apple bobbed up and down as he swallowed. Marcus imagined it sliced by the killer's knife, and saw the man's blood spray across the table. He closed his eyes for a beat to wash his mind of the sight of death. He'd never look at necks the same way again.

'What do you mean?'

'The other women. Murdered in cold blood.'

'Do you have evidence for this?' his solicitor asked.

'We have evidence that Dane was at the scene of Josie's attack, which was played out in the exact same way as two murders in the last two weeks. And ...' Lisa drew it out, playing with them, 'we have been made aware of Mr Hannah's previous sexual relations with each of the women.'

His solicitor shot him a quick look. Dane didn't meet her eye. 'I wasn't aware of that.'

'Let's see what else your client is hiding.'

'My client has denied the attempted murder of Miss Callaghan, Inspector Elliott.'

'And I don't believe him.'

The solicitor sat back in her chair with a quiet sigh, settling in for a long afternoon.

'Did you ever hit Josie, Dane?'

'Of course not.'

'Verbal abuse, perhaps?'

'We had arguments like any other couple.'

'Did she ever hit you?' Marcus asked. Lisa shot him a look.

'She slapped me a couple of times.'

'Why?'

'She thinks my ex-wife and I have an inappropriate relationship.'

'Which you do, right?' Lisa said.

He fell quiet, picking at the skin around his thumbnail. 'No.'

'When was the last time you and Naomi slept together?'

'Is this relevant?' the solicitor asked.

'Very. Please answer the question, Mr Hannah. Remember, lying will only make things worse.'

Dane looked at the solicitor. She nodded. He sighed and looked down at his hands, quivering against the tabletop.

'Not long ago.'

'How long?'

'About two weeks ago.'

'So you were unfaithful to Josie.'

'Yes.'

'Is that why she attacked Naomi?'

'I don't know. I didn't tell her about it.'

'You wanted to stop Josie from hurting Naomi, didn't you?'

'Had I been there, I would have stopped it.'

'But you did, Dane. You saved Naomi's life.'

'I told you, I wasn't there.'

'Then why did we find your watch at the scene?'

'If it really is my watch, someone's framing me.'

'You believe someone is framing you for the attempted murder of your girlfriend for harassing your ex-wife, your current lover? Why would someone do that? Who else would have a plausible reason to intervene the way you did?'

'I know how it sounds.' He looked from Lisa to Marcus. 'But I promise you, I wasn't there. Someone is setting me up.'

'I'll need a better answer than that.'

'I don't have one.' His voice grew louder, defensive. 'All I know is, I wasn't there. I was at home.'

'Alone?'

'Yes.'

'So no one can verify your whereabouts the night Josie left your flat, entered the woods with your ex-wife, and almost died?'

He looked at his solicitor again, who nodded at him to continue.

'No. No one can.'

'So for all we know, you could be lying.'

'I'm not lying!'

'But you lied to Josie, didn't you? You were having a relationship with your ex-wife behind her back. I'd say that makes you a pretty good liar.'

'You're twisting everything ...' His words caught in his throat.

'No, Mr Hannah, I'm trying to get the truth out of you.'

'I didn't hurt Josie!' he yelled, and slammed his fist on the table. The solicitor's coffee jolted in the Styrofoam cup and spilled onto the table.

Lisa didn't even blink. 'Are you prone to outbursts of anger, Mr Hannah?'

'I'm sorry, I ...' He looked at Marcus. 'I didn't do this. I'd never hurt anyone.'

'Well right now, all we have is you, a man in a relationship with both victims of this crime, and your watch, which was found at the scene splattered with Josie's blood. Not to mention

234

your sexual history with the two murdered women.'

'I slept with over a dozen women after my divorce.'

Marcus wondered what women saw in the man. Whatever charm he had, he had left it outside the interview room.

Dane snatched his hands from his lap and wiped his eyes with his sleeve.

'I didn't kill anyone. I don't even know what watch you're talking about.'

Lisa pushed a photo across the table.

'That is yours, isn't it, Dane?'

'I haven't seen that watch in years.' His solicitor coughed into her hand. 'It might not even be mine. I've had one like it since I was a teen. We all had those kind of watches.'

Lisa sighed and looked down at her file.

'Can you confirm this is a photo of you wearing said watch?'

'Or a replica,' his solicitor added.

Dane took the photo. It shivered in his grip. His pupils danced up and down the photo. He closed his eyes and nodded. Tears shimmered on his cheeks.

'Odd that you don't know where your watch is, isn't it, Dane?' Lisa said.

He looked at her. Fresh tears brewed in his eyes.

'You'd do anything for Naomi, wouldn't you?'

'Yes,' he said, and winced. He was beginning to understand Lisa's tactics. 'Within reason.'

'Is it reasonable to kill her competition at her request?'

Dane bowed his head. 'Of course not.'

'Because I don't believe Josie led Naomi into the woods. I believe it was the other way round.'

'What?' Dane shot her a look.

'I believe Naomi asked you to wait for her in the woods, so that when she led Josie to you, you'd be there ready to get rid of her.'

'That's not true! Naomi would never hurt anyone.'

'Then why can't we find the cricket bat that Naomi claimed Josie threatened her with?'

Dane let the tears fall, too shocked to wipe them away.

'Do you need a break?' his solicitor asked.

'Answer the question, Mr Hannah. Why doesn't your story match up?'

'I didn't do this!' He covered his face with his hands and muttered into his palms. 'I didn't ... I didn't ...' He sobbed, a sound so deep and torn that Marcus's throat began to burn. Whenever he heard a man cry, he thought of his father, who had wept as he begged for forgiveness after a bottle of Scotch, his fists swollen from pummelling his son's ribs. He pinched his thigh to bring him out of the memory and back into the room.

'You didn't have anything to do with Hayley Miller's disappearance either, did you, Dane?' Lisa said. 'You're just an innocent man who keeps being linked to crimes you didn't commit.' She leaned over the table, her words close to the top of Dane's head. 'Look at me.'

He looked up with bloodshot eyes.

'You need to start telling the truth, Dane, or it'll eat you alive.'

His lips twitched. A tear slipped down his cheek and onto the table. His solicitor cleared her throat.

'My client and I need to talk alone.'

THIRTY-SIX

The solicitor smelt stale, as though his suit had been pulled out from the back of a wardrobe and patted down to beat off the dust. His breath had a sour tang to it when he spoke, even behind the sugary scent of the cough sweet that rolled around his mouth and clinked against his teeth.

'I didn't attack Josie,' Naomi told him. 'She tried to kill me.'

She sat in the chair with her hands clamped beneath her thighs to stop them from shaking. Her wrists still ached from where the handcuffs had gnawed at her skin and pulled at the hairs.

'I believe you, but I'm not the person you need to convince. You must make the police believe you.'

'I'll tell them the truth.'

'Let's hope that works.'

'Why wouldn't it?'

'The police can believe what they want to believe, just like a jury but with more rules to skirt around. Whatever you're feeling, exaggerate it. Tears, pleas for justice, fear until you shake.' He paused, as if looking at her quivering body and realising she was already there. 'You need to rid them of any doubts they might have.'

'But how can they have arrested me? Doesn't that mean they have evidence?'

'The circumstances might be all they need at this stage.'

A knock on the door. Naomi's head shot towards the sound.

'It's all right, Ms Hannah. You'll be all right.'

She felt his meaty hand pat her thigh. She quivered and moved her leg away from him.

'Come in,' the solicitor said.

Shoes scuffed against the floor. The door clicked shut. Two more mouths were breathing in the room.

'Naomi,' DI Lisa Elliott said. 'I'm here with DS Marcus Campbell. We need to ask you some questions.'

Chair legs dragged against the floor.

How much of her could they see? Could they see that she was shaking? Could they see that her heart was pounding against her ribs?

'Hi, Naomi,' Marcus said.

Naomi nodded her head. She couldn't trust herself to speak. Fear rattled through her body, but beneath it was a growing rage.

The tape recorder turned on with a click, and Lisa introduced everyone in the room.

'Naomi, I'm going to cut to the chase,' she said. 'Your ex-husband's watch was found in the woods, splattered with Josie's blood.'

'Dane?'

'And how does that link my client to the crime?' the solicitor said.

'Given their relationship—'

'You mean their past relationship?'

'You've been sleeping together, haven't you, Naomi?' Lisa's question was light, as if she needed a friend to refresh her memory, but it brought everyone's attention to Naomi like flies landing on her skin.

'No.'

'Are you sure?'

'My client said no.'

'And I'm asking her again. Naomi, have you slept with Dane recently?'

The silence ate away at her. Her skin itched as everyone in the room waited for an answer. Her solicitor had told her that Dane was just across the corridor, locked in another room. She had no idea what he had told them.

'Once.'

'When?'

'After I found the body.'

'For the tape, Ms Hannah is referring to the discovery of the body of Amber O'Neill.' Marcus's tone was grave.

Do you believe me, Marcus?

'So after you found the body,' Lisa said, 'you came home and slept with your ex-husband. Forgive me, Ms Hannah, but that sounds rather morbid, doesn't it?'

'I was distraught. I needed someone to—'

'You don't need to go any further,' her solicitor said, and patted her thigh again. She had to stop herself from digging her fingernails into the back of his hand.

'So you slept with Josie's partner.'

'My ex-husband, yes.'

'Who is the love of Josie's life.'

'I don't think judgements of that nature are necessary, Inspector Elliott.'

'I'm simply getting a picture of what happened, Mr ... Winer, is it?' Lisa sighed, dismissing him. 'So, Josie just turned up at your doorstep?'

'Yes. She knocked on my door and pressed a cricket bat against my temple.'

'We didn't find a cricket bat at the crime scene.'

'Well ... the killer must have taken it. All you have to do is look at the bruises and scratches all over my body.'

'There are many ways someone can get injuries like those. Self-inflicted, even.'

'Now's not the time to speculate,' the solicitor said.

'Again, Mr Winer, I'm painting a picture.'

'Well hurry. Because the paint is drying.'

A silence fell between them before Lisa spoke again.

'Did you hate Josie for taking Dane away from you?'

'She didn't take him away. They began their relationship after the breakdown of our marriage.'

'You're awfully close for a divorced couple. Didn't your ex-husband drop you off at work the day the brick came through the window?'

'That happened once.'

'A lot of things seemed to happen just the once.'

'I'm telling the truth.'

'So you didn't hate Josie before the supposed attack?'

'I didn't know her. I hadn't met her until the night in the woods.'

'But you knew it was her, that night?'

'Yes. She told me who she was before she attacked me.'

'Why didn't the person who tried to kill Josie attack you?'

'He chased me through the woods until I hid.'

'Your husband is obviously very fond of you.'

The question and the statement so close to one another made her realise what was going on.

'You really think Dane and I did this together?'

'It's only a matter of time before Dane confesses.'

'You think I helped him try to kill Josie?'

'Did you?'

'No!'

'And what about Amber in the alley? You just happened to stumble across her body right after she was killed, and somehow lived to tell the tale?'

'Yes, that's exactly—'

'Because I don't believe that,' Lisa interjected. 'I don't believe that a ruthless killer wouldn't hurt you like he did the others. Two women are dead, and one is fighting for her life, and yet you're still here and you can't tell me why.'

The room fell silent. Naomi's heartbeat echoed against the back of the chair.

'Do you know what I think?' Lisa said. 'I think you and Dane were in on this together.'

'Inspector Elliott—' the solicitor said.

'I think you manipulated Dane into attempting to kill Josie Callaghan so you could have him back.'

'Inspector Elliott, this is really—'

'I think you pretend to be helpless to hide the fact that you're ruthless in getting your own way. You lured Josie into the woods that night so Dane could attack her. You stayed behind, injuring yourself and waiting until dawn so you could pretend that you too were a victim—'

'Shut up!' Naomi yelled, shooting up from her chair. 'You're making me out to be a monster, when all I've done is try to help you and tell you everything I know!' She stood gripping the table, shaking uncontrollably. 'I don't deserve to be punished for stumbling across your colleague's body. I don't deserve to be blamed for the attack on Josie when she was the one who led me into the woods in the first place. The only thing I've done wrong is believe that you would help me, that you were on my side. My whole life I've let people walk all over me, control every aspect of my life, but I'll be damned if I'll let you condemn me for crimes I haven't committed!'

'Naomi, sit down,' her solicitor whispered. She felt his hand on her wrist.

'Don't touch me!' she yelled, and snatched her hand away. 'You should be ashamed. You're nothing but a fraud. Once the truth is out, I will tell everyone I know that you're the real monster here.'

A knock on the door broke through the tension in the room.

'One moment, please,' Lisa said. Her chair dragged across the floor and her footsteps made their way to the door.

'For the purpose of the tape, DI Elliott has left the room momentarily.'

Naomi remained standing and noticed how much she was shaking. Lisa had been goading her so that she would snap, and she had given the detective exactly what she wanted. She sank into the chair and put her face in her hands.

The three of them sat in the room in silence, breathing in the hot recycled air. Naomi couldn't get enough of it into her lungs. She could taste the men in the air and fought the urge to spit them back out.

'There, there,' the solicitor said, and tapped her thigh.

Naomi grabbed his hand and squeezed until her nails broke the skin.

'Touch my leg again and I'll break your fingers.'

The solicitor yanked his hand away, breathing quickly through his teeth in a hiss.

Naomi went numb. The tape had recorded it all, ready to use against her. And Marcus – would he think she was capable of the crime now? How much would it take to lose his trust? She wanted to defend herself, but all she was doing was digging herself a deeper grave.

The door clicked open and someone stepped into the room. The chair didn't move; Lisa hadn't sat back down. The person was standing close to Naomi, looming over her.

'Ms Hannah, is there any reason why a kitchen knife would be missing from the knife block in your kitchen?' Lisa sounded victorious.

'No ... No, of course not.' A bead of sweat slid down Naomi's face. Her throat tightened.

'Because we've researched the brand of knives online. The knife that's missing, the knife that can be found nowhere else in your home, is the exact size of the weapon that was used to attack Josie Callaghan.'

The sounds in the room began to blur; Naomi's mind felt like it was spinning. Everything was wrong. So wrong.

'Can you explain that for us please, Ms Hannah?'

'I ...'

I'm innocent. I haven't done any of this. You've made a mistake.

'No comment,' she said suddenly, as no other words came to her.

Someone sighed at the table. She couldn't have said anything more incriminating.

'Hit a nerve, did we?' Lisa asked, through what sounded like a smile.

THIRTY-SEVEN

Naomi woke up to the cold. The sound of her breathing echoed against the wall.

The sheet was stuck to her skin with the adhesive of dried sweat. She peeled herself away and sat up, feeling for the nightstand. There was nothing there but a hard wall. The sheet beneath her wasn't cotton, but cold plastic. The wall wasn't plastered, but made up of breeze blocks.

She wasn't at home.

A shiver rushed through her. She prised herself off the bed and stood up. The floor was covered in a film of dirt and dust that stuck to her bare feet. The air smelt of stale sweat.

She pressed her hands against the wall and followed it around the room, feeling for a door, a window, anything that could tell her where she was. Anxious breaths bounced off the walls and warmed her face. Iron bars shielded the only window. She felt them in her palms, the cold paint that had flaked off in sharp peels.

She was in a prison cell.

Tears filled her eyes as she carried on around the room, feeling the cold walls, the sticky steel toilet without a lid, the locked door.

She backed away and stood in the centre of the room.

The clothes she was wearing weren't her own: a large sweatshirt hung from her shoulders and bulged around her middle; a T-shirt was tucked into the waistband of loose sweatpants, balancing on her hip bones.

And slowly she began to remember.

Your ex-husband's watch was found in the woods, splattered with Josie's blood.

It's only a matter of time before Dane confesses.

Is there any reason why a kitchen knife would be missing from the knife block in your kitchen?

She didn't know how a knife could have gone missing. She couldn't even recollect owning that knife. Each kitchen knife felt the same. Had she even noticed one was gone?

The only person she could think of who would want to frame her for the crime was Josie, but she could hardly have cut her own throat in the woods and chased her between the trees. Someone else was involved.

'I'm ... I'm innocent ...' Naomi approached the door with her hands in front of her, and only stopped when she felt the cold metal. '*I'm innocent! I'M INNOCENT!*' She screamed the words, thrashed her fists against the door until they throbbed. She had been accused of a crime she hadn't committed. With each blow she imagined the door was the inspector's face. She banged and yelled until her voice cracked, then slowly lowered her hands to her waist, holding herself tight as fear seeped in. No one believed her. To lock her away like this, they had to believe she was guilty. Everything she had done to prove her innocence had worked against her.

She stumbled blindly back to the bed and crawled up onto the mattress until she was tucked into the corner of the room in a foetal position.

'They won't get away with this,' she whispered to herself. 'They won't.'

She had very few memories of her birth mother, but one had stayed firmly in her mind. Her mother had told her never to trust the police. *It don't matter if you're right and they're wrong. You're black and they're white. That's all that matters to them. If something goes wrong, you deal with it yourself. Don't go crying to them, or they'll find a way to spin it on you.*

Even though she had been brought up by a black family, Rachel had taught her that the police were there to help them, even if she had her own doubts. But Naomi had always wondered about what her birth mother had said. Now at last she knew that her birth mother had been right.

But if she couldn't trust the police to protect her, then who?

Everyone she knew and loved had secrets, secrets that had helped put her in this cell. Dane's watch had been found in the woods, splattered with Josie's blood. Grace had had an argument with Hayley Miller that continued to push them apart. But they weren't the only ones with secrets. Naomi closed her eyes and thought of her own.

THIRTY-EIGHT

The chair felt cold against Naomi's back, bare behind the ties on the gown that wrapped around her like a limp hug. Her legs shook until the stirrups squeaked.

The chill of the room crept beneath the gown and touched her where only Dane had touched. To think that their love and need for one another's bodies had brought her to this. The guilt she felt wasn't because she was about to terminate a healthy foetus, but because she was going to destroy something that was a part of him.

Ever since the meeting in the doctor's office, she had been unable to get the sound of the baby's heartbeat out of her head.

She tried to steel her muscles to stop them from shaking so the doctor and nurses wouldn't see how nervous she was, but despite her efforts, the chair shook until it rattled on its hinges. The drugs they had fed through the drip were worthless. She could still feel her racing heart and the ache in her abdomen. It was like her body knew.

The doctor spoke softly with a nurse, their backs turned to her to shield their words, as equipment was set up around her. Something knocked into the side of the chair.

'Are you ready, Naomi?' the doctor asked.

Naomi nodded and clenched her jaw. Even a flicker of softness would bring her resolve crumbling down.

'It says on your record that the father isn't aware of the pregnancy.'

Naomi nodded quickly and bit back the tears. She thought of Dane at home, oblivious to the fact that she was pregnant with the child he craved, and sitting in a chair with her legs open, ready for the doctor to rip it out of her.

'There are often side effects after the procedure, and this is something your husband will be witness to: bleeding, cramps, and in rare cases, diarrhoea and nausea.'

'My periods are heavy anyway; it won't seem odd.'

'And I'm sure you've been told this, but remember that you will be overly fertile after the procedure, so take the necessary precautions should sexual intercourse occur within the first few weeks.'

I did, she thought. I was so careful.

The tears fell from her eyes at the thought of Dane touching her again, the man who had put this thing inside her. They dripped down to her jaw and landed cruelly on her stomach, where the baby was growing. She had promised herself she wouldn't cry, and yet here she was, breaking like a dam.

'Are you okay?'

'I'm fine,' she said, wiping away the tears. 'I want this.'

'Okay. Lie back for me.'

Naomi lowered herself down, listening to the shaking of the stirrups. She clamped her eyes shut and dug her nails into the side of the chair.

Dane, I'm so sorry.

'The procedure shouldn't take long, only ten to fifteen minutes, and then we can get you a room to rest in before you leave.'

'Is this it? The drugs, I mean?'

'You shouldn't feel any pain, just discomfort as I manoeuvre the vacuum into the uterus. You've been given a sedative through the drip there, and I will inject a local anaesthetic into the cervix so the area is numb.'

She had imagined the drugs would wipe her out and blur the procedure as though she were sleeping through a nightmare. She dug her nails into the palms of her hands. She would remember it all.

'Shall we begin?'

She nodded.

'I'm going to do an internal examination first, and then I will fit the speculum, okay?'

She nodded again. She couldn't bring herself to speak.

Two gloved fingers felt around inside her as the doctor's other hand pressed down on her abdomen, as if she was trying to make her hands meet.

'Everything seems fine. I'm going to fit the speculum now.'

The cold steel instrument was placed inside and slowly began to crank open.

'Try to relax, Naomi, otherwise it might hurt.'

The doctor's words were warm on her inner thighs, an unwelcome caress.

She longed to cover her face so they wouldn't witness the pain etched into it, but she couldn't give them a reason to stop.

She relaxed her muscles and felt the speculum crank again with a small sound, like the breaking of a wishbone, and then it was done, she was exposed, vulnerable in front of complete strangers.

'Now I'll administer the local anaesthetic … You might feel a pinch.'

Naomi nodded once more, feeling the heat from the overhead lights on her face. Someone dabbed a tear from her cheek with a paper towel.

'Are you all right, Naomi?' the doctor asked.

'I'm fine. Please continue.'

The needle penetrated the wall of her cervix. The doctor pulled away and placed the syringe on a metal table with a quiet clank, before asking a nurse to pass her the device that would suck the life from inside Naomi, the thing that was a part of Dane, a part of her, a jumble of cells that should never have been formed.

'You should be numb now, Naomi. I'm going to begin.'

She couldn't feel anything at first, but after a few seconds she was aware of the tube deep inside her, pushing through to her womb.

The machine whirred; she jolted in the chair.

'It's just the suction, Naomi, no need to worry.'

The tube tugged beneath her skin, as though it had bitten down on her insides and latched onto the living thing inside her, teeth on bone.

Think of Max. Think of … No, don't think of Dane. Anything but Dane.

The suction filled the tube with squelching liquid and

devoured the life inside her with limitless hunger, until she
felt she had nothing left to give, and longed for the tube to
suck her up too.

She couldn't block it out any more. Trying to distract herself with other thoughts was impossible. She tried to envisage herself at the beach, but the smell of the sea was tainted with the medical tang in the air. When she thought of the waves rolling in towards the shore and rippling the sand on the beach, the sound of the vacuum gargled up the water and dragged her back into the room.

She lay back in the chair with her eyes closed, too exhausted to stop the tears from coming, and listened to the rumbling from the machine and the rattle of the tube, knocking against the walls of her cervix and pulling at her insides.

I'm so sorry, Dane.

'Naomi? I said it's all done.'

'It is?'

She would have slapped herself if she could. Her tone was weak, childlike. She cleared her throat.

'I'll just need to do a further examination, and then we can take you somewhere to rest.'

She longed to stay there for ever, hidden behind the walls of the clinic so she didn't have to face what she had done. She wondered if people would see her differently now, as if they could somehow spot that she had terminated a healthy baby, her womb its own little death row.

She covered her face with her hands and let the silent tears fall. She would never be able to look Dane in the eye again.

It's over. My marriage is over.

THIRTY-NINE

Marcus walked through the doors to the ICU with Lisa leading the way. They hadn't spoken a word on the drive over.

'We're here to see Josie Callaghan. It's urgent.'

'She's only just woken up. She needs rest,' the nurse said without looking up from the computer screen.

'She's a witness in a murder investigation,' Lisa said, thrusting her warrant card across the desk. 'Keeping us away could mean another woman is attacked, even killed. Is that what you want?'

The nurse looked up then and eyed Lisa's credentials. Then he got up.

'This way.' He led them through the ward. 'She has her own room; the injury to her neck was ... frightening other patients.'

'They're in the ICU,' Lisa replied. 'Shouldn't they be too ill to notice?'

'It was more the visitors, really. They wouldn't stop staring.'

They passed unconscious bodies lying in beds with tubes up their noses and down their throats. The light at the end of the corridor was flickering off and on.

'Just here. Her family usually arrive around ten.'

'If we aren't done, they'll have to wait,' Lisa said.

'I don't think they'll accept that.'

'Then don't think.'

Lisa opened the door to Josie's room and stepped inside. Marcus nodded to the nurse, in both thanks and apology.

There was nothing welcoming about the room: not the incessant beep of the heart monitor, nor the cold lino floor, nor the flowers already shrivelling in the vase beside the bed. Josie was sitting up, staring at them with those icy blue eyes. The wound on her neck looked like a red choker emblazoned into the skin. Thick stitches kept it together. Marcus tried not to remember how it had looked torn open and packed with dirt.

'Her voice box was severely damaged and needs time to heal,' the nurse said, and picked up a small whiteboard and pen from beside the bed. 'If you want to communicate with her, you'll need to ask her to write it down.'

Lisa took the board and pen and turned her back. The door clicked shut behind the nurse.

'Josie, we're here to find out what happened to you. We've spoken to Naomi. Now we want to hear from you. All right?'

Josie hesitated as she took them in, and eventually nodded.

Lisa sat beside the bed. Marcus stood at the foot and watched the woman closely. He knew she was about to weave lie after lie; he could see it in her eyes.

Josie took the whiteboard from Lisa. She struggled to hold the pen with the heart monitor clip on her finger. She switched the clip to her other hand, with a brief bleep from the monitor. Marcus noticed the steadiness of her hands.

'What happened, Josie? How did it all start?'

Josie began to write. The squeak of the pen made Marcus's teeth ache.

I went to confront Naomi about the affair. She told me to come back later. She said we should go for a walk.

Bullshit, Marcus thought, and gripped the bed frame.

Josie rubbed the writing away with the side of her palm and started again, skirting through grey clouds of ink lingering on the board.

She took me into the woods, said we would have privacy there. I wasn't scared until she pulled out the knife.

Marcus went to speak, but Lisa raised a finger to silence him. Her eyes never left the whiteboard.

I ran away. I didn't think she would catch me, but I tripped and fell. Naomi came up behind me and grabbed my hair until my head was off the ground.

You're lying, Marcus thought as he watched her hand slide across the board. She wrote with such ferocity and flow, he wondered if she actually believed her own lies, or whether she had been planning what to say from the moment she woke up. She flipped the board over to write more, too impatient to wait.

She cut my throat and left me there. I couldn't stop the blood. I packed it with mud. Everything went dark.

He couldn't restrain himself any longer. 'Bullshit!'

'Marcus, leave the room.'

'She's lying to our faces and you're letting her!'

'Get out!' Lisa stood from her chair.

'I won't let you get away with this,' he said to Josie. 'I swear to God I won't.'

Josie tried to speak. Her hand rose to her neck.

'Marcus, leave. Now.' Lisa pointed to the door.

Josie sat up and gripped the bed sheet. 'Naomi ... tried ... to kill ... me.' Her voice cracked with the strain.

'You're lying,' Marcus spat.

'NAOMI TRIED TO KILL ME!' Josie screamed. 'NAOMI ... TRIED ... TO ... KILL ... ME!'

Blood began to stain her teeth. She coughed violently. It splattered on the white sheets and bled from the wound on her neck, oozing around the stitches and dribbling towards her chest.

'Get help!' Lisa ordered. 'Get help now!'

Marcus barged his shoulder into the door frame and stumbled back through the ward. As he placed his hands on top of the nurses' station, he noticed that Josie's blood had splattered on the back of his hand. The nurse spotted it and his face went white. Marcus didn't need to say a word. As the two men ran towards the room, Marcus realised that Josie had orchestrated the whole thing. She knew Marcus could see right through her. She was getting him out of the way.

The nurse burst through the door. The heart monitor was racing and blood was flying from Josie's lips in hacking coughs. He pressed a button on the wall and an alarm sounded above their heads. Josie began to choke on her own blood.

'Leave!' Lisa shouted over the cacophony.

Marcus looked at Josie, at the blood spitting from the wound in her neck, and was sure he could see the twinkle of a smile in her eyes.

He turned and left with his heart beating in his throat. He stared down at his bloodied hand as nurses raced towards Josie's room, and wondered how he had let himself be so easily manipulated. He was a detective, for God's sake, and he had been led right into her trap. He was a damn fool.

Beneath the shame, fear began to spread.

If he was taken off the case, who would protect Naomi?

FORTY

Marcus sat before Lisa's desk in silence.

They had barely spoken since the visit to the hospital, and he had been left with paperwork to attend to for the rest of the day. He hadn't noticed the pivotal moment when Blake stepped into his shoes beside Lisa, accompanying her out of the office and having meetings behind closed doors. Lisa had gradually teased Marcus's responsibilities from his grasp, until Marcus found himself completing Amber's old duties: sifting through paperwork, answering the phones that never seemed to stop ringing. He hated it, but if Lisa had pulled him into her office for an apology, she would be waiting a very long time. He couldn't persecute an innocent woman, even if it meant saving his own neck.

'You can't seriously believe Naomi attempted to kill Josie?' he said finally.

'No, I don't,' Lisa replied, her hands laced together on top of the desk. 'I believe she colluded with her ex-husband. I don't think she did it alone.'

'But it doesn't make sense. Dane would have taken her back in a heartbeat; they wouldn't have needed to hurt anyone.'

'You've met Josie,' Lisa replied. 'She's not exactly easy to get along with. You think she was just going to comply with their wishes?' She sighed. 'You need to remember that sociopaths think differently to the way we do. Just because we can't fathom the reasons behind the crimes, it doesn't mean that the accusations are wrong.'

Marcus went to respond, but she raised her hand.

'I didn't call you in here to talk about whether you believe her or not. Blake's on the case. This is about the situation at the hospital.'

'She was lying to our faces. I couldn't stand back and watch as you lapped up every word.'

'The woman survived the attack. Why the hell would she pin it on Naomi if she knew that the person who had really tried to kill her was still out there?'

'You said sociopaths think differently,' Marcus replied. 'And that if we can't understand their reasons, it doesn't mean—'

'You think a young woman who had her throat slit from ear to ear would lie about the person who was holding the knife? She told you it was Naomi over and over, until a stitch in her neck snapped, for Christ's sake.'

'She's lying. Why would she only blame Naomi? Dane's watch was found at the scene. Why let him walk and pin it all on Naomi?'

'She's young and in love, which makes her stupid.'

'It means she's unreliable. If the person I loved tried to kill me, I don't think I'd let that slide. Would you?'

'Maybe Dane wasn't there at all. Maybe Naomi planted the watch. He obviously believes he's being framed.'

'Josie is hiding something from us and you don't even care.'

'I don't care?' Lisa stood up and peered down at him. 'I'm here fourteen hours a day, often seven days a week, because all I *do* is care about this town. I've been doing this job for years, working on cases just like this. You think you know better than me?'

'I know that you're trying to bury the Hayley Miller case, hoping it will disappear. The only reason you took me to see Josie was because you don't want Blake near her. Probably wise, since he was a suspect in her sister's disappearance. Is that why you're pinning this on Naomi? So the truth won't lead back to him?'

'And here I was giving you the opportunity to apologise.'

Marcus stood up and adjusted his jacket. Lisa walked around the desk without taking her eyes off him, and stopped in front of him.

'You're assigned to desk duty unless I say otherwise. I'm going to bury you in so much paperwork that you'll be begging me to forgive you. Once I'm through with you, you'll be willing to incriminate your own damn mother if I tell you to.' She jabbed his chest with her finger. 'Now get out of my sight.'

Marcus stared into her eyes. Lisa was cruel and corrupt; even her touch made him feel sick. She was never going to back down.

But neither was he.

He stormed out of her office and headed for the door. He needed fresh air, to get away.

If Lisa planned to incriminate Naomi for crimes she hadn't committed, he'd have to do everything he possibly could to prove her wrong, before it was too late.

FORTY-ONE

Naomi opened the front door and listened to the light patter of the rain.

The week she had spent locked up inside her house after being released on bail had felt like months. Seven days breathing in the same stale air, wandering from room to room. She was terrified at the thought of stepping out into the world again, but she couldn't be alone any more. With only her own thoughts for company, she found herself dragged into the darkest depths of her mind, where the cliffs called to her. She couldn't stay inside the house a minute longer.

Dane was out on bail too, the newspapers said. Her mother would read the articles aloud, even when Naomi asked her not to. Rachel had been the one to pay her bail, selling her car and her jewellery, taking out a second mortgage on her house. Grace wasn't to know.

The journalists hadn't been here for a couple of days, but she knew they would be back the moment they heard she had stepped out into the world again. *The Blind Widow*, the papers were calling her, likening her to the killer spider, small and unintimidating until it bit.

For the first two days she had cried whenever she heard the journalists heckling her, taunting her as though she were an animal in a cage, rattling the bars, waiting for her to break, cameras poised to capture the second her eyes changed and madness seeped in. But then she hardened herself against their presence, immune to the hostility leaking through the walls. She was fair game, someone they could bully and torment, because who would pity a killer?

Rain pattered against her face and soaked through her jeans.

Peggy had told her to stay at home and rest, but they would be struggling at the café without her. They must need her help.

Naomi gripped the cane and stepped out into the blustery day.

Her foot landed on something soft. She took another step. Something crackled beneath the sole of her shoe.

She bent down and felt paper, covering the concrete path from her gate to the front door. She rifled through it, the pages flittering in the wind. Newspapers. Was she on the front? What were the damning headlines today?

She scooped up the papers, some dry and fresh, others soggy from the rain, and collected them in her arms before rushing back inside and shoving them into the fireplace. It took a while to get the fire started, her hands shaking so violently that she struggled to light a match, but it wasn't long before she heard the flames devouring the lies the media had spewed.

Don't let them win, she told herself once the papers were gone and she had extinguished the fire. Don't let them get to you. She made her way back to the front door and stood in the doorway.

She took a deep breath and shut the door behind her.

Her week inside the house had left her feral. She startled at the slightest sound, flinched from the lightest touch from the wind. With every car that passed, she wondered if the people inside were talking about her behind the glass.

The wind was harsh and fast, blowing against her until her eyes streamed, as though it was trying to force her back home.

Shoes scuffled against the path, approaching her quickly. She lowered her head and continued to drag the cane across the ground. Her heart began to race.

A hard shoulder shoved against hers and sent her stumbling into the road.

A car horn blasted.

It was an accident, she told herself as she stumbled back onto the kerb on shaking legs. She waited for the culprit to turn and apologise. All she heard was the stranger's dissipating footsteps.

She kept walking with her head down until she reached the high street. Unusually, it was heaving with people. Gradually she began to hear gasps and muttering as she passed. Her cheeks burned and she lowered her head further.

'She's got a nerve, showing her face,' a woman muttered under her breath.

The muscles in Naomi's chest tensed. Someone kicked her cane, throwing her forwards and into a stranger's back.

'I'm so sorry,' she muttered, the words trembling.

'It ain't me you should be apologising to.'

The man hated her. She heard it in his voice. Venom dripped from every word.

She felt the wall beside the path and realised that she was outside Wilson's house. She could smell cigarette smoke.

'Wilson, is that you?'

She heard a cough crackling with phlegm. He mumbled something and a door slammed shut.

'You should be ashamed of yourself!' a woman said behind her. Naomi turned just as a wad of saliva splattered on her sleeve.

She covered her face until the woman passed, then wiped her sleeve on her coat. Someone had actually spat on her.

She headed up the road as quickly as she could, dragging the cane fast against the ground, bashing it against garden walls and bins, a shop's sandwich board that swung violently in its frame.

One more turn.

The moment she felt the café's gravelled parking lot beneath her feet, her shoulders relaxed and air rushed back into her lungs.

The bell chimed above her head. Customers' words overlapped and muddled together. It hadn't been this busy in a while. The smell of food in the air and the warmth drifting in from the kitchen made her feel at home, but slowly the murmur of conversation stopped, and cutlery clattered onto plates. Silence whistled in her ears. She stood in the doorway feeling the heat of dozens of eyes burning on her skin.

'Naomi,' Nick said in a high-pitched tone.

Promoted to waiter and I didn't even have to die.

'Hi, Nick. I'll go through to the back.'

Peggy and Mitch were squabbling in the kitchen by the

stove when she appeared on the threshold. She breathed in the familiar scent.

'Naomi,' Peggy said, her voice high like Nick's. 'What are you doing here?'

Naomi shrugged out of her coat and approached the hooks on the wall to hang it up and grab her apron. Her apron wasn't there.

'I was driving myself crazy at home. I need a distraction. How's everything going? It sounds busy. Where's my apron?'

'You're supposed to be resting.'

'My hands are better now.' She put the cane under her arm and held out her palms. 'I've had the stitches out already.'

The buzz of the diner trickled through the open doorway. They were all talking about her.

'Naomi, you can't be here,' Mitch said.

'Why?'

'I'm sorry, darlin',' Peggy said. 'But people don't want to be served by a mur—' She stopped mid-word.

'I didn't hurt anybody. Josie's lying.'

'But they don't know that.'

'Then tell them.'

'It will make people feel uncomfortable,' Mitch said. 'We can't afford to lose any more business, not when we've just got up and runnin' after the broken window.'

'Most of the customers in there are here because of me, can't you see that? You haven't filled that many seats in years.'

They fell silent.

'Are you firing me?'

Mitch hesitated. 'Not right now.'

'Oh.'

'It might not come to that,' Peggy added.

'If I'm proven innocent, you mean.'

'Naomi, we can't take the risk.'

'I've worked here for twenty years! You know me!'

'Naomi.' Mitch's voice was firm. 'You need to go home.'

Naomi stood shaking on the spot as tears filled her eyes.

'Of all the people ...' she said faintly. 'After everything we've been through together, all these years of hard work ... You should be ashamed.' She snatched her coat from the hook.

'Naomi ...'

'No, Peggy. You've made your opinion of me very clear.'

She walked out into the diner. The chatter died down again, eyes collected on her skin like flies crawling across her face and neck. She stopped in the middle of the room.

'What?' she demanded.

A woman gasped. Another whispered. Slowly the mutter of voices began to grow. She wasn't a human being to them any more. She was a myth they all had to fear.

She strode towards the door and out onto the gravel, a sob bursting from her lips the second the door slammed shut behind her.

Screw them. Screw them all.

FORTY-TWO

Peggy and Mitch had been family. Naomi had trusted them, loved them, stayed late without being asked, covered shifts when other staff called in sick. She had given them everything, and in the end it had amounted to nothing but a shove out the door.

She walked along the street, too busy thinking of the betrayal to hear the angry footsteps behind her.

'How dare you!'

She stopped suddenly. A hand grabbed her shoulder and turned her roughly.

'Of all the days,' he hissed. Saliva sprayed against her face.

'I'm sorry, I don't know what you're—'

The hand grabbed the nape of her neck and dragged her forward. Passers-by ignored her screams. Her cane fell to the ground as she stumbled off the kerb. It felt like she was falling, lurching across the wet road with only the man's grip keeping her from falling face first on the wet tarmac.

Her forehead landed against a car window, wet with rain.

'You know what's in there?'

She tried to shake her head. The moist glass squeaked beneath her brow.

'My daughter. The girl you killed. You and your husband killed my Cassie.'

Cassie's funeral procession was making its way towards the church. She had walked right through it. That was why the street was packed with townspeople. Of all the newspaper articles her mother had read to her, the announcement of the date that Cassie was to be laid to rest was the story Naomi had forgotten. No wonder they hated her – they thought she was there to gloat, relish in their misery.

She tried to remember his name after years of serving him on Friday afternoons at the café, but his grip tightened and squeezed the blood from her neck.

'You killed my baby girl and yet you're walking free. Tell me how that's fair.'

'I didn't kill anyone!'

The hand pulled her away from the glass and turned her roughly. Her back slammed against the hearse and rocked the vehicle. She thought of Cassie's body knocking against the sides of the coffin, petals falling from the wreath.

'Don't fuckin' lie to me!'

His words were close to her nose. His hand snaked around to her throat and clamped down.

'My wife and I have to bury our daughter today because of *you*. We've had to wait all this time for her body to be released, and now you're here to destroy our last day with her.'

Naomi remembered an article on Cassie's body being withheld after the pathologist ordered further tests. She wasn't to blame, but she might as well have been, from the sound of his voice and the strength of his grip.

'Why is my baby girl dead and you're alive? Tell me how that's fair.'

'Leave her alone!' a man's voice said, before the hand was ripped from her throat and she heard the sound of two bodies thumping against the road.

She knew that voice.

'Dane?'

People started to gasp and shout.

'Someone stop them!'

'They should be locked up!'

'Call the police!'

Naomi stayed flat against the car and listened to the punches, the crunch of someone's nose, the thud of a skull hitting concrete. She slid along the wet metal until she reached the end of the vehicle and stumbled down the road, her hands desperately feeling the air.

A wad of spit landed just below her eye.

'I hope you rot in prison for what you did,' a woman hissed, her voice shaken with furious tears. 'If they don't lock you up for killing my daughter, I'll kill you myself!'

Naomi staggered away, wiping the spit from her face with her sleeve. She reached the kerb and tripped, landing on the pavement with a heavy thud. Blood swelled from a graze on her cheek.

She reached out for something to grab onto. No hands reached down to help. Bodies shoved past her; a knee jolted her elbow, a foot stepped on her fingers. She felt the cold exterior of the bus shelter and followed it upwards with her hands, pressing her weight against the glass. She moved round it with rainwater weaving between her fingers and down the backs of her hands.

She was back where everything had started.

'Someone ...' She was sobbing, could barely speak. 'Please can someone help me ... help me get home.'

The street swirled around her: the echoes of the fight still going on in the road, the whispers of people as they passed her. Someone laughed. A bag knocked against her. She put her hands out in front of her and headed blindly for home. She felt a lamp post and clamped herself around it. She hadn't been counting her steps. She had no idea where she was going.

'Naomi!'

Her name echoed up the street. Footsteps pounded against concrete and splashed through puddles.

She pushed away from the lamp post and lurched off the pavement, slamming to the ground. A car horn blasted in her ears.

Strong hands grabbed at her shoulders and pulled her roughly, tugging at her until she stood, bleeding at the knees. She screamed and hit the stranger with clenched fists, feeling the hardness of a collarbone beneath her knuckles, a shirt covering a broad chest.

'LEAVE ME ALONE!'

Someone was shouting. A car door slammed.

'I'm sorry,' a familiar voice said.

No. Not Dane. Anyone but Dane.

Naomi's hand grazed the wet bonnet of a car as Dane guided

her out of the road. She had almost been run over. He had followed her, helped her when no one else would, but all it had done was shake fear into her.

'Leave me alone!'

'I'm helping you home.'

'We can't be seen together or we'll be locked up again. I can't go back in that cell. Please don't let them take me back.'

She tried to pull away from him, but he yanked her back towards him. His breath was hot against her face.

'You can't make it home on your own.'

'Killers!' someone shouted from across the street.

'You're making it worse,' she whispered. Tears trembled on her jaw.

Dane pulled her closer. Something dripped down the side of her face. At first she thought it was rain. She wiped it away and felt the familiar warmth of blood.

'You're ... you're bleeding,' she said.

'We both are, Ni.'

He led her through the dark, the beat of his heart echoing in her ear. She had missed his touch and the sound of his voice, but after all the secrets he had kept, she couldn't let herself trust him. She couldn't let him in.

When they turned into her road, she pushed away from him and put her hands out to feel her own way home.

'Naomi, please ...'

'I told you to leave me alone.'

'I helped you.'

'I wouldn't need your help if you hadn't got me into this mess.'

'I didn't do it!'

'Then what about the watch, Dane?'

'I thought I'd lost it, I hadn't seen it in years. We all had that bloody watch as teens – they can't even prove it's mine.'

'Don't lie to me!'

'I'm not lying to you! Someone is framing me. Maybe it's *you* who's lying to me.'

'Screw you.'

She stumbled up the street, her hands swiping through the cold air until they were numb. Her knees banged into a parked car. The alarm blasted and echoed down the street. She followed the bonnet until she felt the kerb, and stumbled across the road.

'I didn't do it, Naomi. You have to believe me. Someone has set us both up.'

She stroked her hand against the brick walls of the front gardens framing the street, searching for the familiar deep chip on one of the pillars. When she found it, she pushed the gate open. Dane grabbed her shoulder and pulled her round towards him.

'You can't push me away any more. We've only got each other.'

His lips pressed onto hers. She squirmed against him and bit down on his bottom lip.

'Leave me alone!'

She walked down the path, fumbling for her keys, and dropped them at her feet. His hands supported her hips as she bent down to get them.

'Don't touch me!'

She snapped up and slid the key into the lock.

'I'm sorry,' he said, so quietly she barely heard him.

'I'm sorry too,' she said, stepping inside. 'I'm sorry I ever met you.'

She slammed the door behind her, then slid down the back of it and sobbed into her hands.

FORTY-THREE

I t was almost five. Lisa and Blake were still out of the office, working on the case that Marcus had once been a part of. He sighed and rubbed his eyes with the base of his palms.

Craig Kennedy's file was clean. He was a model citizen, husband and father. But Marcus knew that people were capable of hiding in plain sight. He would talk to Craig somehow, even if Lisa was determined to keep him at his desk. He looked around the empty office.

This place had once excited him. He had seen his future here, and thought of all the cases he would solve, the lives he would save. Now it reminded him of Lisa. But even so, it was better than going home, where Natalie would be waiting for him with an eye on the clock. All he did was push her away, and yet there she was, digging in her fingernails. He didn't need to work late tonight, but he would.

He heard them before he saw them. Lisa and Blake were laughing as they made their way down the corridor towards the office.

They didn't greet him as they walked in. Blake shrugged off his coat but still wore his smile. Marcus wondered if his cheeks hurt from keeping the false expression on his face all day, so eager to please the boss that he followed her around like a dog, coming to heel when asked, sitting when commanded.

'Good day?' Marcus asked.

'Fine,' Blake replied as he sat at his desk.

Lisa headed into her office and shut the door.

'Any leads?'

'Josie Callaghan is doing better.'

Marcus dropped a file on his desk with a heavy thump.

'I'm glad to hear it.'

He made his way to Lisa's office and knocked on the door.

'Yes?' she said without looking up from her desk.

He stepped inside. 'I was wondering if you'd thought about further police protection for Naomi Hannah.'

'Why would I think about that?' she asked, looking up at him over her reading glasses, a page poised in her fingertips, ready to be turned. 'I already told you no the first time.'

'Well, I thought after what happened today, with Cassie's family ...'

'You mean where one of our suspects got in a fist fight with a grieving man during his daughter's funeral procession?'

'It wasn't Dane who started the altercation.'

She looked back down at the page. 'They're lucky I haven't locked them both up until their court dates.'

'So she isn't allowed to walk down the street any more?'

'She can do what she likes as long as she doesn't breach her bail conditions.' She sighed and took off her reading glasses. 'Look, if you feel so strongly about police protection for Naomi Hannah, why don't you do it yourself?'

'And work around the clock? When do you expect me to sleep?'

'I don't expect anything from you. It's your idea, your problem.'

'But if Naomi is attacked again—'

'If she stays at home until the court date, she'll be fine. She's a grown woman, Marcus. She should be able to handle herself.'

'I think you're making a mistake.'

Lisa shut the file and clasped her hands together, her steely eyes zoning in on his.

'No, Marcus, you're the one making a mistake. You won't get far as a detective if you refuse to take orders, trust me on that. You're making the decision to let you go after your six-month probation extremely easy. Look at Blake, for instance. He might not be the best detective out there, but he falls in line when he's told, follows every order he's given.'

'So do dogs, boss.'

'Call him what you like, but he'll go far while you're still pushing paper around because your superior cannot trust you to follow the simplest command.'

'It's not authority I have a problem with, boss, it's injustice. I can't stand by while an innocent person is persecuted for a crime she didn't commit.'

'And you know this how?'

'I just do.'

'Not exactly concrete evidence,' she scoffed, and opened the file again. 'And all I have is a victim who swears Naomi slit her throat. What a fool I've been.'

'You can't trust Josie. She's lying to you.'

'No, Marcus, I can't trust *you*.'

Their eyes met again.

'Why can't you be like Blake? Follow orders and keep your head down? You're making it hard on all of us. It's detrimental to the investigation.'

'You want me to be like Blake? Have my daddy hide evidence to keep me out of trouble? He should never have been allowed on the force. This whole place is corrupt.'

'What did you say?' Blake said behind him.

'I'm not talking to you.'

'You're talking *about* me. Why don't you turn around, say it to my face?'

Marcus turned. Blake was standing in the doorway. His face was red. Veins were elevated in his neck.

'You shouldn't even be a detective,' Marcus said. 'The superintendent worries about losing the trust of the town, and it's because of what you and your father did. How can any of us expect respect when you're here cosying up to the lead detective on this case? You shouldn't be on the case at all; you should be investigated yourself.'

'That's enough, Marcus,' Lisa said.

'What evidence did you and your daddy dispose of, Blake? What are you hiding?'

'Shut up,' Blake spat. 'Shut your damn mouth. It never happened. It was a rumour, a rumour that almost cost me my career before it had even begun.'

'Tell the truth. What happened to Hayley Miller? What did you do to her? And Amber, what were you two arguing about just hours before her murder?' He looked at Lisa, who was eyeing Blake with a new sense of doubt. 'Oh, you didn't know about that? Just hours before Amber was killed, the two of them were arguing in this very building. She was begging him for help and he shrugged her off.'

Blake lunged forward, his fist heading towards Marcus's jaw. Marcus ducked out of the way, grabbing Blake's wrist with one hand and his collar with the other, and launched his head into the front of Lisa's desk. A glass was knocked onto its side, spilling water over the file Lisa had been reading.

'Get off him!'

Lisa lunged over the desk to split them up, just as Blake stumbled to his feet and thrust his forehead against Marcus's nose. Marcus stumbled back, narrowly dodging another punch. Blake's fist cracked into the wall. Marcus jabbed two punches into his ribs before Blake was yanked away. Lisa pushed him to the floor, then pressed Marcus against the wall with her forearm.

'Keep going, fucker,' she hissed. 'Give me a reason to kick your teeth in.'

Marcus panted and licked blood from his lips. The skin on his knuckles was pulsing. Blake stumbled to his feet. Blood dripped from a cut on the bridge of his nose. Lisa stood between them with her hands on her hips.

'None of us have to like each other, all right?' she said. All three of them were breathless. 'But we do have to work together. I haven't got time to waste as you boys measure your dicks to see who's the bigger man. This isn't about us. It's about the victims.'

Blake stared at Marcus, panting heavily. A drop of blood fell from the tip of his nose onto the carpet.

'If anything like this happens again, I'll drag the pair of you outside and knock ten tons of sense into you. Understand?'

Both men nodded, wiping blood onto their sleeves in red streaks.

'Get out,' she spat as she sat behind her desk again and picked up the wet documents.

Marcus and Blake left the room, bleeding and panting. As they sat down at their desks, they kept their gazes fixed on each other, both refusing to be the first to look away.

FORTY-FOUR

Naomi woke to the sound of a crash.

She screamed and ducked her head beneath the sheets. Something had hit the window; she could hear the glass slowly cracking in the pane, like small bones being crushed.

'KILLER BITCH!' a voice shouted. The words echoed down the empty street.

She covered her ears and clamped her eyes shut.

With the next bang, her bladder clenched with the shock and released. Urine poured down her thighs and soaked into the sheets.

'Hey! Get out of here!' a different voice shouted.

Multiple pairs of footsteps pounded against the road until everything went quiet.

I'm safe inside. They can't get in.

Silence fell. The house grew colder. The chill crept into bed with her and cooled the urine on the sheets.

Someone will call the police. They will be here soon. They will help me.

Hours passed. The street was silent except for the hum of the street lights and the whistle of the wind, but she was too frightened to lift her head above the duvet. Her nightgown stuck to her thighs. It reminded her of the night at the bus stop, shivering in the dark with the scent of urine filling her nostrils. Eventually she peeled the covers back and got out of bed with her hands outstretched. She pressed them against the window. Faint cracks ran through the glass.

A gust of wind caressed the skin on the backs of her legs. Her teeth chattered as the cold night drifted through the door from the landing; the outside had made its way in and was curling up through the house.

She crept to the en suite, stripped off her nightgown and dropped it in the bath with a weighty splat. Then she snatched her dressing gown from the door, wrapping it tightly around her body, and stepped into her slippers.

The house felt abandoned: the night air had chilled the banisters, the floorboards, the paint on the walls, until everything felt damp. She stood at the top of the stairs and listened. Gusts of wind whistled through the ground floor. The curtains flapped with the breeze and strands of hair fluttered against her face.

The stairs creaked beneath her feet. As she reached the bottom, she grimaced, covering her nose and mouth as a foul smell drifted towards her. She sniffed the air and gagged. Excrement. Someone had put faeces through the letter box.

She stumbled away and leaned against the stair post, trying not to heave.

Glass crunched under her slippers as she moved through into the sitting room and stopped before the window. The cold night air tightened the pores on her face. She stepped back and hit something hard with her foot. She bent down and felt a rock lying on the floor.

George hadn't checked on her, hadn't protected her from the yobs who had attacked her house. Had he stayed in bed listening to the attack, their shouts, and waited for the night to fall quiet again before turning over and going back to sleep? Maybe he believed the papers and the talk of the town. Maybe she was guilty in his eyes too.

She stood before the broken window, frozen to the spot.

She couldn't call her mum. Grace was right: Rachel was too fragile to be put through such hell. She made her way to the side table and held the phone in shaking hands. She keyed in her sister's number.

'Hello?' Grace's voice was thick with sleep.

'Grace, it's me,' whispered Naomi, as though the whole street could hear her through the broken window. 'Something's happened. Will you come over?'

Marcus arrived at Naomi's house at dawn. Exhaustion blurred his vision. He had two black eyes and a nose swollen to twice its usual size.

He looked at the house and sighed. The living room window was shattered, covered with a white tarpaulin sheet from the inside, glass littering the grass beneath like frost. One of the windows on the top floor was cracked. But it was the front door that was the most menacing. The red letters were large and jagged, like they had been cut into the flesh of the door, causing it to bleed. The red paint had dripped down to the doorstep in thick streaks and pooled on the concrete path.

KILLER

A police patrol car was parked outside the house. He glanced inside. If he hadn't known that it was PCs Billy Edwards and Kate Finch who had attended the call-out, he would have worked it out from the sight of the McDonald's bags shoved into the footwell. He had received Billy's call at 5.30 that morning.

He was the only detective who had picked up. He had slept on the sofa again to avoid Natalie.

A lone paparazzo was lurking outside the house, waiting patiently for a glimpse of the Blind Widow.

'You want to make a comment?' the man asked. He sounded Eastern European. His gut folded over the waist of his jeans.

'You're not a journalist,' Marcus said. 'Leave the questions to them.'

The man snorted and dragged on his cigarette. 'Prick.'

Marcus pushed open the gate and looked up and down the street. Figures stood at windows watching the activity. The town was waking up. It wouldn't be long before journalists flocked to the house.

He found a dry spot on the door and pushed it open. Glass sparkled on the floor and reflected the orange of the sunrise beaming through the door. He spotted a large rock on the rug in the sitting room.

'Five hours is a disgrace,' a woman said from the kitchen. 'The station is up the bloody road.'

'We're here now,' Billy said, his back to the door. Kate stood beside him, jotting something down in her notepad.

'Yeah, and we're freezing.'

'Grace, it's all right,' Naomi said.

'No, it's not all right. This is serious. It could have been life-threatening. What if the rock had hit her?'

'We take crimes like this very seriously.'

As Marcus stepped through the doorway to the kitchen, Billy and Kate looked round. Billy frowned, taking in the swollen nose and black eyes. 'Jesus, what happened to you?'

'Later,' Marcus said.

'DS Campbell?' Naomi said.

'Hello, Naomi.'

'This is my sister, Grace.'

Grace was an attractive woman, but evidently exhausted, with untamed brown hair and odd socks on her feet. She wore a tracksuit beneath her coat. She was older than Naomi, maybe by a couple of years or so, and her skin was a darker shade of ebony. Grace stood an inch or two taller beside her sister with her arms crossed over her chest.

Marcus thought of the Hayley Miller file. He tried to compare the woman standing in front of him with the young girl from the police interview. She looked strong, together, unrecognisable from the terrified teenager documented in Hayley's file. With Grace here, her husband Craig would be alone. Marcus decided to call in on his way back to the office. It might be his only chance to talk to him.

'I'm sorry you're going through this, Naomi,' he said. 'Do you know who it was who—'

'It's got to be someone close to Josie,' Grace interjected. 'Her whole family is a bunch of scumbags.'

'I'll make sure they are looked into.'

'But it's not just this,' Grace said. 'Our mum has been subject to abuse too.'

'What?' Naomi said. 'What kind of abuse?'

'Letters about her raising a monster. Some were racist.'

Naomi looked away. Her jaw clenched beneath the skin.

'I'll need to see the letters,' Marcus said.

'Why didn't you tell me any of this?' Naomi asked.

'You're going through enough,' Grace replied dismissively. She looked at Marcus. 'Could Dane have done this?'

'I'll certainly investigate that possibility. I will make sure you're safe, Naomi. I'll look into protective housing. I can't make the final call, but I promise you I'll do everything I can.'

Naomi nodded silently.

'That's a bit drastic, isn't it?' Grace asked. 'Would it be local? We'd need to be able to reach her if she needed us.'

'Naomi's safety is our prime concern. Right now, it seems she would be better off away from Balkerne Heights.'

Grace sighed. 'Can we clean up the mess now? You've taken enough photos. This place is bloody freezing.'

Marcus looked at Billy.

'We've got her statement,' he said.

Marcus nodded at Grace, then turned to Naomi.

'Naomi, remember the card I gave you. If you need me, call.'

She looked in his direction, but didn't reply.

Billy followed him through the house as Kate nosed around the living room. He hadn't even noticed that she had slipped past him as he stood in the kitchen. He had been too focused on Naomi, at the anger flickering in her eyes. He was losing her trust.

'Kate,' Billy said quickly.

She put the photo frame back on the mantelpiece and pointed her thumb over her shoulder as she headed for the door. Marcus glanced at it: a picture of Naomi, Dane and Max, a small but happy family. Marcus wondered if she knew it was still up there, the past staring out at her whenever she passed.

He opened the front door. Cameras flashed. The press had heard about the attack. A neighbour had probably called it in.

No one had bothered to ring the police, but they'd had time to contact a journalist to line their pockets.

Marcus walked up the path, blinking away the blots in his vision. When he got to the garden gate, he saw them: seven neighbours wrapped in dressing gowns and winter coats, frowns creasing their brows. The photographers lowered their cameras. Children watched from windows, rubbing sleepy eyes.

'We want her out of here.' Their spokesman was a man wearing a coat over his pyjamas and wellies on his feet. 'We've got kids, mate. We can't have journos and photographers blocking the road and yobs shouting in the night.'

'I understand,' Marcus replied. 'We are assessing how best to make sure that Ms Hannah and her neighbours feel safe during this time.'

'I don't give a flying f—'

'Daniel!' The woman next to him poked his arm.

'I don't care how she feels. My family don't need this crap.'

'She needs to go,' an older woman said, puffing on a cigarette between thin, wrinkled lips. The back of her hand was covered in sun spots.

The others murmured in agreement.

'We are doing everything we can,' Marcus said, and opened the gate.

The man moved in front of him. 'We need more than that.'

'Daniel!' The woman pulled at his arm.

'Don't do something you'll regret,' Marcus said. He held his palm out behind him to Billy as he heard him open his cuff case.

Billy's fluorescent jacket reflected in the man's eyes. The man backed away with his hands clenched by his sides.

'It's in hand,' Marcus said.

Tyres screeched on the road as a broadcaster's van turned the corner wildly and slammed on the brakes in a space across the street.

'Question as many neighbours as you can,' Marcus said to Billy and Kate. 'Maybe one of them saw who did this. Remind them that if they cooperate, it will make this whole thing go a lot faster. And let them moan, because they will. They'll want to feel that they're being heard. Call me if you get anything. Once you're back at the station, leave a copy of the reports on my desk.'

The door to the van slid open and a woman in her thirties clambered out, her long black hair blowing in the wind, followed by a man with a camera on his shoulder and a tripod tucked under his arm. Her microphone was powered and poised.

As Marcus lowered his head and walked towards his car, the reporter ran after him, shouting questions at his back, her high heels clacking against the pavement.

'Who was behind the attack on the Blind Widow, Detective Campbell? Is it true that Naomi Hannah attempted to kill Josie Callaghan? Is she suspected of killing the other women? How are the people of Balkerne Heights meant to feel safe in their own town when suspected killers are allowed to roam the streets? Is the case connected to the unsolved disappearance of Hayley Miller?'

'No comment,' Marcus said, and slammed the car door behind him. He didn't have time for the press. He had to talk to Craig Kennedy before heading to the office. He had to find some sort of lead. Naomi's fate depended on it.

FORTY-SIX

Marcus pulled up outside the Kennedys' house. It was a new-build property with large bay windows and two potted shrubs outside the front door, groomed into perfect swirls curling up the trunks.

He hovered his hand over the doorbell and glanced at his watch. It was early, but he remembered that the Kennedys had young children. They would likely be awake, which meant Craig would be too.

He caught movement from the corner of his eye and looked at the bay window. A man was staring out at Marcus's car parked outside the house. As their eyes met, he realised he was looking at the young boy in the school photo, all grown up.

Craig left the window, and shortly afterwards, the door opened.

'Can I help you?'

He wasn't a scrawny young kid any more. His shoulders had filled out and he had a broad, sculpted jaw. His hair was tousled from sleep and he wore creased navy pyjamas.

'I'm Detective Sergeant Marcus Campbell. I'm sorry to disturb you so early in the morning.'

'Is it Naomi? Is she all right?' Marcus noticed genuine concern in the man's eyes.

'Naomi is fine. Your wife is with her. Do you mind if I come in? I have some questions to ask you about Hayley Miller.'

Craig frowned and blinked furiously, as if to wake himself up.

'Hayley Miller? Christ, I haven't heard that name in a while.'

'I'm sorry to dig up the past, but with the new attacks, we're considering every line of inquiry.'

'Come in,' Craig said. 'The kids are still asleep. The one time they decide to have a lie-in and I'm up at the crack of dawn.'

He led Marcus through the house towards a bright white kitchen. Fresh flowers sat in a vase on the breakfast table. Marcus could feel the under-floor heating warming his feet through his shoes.

'Would you like a drink? The kettle's just boiled.'

'I'm fine, thank you.'

'Please,' Craig said, indicating the island unit.

Marcus settled on one of the stools as the other man made himself a coffee and tried to hide a yawn.

'Are you new in town?' Craig asked with his back turned. 'I haven't seen you around.'

'Two months,' Marcus replied. 'Nice town.' He noted the insincerity in his tone and coughed. 'The scenery is beautiful.'

'You get immune to it after a while,' Craig replied. 'I just see it as home.'

The sun shone through the windows and gleamed on the granite worktop. Craig turned and stood at the island, a mug of coffee in hand. He took a sip and winced at the heat. Marcus smelled the coffee and wished that he had taken up the offer after all.

'How can I help?'

There was something about questioning a man in his own home that made Marcus uneasy. There was a level of respect that had to be maintained, balancing authority with courtesy so he wouldn't be asked to leave. The look in a suspect's eyes could change with a single word.

'I saw a photo of you and Hayley attached to an old newspaper article.'

'Yes, I remember that,' Craig said, and took a sip of coffee. 'First time I'd been in a newspaper.'

'Were you close?'

'I was too shy back then to be close to anyone,' Craig said, and chuckled. 'I rarely spoke a word. I only came out of my shell when I began seeing Grace.'

'You were class partners with Hayley at one point, weren't you?'

'If you can call it that. She would doodle in her notebook while I did all the work and got us an A.'

'I see. She didn't confide in you at all? Talk about who she was seeing?'

'People tended not to talk to me. I was too shy. She told me to do the work and I did as I was told. The only time we saw each other outside school was the day of the presentation we had to give in front of the class. She told me to come to her house before school started and I could catch her up on what to say. There was no way I would be able to speak.'

Marcus thought back to Anita's description of Craig. She must have seen him that morning.

'Grace and Hayley were close, weren't they?'

'I know what you're thinking,' Craig said. 'This town is so small that we're all in each other's pockets.'

'The thought had crossed my mind,' Marcus confessed.

'It's true that we all know each other, but secrets are still kept. Grace has always been protective about her friendship with Hayley, and because I love her, I never pushed it.'

'What do you mean by protective?'

Craig sighed. 'If Hayley ever comes up in conversation, Grace stiffens and changes the subject. Hayley's disappearance really affected her. I tried to persuade her to go to therapy, but she refused.'

'Do you think she would speak to me?' Marcus asked.

'With everything that's happened lately, she's become defensive again. I think talking about it would tip her over the edge.'

'I understand,' Marcus replied. 'Are any of Hayley's other school friends still in town? I'd like to talk to as many people as possible.'

'I'm not sure you could call them friends,' Craig replied. 'After she began to garner a certain reputation, all her friends turned on her. Except Grace.'

Children's laughter echoed above them.

'Time to put my dad face on.' Craig laughed.

'Thanks for seeing me. I won't disturb you again.'

Craig led him to the door. Marcus stepped out into the cold, blustering day, then stopped and turned.

'Craig,' he said. 'What do *you* think happened to Hayley?'

Craig sighed. He looked over his shoulder towards the stairs as the children shouted from upstairs.

'I don't know. I've been asking myself that question for the last twenty years.'

Marcus nodded and thanked him again for his time. As he unlocked the car door, he looked back at the house. Craig was standing by an upstairs window with a child of about five in his arms. The child waved at him with a gap-toothed smile. Marcus waved back.

Grace had done well for herself, he thought. He wondered what Hayley might have achieved had she been allowed to. But behind the perfect home and family, Marcus had noticed the cracks. Grace Kennedy was hiding something.

FORTY-SEVEN

Naomi swept up the last of the glass from the living room floor. Stray shards fell between the floorboards. If only it were that easy for her to disappear.

The board Grace had nailed across the broken window creaked with the wind. She stayed sitting on the floor and closed her eyes to calm her racing heart. Even with the doormat in the bin outside, and the inside of the door scrubbed clean, she could still smell the stink lingering in the air. Someone had purposely bagged up their dog's faeces and emptied them through her letter box. At least she thought it was dog faeces.

The front door opened to the sound of clicking cameras, then quickly slammed shut.

'Bastards,' Grace spat, breathing heavily. 'Bloody bastards.'

'Are you all right?'

'They're pigs,' she said as she walked to the kitchen and ran the tap.

Naomi got up and followed her.

'What did they do?'

'It doesn't matter,' Grace replied as she washed her hands.

She had been scrubbing at the graffiti on the front door for over an hour.

'I'm sorry I've dragged you into this.'

Naomi stood in the doorway and listened to the broken glass rattle in the dustpan. It had been over twelve hours since the rock had clattered against her bedroom window, and she was still shaking. It was only then that she realised she hadn't eaten since the previous day. She emptied the glass into the bin and left the dustpan and brush on the kitchen counter.

Grace turned off the tap and dried her hands.

'Are we okay?' Naomi asked.

'Why wouldn't we be?'

Grace passed her and went into the living room. Naomi heard the spark of a lighter.

'You don't mind, do you?'

Naomi shook her head. Her house was hardly a sanctuary any more. Her sister could pull down her trousers and urinate on the rug and it wouldn't make any difference.

'I thought you'd quit,' she said. The words sounded forced, but she had to say something. The tension between them felt so much thicker when they were left alone.

'This is my guilty pleasure. Don't tell Mum.'

'You know I won't. I've kept all your secrets.'

She listened to Grace drag on the cigarette and smelt the smoke in the air.

'Are you ever going to tell me?'

'No,' Grace replied. 'And now is hardly the time to talk about this.'

302

'There will never be a good time.'

'Naomi, just leave it.'

Naomi edged closer. The floorboards creaked beneath her feet.

'I'm tired of leaving it. I want my sister back.'

Grace shifted in the armchair.

'I'm right here, Naomi. I've spent the day nailing boards over the windows and scrubbing paint off the door. What else do you want?'

'I want to know that you love me.'

'Of course I love you,' she replied with a huff.

'Do you? Because for the last twenty years it feels like you've barely tolerated me.'

Grace sighed and flung the cigarette end into the fireplace.

'What have I done? Why won't you let me in?'

'It isn't about you, all right? It's me.'

Grace got up and moved about the room. Naomi listened to her slip into her shoes and shrug on her coat.

'I should go. The kids will need dinner.'

'Grace—'

'Just leave it, Naomi. You're not the only one going through shit.'

'Then let me help you like you're helping me.'

'I don't need help.' Grace slung her bag over her shoulder. 'All I want is to leave the past in the past.'

'And that's where you're going to leave us, then?'

Grace unlocked the door and hesitated. Naomi stood in the centre of the room. She longed for her sister to take her coat off and sit back down.

'You remind me of ...' Grace's voice broke. She cleared her throat. 'Every time I look at you, I remember.'

'Remember what?' Naomi asked. 'Remember what, Grace?'

Grace opened the door. The heckling of the photographers slipped through briefly before it slammed shut again.

Naomi stood in the silence, breathing in the scent of cigarette smoke, as her new-found strength began to crack at the seams.

FORTY-EIGHT

The cliff had been waiting for her.

The salt on the breeze, the chill of the night, the dirt crumbling beneath her feet: it was as though she had never left. Thunder clapped above her head and echoed along the shore.

Naomi swigged the last of the brandy from the bottle and launched it over the edge with a scream. She was screaming at the injustice of it all, screaming for the murdered women, for the life she used to live, until all her anger and fear rattled up her throat. She felt the edge of the cliff crumble beneath her weight and stepped back.

She wasn't there to die.

She sat down on the wet grass and listened to the storm grumble overhead. She felt free up there on the green, away from the confines of home with the photographers pacing outside. The night air felt cool in her lungs. She breathed it in and tasted the saltiness of the sea.

She thought of everything that had happened during her month away from the cliff edge, the lives that had ended and the hate the town had spewed upon her. She remembered Max's bloody fur, his yelps as the knife slipped between his ribs, the weight of him as she carried him along the beach below.

Before it had all begun, the loneliness had been enough to devour her from the inside and pull her towards the cliff, but now something had changed. Now she had something to fight for. She wouldn't die with a crime linked to her name, a crime she hadn't committed. She had people to avenge. Max hadn't deserved it. The murdered women hadn't deserved it; even Josie, lying in a hospital bed with her neck stitched from ear to ear.

The brandy on her breath mixed with the saltiness of the breeze; she closed her eyes and licked her lips, tasted it.

'Don't do it.'

Her eyes snapped open, and she whipped her head around to listen, but she only heard the crashing waves.

'Who's there?'

'It's George.'

She wondered how long he had been there behind her; whether he had heard her scream into the wind and watched her throw the bottle. Maybe he had been following her since she stepped out of her front door.

'I'm not here to jump,' she said. 'I just needed space.'

'Space from what?' He was closer. 'Can I sit?'

She nodded and hugged her knees to her chest.

'All of it. The town. The hate. The journalists. My home feels like a prison now. I needed fresh air.'

He sat beside her. His arm brushed against hers.

'I can go if …'

'No,' she replied. 'You can stay.'

They sat quietly and listened to the waves, to the storm

rumbling out to sea. It felt good to be close to someone. She could feel the warmth of him against her body.

'I'm not usually a big drinker.'

'You don't have to justify yourself to me. I would have hit the bottle a lot sooner than this.'

'I'm just ... I'm trying to understand them.'

'Who?'

'The people who are doing this to me.' She was slurring. She closed her eyes and focused on pronouncing every syllable. She should have eaten. 'Did you hear about what happened?'

'With that woman in the woods? Yeah. I read it in the paper.'

'She told the police I did it, that I was the one who attacked her. She's my ex-husband's partner, and she ... she hates me because of something I did. I can't say I blame her, but to tell the police I hurt her and let the real attacker walk is just crazy. It means she hates me more than the stranger who tried to kill her. How can someone do that? Let a murderer roam free so an innocent person can be framed? Just to get back at me.'

'I don't know,' he said. 'There are some crazy people in this world.'

'I'll take your word for it,' she replied. 'I've never left Balkerne Heights.'

'Never?'

She shook her head. 'It's different for me. There's a whole world out there I'll never see. I know I sound bitter, but ... I don't want to know what I'm missing. It's been so long now. To go out there and realise that it's all the same ... I'd rather imagine the grass is greener than understand that this is all there is.'

'There's a lot more to life than this place, Naomi. The world might not be perfect, but it has a lot to offer. Maybe it would be good for you to get out there and make a fresh start.'

'Maybe,' she said. 'What made you come here? Balkerne Heights is so small, so ... insignificant.'

'That's what attracted me. I lived in London for over ten years, and the whole time I craved peace. Life without nature, the sea, the trees, it was draining. Since I came here, I finally feel like I can breathe again.'

'Don't stay too long. Balkerne Heights has a way of sucking the life out of people.'

There was a sweet smell to him, almost feminine. She longed to lean into him and feel his arms wrap around her. Out of all the people in her life, it was a stranger who made her feel safest.

'What are you going to do? About the police?'

'I don't know. They think I did it.'

'Surely they can't believe you hurt that woman.'

'Women,' she corrected. 'The attack on Josie was similar to the two murders. I think they want to pin those on me as well.'

'What about your ex-husband? Wasn't he arrested too?'

She nodded. 'We've lived in this town for decades, and now it's turned on us.'

'The truth will come out.'

'I hope so. I used to think the system protected the innocent, the people who told the truth. But now it feels like I have to do anything and everything I can to survive it.'

She listened to his calm breaths and wondered what he looked like. Maybe he had plump lips and stubble on his cheeks. He was a runner; she imagined a toned body beneath his clothes. If none of this had happened, if her heart hadn't been claimed by another man, maybe they could have been more than just friends.

'What made you follow me here?'

'I was returning from a business trip and saw you walk out of your door with the bottle. I'd just read the newspaper articles on the train journey back, and seeing you going off alone made me worry. You've been through a lot.'

'A month ago you would have been right to worry, but all this, this mess, it's changed me. I won't give in to it. I won't let them break me.'

After a brief silence, he spoke again.

'Can I ask you a question?'

'Go ahead.'

'What made you blind? Did you ever have sight, or ...?'

Naomi sighed. She couldn't tell him that she was blind because her birth mother was a drug-taking prostitute, and an untreated STI had given her an infection as she was born. She couldn't tell him that her mother was so ignorant and neglectful that she'd ignored all the symptoms and only taken her to the hospital when it was too late. She could barely bring herself to mention it in the confines of her own mind.

'Birth defect,' she replied finally.

She felt the first spit of rain against her face.

'We should probably go,' he said.

She nodded and pushed up from the wet grass. The muscles in her legs felt soft. She stumbled to her feet and laughed.

'I'm drunker than I thought.'

'A bottle of brandy will do that to you. Here.'

He placed his coat over her shoulders and hooked her arm through his. He picked up her cane and put it under his arm.

'Thanks.'

They headed off across the green with the sea breeze blowing the rain against their backs. George pulled her close, and as she shut her eyes and leaned into his warmth, she realised that there really was more to life than Balkerne Heights. She thought about what he had said about a fresh start, and took a deep breath. For the first time in a long time, she felt as though she could breathe properly too.

FORTY-NINE

Marcus stepped into his apartment building and let the silence wash over him. The keys trembled in his hand. He hadn't eaten much; the tension in the office was so profound that he was reluctant to leave his desk.

Lisa had chosen not to speak a single word to him since the fight. While she had locked herself in her room, Marcus and Blake had shared the open office in silence. If Marcus dared to look up from his work, he often saw Blake eyeing him from his desk before he quickly looked away. Around noon, he glanced through the window of Lisa's office and met her glare. She continued to talk into the phone pressed to her ear without taking her eyes off him. When he finally looked away, he wondered who she was talking to, and whether they were discussing him.

He faced the stairs and toyed with the idea of turning back and jumping in his car again. But exhaustion stung the backs of his eyes. He needed his own bed, even if it meant facing Natalie. He tried to remember the last time he'd seen her, and how they had left things between them. He often got home after she had fallen asleep, and woke before she did. They fought so often, he struggled to remember a time when they hadn't been at each other's throats.

At the door to the flat, he closed his eyes and took a deep breath before turning the key in the lock. The door refused to open more than an inch. He pushed it, and heard the chain rattle and snap with the motion.

'Natalie, you left the chain on,' he called. He peered through the gap; she was sitting on the sofa in front of the television. 'Natalie ...'

'Fuck off, Marcus,' she spat over her shoulder. 'You don't live here any more.'

'What? Natalie, let me in, it's late.'

'I don't give a damn that it's late.' She spun round. 'You don't live here any more.'

Even from where he was standing, he could see that her eyes were red raw.

'You can't decide that,' he said, and pushed against the door. The links in the chain creaked. 'Let me in.'

'It's not like you're ever here anyway.'

'Natalie, I'm not arguing through the door. I've had a shit day, all right? I just want to go to bed. We can talk about it in the morning.'

'No, Marcus. I'm done talking.'

'Natalie,' he said. 'Open this door.'

'Or what?'

'Or I'll break it down.'

'You're a cop. Isn't breaking and entering against the law?'

'It isn't if I own the bloody property!' He glanced down the corridor towards his neighbour's door and lowered his voice. 'Open the door.'

'I'll make this easy for you.' She stood up from the sofa with a glass of red wine in her hand. 'There is no way in hell you're getting in here.' She stormed out of the room.

Marcus pushed against the door again. The chain tugged at the frame until he heard paint chip away. Natalie came back into the room with a bundle of suits and shirts in her arms.

'Here.' She started to shove them through the gap. 'It's all you wear anyway, working day and night. You can sleep at your damn desk.'

He reached through the gap and grabbed her wrist, pulling her against the door. 'Open it!'

'Get off!' Her cheek was pressed against the door, distorting her face. The sight of it made him feel sick. 'You're hurting me!'

He let go, then stood back and kicked the door. The chain ripped off the wall. Splinters of wood burst from the frame. Natalie screamed and staggered back. Red wine splashed across the carpet.

'Trust me, I'll be glad to go, but not without my stuff.' He snatched up his suits and stormed past her towards the bedroom.

'Good,' she slurred, 'because I'll be changing the locks first thing tomorrow!'

'Do what you like,' he spat as he yanked open the wardrobe doors and threw clothes onto the bed.

'I don't even know you any more,' she said. 'You're never home. I only know you've been here by the plates in the sink and the blanket on the sofa. It's like living with a ghost.'

Marcus grabbed toiletries from the cabinet above the basin and shoved them in the nearest washbag. Natalie stood in the doorway.

'I hate you,' she said. 'I really hate you sometimes, Marcus.'

He turned back towards the door, and she stepped aside and watched him stuff the toiletries in his overnight bag.

'Do you even care? Four years of our lives gone, and you can't even talk to me.'

'What's the point?'

'You're not even going to fight for it?'

'I'm done fighting,' he said, and started to close the bag. A shirt caught in the zip. He tugged it until the lining of the bag ripped. 'I'm done with you.'

He slung the overnight bag over his shoulder and walked out of the room. Natalie followed, breathing heavily.

'You're a worthless prick, Marcus,' she spat. 'You hear me? A worthless prick!'

The glass smashed against the wall just inches from his head. Red wine bled down the wall and soaked into the carpet.

He turned and looked at her. Tears rolled down her cheeks. Red wine stained her lips. He had spent four years of his life with this woman, but he couldn't explain why. Loneliness, maybe. Maybe he'd believed he didn't deserve any better and was destined to be with a woman who put him down so often that he was afraid to go home. But at this moment he realised that he didn't love her, and that he never had.

'Goodbye, Natalie.'

He held his breath until he was outside the building, then

gulped in lungfuls of the cold night air. He'd thought he would feel free, but all he could think of was the destruction the case had caused: his job, his home, his relationship, all of them gone or broken beyond repair.

He walked towards his car and kicked a dent in the door. Then he ripped off his jacket and crawled onto the back seat.

It was cold inside the car, bathed in yellow light from the street lamp above. He locked the door behind him, bunched his jacket up beneath his head to act as a pillow, and closed his eyes.

FIFTY

Naomi woke at dawn. The cool morning air whistled around the board on the bedroom window. Pain pulsed at her temples and her breath smelt of stale alcohol and something sour. She patted the bedside table for water, latched both hands around the glass, and drank until the last of the water dripped from her chin.

She turned and felt the other side of the bed. Her fingertips grazed his arm below his rolled-up sleeve. George's skin was soft and warm, decorated with silky hairs, unlike Dane's, which were coarse. He was still dressed in his shirt and jeans.

It all came back to her. They had just reached their street when the nausea had come. George had held the lid on a neighbour's wheelie bin as she vomited up the brandy, the hot, sweet stench rising up to meet her. He had helped her into her house and up the stairs, and waited behind the bathroom door as she hugged the toilet bowl. He must have stayed to make sure she wasn't sick during the night. Through all the hate the town gave, there was someone good, someone who cared.

She remembered dressing herself for bed. The nightgown was back to front, the label digging into her chest.

She inched from beneath the duvet and crept towards the door, flinching as the floorboards creaked under her weight. She wrapped herself in her dressing gown and fastened it with a double knot. The door handle was freezing. She stood at the top of the stairs, arms hugged around her body, listening to the silence of the house.

The photographers wouldn't be outside yet. It almost felt like everything had returned to normal, and that it had all been a dreadful dream. But Max wasn't in his bed, and the boards on the windows still creaked against the wind, and come eight o'clock, she would hear the journalists' cars grumbling up the road and the murmur of voices collecting outside.

She made her way downstairs and sat in her chair by the fireplace.

The house had been her home for sixteen years, but with Dane and Max gone, it was a shell of what it used to be. All the memories she had accumulated over the years had shattered. George had been right about making a fresh start. If she wanted to survive this, she had to take matters into her own hands.

The police weren't protecting her. She and Grace could barely occupy the same room. Her mother wanted to help her, but Naomi couldn't put her at risk. The police, the town, they all wanted her to suffer. If they wanted to destroy her, she would make it difficult for them. As soon as George woke and left, she would pack a bag and run.

FIFTY-ONE

Marcus and Blake sat in the conference room in silence.

Marcus hid a yawn behind his hand. He felt filthy after spending the night curled up on the back seat of the car, even after the quick wash he'd had in the gents'. His suit was creased from where Natalie had bundled it through the gap, and he remembered how he had kicked the door open. He had never been violent before. The memory of it twisted his stomach. He had acted just like his father.

Lisa walked into the room with Sergeant Belinda Shaw, a hard-faced woman with thin lips and sandy blonde hair with hints of grey at the roots. As if Lisa didn't have enough allies, she'd brought in another one to stare him down. She didn't trust Marcus, she had said so. Now she had a witness in case he acted up again.

Marcus almost craved her anger, wanting to hear every scathing, unrestrained word she had to say to him, but what she did instead was worse: she pretended he wasn't there. If he spoke, she directed her answer to Blake. She wouldn't even look at him any more.

Lisa stood on the other side of the conference table. Belinda leaned against the wall and slowly tapped her fingernails against it, like a cat sharpening its claws.

'I've had a meeting with the super,' Lisa said, her eyes on Blake. 'He has instructed that we keep Ms Hannah safe. Whether you believe this is the right way to go is irrelevant: the superintendent has spoken, so we must follow his word.

'Need I remind you, I'm still your boss, and you both still report to me. I won't tolerate backchat, going against orders, or fighting. One more step out of line and I will be taking disciplinary action. Do you both understand?'

'Yes,' Blake said.

Tap, tap, tap, tap.

Marcus looked at Belinda's nails drumming against the wall and imagined snapping her fingers at the knuckles.

'Marcus?' Lisa asked, one eyebrow raised.

'Yes,' he said.

'Good. Now, Blake, you'll be with me. Marcus, man the office. Blake will call you if there is anything we need.' She looked at Belinda. Their eyes met as though words flitted between them. Marcus's cheeks burned.

Blake rose and followed Lisa out of the room. Belinda lingered on, her fingers still tapping, her eyes on Marcus. He returned her gaze, steeling his muscles against the animosity. Belinda smirked and left the room.

Marcus took a deep breath and flexed his hands, watching the blood seep back into his whitened fingers.

You can survive this. Wait for the case to close and then request a transfer. You can stick it out.

'*What?*' he heard Lisa shout from her office. A door slammed, and she was back, leaning over the table. A lock of hair slipped from behind her ear and moved with her breaths.

'Dane Hannah is missing.'

No.

'He didn't report here this morning like he was supposed to. You still sure the Hannahs are innocent, Marcus?'

She smirked and left the room.

His phone began to vibrate in his jacket pocket. He didn't even have time to catch his breath.

'Detective Sergeant Marcus Campbell.' Anger had clotted in his throat. He coughed.

'Sir, it's Edwards. I just passed the train station on patrol and saw Naomi Hannah walking inside with a suitcase.'

Marcus covered his face with his spare hand. It was shaking.

'You're sure it was her?'

'She had a cane and everything. You want me to go after her?'

'Follow her inside and keep me updated. Don't approach unless she is about to board a train. I'll be there in ten.'

He was about to hang up, but put the phone back to his ear.

'And Billy ...'

'Yeah?'

'Don't say anything to Lisa.'

He rammed the phone into his pocket, then leapt from his chair and escaped through the fire exit to avoid being seen.

For the first time since the investigation had begun, a new possibility clawed at the back of his mind. He wondered if he was wrong. He wondered if Naomi and Dane really were guilty.

FIFTY-TWO

aomi stood on the platform with her head down. It was a cold day. Her eyes watered with the wind and her cheeks were flushed. She hid her collapsible cane behind her back. She never had got her other cane back after the ordeal at Cassie's procession. If she lost this one, she would be completely helpless.

The last time she had gone to a railway station to escape, she had been intending to jump onto the tracks, but now escape meant something entirely new to her: it meant hope.

She thought of the haunted woman she had once been, the woman who had had nothing left to live for until Dane had slipped his hand into hers. She and her younger self seemed like such different people now.

A woman laughed across the tracks. Naomi imagined being spotted, the Blind Widow fleeing her crimes, and lowered her hood.

Doubt lingered beneath her new-found strength. Maybe she would always be running, fleeing crimes she hadn't committed. The plan was to travel into London and take the tube to Paddington, where she would head for the Welsh coast.

At first, the idea of stowing away in a cottage by the sea felt peaceful, but as she stood on the platform, she couldn't escape the thought that she was simply exchanging one small town for another, facing a different ocean that made the same sounds, and that the loneliness she was trying to flee would be waiting for her wherever she went. And in a new town, she wouldn't know anyone. She would truly be alone. But she had faced so much since she first went to the cliff all those weeks ago. The old Naomi was dead, as though she really had leapt from the edge. Once she boarded the train, the town would be dead to her too.

Each time she considered turning back and returning home, she thought of Amber dead in the ground; of the jagged scar fused into Josie's neck. Her sister couldn't even look at her – Naomi reminded her of something she couldn't face. Her mother was too fragile and had to be protected. Naomi couldn't go home.

'The next train to arrive at Platform Three is the Greater Anglia service to London Liverpool Street.'

Naomi took a deep breath and listened as the train approached in the distance.

There was something exhilarating about finally leaving Balkerne Heights, but it was a mere simmer beneath the fear of all the new obstacles she had to face: the countless escalators, the rush of strangers pushing past her, the numerous platforms she had to find; and that was just the journey. All the while, she would need to keep her head down. The story of the Blind Widow had spread further than the town she had always known. National newspapers had caught onto the story. She would lose the security that came with Balkerne Heights. She knew which doors led to the ladies' in restaurants and pubs; how many steps to walk down to get from the high street to East Hill. She knew every step to take. With her new hope came an old fear: she would be lost in the dark again, like she had been at the bus stop, but this time there would be no one to find her.

She listened to the approaching train, the chug and whine of its wheels, and thought of how just a month before, she would have longed to step off the edge of the platform.

The train pulled in with a cold gust of wind and the piercing squeal of its brakes. Her heart beat faster.

The doors opened. Naomi felt the step up with her cane and placed one foot inside.

A hand landed on her shoulder.

She froze with her hand on the railing inside the train. One foot on the platform, the other aboard.

'Don't do this, Naomi.' It was Marcus.

'I can't stay here, Marcus. It's not safe.'

'I'll make it safe, I promise.'

She gripped the railing until the blood was squeezed from her hand and pins and needles pricked her fingertips. Her escape was right in front of her, but her past was there to drag her back.

'I'm sick of your promises, Marcus. You don't know what might happen to me if I stay.'

'I know what will happen if you go. You'll look guilty. You'll have broken the bail conditions and you'll be confined to a cell until the court date. They'll come looking for you.'

Naomi lingered. Her legs began to shake.

'If you stay, I can protect you. If you go, you'll always be running.' He sighed. She felt the heat of it on the side of her neck, smelt the coffee he'd drunk. 'We can't find Dane, Naomi. We think he's gone. He looks guiltier than ever, and I can't protect him any more. If you go too, I can't protect you either.'

Even though she too was planning her escape, hearing that Dane had fled without her made her heart jolt with an irregular beat. The man she had trusted with her life for so many years had left her behind.

'You gettin' on, lady?' a man called from down the platform. 'This train's gotta leave.'

With Dane gone, she had all the more reason to step aboard the train and make her fresh start. There was nothing left for her in Balkerne Heights. She wondered what Marcus would do. Would he let her go? Or would he drag her away in handcuffs?

She stepped away from the edge of the platform to the sound of the conductor's whistle. The doors closed behind her, breathing a puff of air on her back.

'I'll make sure you're safe, Naomi. You'll have police protection outside your house around the clock while I find out who is behind all this.'

The train crept away. Her fresh start was escaping down the tracks.

'I hope ...'

'Yes?' Marcus said as he guided her down the platform towards the exit.

'I hope you're right.'

FIFTY-THREE

The suitcase fell on its back with a bang. Naomi left it there. She couldn't return it to the back of the wardrobe to grow a new sheath of dust. The thought of it waiting by the door for another escape gave her comfort; the feeling that she still had a sliver of control.

She listened to the small noises of the house: the click of the pipes, the water dripping from the kitchen sink, the board on the window breathing against the nails. She was back there again, banished behind the walls.

There were things she couldn't ignore any more. Before her attempt to escape, all she had focused on was the day the police realised that they were wrong, that she was innocent as she proclaimed, but being home again, she had to face the fact that it had been blind hope, a primal survival technique. There would be a trial. She would be ushered up onto the stand and torn apart. A jury would watch her, take in every crack in her voice, every nervous twitch. Her family would watch from the wings, and the townspeople would crowd outside waiting to condemn her; a modern witch hunt. She wondered if Dane would be in the dock with her, or whether he would still be running.

Dane had managed what she couldn't. He had escaped. She imagined what his new life would look like. Would he go to another small town, like she had planned, or would he lose himself in the bustle of a city? Did he see a new woman in his future, or would he continue to think of her and come back for her when it all died down? Even with everything that had happened between them, she still loved him, and feared that she always would.

She walked through to the kitchen and sat down at the table.

'You're safe,' she whispered. 'Marcus will keep you safe.'

'Will he?'

She jolted, the question like a cattle prod jabbing into her spine. Josie's broken breaths crackled from where the knife had split her throat in two.

Naomi opened her mouth to speak, but stopped the second she felt the cold metal of a blade rest against her cheek.

'Do you enjoy breaking people's hearts?' The blade lowered to Naomi's neck.

The police would turn up soon. They would come to the door to check on her. Would they get there in time? Or would they arrive only to photograph the blood on the walls?

'What happened between Dane and me, it's over.' Naomi swallowed, felt her throat move against the blade. 'I don't want him, I just want—'

'You've wanted to break us up from the beginning.'

'I wanted to move on, Josie, but he kept coming back, he wouldn't let me.'

The knife pressed deeper.

'Don't lie to me. He was the only person who'd ever want

you. You knew you didn't stand a chance of meeting someone else, so you took him back. You took him away from me.'

'If I'd wanted him, I would have run off with him, wouldn't I? We would've fled together. But we didn't. He went without me.'

Josie laughed. The sound rumbled in her throat as if it were full of blood.

'That's what you think? That he ran away?'

Naomi's gut plummeted.

'Where is he, Josie?'

The butt of the knife thundered against Naomi's skull. Her head bounced off the tabletop and blood snaked along her scalp. Josie grabbed her hair and pulled her back in the chair. She took Naomi's wrists and yanked them behind her back. Rope pinched at her wrists, twisting around them until her skin burned, but all she could focus on was her pulse drumming against the top of her skull. Everything was spinning.

The chair turned violently on its hind legs and screeched against the floor. Naomi lolled in her seat.

'What are you going to do to me?' she whispered.

Josie knelt down at her feet, tugging at her legs, and tied rope around her ankles.

Something wet and sour slipped from between Naomi's lips and dripped down to her lap in thick strings.

Josie gripped the back of the chair and dragged it from the room. The back legs bumped against the ridges between the floorboards and jolted over the threshold of the doorway, a bright trail of blood left in their wake. The chair crashed back onto all four legs.

'I've got some things to show you,' Josie said, circling the chair. 'Wake up!' A slap stung Naomi's cheek. Josie leaned in and rested a hand on her knee. 'Are you going to concentrate?'

Naomi nodded, and felt something light being placed on her lap, a postcard or a photo. Then another, and another, and another, and objects she couldn't work out, until the pile slipped off her lap and scattered across the floorboards.

'Do you know what they are?'

Naomi shook her head and clenched her teeth against the nausea rising from her gut.

'It's all yours. Photos of you and him together, your underwear, your hairbrush, your perfume. Dane kept it all under our bed, the place where he fucked me, but he was thinking of you. You were always there, lurking beneath us. We never stood a chance. I was such an idiot falling for him and his lies. He told me he was over you, that he felt sorry for you. Like a fool, I believed him. Well, I'm not as weak as you both think.'

'Did you ...' Naomi couldn't say it, couldn't bring herself to hear the answer. 'Did you hurt Max? My Max?'

'I would have. You deserve to know how it feels to have everything taken away from you. But obviously I'm not the only one who sees right through you. How many other guys have you been screwing? How many other hearts have you broken?'

'What are you going to do?'

Josie grabbed Naomi's throat. Long fingernails broke the skin.

'I'm going to make sure you feel the same pain you've caused me,' she spat. Her face was so close to Naomi's that the words warmed her skin. 'When I'm done, you'll be begging me to kill you.'

Numbness snaked through Naomi and dulled the throbbing of the wound on her head. Her limbs felt heavy and her neck weak, as the paralysis dragged her under and everything went silent.

FIFTY-FOUR

Naomi awoke to a deep demonic voice. Something was drumming against her head.

Bang-bang, bang-bang, bang-bang.

It took her a moment to realise it was the beat of her own heart. She remembered being hit by something, hard and fast.

'What did Dane see in you?' the voice asked. 'You're so weak.' The crackling sound was difficult to distinguish. She couldn't tell if it was a man or a woman.

She went to wipe away the blood trailing down the back of her neck. Her wrist snagged against rope.

'He always felt sorry for you,' the voice said.

And then she remembered.

She tried to find the voice in the room, but her senses were bleeding together.

'He would still talk about you to anyone who would listen. Talk about you right in front of me. All he did was push me away, and all I could do was watch as you stole my life.'

Naomi jolted backwards and slammed down on the floor. Her head cracked against the floorboards. Pain gushed through her like a wave.

'IT WAS MY LIFE!'

'I'm sorry ...' she murmured as the room spun.

'It's too late for that.'

Josie ran the blade of the knife around the edge of Naomi's face. The tip just scratched the surface.

'I let it go on for so long,' she whispered. 'I hoped that one day you would leave us in peace. But you didn't, and Dane continued to say your name as he dreamed, and call me Naomi by mistake. He looked at me as though I would never be enough for him, enough to fill the hole you left.'

She lifted the blade away and smeared the blood on Naomi's cheek. Tears stung Naomi's eyes.

'I cried when we had sex. Even after he had turned off the lights, I could still see his eyes were closed as he thrust into me and thought of you. I was nothing to him, a bag of flesh to make up for the real thing he craved. And when he was done, he would roll off me and turn his back to shut me out as he tried to hang onto the thought of you lying beside him instead of me.'

'Josie, I—'

'DON'T!' she boomed, and thrust a finger into Naomi's face. Her fingernail swiped the tip of her nose. 'For once I'm going to be heard. I'm not going to stand in your shadow any longer.'

The floorboards creaked as she paced back and forth. Naomi had to clench her teeth to keep from being sick.

'Just when I thought I couldn't hate you any more, he would enter me again and yet somehow be so far away. He would be inside me, but he wasn't there at all, hiding behind his eyes in a world that I could never reach. It was like a stranger was pressing down on me, dripping with sweat, breathing against my face.

'Whenever I looked in the mirror, I tried to find parts of me that I could change so he would love me like he did you. I used to watch you, did you know that? I watched you live your pitiful life and tried to learn from you. I copied the way you walked. I listened to how you spoke to people, trying to reach the same pitch, dip and rise in the same places you did. I held myself like you and presented these traits to him in the hope that he would see you in me and fall for the both of us, wrapped up in one body, so he would only need me. I tried to make room for you in me, so I could have all of his love, his attention, really have him. But whatever I did, no matter how hard I tried, I just seemed to push him further away.'

'Josie ...'

She heard the knife swiping through the air as Josie paced back and forth, gesticulated, spat out her words.

'That was when I realised. I hadn't lost him; I'd never had him to begin with. He was still wrapped up in you. I loathed you for that and wanted you to feel every speck of pain I felt. I wanted to hurt you so badly when I came to your door that night, but your damn dog was there, barking at me. And then I watched as Dane knocked on your door and took you to work, held the car door for you, looking at you in a way he never looked at me. I threw the brick and I missed you. Every single time I wanted to get back at you, you managed to slip away. But then the murder happened and you stumbled across the body. It always has to be about you, doesn't it? Women can't even be murdered without you turning up to bask in the limelight.'

The knife clattered against the floor. Josie bent down and picked it up again.

'But it was perfect. Someone was killing women, and you had pretty much made yourself the next victim. All I had to do was take your life like you did mine, and the police would think it was the same person who killed those women.'

'But the woods ... Dane's watch ...'

Josie snatched Naomi's jaw, took a rattling breath.

'I don't know what to believe any more,' she whispered. 'When I was in hospital, I tried to work out whether I would have known his touch if it had been him who attacked me. Would I have recognised the sound of his breaths, the scent of him? All I saw was you beneath me, covered in blood. I fell to the ground and watched you run under the light of the moon, saw the man follow you. I couldn't work out if it was Dane; all I saw was a silhouette against the night. And then you both left me there, bleeding into the earth, choking on the mud.'

Her voice grew quiet as she remembered the night that had altered both of their lives. 'I was losing so much blood. My body felt so weak I could barely pack the mud into the wound. You think you're in pain from a knock to the head? Try shoving mud and stones into your own throat and packing it shut. Imagine lying on the ground as every drop of heat leaves your body and the night gets quieter, waiting for you to die. I couldn't feel anything but the cold claiming me and the lump of earth in my throat. I didn't think Dane could leave me there like that, but then I had made him choose, hadn't I? It was you or me.'

'Why? Why did you tell the police it was me?'

'It's always about you, isn't it?' She snatched Naomi's hair and yanked her head back, pressing the blade to her neck. 'LISTEN TO YOURSELF!'

'I'm sorry,' Naomi whispered.

'You ...' Josie let go of her hair. 'You started it all. You're the one who kept him from me. You were the one he chose. I can't let you get away with what you did to us. Prison is too good for you.'

'It was Dane who hurt you, not me. I didn't do anything to you.'

'You fucked him, right here in this house!' Saliva sprayed against Naomi's face. 'You gave him hope. You gave him a reason to push me even further away, until I was living with a man who looked through me, not at me, who existed in silence as though I wasn't there at all. Just when he had started to give up the idea of getting you back, you reeled him in again. I'd almost had him. It's like you knew.'

'I didn't, I swear,' Naomi stuttered through dry lips. 'It was a moment of weakness. I had just found Amber's body. I was a mess. I wanted to feel safe.'

'So you took the only thing I had.'

'I'm so sorry.'

'That's not enough.' Josie sniffed back tears and took a deep breath. 'You'll be treated as a martyr for a little while, but I'll be ready for that. I'll be there for when he needs me, and soon he will realise what he has, who he has, right in front of him. He'll forgive me for what I did to him; he'll understand I was angry.'

'What did you do to him? Where is he?'

'He won't tell ...' she whispered. 'He won't tell them that it was me. He'll understand why I had to do it.'

'You're crazy,' Naomi said.

'You made me like this. This is all because of you.'

The knife pressed against Naomi's neck.

The doorbell rang through the room. The shrill sound drilled into her ears and made her feel sick again.

The knife rose from her neck. Josie shoved something into Naomi's mouth until it scratched the back of her throat. She gagged, her eyes watering.

'Make one sound and I'll kill whoever is on the other side of the door.'

Josie pulled a zip from the bottom of her jacket to the neck and walked towards the door.

'Hello?'

'Hi, I'm George, Naomi's next-door neighbour.'

George.

'I'm Naomi's sister. Nice to meet you.'

Listen to her voice, George. Look for the scar on her neck. See the truth.

'You too. Is Naomi around?'

'She's asleep.'

If George left, Naomi would die. The gag was too big to spit out. She rocked on the chair legs until she crashed back onto the floor with a loud bang.

'What was that?' George asked.

A beat rested between them; Naomi could hear the buzzing tension, like static crackling in the air.

'I'd like to see Naomi.'

'I told you, she's asleep.'

Naomi screamed as loudly as she could behind the gag. Her head filled with blood.

There was a scuffle at the door. Two bodies clashed with shouts and shoves. Josie cried out as something boomed against the wall and the door slammed shut.

'What the hell is going on here?' George asked, standing above her. The floorboards quivered beneath her with approaching footsteps, and a faint groan slipped from someone's lips.

And then everything fell silent.

Naomi moved her vacant eyes, and listened to the faint gargling sound coming from somewhere in the room. She managed to manoeuvre the gag from her mouth, regurgitating a thick sports sock damp with saliva.

'What did you do?' she asked.

Something heavy fell to the ground. Air darted into Naomi's face.

'*What did you do?*'

'I just made this a lot more interesting.'

Marcus sat at his desk scrolling through the CCTV footage. His eyes burned from staring at the screen and scanning so many faces, none of them Dane's. Not only had Dane escaped the town, he had done so undetected.

Lisa turned off the light in her office and locked the door behind her.

'My phone's dead, and it's staying that way until morning. I need a good night's sleep.'

He nodded without looking up from the screen.

'How does it feel being wrong?' she asked.

'I'm not wrong.'

'Our prime suspect has fled.'

'*Your* prime suspect, not mine.' He looked up and their eyes met.

'Don't stop looking until you've found him. I don't care how long it takes. You made this mess, you'll fix it. Understood?'

It took all of his strength to nod.

'Be in my office at eight a.m. We need to talk about your future here.' She turned and left before he could even blink.

He sighed and rubbed his eyes.

The hours were ticking away like minutes; he didn't have long to find the real culprit. If he was taken off the case, lost his job before he could make it right, Naomi would go to prison, that he was sure of. He had lost faith in the justice system under Lisa's command.

He opened the drawer in his desk and removed some files, bulging with details of the people in Naomi's life, exposed in healthcare records, previous convictions. He looked down at the list of names and sighed. Stale breath ruffled the page. Each name written in black ink had been crossed out in red after finding nothing that could link them to the abuse Naomi had received, the indentations in the page getting deeper and deeper as the list went on, his frustration etched onto the paper. He had read the files before, but here he was again, scouring through the strangers' lives as though the truth would bleed from the words.

The person who had killed Cassie and Amber, who had attacked Josie in the woods, was responsible for the disappearance of Hayley Miller. He knew it. He just had to prove it.

Dane's watch had been found at the scene, Josie's blood splashed onto the face.

Grace Kennedy had been Hayley Miller's best friend, and held a secret from everyone, even her own husband.

Hayley's own sister was in a relationship with a man who had been questioned over her disappearance. Josie hated Naomi and had clearly lied to the police about who had attacked her just so she could get Naomi out of their lives.

And Blake, a man close to the investigation, who knew every lead the inquiry took, could cover his tracks before he was discovered.

The whole thing was a mess.

Marcus went to the kitchen to refill his coffee mug, and pulled out his phone.

He thought of Billy and Kate sitting in the patrol car outside Naomi's house, munching on fries and adding to the fast-food bags bulging in the footwell.

'Billy. How's she doing?'

'We've ... er ... we've gone to grab a coffee.'

'How long ago?' Marcus asked.

'About fifteen minutes.'

His grip steeled around the handle of the mug. 'Get back there and check on her the minute you arrive. Next time, pack a flask.'

'Sorry.'

He ended the call and sighed. He could almost understand why Lisa was so aggressive. Almost.

He took the coffee back to his desk and eyed the CCTV footage still running on the computer screen. He needed to sleep off the day, but he couldn't let Naomi down; he couldn't let Lisa win. All that was waiting for him outside the office was the cold back seat of his car and the night sky staring in through the windows.

He took a gulp of coffee, opened a file and began to read, repeating any standout facts in his head until his eyes blurred.

The phone cut through the silence like a scream.

Marcus rubbed his eyelids until his eyeballs squeaked beneath his fists and picked up the phone.

'Hello?'

'Is this,' the woman fell silent for a second, as if reading his name from a page, 'Detective Sergeant Marcus Campbell?'

'Speaking.' He stifled a yawn behind his hand.

'I'm Alison Moore, head nurse on the ICU ward at Balkerne Heights Hospital. I'm afraid this call is coming quite late ...'

'It doesn't matter about the time. I'm at the office anyway.'

'No ... I mean, one of my colleagues should have called before, but it was overlooked.'

'What was?'

'On Josie Callaghan's file, it states that you and an Inspector Elliott wished to be informed if anything changed with the patient's care.'

'That's correct.'

'The patient discharged herself.'

Marcus instinctively clutched his stomach. His mouth dried.

'But ... is she well enough to do that? Couldn't you stop her?'

'We tried, but she was adamant. We couldn't keep her from leaving, not unless we had a reason to believe she was a danger to herself or others. She was going to be moved to another wing anyway, now that she's no longer at death's door, but she began to make a scene.'

'What time did she discharge herself?'

'Just after three p.m. ... yesterday.'

'*Yesterday?*'

'I'm sorry you weren't called sooner. I tried to get hold of Inspector Elliott this evening, but the call went straight to voicemail.'

'Thanks for calling.'

Marcus ended the call and stared out into the empty office. Dane was gone. Josie was out there. Naomi was alone.

He stood up from his desk, gulped down the cold coffee and snatched his coat from the rack.

It was time to talk to Josie.

FIFTY-SIX

George was lying beneath the window, his breaths wheezing in and out of his lungs. Josie let the knife clatter to the floor. Something wet and warm splattered against Naomi's face. Josie grabbed the chair and dragged it up onto all four legs.

'*Why?*' Naomi shouted. Tears streamed down her cheeks.

'You need to know what it's like to be me,' Josie spat. She gripped Naomi's chin. 'To have everyone that you hold dear taken away.'

'What did you do to him?'

Josie paced the room. The floorboards creaked beneath her weight.

'WHAT DID YOU DO?'

'I aimed to stab him in his lower back, but the blade darted between his ribs. It sounds like I might have nicked a lung. Breathe for us, George. Let us hear where we got you.'

George breathed quickly, rasping and desperate.

'Yeah, sounds like a pierced lung. Not a nice way to go, but then he shouldn't have interfered. This is what happens when people let you into their lives, Naomi. You destroy them.'

'You're despicable!' Naomi lunged forward in the chair. The rope tugged at her wrists.

'Take some responsibility!' Josie spat. 'You are the reason for all of this, don't you see that? None of this would have happened if you'd let Dane move on. If you'd let me have him.'

'You blame me,' Naomi said. 'But you got yourself into this mess. You're the one who is so obsessed with a man that you don't realise how weak you really are. No woman needs a man to define her, and yet here you are, throwing your life away and destroying others just because you can't get your own way!'

'You have no idea what I've been through,' Josie replied. 'You have no idea how much it took to survive, to get this far in life. After years of abuse from my brothers, neglect from my drunk of a mother, living in my dead sister's shadow, I was just starting to make something of myself. I met a man who finally understood my pain and who wasn't frightened by it. He knew what it felt like to wander through life covered in wounds. We understood each other, we loved each other, and then you took the only good thing in my life away from me.'

She bent down by the chair, sniffling back tears.

'Feel,' she said, and ran her arm beneath Naomi's bound hands. The surface felt warped in places, like fleshy studs in her skin. 'Feel that? My brothers used to burn me with cigarettes, just because they could. Mum was always too drunk to hear me scream. When my sister disappeared, my mother's mind went with her, and things got even worse. I spent so many years alone until I met Dane. I can't let you take him away from me, Naomi. I won't be alone again. I'd rather die.'

Naomi could hear George's breaths growing more ragged. They sounded wet with blood.

Suddenly it hit her. The police weren't coming, and Marcus would never unearth the truth. She and George were going to die.

The doorbell rang, and everyone in the room fell silent.

FIFTY-SEVEN

Josie and Dane shared a flat on the rough side of town, where the roads were scarred with potholes, and weeds were left to grow hip-high on the lawns. The block of flats would have been enviable once, but three decades on, the bricks were stained with green moss and crumbling from years of rain and frost. The drainpipes were blocked with decaying leaves. Rainwater trickled out like pus from a wound.

Marcus stood before the front door and pressed the buzzer for Josie's flat. She had been desperate to leave the hospital, but looking up at the block, Marcus wondered why.

He peered through the cracked glass in the door and into the communal hallway. An abandoned sofa had been shoved beneath the stairwell, moth-eaten and frayed. A pair of green cat's eyes stared out from the shadows and watched him on the other side of the glass.

He pressed the buzzer again, just as a gust of wind blew against the door and caused it to open and shut in a succession of shivers. He pushed it open, eyeing the staircase, then looked back over his shoulder at his car parked on the road. He felt sick with hunger. Coffee churned in his stomach and exhaustion burned the backs of his eyes. He was thinking of turning back to the warmth of his car when the first spit of rain blew against his neck and coaxed him inside.

The air smelt of damp, which speckled the walls and ceiling like flicks of brown paint. Cigarette ends swam in a child's cup by a stranger's front door, filled with water that was black with tar. He listened to the silence of the building and the creaking of the door behind him. Something was unsettling him, tightening around his throat like a noose; all he had to do now was jump.

He took the stairs and paused at the first landing, listening to the lives hidden on the other side of the walls. Even without seeing their faces, he pitied them. Of all the things they could have done with their lives, they had chosen to stay here.

An argument erupted behind the door of flat number 14. Marcus flinched and tightened his hands into fists. He took a deep breath and kept walking, up the next flight of stairs.

It was a completely different atmosphere on the second floor, as though nothing lived there but trapped air and echoes from the lives below. Water dripped from a hole in the ceiling and soaked into the carpet.

Marcus had learned to listen to his gut over the years. And it was then, as the hairs on his arms rose and his stomach began to churn, that he knew there was something wrong going on behind the silence.

He stepped towards flat 18, stopping the second he saw the door was ajar. He didn't know his hands were shaking until he pushed at the door with the tips of his fingers. It creaked on its hinges. Open doorways stood out against the dark.

'Ms Callaghan?' He rapped his knuckles against the door. The sound echoed through the flat. 'It's DS Campbell. I'm going to come inside now.'

He took a step forward and flicked the light switch on the wall. Nothing. He tried again, flick, flick, flick, flick, but the darkness seemed to get thicker. He took the small torch from his waist and shone the beam at his feet. The light crept along filthy carpet and up walls covered in tobacco-stained wallpaper that had peeled away from the skirting boards. He traced the beam of light across the carpet and stopped when he saw dark stains dried into the fabric. Cool sweat broke out on his back and forehead. He took a step forward and crouched down, studying the crimson flakes peeling up from the carpet. He scratched at one and felt it dig beneath his fingernail. Blood.

'Josie?'

He stood on weak legs and raised the torch. The beam danced against a wall in the next room, quivering in his unsteady hand. He stood in the doorway and moved it around, darting over a sofa, a television, a coffee table piled with crockery covered in scraps of food, growing mould like coats of fur. Flies buzzed around in the darkness, darting briefly before the light and flashing beastly shadows against the walls. Marcus batted them away with the back of his hand.

A sound made him stop mid step: a distant clink of metal. He fought the urge to hush the flies buzzing around the head of the torch. There it was again. He walked back towards the entrance hall, his head cocked to the right, and followed the sound towards a closed door.

He was alone, in a flat he hadn't been invited into, with only his word that the front door was open when he arrived, following a hunch that Josie was hiding more than she was telling them. If he found something, he would have to explain it, and if he was hurt, no one would know to look for him there. So many things could go wrong.

He placed his hand on the door handle. The door creaked open and the smell hit him instantly.

Blood. Urine. Faeces. Sweat turned putrid in the hot room. The torchlight crept up the carpet and fell on a bare foot. It moved upwards, onto a man's calf covered in inflamed welts. The rattling sound started up again. Marcus followed the sound with the torch beam and took in the sight of the naked body of a man, handcuffed to a pipe beneath the radiator. His wrists were bloodied around the metal cuffs, which he continued rattling against the pipe. An iron lay beside him with flesh melted onto the metal, matted with hair and blood.

The man's eyes were swollen shut and bruised black, and his nose was covered in a layer of dried blood that had blocked his nostrils.

'Help … me …'

It was only then, as the words were forced through the split lips, that Marcus realised he was staring at Dane Hannah.

FIFTY-EIGHT

'M s Hannah, It's PC Edwards,' a voice said outside the door. The letter box opened briefly with a screech. 'We just want to check you're all right.'

The words filled Naomi's throat, ready to be screamed from behind the gag that Josie had shoved back into her mouth, but the thought of the knife plunging into George's neck forced her to bite down on the fabric. The letter box banged shut.

'Say one word and I'll kill him,' Josie whispered. She was crouched beside George, who lay on the floor by Naomi's feet, so close she could hear the blood bubbling in his throat every time he breathed.

She tried to speak behind the gag. It slipped further down her throat and made her retch. Josie yanked the sock from her mouth.

'They won't leave until I confirm I'm all right.'

George coughed violently.

'You'll tell them everything's fine if you want him to live,' Josie said, pulling at the rope around Naomi's ankles until the blood rushed back into her feet. 'Keep the light off and only open the door a crack.'

Naomi nodded as she tried to think of a way to save them without sending George to his grave.

'Pretend you were asleep,' Josie whispered as she untied her wrists. 'Tell them you're fine and you're going back to bed.'

Naomi nodded and flexed her wrists as the rope began to loosen around her ankles. It was night-time, then. She wondered how long she had been unconscious from the blow to her head.

The doorbell rang again. George groaned deeply by her feet. His breath tickled the skin on her ankles.

'Shut up,' Josie spat, and kicked him in the stomach. He groaned and coughed up blood, spewing it against the floorboards and Naomi's bare feet.

Naomi rubbed her wrists and wiped George's blood from her face.

'Go!' Josie hissed.

Naomi lurched to her feet and stumbled, her head not yet connected with her limbs. She scrabbled at the locks on the door, smearing blood on the metal. Cool air drifted in.

'Yes?' she said through the crack in the door.

'Ms Hannah, it's PCs Billy Edwards and Kate Finch. We wanted to check you were all right.'

'I was sleeping.'

Naomi heard George's voice, smothered by a gag or a hand.

'I'm sorry,' PC Edwards replied. 'We won't disturb you again.'

'It's all right, it makes me feel safe.'

Hear the fear in my voice. Smell the blood.

She followed her hand up the wall and felt the light switch

beneath her fingers. If she turned on the light they would see the blood, but George would be dead, the knife in his neck. She imagined the handle quivering with the beat of his heart as blood spurted up the wall. She lowered her hand.

'We'll be here all night. We're parked just outside if you need us.'

Naomi nodded, and stood in the doorway even as they began to walk down the garden path, lingering in the hope that they would notice she didn't want them to go.

'Close the door!' Josie hissed. Her voice was only a whisper, but Naomi jolted at the sound and shut the door.

A whimper escaped her lips the moment the hand clasped around her throat and pinned her against the wall.

'Nice try, but they're thick as shit,' Josie said, her words so close to Naomi's face that she could taste them. 'They won't check again until morning. Think of the fun we're going to have before then.'

FIFTY-NINE

Marcus ended the call to his colleague at the station and thought of the last words he had said. *And bring bolt cutters. He's been handcuffed.*

The urine soaked into the carpet had seeped through the knees of his trousers. By the smell of him, Dane had been there for hours, festering in his own waste and blood, with sweat growing cold on his skin. Marcus focused on the man's face: behind the mask of puffy, broken skin, Dane looked terrified.

'You're going to be okay, Dane. My colleagues will be here soon to get you out of these cuffs. Who did this to you?'

'She's crazy,' Dane said, sounding like he was talking around a mouthful of dislodged teeth. 'She's going to ...'

'What? What is she going to do, Dane? Who did this?'

'Josie,' he replied through gritted teeth. A tear plummeted to his jaw. 'She's ...'

'She's gone now. You're safe. We'll find her.' Marcus felt sick with guilt. They had suspected Dane when they should have been protecting him.

He felt for Dane's pulse at his wrist. His heart was racing sporadically. Shock was taking over.

'Naomi …' Dane said, his voice fading. 'Save Naomi.'

Marcus held Dane's head up as it lolled against the radiator. 'What's going to happen to Naomi?' he asked. 'Dane … what's going to happen to Naomi?'

'Josie …' The words sounded difficult to muster, as though each letter cost him seconds of consciousness. 'She will hurt Naomi.'

'Did she tell you this?'

Dane swallowed loudly. He nodded so briefly that Marcus had to ask him again to be sure.

'Yes.'

Marcus snatched up his phone with his free hand and called Billy.

'Is Naomi safe? Did you check on her?'

'Yeah, she's all right. She was asleep, we woke her up.'

'How long ago?'

'Huh?'

'Damn it, Billy. I asked how long ago.'

'Half an hour or less. She's gone back to bed.'

'And no one else was in the house with her?'

'Well we didn't search it, we just spoke to her at the door.'

'But did you get the impression that there was anyone else inside?'

'No, she was alone. What's going on?'

'Dane Hannah has been assaulted and handcuffed to a radiator in his flat. There's an ambulance on its way. Josie Callaghan did this.'

'Do you need us there?'

'No, I need you to protect Naomi. Dane said Josie is looking to hurt Naomi, so keep an eye out for her.'

'Isn't she in hospital?'

'Not any more. Call me if anything happens.'

He ended the call, then tried Lisa's phone, just in case she had switched it on, and cursed her as it went straight to voicemail.

Outside the flat, multiple footsteps echoed up the stairs. Marcus looked down at Dane's swollen face, ghoulish in the torchlight.

'The paramedics are here now, Dane. We'll get you out of these cuffs and cleaned up in no time.'

There was no response. Dane had mercifully lost consciousness.

'We'll get her, Dane,' Marcus said softly. 'We'll get her.'

SIXTY

Naomi sat tied to the chair by the fire, screaming behind the gag. Pain scorched all over her body. Josie had dragged the poker down her arms, across her chest and stomach. She had run it along Naomi's ribs and scorched down to the bone. Every single wound pulsed like it had its own small heart. Naomi had cried for so many hours that there were no more tears to shed. The scent of burnt meat filled the air. It had taken her a while to realise the smell was coming from her.

George had been quiet for too long. He hadn't even woken to the sound of her muffled screams. He had left her alone with the madwoman.

Josie sat in front the fireplace and took a gulp of vodka from the bottle as she shifted the burning wood with the poker. She had raided Naomi's drinks cabinet just before the torture began. Naomi suspected that by morning, the cabinet would be empty and she herself would be dead.

She would never forget Josie's glee during the attack. She had breathed heavily through a smile, licked her lips, laughed loudly when Naomi squealed behind the gag, and poked the wounds with her finger to hear her scream.

But as the hours passed Josie grew quieter, and through the pain and the blips of unconsciousness when it all got too much, Naomi figured out why. She had strayed from the killer's pattern. The other victims hadn't been burned or mutilated like this. Josie had screwed up. The police wouldn't link this case to the earlier murders; they would look for another killer – for her.

Josie had wanted Naomi to feel the pain she herself had been dealt. The burns singeing down to Naomi's bones mirrored those Josie's brothers had given her as a child. They were the same now.

'Do you ever think of your mother?' Josie asked. She sounded tired and distant. Maybe she had been crying too. 'Your real mother?' She stumbled to her feet and yanked the gag from Naomi's mouth. The fabric left a dry fur on her tongue where the sock and muscle had stuck together.

Naomi tried to find the strength to speak, but the screams had left her throat scratched and sore and the gag had leeched all the moisture from her tongue.

'No.'

Josie snorted. 'Liar.'

The vodka sloshed up the bottle as she tipped it to her lips, gulped twice.

'What do you think drove her to do it? Leave you there in the middle of the night? Dane said he thought that's why you're so defensive and struggle to let people in. Not that I agree with him: you let him between your legs easily enough.'

Naomi didn't reply; she couldn't. Her back was slumped and her head hung forward. She fought to keep her eyes open as her body longed to shut down and block out the pain.

A stray sound rumbled up George's throat, birthed from somewhere deep inside his torn-up lungs.

Fight for him.

The idea of moving her burnt limbs sent tears from her eyes to her lap.

Fight for yourself.

She began to pull at the rope around her wrists, hidden behind her back. She gritted her teeth as it sawed at her skin.

'Was it drugs that made her do it? Money problems? Or was it you?'

Naomi longed for the poker again. She'd welcome the scorching of her skin until it bubbled up in blisters. Anything but talk of her mother.

'She probably couldn't stand the sight of you.'

The poker chimed against the rack as Josie hung it back up beside the fire.

'You've really got to hate a kid to leave them alone at night like that and never come back. Anything could have happened. Did she ever try to contact you?'

Naomi lowered her head until her chin pressed into a burn on her chest and a blister popped, oozing liquid down between her breasts. The pain was easier than showing Josie that her words had got to her, that tears were streaming down her cheeks.

'She didn't, did she? Just shows you then. *You* were the problem. You destroy people's lives.'

'You're crazy,' Naomi whispered as she pulled her left hand against the rope until her fingers swelled.

'Everyone's crazy, Naomi. It's all a game of who can hide it best.' Another swig from the bottle. 'I mean, look at you,' she said, swallowing. 'You would've killed yourself if Dane hadn't stopped you. If only you had. It would have saved us all so much grief.'

Dane had told Josie so much about her. Had he only spoken about her when asked? Or did he constantly bring her up, just as Josie said?

'I pity you,' Naomi said, her voice so hoarse that the words sounded like growls. 'I pity you for wanting someone who clearly doesn't give a damn about you.'

Josie was quick to her feet and gripped Naomi's jaw in one hand.

'Shut your mouth.'

'He's seen you for what you really are; he must hate you just as much as you hate me.'

The vodka splashed onto her burns and seeped into the broken skin. The pain was so agonising that she couldn't even find the strength to scream. The liquid dribbled down her semi-naked body, rolling down her front and her back, all the way to her bound wrists, moistening the skin and the rope. She was sure she could hear it hissing on her wounds.

Josie sat back down by the fire and threw the empty bottle to the floor with a heavy clonk.

'You have no idea what Dane and I have,' she said, her tone low and grave. 'He'll forgive me for hurting him, and one day he'll thank me for getting you out of our lives. He doesn't know it yet, but you've destroyed him. He'll see the truth. I'll wait as long as it takes.'

Naomi pulled at the rope again and felt the instant release of pressure as one hand slipped free.

'I could never bring myself to hate him,' Josie whispered, her voice quiet as she faced the fire. 'I wish I could, but I can't. It wasn't him who made him act the way he did. It was you. I can't hate him for that.'

Naomi freed the other wrist quickly, then bent down and untied her ankles from the chair legs, biting down on her bottom lip as the burns folded with her skin.

'He'll love me again, Naomi. I know he will. When you're dead, everything will be right again.'

Naomi lunged forward with her hands out and shoved Josie with all of her strength, launching her head-first into the fire. Sparks blasted out into the room and stung Naomi's skin. The fire roared furiously around Josie's body, and she screamed and kicked wildly against the flames, knocking the poker rack over with a clatter. She sounded like an animal, wailing with a mouthful of flames.

Josie banged her head on the mouth of the chimney. As she fought against the fire, she swiped at Naomi's face with her nails.

Naomi's legs buckled beneath her as her lungs filled with black smoke. Josie screamed in agony and twitched violently as the fire ate away at her, but she still found the strength to latch both hands around Naomi's throat and squeeze.

'Die!' she screamed. Hot tears dripped from her eyes and fell onto Naomi's cheeks.

Naomi felt around her with her hands, wild and frantic as sparks and burning ashes fell on her. She felt the cool glass of the vodka bottle against her fingertips and grasped hold of the neck.

The bottle smashed against Josie's head. Glass and sparks exploded. Pinches of flame scorched Naomi's skin and shards of glass caught in her hair. Josie groaned through gritted teeth and lifted her hands to her head.

Naomi clawed the air in front of her and snatched a handful of hair, hot and shrivelled in the palm of her hand. She dragged Josie to the ground and pulled herself on top of her, pushing her into the floor with her hips as she frantically searched the floor for the neck of the broken bottle, anything to protect herself. Her fingers found the poker lying on the floor beside the overturned rack just as the knife penetrated the flesh above her belly button.

'*Just die!*' Josie rasped.

The blade felt cold inside her, even as the warm blood slipped down Naomi's stomach. Her muscles clenched around it like pursed lips and retracted when the blade sliced into them. Tears slid down her cheeks as she took the poker in both hands.

'No, Josie.' She sniffed away tears. 'I'm going to live.'

She raised the poker above her head, screaming as the blade moved within her, and brought it down with the last of her strength.

Josie loosened her grip on the knife; her hand fell limply to the floor. The knife dangled in the wound, pulsing with Naomi's heart. Naomi gripped the handle and screamed as she eased the blade out. Blood coated her hands and dripped from her fingers. The knife fell to the floor with a clatter.

The room was quiet. Wood crackled in the fireplace. Blood gargled in Josie's throat. Naomi felt the poker standing erect in the air, shuddering from the blow, and followed it down until the warmth of Josie's blood bubbled beneath her fingertips. The poker had plunged into her neck and lodged in the bone, choking her.

She whimpered and covered her mouth. She could taste Josie on her lips.

She lay and listened to the blood filling Josie's mouth and her throat contracting around the poker. Josie's pulse slowed against Naomi's thighs. Her last breath was far more desperate than the rest, ripping at the air in one final bid to live, before rattling out again in a collection of sighs. Then she shuddered and fell still, with a final retch of blood spilling from her lips and dribbling onto the floorboards.

The agony rushed back into Naomi's body, pulsing at her burns, throbbing from the stab wound. She crawled across the floor with blood seeping from the wound and drooling along the floorboards, and reached up for the phone with one hand as the other buckled beneath her.

She lay against the floorboards as the pain took over. She listened to the sound of the fire, the rasping breaths wheezing in and out of her own nostrils.

Her head felt light. Her lungs filled with the smell of toasted skin and black smoke. Blood swelled in her abdomen. She closed her eyes.

SIXTY-ONE

'A nything?' Marcus asked as he approached Billy Edwards and Kate Finch, stationed outside Naomi's house.

The windows lining the street reflected the rising sun as though the houses were ablaze. When he sniffed the air, he was sure he could smell smoke.

'No answer.'

'Next time, kick the damn door down.'

'Wouldn't we need a warrant?' Billy asked.

'Not if you suspect harm.' Marcus made his way to the front door and banged loudly with his fist. A dog barked from a distant garden. He banged again, then bent down to the letter box and peered inside.

The room was dark except for the embers glowing in the fireplace. The smell of burnt meat hit him instantly. He grimaced, but continued to search for human forms in the room. He homed in on something in the shadows and followed it down to where smoke curled up from a blackened body.

'Shit. Get an ambulance here.' He stood up and stared up at the house, hoping to find an open window. 'We need to get in there.'

'We could rip the board off the window,' Billy suggested as Kate pressed her phone to her ear.

'It would take too long. Stand back.'

Marcus looked at the white door, bathed orange in the glow of the rising sun, and launched a kick under the lock. He kicked again and again, until the lock splintered and the door clattered against the wall, marked with his shoeprints.

He stood in the doorway to the living room and looked down at the woman's body. A poker was lodged in her neck. The skin on her face had melted away, revealing strips of burnt muscle and the white of her skull. But there was just enough left for him to recognise her: it was Josie.

'She's dead,' he said breathlessly as Billy appeared in the doorway behind him, blocking out the light. Marcus searched the wall and flicked the light switch. His fingertips were covered in blood. He wiped them on the back of his trousers and looked about the room.

Naomi was lying by the sideboard with her eyes closed, in a pool of blood. She was just in her underwear, her skin littered with burns, just like Dane. He spotted the open wound in her abdomen, framed by congealed blood. A man was lying beneath the boarded window in his own crimson pool.

'We need two ambulances!' Marcus yelled.

He darted across the room and landed on his knees. He felt for a pulse on her neck, pressing his fingers hard against the cold skin. It was faint, but it was there, like the ticking of a clock stitched deep beneath the skin.

Billy was crouched beside the man, with his hand on his neck.

'He alive?' Marcus asked as he pressed down on Naomi's wound. Fresh blood swelled between his fingers. The tear in her skin felt like lips sucking at his palm.

Billy stared at Josie's body as he waited for the beat of the man's heart. 'Just.'

Sirens called in the distance.

'They're coming,' Billy said, glancing up anxiously.

'Not fast enough,' Marcus replied, wiping sweat from his brow.

'Shit,' Billy whispered as he checked the man's neck with both hands, his eyes wide and searching.

'What?'

'I can't feel a pulse any more.'

'Take over here,' Marcus said. He waited for Billy's hands to replace his own on Naomi's abdomen before darting across the floor on his knees. He listened for breath at the man's mouth and looked down at his chest for movement. Nothing.

'Where are the paramedics, Kate?' he called towards the door as he laced his fingers together and began to perform CPR.

'Here! I can hear them!'

Marcus pumped his hands into the man's chest and watched as his head lolled against the hardwood floor. Prising open his mouth, he breathed heavily and filled the man's lungs. Stubble scratched against his lips. He pumped again, sporadically checking for a pulse. Each time he pressed his hands into the stranger's chest, the pool of blood seeped further around him, coating his knees. He knew he had to keep going. Without blood and oxygen to his brain, the man would die. Keeping the blood flowing was the priority. He continued to work even when he felt ribs crack beneath his hands and sweat dripped into his eyes.

He looked up to see a woman in green kneeling beside him. She had warm brown skin, and long dark hair held back with a band. She looked at him with kind eyes.

'Take a break,' she said. 'I've got this.'

Marcus pressed himself against the wall and heaved for air as he watched the paramedic push down against the man's chest with all her weight, as another paramedic fitted a clear shield into the man's mouth for her to breathe air into. Marcus wiped his lips with the back of his hand and eyed the room, taking in the smell of burnt flesh, the sour tang of blood, the smoke curling up from the body. Josie's burns were worse than he'd thought. It wasn't just her face and neck, but her whole body; the fire had eaten away at her until her clothes melted into the skin and crisped against her bones.

Billy was looking at him, waiting for him to speak.

'Did someone ask me something?' Blots of white light were flashing in his eyes.

'What are the injuries?' the paramedic asked again, pumping her hands against the man's chest.

'Both victims have stab wounds,' Billy said as he eyed Marcus's heaving breaths. 'The man was stabbed in the left side of his back, the woman in the centre of her abdomen. The third ...'

He didn't need to say any more. Everyone in the room could smell the death on her, taste it with every breath they took.

'I'm sorry,' the woman in green said. 'We've lost him.'

Marcus's eyes darted to her face. She nodded to confirm, and he looked down at the blood dripping from his shaking hands. It hadn't been enough.

'You did everything you could.'

Marcus sighed, bowed his head. 'And Naomi? The woman?'

'Not as stable as I'd like,' the male paramedic said as he set up a gurney beside her.

Marcus nodded and tried to stand, but his legs were weak. Blood dripped from the hem of his trousers. He was so exhausted that he could have slept right there in the corner of the room, surrounded by all the blood and death, but he fought his legs and made his way to the door.

'Good work, Billy,' he said, slapping him on the back as he stepped outside, leaving a bloody handprint on his high-vis jacket.

The sun was higher in the sky. He squinted against the glare, raising his hand to shield his face, and saw that residents of the street had congregated outside the house.

'Please go home, we've got this under control,' Kate was saying. She turned at the sound of him and her face drained of colour. Marcus looked down and saw the blood coating his trousers and dripping onto the concrete path. His hands were smeared red.

They all stood silently, staring past Kate at the open door, which revealed splashes of blood, the smell of cooked skin. Marcus eyed each neighbour in turn.

'You could have done something,' he said. 'You could have helped her. But you didn't. You left her.'

They stared back at him, eyes wide and unblinking. One

woman wiped away a tear. The man named Daniel, who had been the spokesman for the group before, was fixated on the blood soaked into Marcus's trousers.

'You believed the gossip, and now she's fighting for her life and an innocent man is dead. If anything comes from this, I hope it's a lesson for you all to have some fucking compassion.' He turned at the touch of Billy's hand on his shoulder. 'I'm fine.'

He sat on the kerb and buried his face in his hands.

'Go home!' he yelled, spraying saliva down to the tarmac. 'You've done enough!'

Feet scuffled against the pavement as hushed whispers crept down the street, until door after door clicked shut and Marcus was left alone, quivering in the gutter, dripping with blood that wasn't his own.

SIXTY-TWO

Marcus woke up with his head pressed against the car window, which had steamed up with his breath. It was dark outside, lit faintly by the flickering street lamp in the hospital car park. It took him a moment to remember where he was. He wiped away the film on the window and peered out at the night. The knot of his tie dug into his throat. His tongue was rough against the roof of his mouth.

He had worked into the afternoon until his hands shook and every blink had been slow and forced. The sun had been setting in the sky as he closed his eyes.

A packet of cigarettes rested on the passenger seat, the lid gaping open to reveal just two orange tips protruding from the carton. He hadn't smoked since college, yet the pressure to keep going through the day had dragged him to the corner shop to buy a pack. He loathed the taste and the way it coated his teeth in fur, but the moment he stubbed one out, he wanted another, and another. He couldn't remember the last time he had eaten something or drunk anything except instant coffee.

He rubbed his eyes. Nausea splashed around his stomach in waves.

Josie Callaghan was dead. There was nothing to link her attacks on Naomi and Dane with the murders of Amber O'Neill and Cassie Jennings. And the disappearance of Hayley Miller still gnawed at his brain. It was all connected. He felt like the answer was right there in front of him, but he was too exhausted to see it.

He turned on the engine, opened the window, and lit a cigarette. The night air was refreshing, each gust stroking against his hair like his mother used to do to send him to sleep after his father had beaten them both. Hospitals always reminded him of her and the way she held him as they sat in A&E in silence, waiting their turn.

He checked his watch. It was gone nine, which meant he'd only had a few measly hours of sleep, crumpled behind the wheel. The exhaustion filled him up until he felt sick with it.

Talk to Naomi. Find out what she knows and go from there.

He sat beneath the flickering street lamp until the cigarette burned down to the filter. He threw it into the shadows beneath the neighbouring vehicle and closed the window, then got out of the car and stretched, his shirt spilling from the waistband of his trousers. He locked the car, then walked down the dark path towards the hospital. Distant sirens wailed in the distance.

A security guard stood outside the entrance, nonchalantly smoking a cigarette by the non-smoking sign. As he looked Marcus up and down and opened his mouth to speak, Marcus flashed his warrant card and walked inside. He didn't blame the guard for his doubts – he didn't look like a police officer tonight; just a desperate man in a crumpled suit.

The fresh air had breathed some life into him, but he still bought a coffee from the dusty machine in the hallway. It tasted burnt and scalded his tongue, but he drank it down anyway. Dribbles of black coffee seeped from the corners of his lips and onto his shirt. He threw the empty cup into the bin by the lift and travelled up one floor. He popped a mint in his mouth and checked his underarms with his nose.

The hospital was eerily quiet at night except for the buzzing of the strip lights and the faint bleeping from behind closed doors, some machines pumping oxygen and blood, others just waiting for hearts to stop.

He checked his phone for the ward name and followed the signs until he stood outside the double doors. What if Naomi wanted answers that he couldn't give her? What if she was angry at him for failing her?

He took a deep breath and walked through the doorway. His footsteps echoed in the quiet ward.

'Can I help you?' the nurse asked from behind the desk, shoving a magazine out of sight. Her black hair was tainted with grey streaks.

'I'm here to see Naomi Hannah.'

'Visiting hours ended a while ago.'

He showed her his warrant card and watched her brow crease.

'There's already a detective here.'

'Well now there are two.'

He wasn't himself – exhaustion was curdling his brain. He was beginning to understand Lisa's coolness, and wondered if he was already starting to morph into her.

'Down the corridor,' the nurse said dismissively. 'Second door on the left.'

He nodded curtly and followed the directions. He stopped the moment he saw her.

Lisa was sitting outside Naomi's room, biting her thumbnail. When she looked up, her icy blue eyes sent a shiver down the flesh on his back.

'I knew you'd come,' she said. 'Took your time, though.'

'Is she ...'

'She's asleep. Her mum's in there. Refuses to leave.'

They occupied the hallway in silence. A clock was ticking. Marcus heard the nurse flicking through the magazine again.

'Why are you here?' he asked.

Lisa looked down at her feet. She chewed on her bottom lip and tapped her foot against the floor. 'I fucked up. I got it wrong. She deserves an apology.'

'I wasn't expecting that.'

'Then you don't know me very well.' She glanced up and ran her eyes over him. 'You look like shit,' she said.

'You too.'

Laughter reverberated up her throat. 'So you've grown some balls, being boss for the night. Found the killer yet? The real one, I mean.'

He looked away.

'Not so easy, huh? TV shows and books make it look simple. The detectives always find the killer in the end. But that's not real life, is it?'

She got up and walked towards him. He fought the urge to step back. She looked older up close: the crow's feet at the corners of her eyes were deeper, and the whites of her eyes were turning a dull, sickly yellow.

'The superintendent will want the killer caught quickly, especially after last night. What will you say to him? Or better yet, what will you do to cover your tracks?'

'I don't know what you mean.'

'You know exactly what I mean.' She looked up at him with hatred in her eyes, the corners of her lips turning upwards. 'Who will you blame for the murders, Marcus? Who will be your scapegoat?'

'I'm not like you,' he said.

'You follow the rules,' she said. 'And look where that's got you. Josie Callaghan didn't kill Amber and Cassie, did she? But I'm sure you could make it look that way.'

'And let the real killer walk? No way.'

'He already has,' she replied. 'There hasn't been a murder in weeks, not that fits the killer's pattern. He's gone, and you've missed your chance to be the hero. So what are you going to do?' She peered up at him, unblinking.

'I'm going to do the right thing.'

'The right thing,' she scoffed. 'And who does that help? The case will die off without a conviction, and the victims' families will forever wonder if they're safe, if the killer is out there stealing the lives of more innocent women, if they can ever trust the police again, just like Hayley Miller's case. It wouldn't do your reputation any good, would it? Not the best way to start your career here. Does that sound like the right thing?' She stepped back. 'Or you could do the respectful thing. You could pin the responsibility on a psychopathic dead woman who will never be able to plead her innocence, save the families any more pain and suffering, and keep your career afloat.'

'That's not the way I work,' he said.

'Wake up, Marcus. We're not the good guys; we're at the front line of something much bigger. We enforce control on society so that people don't turn against the system. We lie so that civilians can sleep at night. We tell them what they need to hear so we can keep the peace. It's not our job to save people; it's our job to protect the system, and the sooner you realise that, the easier all of this will be on you.'

'It certainly looks to have taken its toll on you,' he said, looking at her drawn features.

'Come and talk to me when you've been in the job for over a decade. We'll see how great *you* look. That's if you haven't been demoted like me.'

He stared at her, trying to decide whether to believe her or not.

'Don't look so surprised. It's exactly what you wanted. I'll be chained to a desk come the end of the month, after Internal Affairs have had their say.'

'All I wanted was justice for the victims,' he said. 'You were trying to pin the murders on an innocent woman. We could have worked together on this, but you chose to see me as the enemy.'

She scoffed. 'You're just another man who wanted to undermine me. Men always find a way to pick away at women in the workplace. Do you know how hard it is being a woman in this job? And a gay one at that? I've had to fight for respect, shrug off the PMT jokes and being called a dyke behind my back, while you receive instant respect just for having a dick between your legs. I wasn't going to give you or anyone else a reason to push me out. But somehow you still managed it. Well, I won't be some desk-twat filing your paperwork. I'm moving divisions after my compulsory leave is over.'

She clenched her hands into fists at her sides. Marcus wondered how hard she could throw a right hook.

'You think you can stick around and do my job? Be my guest. But it's already tearing you apart. I'd get out while you still can.'

For the first time he saw something else in her eyes, behind the hatred and the hardness. Fear. She cleared her throat and tucked a lock of hair behind her ear. Then she patted a pocket, took out a packet of cigarettes, and walked away.

'Get some rest, Campbell,' she called over her shoulder. 'And think about what I said.'

'Lisa?'

She turned back at the sound of his voice, a cigarette already in her fingers.

'Hayley's disappearance is connected to all of this, isn't it?'

She paused for a beat, looking him up and down.

'I think so.'

He stood in silence and listened to the sound of her footsteps echoing down the corridor. He had survived Lisa Elliott.

His phone rang shrilly in his jacket pocket. The nurse peered over the desk and pressed a finger to her lips.

'Sorry,' he whispered, and answered the call.

'DS Campbell.'

'Marcus, it's Dr Ling. There's something here you should see. I would usually call Lisa, but after what's happened with her, I didn't know who else to contact.'

'I can be there in fifteen minutes. What is it?'

'This is big, Marcus.'

'I'll make it in ten.'

He ended the call and raced down the corridor, ignoring the nurse's disapproving frown as the soles of his shoes squealed against the lino floor.

SIXTY-THREE

Marcus blinked away the sweat as Dr Ling led him down the corridor. He had run from the hospital ward to his car, and sped through the streets. It was only now, as Dr Ling led him down the corridor nine minutes after she had called, that he had a chance to catch his breath.

'Just in here,' she said and held the door for him.

The room was dominated by a large steel table covered with clear plastic evidence bags containing bloodstained photos, underwear, a bottle of perfume.

'We collected these items from the crime scene at Ms Hannah's house,' Ling said, standing on one side of the table. Marcus stood on the other. 'They appear to belong to Naomi, at least at some point, and were found scattered over the floor, seemingly brought into the house in an empty shoebox we also found. But one item stood out.'

She slid an evidence bag across the table. Inside was a photo, the corner of it red with blood. Marcus picked up the bag and held it between his fingertips. The cold wave of shock almost made him drop it back onto the table.

The photo was of Hayley Miller, Grace, Dane and Blake.

'Now you understand why I didn't know who to call,' Dr Ling said.

'This ... this was found at Naomi's house?'

Ling nodded.

'The watches Dane and Blake are wearing in the photo, are they the same as ...'

'They appear to be identical,' Dr Ling said.

Marcus stared down at the photo, at Dane's arm hanging over Hayley's shoulder, the steel of the watch gleaming in the flash of the camera. Blake was on the other side of her, holding Grace in a seemingly friendly chokehold with an identical watch wrapped around his wrist.

'What are you going to do?' Dr Ling asked.

Lisa was gone. Blake couldn't be trusted. It was down to him and him alone.

'I'm going to speak to Grace Kennedy.'

SIXTY-FOUR

Marcus stood outside Grace's front door and took a deep breath. The coffee he'd drunk at the hospital had worn off, and his body was running purely on adrenalin.

The door opened and shed a warm sliver of light. Grace stood there in the doorway with tears shimmering on her cheeks.

'Is it Naomi?' she asked, and rested her hand on her chest as though she was bracing her heart for the answer. The hospital would only allow one visitor to remain with Naomi. Grace had been forced to stay at home and wait for news.

'She's stable,' he replied. 'I'm here about Hayley.'

She stared at him silently. A visible shiver shook through her.

'It's time, Grace. We need to know what happened to her.'

Grace nodded silently and stood aside to let him pass.

'I'm getting a drink,' she said as she closed the door behind him and wiped her face. 'Want one?'

'I shouldn't really,' he said.

She led him down the warm hallway. The walls were lined with maroon wallpaper with velvet floral designs in a lighter shade. The carpet beneath his shoes was the purest of creams. He peered down the hall at the kitchen where he had spoken to her husband.

The drawing room was quaint and homely, with two armchairs by a lit fire and bookshelves on either side of the chimney breast. A burgundy chaise longue rested in the bay window with a throw dangling off the edge, as if she had been curled up beneath it before he arrived.

'Take a seat,' she said as she opened a cupboard below one of the bookshelves and retrieved a bottle of Scotch and two tumblers. 'You'll need this,' she added.

Marcus sat down in one of the armchairs and watched as Grace poured amber liquid into the glasses. She handed one to him, then sat opposite him and knocked hers back without even flinching. She poured herself another straight away.

Marcus took a sip of his own drink and relished the warmth of it seeping down his throat.

'Hayley was raped,' she said suddenly, as though the secret had been sleeping beneath her tongue for twenty years. 'By Blake Crouch.'

She was right. He needed the drink. He knocked it back and let her pour him another. The bottle shook in her hand.

'Two nights before she disappeared, there was a party at Blake's house with all his friends, laddish types who goaded each other into things. Hayley had a reputation for being ... Well, I'm sure you've heard. They invited both of us to the party. I think they thought we would be easy lays.

'I knew Dane and Blake through Hayley; they were older than we were. Hayley and Dane had been an item on and off while Hayley was at college, and Dane was always trying to set Blake up with me. We went on a few double dates, but it was clear we didn't fancy each other. I always thought Blake wanted Hayley himself and resented having to entertain me.

'I didn't want to go to the party. I didn't think it was a good idea. Dane wasn't going, it was just Blake and his friends, but Hayley was adamant, and she said if I didn't go, she would go on her own.

'When we turned up, there were eight boys there. A spliff was doing the rounds and booze was lined up on the side table. Hayley was in her element. The boys flocked around her, plying her with drink and drugs. They were like dogs crowding around a bowl, drooling and scraping at each other to get in beside her.

'I felt uncomfortable and wanted to go home. I finally pulled Hayley aside and told her I wanted to leave, but she just laughed. She was wasted and wouldn't go with me. I couldn't leave her there like that. I didn't trust the boys one bit.

'Hayley dragged me down next to her on the sofa and pressured me into joining in. The boys chanted until I had chugged down half a bottle of wine and taken a deep drag on a spliff. It wasn't long before I had to run to the cloakroom to throw up.

'I don't know how long I was in there, but when I came out, the living room was empty. I could hear them upstairs.'

Marcus felt sick. He noticed the empty glass shaking in his hand.

'They gang-raped her, Detective. I walked in and saw them, like a sea of skin, boys waiting beside the bed with their trousers around their ankles, holding themselves, waiting for their turn.

389

'Blake was on top of Hayley. She had sick in her hair and her eyes were rolled back in her head. It wasn't consensual. They were raping her, one by one.

'I don't know what came over me. One minute I was in the doorway, and the next I was on top of him, punching the back of his head, scratching at his eyes, snatching at his hands to get them away from her. The boys grabbed me and yanked me off him. Five of them dragged me downstairs by my hair. I fought them – I couldn't leave her there unconscious, at their mercy – but I was no match for them. They hit my head against the wall and cracked the plaster. One of them punched me in the ribs. I was thrown out of the house, then they shut the door behind me and went back upstairs.

'I lay there on the pavement, sobbing hysterically. I only realised I had Blake's watch in my hand when I went to wipe away tears. I had ripped it off his wrist in the struggle. All the boys had the same watch, like they were some band of brothers or something. They got them before their first lads' holiday. Blake's watch had Hayley's blood and sick on it ...'

She covered her mouth with the back of her hand as though the Scotch was going to lurch back up, and shook her head.

'I didn't know what to do. I was so young and stupid, I thought Hayley and I would be in trouble if we told our parents. I'm so angry with myself now for what I did, but I was so scared and shocked that I did the only thing that would make me feel safe. I went home.'

'You didn't report the incident to the police?'

'I went the next day. I gave them the watch and a witness statement. They took a photo of my bruised ribs, the bump on my head. I was covered in scratches from the struggle. They said they'd go to Hayley's house to get her side of the story.

'I couldn't go home again. I was too scared, in case my mum found out. I'd managed to avoid her that morning, but I knew she would be there when I got home. She'd only have to look at me to see something was wrong. I sat up on the cliff and waited until the sun set, then I went to Hayley's house.'

Tears shimmered in her eyes. Her chin trembled.

'Hayley denied it,' she said, and looked down at her lap, shedding tears on her jeans. 'She lied to the police. She told me that if she admitted that she'd been raped, they would do tests and examinations, tests that would confirm she was pregnant.'

'Hayley was pregnant?'

'It was either Dane's or Blake's. She had slept with Blake after breaking up with Dane. Her father would have killed her if he'd found out. He was a raging alcoholic and handy with his fists. Her mother lived in his shadow. So she denied it to protect herself from her own family.'

Marcus thought of his father. He would have acted the same way as Hayley at her age. Men like their fathers longed for a reason to use their fists. A truth like that could have killed her.

'She was scared that the police wouldn't believe her because of her reputation, and how the boys might have spun it. It was all of their voices against ours. We had gone to that party voluntarily, put ourselves in that situation. The boys all came from good families. Hayley didn't. It's a small town, Detective, and you've seen for yourself how quickly the community can turn on someone. Hayley was terrified they would hate her for reporting them.

'I was so angry. I had seen Blake rape her, and the others waiting their turn, and suddenly I'd have to meet them in the street, and remember what they'd done every time I looked into their eyes. I begged her to tell the truth, but she wouldn't. I called her a coward and stormed out of the house. Hayley called after me and pleaded with me not to tell. Her mother was just coming up the drive and I pushed past her when she asked if I was all right. The next day, Hayley disappeared.'

Grace released a shudder of a breath, wet from tears.

'I looked into Hayley's case, Grace. There wasn't a report on the rape.'

'That's because Blake's father stepped in.'

She wiped her tears and blinked furiously. Her jaw clenched beneath the skin.

'The day after Hayley went missing, Mr Crouch had a police officer collect me from my home and bring me to the police station. I was locked inside an interview room. He told me he had got rid of the report of the rape, the photos of my injuries, and the watch. He made them all disappear to protect his son, in case the rape was linked to her disappearance. He threatened me, Detective. He said he could frame me as easily as he could make evidence vanish.'

'Nathan Crouch threatened you?'

She nodded, trembling in the chair.

'And you never told anyone?'

'Who were they going to believe? The head of police or the girl who argued with the missing girl the night before she disappeared?'

She sighed into her hands, then poured herself another

drink. She was shaking so badly that most of the Scotch missed the glass. She knocked it back, and when she lowered her head, Marcus saw that the alcohol had hit her. Her eyes were swimming.

'But when the murders happened, when Naomi and your brother-in-law were arrested, and the watch was found in the woods ...'

'I have a family of my own, Detective. I wasn't going to be framed for Hayley's disappearance. Blake's a cop himself now. He is just as capable of setting me up as his father was. I have children to protect. They need their mother.'

'Did Naomi know any of this? Is this why the killer harassed her?'

'She knew that Hayley and I fought, but not the reason why.'

'Was anyone else aware that she knew of the falling-out?'

'Yes.' She downed another drink and coughed as it burned her throat. Marcus reached across and took the bottle away. 'Nathan Crouch knew. He warned me to keep Naomi quiet.'

'So if Blake's father knew, that means that ...'

'Blake knew too.'

Something must have happened for Blake to think the truth was going to come out.

'But that still doesn't explain why Cassie and Amber died,' he said.

Grace hesitated. 'They came to me.'

'What?'

'Cassie and Amber, they came to me about a month ago, asking about Hayley.'

He wanted to shake her, ask her why the hell she hadn't

reported it to the police after their murders, but he bit down on his tongue and clenched the arms of the chair.

'They were looking into her disappearance. Cassie was a reporter and wanted to crack the story, said it would land her a job in London for one of the top newspapers. Amber wanted to make detective, and thought solving the case would get her there quicker. Cassie had the investigative skills, and Amber had the resources.'

'How did they know to come to you?'

'Amber found a copy of my witness statement reporting the rape. Blake's father obviously didn't hide the evidence well enough. She and Cassie suspected that one of the boys had killed Hayley to keep her quiet about the rape. They wanted me to go to the police again. I told them to keep me out of it.'

'And then they were both murdered.'

She eyed the bottle in his hand, and then her empty glass.

'You kept all of this quiet, even when they were killed? When your sister was arrested and then nearly died?'

'Are you a parent, Detective?' She looked up at him and read the answer in his eyes. 'I didn't think so. You have no idea what it means to protect your children. If Blake framed me, my children would lose their mother. I will always put them first, before myself or anyone. My father died when I was just a baby. I know how life-shattering it is to lose a parent. I would never let my children go through that.'

'Why tell me now?'

She struggled to compose herself, taking a deep, rattling breath and wiping away the tears.

'Because I'm sick of looking over my shoulder. I live in the same town as those rapists, Detective. I see them every day, on the school run, at the supermarket, crossing the street. They look at me with such hate, as if they are telling me to keep my mouth shut, like every glare is a threat to me and my family. I'm sick of swallowing down this secret. It makes me ill, physically ill, whenever I see them, even after twenty years.'

She sobbed into her hands and slumped back in the chair.

Marcus clenched his teeth until blood rushed in his ears. If Grace had spoken to him sooner, they might have been able to save Amber's life. Naomi wouldn't have found her body, the night her harassment began. All of this could have been avoided. But he wasn't angry with Grace; he was angry at the system he was a part of that stopped victims from coming forward. No one should fear the repercussions of rape as much as the act itself.

He stood up, placed the glass on a side table, and left the house, shutting the front door behind him.

SIXTY-FIVE

Marcus stepped into the office and listened to the silence ringing through the room.

He looked down at Amber's desk, where her belongings were gathering dust. None of them had wanted to clear them away. Photos were pressed into the back of the room separator with pins; one lone red pin had a piece of a Polaroid print stuck around it, as though the photo had been ripped off in a hurry. A pink coffee mug filled with pens sat behind the computer monitor.

Marcus pulled at the drawer beneath the desk. It was locked, but he had prepared for that. He placed the crowbar between the groove of the drawer and the desktop and pushed down until it cracked open, spitting splinters of wood in the air. The crowbar dropped to the floor with a clang as he ripped the drawer free and emptied out the contents.

Paper clips, Post-it notes and pens clattered onto the desk, and paperwork flittered to the floor, darting under desks and across the lino. A photo stared up at him, the top of it torn where it had been ripped from sight and stuffed into the drawer. It showed Amber and Cassie slurping on cocktails and giving the camera the peace sign.

He locked the photo in his own desk drawer and scrabbled around for the fallen paperwork, then leafed through the pages, scanning the words until the backs of his eyes burned. At last he found what he was after: the copy of the rape report.

Grace had been right. Cassie and Amber had been looking into Hayley's disappearance. And if she was right about that, she was right about Blake.

Marcus looked up to the doorway of the kitchen and remembered the argument Blake and Amber had had just before she was murdered.

Tell me what to do. Please, just tell me what I should do.

Why should I help you? What you did could have destroyed my marriage, my career. I don't owe you anything.

Had Blake caught her looking into the case?

He got up from the floor with the report shaking in one hand and his phone pressed to his ear with the other. He tapped his foot as the phone rang. He didn't even give Billy a chance to finish his greeting.

'Billy, pick Kate up and meet me at the station. I don't care how late it is, you need to get here now ... And dress for duty. We'll need handcuffs.'

SIXTY-SIX

Marcus stood on Blake's doorstep and rang the doorbell. He took one last look down the street at the patrol car; Billy and Kate were waiting to drive up and park in front of the house once he was inside.

The lights were on behind the curtains in the living room, illuminating the hallway. When a shadow of a figure appeared behind the glass panels in the front door, his heart began to race. This was it.

A dark-haired woman stood in the doorway in silk pyjamas; her face was clear of make-up, revealing every fine line.

'Yes?'

'My name is Detective Sergeant Marcus Campbell. I'm here to speak to Blake.'

'It's very late. We were just about to put my father-in-law to bed.'

'He might want to stay up for this.'

She hesitated before calling Blake's name over her shoulder.

Blake appeared from a doorway off the hall and froze when he saw him.

'Go to bed, Elaine,' he said as he approached the door.

'But I need to help with your father—'

'I said go to bed,' he snapped. 'Don't come down unless I tell you to.'

She eyed her husband, appearing both offended and frightened by his tone, before turning for the stairs. She glanced back at Marcus in the doorway as she ascended into the darkness of the first floor.

'What are you doing here?' Blake asked.

'You know what I'm doing here.'

Blake looked ill, and Marcus knew why. His secrets, everything he had done, had been eating away at him from the inside. He looked like he belonged in the morgue, not standing on his own two feet in his doorway.

'Are you going to let me in?'

Blake moved aside. Marcus stepped into the house and followed him towards the lit room.

Nathan Crouch was sitting in a recliner chair in the bay window with a tobacco pipe dangling from his mouth. He was an old man, over eighty now. His head was bald except for a few tufts of white hair, with liver spots on his scalp. His face was creased with wrinkles and spider veins. He pushed his glasses up his nose, and closed the book nestled on his lap.

'And you are?'

'Detective Sergeant Marcus Campbell.'

The man's face went white. He'd heard of him. Marcus wondered if Blake still ran to his father to clean up his messes.

'What's this about, Blake?' Nathan asked.

'It's about your secret,' Marcus interjected. 'And the repercussions it's caused. I'd sit down, Blake.'

'Don't tell me to sit down in my own house.'

'Listen to the man, Blake,' his father said. 'He obviously thinks he has something important to say. Let's hear it.'

Although Nathan Crouch was an old man, he still had an air of authority, as though he was the most important person in the room.

Blake sat down reluctantly with his eyes on Marcus.

'I know what you've done. Both of you. I know about the rape, the corruption, the hidden evidence.'

'I'm afraid I don't know what you're talking about,' Nathan Crouch said. 'You must have made a mist—'

'Let me refresh your memory.' Marcus took a document from his bag and handed it to the old man. 'Here's the witness statement that was taken from Grace Porter, Grace Kennedy's maiden name, after your son and his buddies raped Hayley Miller in this very house, the house that used to belong to you. The very statement that was taken before you hid the evidence, attempted to destroy any record of the incident, and threatened to frame a teenage girl for Hayley's disappearance to protect your own son.'

Nathan stared down at the report. The paper was shaking in his hands.

'This is impossible,' he said. His confidence had vanished. 'I got rid of it ...'

'Not well enough. Amber O'Neill found a copy. That's why you killed her, isn't it, Blake?'

'What?' Nathan exclaimed.

Blake looked sick. His Adam's apple was dancing up and down his throat. His shoulders were shaking.

'It's what you and Amber argued about just hours before she was murdered.'

Nathan looked between the pair of them, his yellow eyes twitching in his skull.

'You had discovered she was working on Hayley's case with Cassie Jennings, the local reporter, who you killed off first. You knew they were close to discovering the truth: that you murdered Hayley to keep her quiet about the rape, maybe even the pregnancy – because there was a chance the baby was yours, wasn't there? You confronted Amber that night in the office, and then you followed her home and killed her.'

'Dad, don't listen to him. He's lying.'

'You couldn't let the murders lead back to the crime that started it all – the rape and murder of Hayley Miller. So, like father like son, you had to find someone to frame.'

'Shut your mouth,' Blake spat as he stood. 'Dad, don't listen to this horseshit.'

'That's why you set Dane up. He was the only one of your friends with a matching watch who hadn't been at the party that night, who hadn't taken part in the brutal rape of a teenage girl. So you followed Josie and Naomi into the woods, attacked Josie and left the watch behind, knowing that Dane would be a prime suspect in the attempt to kill his partner as she attacked his ex-wife, especially as he had a sexual history with the two women you had already killed. You framed your childhood best friend to save your own back.

'And best of all, you were at the heart of the investigation. You knew each lead as it came in. You could cover your tracks before we even got a whiff of them.'

'Blake?' his father asked, trembling in the recliner chair. 'Is this true?'

'I told you not to listen to this horseshit!' Blake spat, so loudly that his father cowered in his chair.

'I didn't rape Hayley,' he said as he turned back to Marcus, his whole body shaking. 'She was begging for it. Craved it. She was making her way through the town. We were just taking our turn.'

'What did you do with her body, Blake?'

Blake walked closer to Marcus until their noses were almost touching and their eyes locked. Marcus saw the familiar rage there, the same rage he had seen before Blake had thrown the first punch in Lisa's office. He knew what was coming, and braced every muscle.

'Where did you bury her, Blake?' he whispered, inhaling the taste of the man's breath. 'After you raped her, and slit her throat, how did you dispose of the body?'

The punch came fast, cracking against Marcus's nose and knocking him to the floor. Marcus let it happen. He let the punches rain on top of his skull until his blood splattered on the carpet. He let the feet stamp on his ribs and his chest. He watched from swelling eyes as Blake's wife burst into the room, screaming at him to stop, and was thrown to the floor by her husband's hands. Her nightshirt ripped open, exposing a pale white breast. He listened to the banging on the door between kicks, and watched as Elaine clutched her shirt together in a fist and darted into the hall.

Blake was tackled to the carpet and pinned onto his front

as Kate drew his hands behind his back, handcuffed his wrists and read him his rights.

As Billy checked his injuries, Marcus locked eyes with Nathan Crouch, who looked so much smaller in the chair now. He raised his bloody hand to move his shirt aside and reveal the small microphone taped to his chest, and watched the old man sob into his hands.

SIXTY-SEVEN

Naomi woke up to a throbbing in her abdomen, as though a second heart had been stitched beneath the skin. Her skin felt taut and immovable.

Tubes slithered in and out of her. Oxygen hissed into her nostrils. A catheter burned between her legs. An IV was threaded into a vein in her hand. A thick tube was drawing something wet out of her abdomen and gargling on her insides. She wanted to rip them all away, but wondered what would be left of her if she did.

'Hello?' Her voice was croaky. She held her neck to ease the burning. The heart monitor clip on her finger was cold.

'Ni ...' Grace said. Her voice was thick from crying. She sniffed loudly and took her hand. 'How are you feeling?' she asked.

'I've felt better,' Naomi replied, and to her surprise, she attempted a laugh.

'You've looked better too,' Grace replied wryly.

Silence fell between them. Naomi realised that after everything that had happened, the past still sat between them, and her heart sank.

'Naomi, I ...' Grace's voice broke. She cleared her throat and tried again. 'I'm so sorry. I've been an awful sister to you.'

'No, you haven't.'

'Yes, I have. You were right, I was pushing you away and you didn't deserve it, not one bit. The secret I was keeping was eating me alive, and every time I looked at you, I remembered. That wasn't fair. None of it was your fault.' She blew her nose loudly and took Naomi's hand again. 'Will you forgive me?'

'Always,' Naomi replied, and sniffled back tears of her own.

Grace kissed the back of her hand.

'What happened between you? Will you tell me now?'

'I promise I will, but right now you need to focus on getting better.'

'Naomi?' Rachel said from the doorway. 'You're awake!'

She rushed to the bed and wrapped her arms around her. Naomi winced and dug her fingertips into her mother's back.

'Mum, be careful,' Grace said.

'I'm sorry!' Rachel said, stroking Naomi's hair. 'I'm just ... I'm so happy you're awake.'

'Water.'

'Of course. I'll just check with the nurse if you can ...'

'Water,' Naomi persisted.

She felt the rim of a bottle brush against her lips, and glugged at the liquid until the plastic crunched in her fist. Then she lay back on the bed and heaved in air, water slithering down her chin.

'How are you feeling?' Rachel asked.

'Tired.'

'You've been asleep for nearly two days,' Grace said.

The pain made it so easy to forget how it had all begun.

George was hurt.

Josie stabbed me.

I killed her.

Her mother wiped a tear from Naomi's cheek.

'I'm so sorry,' Naomi said.

'Why are you sorry?'

'I killed her ... I killed Josie ...'

'If you hadn't, you'd be dead yourself.'

'I didn't want to. I never wanted to hurt ...'

'We know, darling, we know.'

She took Naomi's hand and stroked her wrist.

'Is George okay?'

Her mother fell silent. Her lips smacked together as she tried to find the words.

'Mum?'

'I'm sorry, darling. He lost too much blood.'

George, the man who had sat beside her on the cliff, the man who had left London for the silence, was gone. Her throat burned.

'He didn't deserve to die,' she whispered. 'All he wanted to do was make sure I was safe.'

Her mother stroked her hand and tried to quiet her own tears. Naomi thought of Josie, the woman who had ended George's life just so she could get to her.

'She hated me. I didn't think it was possible for someone to hate that much. She killed an innocent man just so she could hurt me.'

'Some people are made differently, Naomi,' Rachel said, clearing her throat. 'She was one of those people.'

Someone knocked on the door.

'It's DS Campbell. Is this a bad time?'

'Naomi?' Rachel asked.

'I'm fine,' she said, and wiped her cheeks. 'I can talk.'

'Thank you,' Marcus said.

It was good to hear his voice, but there was a solemn undertone to it now, as though something good and sweet had been taken from him.

Her mother fell silent and slipped her hand from Naomi's. 'Are you all right? You look ...'

'I'm fine,' Marcus replied. 'Comes with the job.'

'I'll go and get you something to eat,' Rachel said, and patted Naomi's hand. 'You must be starving.'

'I'll pop home and check on Craig and the kids, but I'll be back, all right?'

Naomi nodded.

Rachel and Grace left the room and Marcus sat down with a quiet sigh.

'I'm sorry about what happened to you. I'm really glad to see you're on the mend.'

Naomi had never felt more broken.

'We found the killer, Naomi.'

She thought of the man in the alley, the man who had started it all. The man who stalked her dreams had been caught. She held her breath.

'Who ... who was it?'

'Blake Crouch.'

'The detective? The man who arrested me?'

'Yes. He killed Cassie and Amber because they were investigating Hayley Miller's disappearance.'

'Why would he do that?'

'Because he was responsible for what happened to Hayley.'

'What did he do to her?'

'He and his friends assaulted her. After the incident was reported to the police by a third party, we believe he got rid of her so she wouldn't talk of the attack herself.'

'Was Dane ...?' She couldn't say the rest. She couldn't imagine that the man she had loved for most of her life could be capable of hurting someone.

'Dane wasn't involved. He wasn't there.'

'But it doesn't make any sense. Why would he want to frame Dane and me? What did we ever do to him?'

'Dane and Blake were best friends. They had matching watches – all their friends did. Dane was the only person in their group who wasn't involved in the assault. By framing him for the murders, Blake was trying to lead us away from what happened to Hayley all those years ago.'

'And me? Why me?'

'Grace reported the assault after it happened. Blake's father, the superintendent at the time, threatened to frame her to protect his son and cover up the crime. He knew that you were aware of the fight Grace and Hayley had had over what happened, which meant Blake knew too. He might have thought you knew more than you did.'

Naomi knew her sister had kept a secret for all those years, but she had never imagined it would be so dark. Her heart broke for her.

'But the knife from my kitchen ... how did that go missing?'

'Blake orchestrated the search of your house, Naomi.'

She closed her eyes. The corruption. The lies. The secrets everyone kept.

'Will you tell me what happened?' Marcus asked.

She took a deep breath and started at the beginning. Marcus probed her story, but his words were soft, guiding her along when the memories got too much. A pen scratched on a notepad.

'So Dane and I are free? We aren't suspects any more?'

'That's right. I'm sorry you went through all that.'

She sighed with relief and sniffed back tears.

'Dane ... what happened to Dane? What did she do to him?'

'I found him in the flat he shared with Josie. He was handcuffed to the radiator and badly burnt. He had been there for some time. He's recovering well.'

Naomi thought of their wedding day, the feel of her dress swishing against her legs, the press of Dane's lips when they kissed for the first time as husband and wife. Neither of them could have ever imagined what was to come.

'What do I do now?' she asked.

'You survive.'

The room fell quiet but for the beeping of the heart monitor. She knew that Marcus wanted to say more, but no words came. What did you say to someone whose life had collapsed around her? He couldn't help her start over; that was up to her.

'Is there anything I can do?' he asked.

'Can you tell Dane I want to see him? When he's able?'

He fell quiet. She knew he wouldn't understand.

'Of course, if that's what you want.'

'It is.'

He got up from the chair and headed for the door.

'Contact me if you have any questions. I'll be in touch to see how you're doing.'

It seemed wrong to part from him, even though she hardly knew him. He had simply been a kind voice amongst the trauma, a sliver of hope in the darkness, and yet the thought of never seeing him again left a dull ache in her chest.

'Marcus?'

'Yes?'

'Thank you for believing me.'

'I know a good person when I see one,' he replied, and shut the door behind him.

Naomi sat in the silence.

You survive.

The cliff would always be there, and the desire to escape would still burn in her like a dormant fire ready to spread and devour her again, but if her ordeal had taught her anything, it was that she was stronger than she had ever given herself credit for.

I'll survive, Marcus, she thought. I will.

SIXTY-EIGHT

Naomi woke with a gasp. The sea was calling to her as though the waves were splashing up against the walls of the house and trickling in through the windows. She was having one of her bad nights.

'You're safe,' she whispered to herself. 'No one can hurt you here.'

She leant down and stroked Max's fur, felt his chest rise and fall; then rolled over in bed and reached out. Dane was still there.

She loved him, always had. He was the only person who made her feel whole. With Dane, she didn't feel so alone in the dark. Even after everything that had happened between them since the divorce, it was Dane she had needed in the hospital. When he was well enough to get out of bed, a nurse had wheeled him into Naomi's room. They had held each other for hours, and when they parted, they both knew there was no turning back. They were together again, the way it should always have been. They were going to start afresh.

Naomi lay in bed and listened to his sleeping breaths as the air began to thin. Her hands gripped the sheets until they twisted around her fists. The past was suffocating her as Dane slept peacefully by her side. She'd thought that moving away from Balkerne Heights would be the answer. She hadn't realised that the past would follow them, leak in through the windows and vibrate against the walls.

She wiped the sweat from her forehead and rubbed her chest with her nightgown until the fabric was soaked. She tried to slow her breaths, and closed her eyes.

'It's just one of your bad nights,' she whispered to herself. 'You'll feel better in the morning.'

'Are you all right?'

Her hand clapped against her chest.

'Jesus.'

'Sorry,' Dane whispered. 'Can't sleep?'

'Nightmare.'

'Come here.'

She hesitated. When she was having a panic attack, the thought of his arms wrapping around her made her feel trapped, as though he was sinking and dragging her down with him.

Slowly she moved into the crook of him. He kissed the nape of her neck and pulled her closer, and it wasn't long before he was asleep again. Naomi lay in his arms and listened to the call of the sea until dawn. Only when she felt the heat of the sun seeping through the window did she trust herself to close her eyes.

She woke to the sound of Max's tail knocking against the radiator. She smiled and patted the bed. He jumped up and rested his head on her hip.

She had only had him back a few months. He was retired from his duties as a guide dog because of his injuries, but he was her companion again – he was finally home. She stroked his fur and cringed when she felt the bald scars hardened against his ribs.

She sat up against the headboard and took a deep breath. She had survived another bad night. There were more good nights than bad after so many months, but the dark part of her was still there beneath the surface. Once each night had passed, however, she reminded herself that she had survived it.

'Here we are,' Dane said as he walked into the room and placed a mug of coffee on the bedside table.

'Thanks.'

He leaned down and kissed her.

'How did you sleep?' he asked, and sat on his side of the bed. Max jumped down and flopped beneath the radiator.

'I had a bad night. First one in a while.'

'It will get better. I get them too. But they're just nightmares. When I wake up with you beside me, I know it was only a dream.'

She took a sip of coffee and placed the mug back on the table.

'I thought that if we moved, the nightmares would stop.'

Every fireplace in the new house had been sealed shut, locking the memories of Josie's screams behind brick and plaster. But some nights Naomi was sure she could hear the crackle of flames, and smell charred flesh in the air.

'They will stop, Ni. Just give it time.' Dane moved up the bed and sat beside her. His weight pressed the headboard against the wall. 'What do you want to do today? The weather's lovely; we could take Max on a hike.'

'Marcus is dropping by, remember?'

He took a loud sip of coffee. 'Can't we just leave the past in the past?'

'I need to hear it from him, Dane. I need to hear him say the words.'

'You're safe now,' he said, and kissed her forehead.

'I need to hear *him* say that.'

Her hand unconsciously slipped beneath her nightgown and stroked the scar where the knife had cut through her. Any sensation that had once been there was dead, but her mind still conjured the memory of it. A dull ache shivered through her whenever her fingertips met the jagged skin.

'We have a new life now,' Dane said. 'We deserve to be happy.'

Dane seemed revitalised having her back in his life. He cherished her, doted on her every whim, smothered her in more affection than she had received during the whole of their fifteen years of marriage, and had promised never to mention parenthood, a promise he had kept. But Naomi couldn't leave the past behind as well as he could. It still had its hold on her. Whenever she thought of the night she nearly died, her scars seemed to pulse with the memory.

'Every time I feel the scars, I remember what happened,' she said. 'I can't even take a shower without it all coming back.'

'Me too,' he said.

They sat quietly for a moment, remembering. Josie would hate it if she knew that sharing scars had brought them even closer.

The doorbell chimed through the house. Max barked and hobbled out of the room.

'What's the time?'

'Nearly midday.'

'What? You should have woken me.'

'You looked so beautiful, I didn't want to disturb you.'

'He's early,' she said, and threw back the duvet.

'I'll go. I'll keep him busy while you freshen up.'

'Tell him I'll be five minutes,' she said, and shut the bathroom door behind her.

She listened to the staircase creak under Dane's footsteps as she stood in the warm bathroom. The air was wet with steam from his shower. As she slipped out of her nightgown, she breathed in his scent, and held it in her lungs. She had loved him all her adult life, but beneath the love, the dark memories simmered, as though her skin was still burning.

She stroked the scars one by one, felt the raised skin warped and numb beneath her fingertips, and hoped that one day she would be able to touch them without remembering how they got there.

She turned on the shower and filled the room with more steam.

The house had belonged to Dane's mother, and Naomi could still feel her presence there, as though her love had stained into the walls. She had died before Naomi and Dane met, but living in her house, it was as though Naomi had known her all her life. The plants in the garden had been nurtured by her hands, the concoction of scents following the breeze in through the open windows, filling the house with the smell of summer. But the house came with memories too, and during her bad nights, life buzzed around her until she wasn't sure she could bear it. Dane had grown up there; it was already his home, but Naomi felt like a visitor, trying to shrug off the past as it clawed at her like hands bursting through the walls.

She stood beneath the water and waited for it to wash away the nightmares that had claimed the night.

Even with her new home in the country, and her old house rented out, she still couldn't defeat the melancholy that had claimed so many years of her life. It sat beneath her skin and burned with the slightest falter. But she was away from the cliffs now. They could call however much they wanted; she wasn't listening.

She wasn't the woman she had been before – she wasn't the woman at the cliff edge or the woman who had begged for death in the alley. She was stronger now, not in physical form, but of heart.

Marcus would be waiting for her downstairs. She wondered if he would recognise the woman who stood before him, scarred but new. She had done what he had told her to do that day in the hospital, and she hoped he would notice. She had done everything she could to survive.

SIXTY-NINE

Marcus drove along the quaint country roads, weaving between endless fields of corn gleaming in the sun. The air was so fresh, it clawed yawns from his lungs. His heart sank at the thought of returning home, where the sky was smothered with a thick coat of cloud and the air was tainted with salt from the sea until everything was plagued with the sickly stench. There was only forty miles between the town and the village, but it was like they were two separate worlds. But the worst part of returning home was facing the memories that waited for him.

Months had passed since he last saw Naomi, and the thought of seeing her again had kept him up into the night, listening to the clock tick on the bedside table by his head until sunlight filtered through the blinds and crept up the bed like fire.

He hadn't known her, not really, but when she had left Balkerne Heights, a part of him had left with her, and he had to face the bleak reality that she was the only redeeming quality the town had had. Even with Blake and Nathan Crouch in prison, along with the rest of the men who had gang-raped Hayley, and the mystery around her disappearance solved, the town still hadn't forgiven the police. They had cracked the case twenty years too late, and the crime had been committed by one of their own.

He longed to see Naomi, but he knew it would be so much harder for him once he left, haunted by the beauty of her face and what might have been.

He checked the directions as he drove down a particularly narrow lane. The car veered to the left and scraped against the hedgerow. He swerved back into the middle of the road, his heart clambering in his chest.

The sun beat down on the car and glared against the bonnet, and hot air filtered through the open windows, unable to cool the sweat trickling down his temples. As he took the final corner, he spotted the house at the end, standing tall and beautiful, just like her. It was made of red bricks, with white sash windows and a dark green front door, rose bushes on either side basking in the sun.

She deserves this, he thought.

He pulled up outside the house and checked himself in the rear-view mirror, smoothing down his hair where sweat had caused it to curl and wiping the corners of his eyes with licked fingertips. Then he stepped out of the car and took a deep breath.

The gravel crunched beneath his feet as the aroma of the roses filled his lungs. He rang the doorbell and waited, patting down his shirt and running his hand through his hair. The bell chimed through the house behind the stained glass, and a dog barked.

As the door edged open, Max's head forced its way through the gap, and he bounded out onto the gravel, tail wagging, barking up at Marcus excitedly. He was slower than he would have been before the attack, but he still exuded joy, like heat radiating from his fur. Marcus bent down to pet him as he looked up towards the door.

Dane, the man who had her heart. He was tall and lean, with sculpted arms and a broad chest hidden beneath a white top, so white that it was almost blinding in the sun. His hair was damp from a recent shower. Marcus thought of Dane and Naomi together beneath the showerhead, their lips locked and their naked, scarred bodies lathered in soap suds.

'Marcus, it's good to see you.'

It felt odd, hearing him use his first name.

'Great house.'

'Gorgeous, isn't it? It was my mother's. I'd been renting it out for years, tucking the money away for retirement, but it finally felt like the right time to come home. Come inside, I'll get us a drink.' He turned his attention to Max. 'You too, mister.'

It was warm and quaint inside, so different from her last house. Maybe it was the jealousy that tinted Marcus's view, but right then, standing in Naomi's new home, he wished it were his. Theirs.

'Tea? Coffee?'

'Black coffee would be great.'

Dane caught his eye drifting up the staircase, each step wrapped in cream carpet.

'Naomi will be down in five minutes.'

Marcus followed him through the house, noticing all the beautiful features that Naomi herself couldn't see, from the art on the walls to the pattern on the runner leading down the hall.

Dane led him into a beautifully lit kitchen where the windows overlooked a long, winding garden. He made conversation as the kettle boiled, and it was clear that he wanted Marcus to like him. Marcus wished he could – he had saved the man's life after all – but he could never like a man who had the heart of the woman he wanted. When he looked at Dane, he saw the sniffling mess in the interview room, the man who had brought Josie into Naomi's life.

'Hi,' she said from the doorway.

The months he had gone without seeing her had only deepened her beauty. Her eyes, her smile, her lips, they were just as he remembered, but there was something different about her now: a hardness, as though taking a life had steeled her heart. If only she knew that she wasn't alone, that the past haunted him at night too.

'Hi.'

She wore a long summer dress covered in a pattern of colourful flowers, complementing the deep brown of her skin, her scars somehow making her more beautiful, a rarity. But her eyelids were swollen from sleepless nights. When he lay awake at night thinking of her, she was awake too, thinking of Josie's body falling limp beneath her, the smell of fire crackling on her skin.

'Here you go,' Dane said, and handed Marcus his coffee. He took a mug to Naomi and waited for her fingers to wrap around the handle. 'You guys catch up,' he said. 'It's beautiful outside; maybe you want to sit on the patio.'

'That okay with you, Marcus?'

'Of course. Lead the way.'

Naomi moved freely through the house towards the French windows, allowing the sound of birdsong to ripple into the house. Marcus wondered how long it had taken her to master her way around and how many bruises she'd had to wear before she could call it home.

Max brushed past him and flopped down on the lawn, his tongue dangling towards the grass.

'He loves it here,' Naomi said as she sat at the table on the patio. 'He'd probably prefer it if I let him roam the fields out back until I called him in for dinner.'

'He looks happy to be back with you,' Marcus said.

'Not as happy as me. I missed him so much.'

He sat at the table and shuffled close, blushing as their knees touched.

'Have you thought of getting another guide dog? The unretired kind, I mean?'

'After what happened ... I just couldn't risk another life like that, not again.'

'But you're free now; no one can hurt you here.'

'I'll never feel safe, even with Blake in prison and Josie –' she flinched with the memory – 'gone.'

'They really are gone, Naomi. Blake will be in prison until the day he dies.'

The case had been drawn out for months. Even with the evidence mounted against him – the photo of him wearing the watch, Grace's testimony about the night of the rape, the corruption orchestrated by Nathan Crouch confessed on tape, the argument Blake and Amber had had just hours before she died, and the investigation Amber and Cassie had undertaken

– Blake still wouldn't admit to what he had done, making it harder to convict without the discovery of Hayley's body. The media had relished it, dragging Naomi back onto the front pages, the Blind Widow approaching the courtroom to talk about her experience in the alley.

She was silent for a moment. The backdrop of the garden glowed in the sun behind her. Bees buzzed from flower to flower.

'Even when you say it, I can't quite believe it,' she said.

'Please do.'

'I just ... I don't understand why Blake didn't kill me like the others.'

'Maybe because you're blind, he didn't see you as a threat in the alley, but then paranoia set in. Maybe he thought you knew more about what had happened to Hayley, so he attacked you and Max on the beach as a threat. He tried to frame Dane; that's why he hurt Josie. Maybe hurting you was part of framing Dane too.'

'Maybe ... maybe ... There don't seem to be any concrete answers. How can I move on when I don't know for sure?'

'Blake is a coward. He still won't accept what he's done. And without knowing where Hayley's body is, we have to try and connect the dots ourselves. You will overcome this, Naomi, but it will take time.'

Even with her scars, she looked more alive than he had ever seen her, even when he noticed the pain dwelling in her eyes.

'You did it,' he said suddenly.

'Did what?'

'You survived.'

'I just take each day as it comes.'

'I'm happy for you.'

'Mum read in the paper that you'll make inspector by next year. I'm happy for you too.'

'Thanks. It still feels new, but I'm getting used to it.'

'And Lisa? Where did she end up?'

'Moved to another town. It was for the best.'

They sat quietly for a moment, listening to the sounds of the garden. He would do anything to stay there with her, but he had to prise himself away before he was pushed. He looked up at the house, at the life Naomi had found for herself, and smiled as he returned his gaze to her.

He stood up. 'Thanks for the coffee.'

She rose and moved towards him, one hand out in front of her. Marcus stayed stock still and waited for her fingertips to meet his shirt just above his heart. The feel of her sent shocks through his skin.

'A handshake doesn't seem appropriate for the man who saved my life.'

He laughed nervously as he opened his arms and felt hers slip around him. They held each other for mere seconds, but it would be enough to carry him home and keep him from thinking of anything else. He tried to engrain the feel of her body into his mind. When she pulled away, he longed to kiss her lips. He bit down on his tongue.

'Perhaps ... perhaps you could come by again,' she said.

He smiled. 'Yes, perhaps I will.'

'Goodbye, Marcus.'

She walked down the brick steps to the grass and met Max there, ruffling the fur on his stomach until he kicked out his legs, beckoning a laugh from her lips.

'It's great to see her happy, isn't it?' Dane said from the doorway.

'It is,' Marcus replied, tearing his eyes away from her.

'Thanks for coming.'

'Pleasure.'

Dane led him down the hall and opened the front door, allowing the scent of roses to trickle in. Marcus knew he'd never be able to smell the flowers again without thinking of her.

Dane shook his hand, his grip strong in the man-to-man exchange, and smiled as he said goodbye, revealing perfectly straight teeth that made Marcus smile back with closed lips to hide his own. He could see it now, the charm Dane had with women, and a sudden thought anchored in him: he wished he hadn't followed the sound of handcuffs rattling against the radiator and had left the apartment instead; maybe then he might have stood a chance with Naomi. He scolded himself by digging his fingernails into his palms.

At least she's happy, he thought as he made his way back to the car. Even if it isn't with you.

He sat behind the wheel, enveloped by the suffocating heat trapped inside the car, reluctant to leave the past behind. He would never see her again, but it was for the best.

Grow up, Campbell, he told himself as he started the engine and lowered the windows, allowing the summer breeze to sweep through.

He pulled out of the drive, turned onto the secluded country lane and promised to try not to think of her on the journey home.

SEVENTY

Dane watched the car pull out of the driveway and stood there for a few minutes after it had gone, just in case Marcus returned. Marcus was in love with Naomi, that he knew. He had seen it from the kitchen as he watched them through the window. The detective's eyes had looked at her longingly, his feelings lost on her, but not on Dane. It made him feel powerful knowing that he had something, or someone, that another man wanted. The feeling was almost as powerful as taking another person's life. Almost.

He had been nervous about having the detective inside the house, but the moment he saw Marcus on the doorstep, and the jealousy in his eyes, he knew that the other man wouldn't be able to look past Dane's luck and Naomi's face. He knew he'd got away with murder.

He stood at the window and reflected on how he had got to where he was now, in a life he had once only dreamed of having. The murders, the police investigation, the hell he and Naomi had gone through, it had all started with Hayley Miller.

He had given her everything he had, and still she'd broken his heart, sleeping with half the town and teasing him with a baby that could have been his. He had swallowed down his anger as she shared her body with his friends, and longed for the day when she would return to him, once she got it out of her system; but when she had told him about the baby, the baby that could have been his or Blake's, he knew what he had to do.

She had met him that night. He had given her one last chance to redeem herself, to understand that he couldn't stand by and watch another man raise his child. He had hoped that when she saw how much he was willing to sacrifice for her, she would finally give her heart to him just as he had given her his. But when he vowed to quit studying and find a job right away so that he could care for her and the baby, she pulled away. There was no way she could have the baby, she said; her father would kill them both if he ever found out. When he suggested that they run away, she refused. She wouldn't give up anything for him or their child. She wanted her own life, the freedom to hop from bed to bed in search of the love that Dane was there to give.

But she didn't want his love; he was merely a distraction until she found what, or who, she was really looking for. He had been used. Finally he saw her for what she was. She didn't have to spell it out for him; he had seen the pity in her eyes. But that pity had soon flashed to fear, which proved to him that she understood what he was capable of, and that she had underestimated him from the very beginning. He wasn't a gullible boy, easily used and discarded; he was a man with a heart capable of love so strong it seared, and in turn, unimaginable hate.

He had watched the look in her eyes change as he pulled out the knife, with the sun setting in the blade. She apologised, begged for his forgiveness until tears filled her eyes; she told him the baby was his, that they could have the life he spoke about. She spoke so fast, so pleadingly, that spit flew from her lips and her words stammered together. But he had seen through her, through the manipulation, the vindictiveness, the lies.

He ran the knife across her throat until blood filled her mouth and silenced her screams. The blood had spoiled the back of his car and dripped up the gravel driveway as he dragged her body through to the garden, where he dug her grave deep into the night.

His mother had forgiven him for what she had witnessed, and vowed to keep his secret as long as he never hurt another girl again. It had always been the two of them together. Deep down, Dane knew that she would forgive him anything to keep from being alone.

He'd promised he wouldn't hurt anyone else – that was, until Cassie Jennings told him that she and Amber O'Neill were investigating Hayley's disappearance.

He hadn't meant to sleep with Cassie again, but after a while, the sight of Josie had brought back all the hate he'd had for her sister. They had the same eyes, the same lips, the same laugh. He had enjoyed being with Josie at first – it had been like a fresh start, washing away the mistakes Hayley had made – but the more he looked at her, the more he saw her sister staring back at him. Cassie gave him the distraction he needed, but her problem was that she liked to talk. She always said too much.

Cassie was ambitious, had her eyes set on London in the hope of working for one of the nationals, and would do anything to get there. By discovering the truth of Hayley Miller's disappearance, she would become a legend and would be offered jobs by all the big newspapers. And with her friend Amber O'Neill working alongside her, they had access to police files and were able to look behind closed doors, doors other journalists could never open. They already knew too much, knew more than Dane in some respects. It was from Cassie that he learned what Blake and their friends had done to Hayley two nights before Dane killed her.

Cassie and Amber were determined to unearth the truth.

So they had to die.

After Cassie was found, he knew that Amber would either stop looking into the case to protect herself, or continue with renewed determination. Either way, he knew he couldn't take any chances. The past had been buried with Hayley twenty years before. There was no way he could allow Amber to dig it back up again. So he followed her home.

Then Naomi had stumbled down the alley.

Her arrival had felt like a meeting of fates. She could be his again if he did it right. After two years, it seemed she was growing stronger without him. To get her back, he had to break her down again. She had to see that living alone was dangerous, and that without him, she could fall victim to someone evil. Everything he'd done, from taunting her in the alley to rearranging the furniture in her house, had all been for her – for both of them.

Max hadn't been too pleased to see him again. Dane had expected that; after all, he had pummelled a knife handle-deep between the dog's ribs. But he'd had to take away from Naomi everything that made her strong. If he was to step in and make her realise that she needed him, she had to be at her most vulnerable.

Naomi had been adamant about getting Max back. After days of the dog walking out of a room when Dane walked in, or growling if he got too close, he knew he had to do something before Naomi started to wonder. He fed the animal treats until he got fat, and walked him alone most mornings to build the trust between them, and eventually Max learned to tolerate him, seeing Dane as a source of food and walks in the countryside. But it was clear he would never forget; Dane could see it in the dog's eyes, the way he watched him as he moved about the house.

He'd thought it was all over after the night in the woods. He had followed Josie out of their apartment that night, had watched her press the bat against Naomi's head and lead her into the woods. Without thinking, he had let himself into Naomi's house with his key and taken the nearest knife, not even thinking of the implications. Then he had followed them, watching as Josie had taunted Naomi.

It had been like attacking Hayley all over again. Josie's blood had sprayed in his eyes and blinded him. He had staggered through the woods, trying to find Naomi to bring her home safely. But he'd still had time to plant the watch. After learning what Blake had done to Hayley, he felt no remorse for framing him for murder. It was the least he deserved. He had kept the photo of the four of them, Hayley, Grace, Blake and himself, in the shoebox of Naomi's belongings, hidden beneath the bed he and Josie shared. If the police couldn't follow the trail to Blake on their own, he would send it the station anonymously. In the end, Josie had taken it right to them.

But he did have regrets. He regretted bringing Josie into Naomi's life. He had been so preoccupied with his own secrets that he hadn't seen Josie unravelling before his eyes, jealousy pumping through her veins, pain and madness simmering beneath the surface. But she was dead now. She couldn't harm them any more.

He also felt remorse for hurting Naomi on the beach, which he had never planned to do. When he realised she had been knocked unconscious, he'd dragged her higher up the beach, away from the waves. He'd tried to wake her by slapping her lightly and calling her name, but the sound of sirens on the road along the beachfront had caused him to flee. He'd only found out later that the sirens hadn't been for them.

As he walked back through the house, he marvelled at the life he had found for himself and Naomi. He stood at the glass doors overlooking the garden, a smile creeping across his face as he watched Naomi play with Max on the lawn. Hayley Miller's bones were buried right beneath her feet.

Naomi would stop obsessing over it all once enough time had passed. She would accept the lie that Blake was to blame, a lie Dane helped to enforce day after day.

Lying next to Naomi at night, he would take her in his arms as she tossed and turned and dripped with sweat, struggling through nightmares that he himself had spawned. That was the rush he craved. He didn't need to kill any more.

He and Naomi weren't so different. They were both covered in burns and had both taken lives; they were bonded by the blood on their hands and their mutilated skin. They shared something no one else did. She would forget about her need for answers when she settled. She would never know about the women he had killed, or the true identity of the man in the alley that night. It would ruin everything they had built together, and all the hard work he had put into getting her back. That was a rush in itself, wasn't it? That the woman he loved, the woman he craved, feared a man that she had no idea was right before her eyes.

ACKNOWLEDGEMENTS

Many thanks to my agent, Sarah Manning of The Bent Agency, for her firm belief in my work and her astounding dedication (she once sent me a string of emails from a canoe). To my editor, Sara O'Keeffe at Atlantic, for nurturing me as a writer and believing in the story I wished to tell, and her editorial assistant, Poppy Mostyn-Owen. To my publicist, Kirsty Doole, for ordering wine at lunch meetings and sending free books when I ask (beg), as well as the wonderful job she does. To Jane Selley, my copy-editor, for spotting where I had forgotten to dot the i's and cross the t's, and, occasionally, make sense. Many thanks to Tracy Fenton and the incredibly supportive readers of The Book Club on Facebook – your support means the world.

I must also thank the wonderful baristas at my local Costa Coffee shops for allowing me to overstay my welcome to meet deadlines, reminding me when I've had too much caffeine, and knowing my coffee order off by heart.

Thanks to my family, for continuing to motivate me when I dare to doubt myself, and for your unconditional love and support: Sandra Jarrad, Pamela Jordan, Gary Barnes, Natalie

Gowers and Carl Jarrad (and many more). And to my friends, for allowing me to be antisocial to meet deadlines, but also knowing when to drag me out against my will, especially Abbi Houghton, who has been by my side for over twenty years.

Lastly, I must give a huge thank you to you – yes, you – for buying this book. Your support is life-changing.

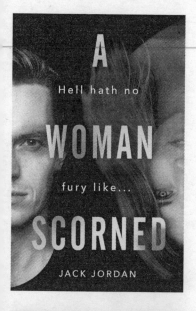
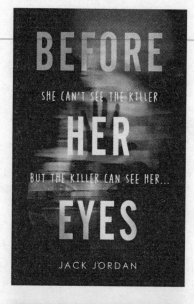
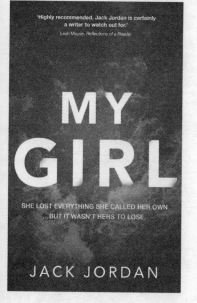